The Russian Resistance

September - December 1940

A Misfit Squadron Novel

Simon Brading

PART 1

REBUILD

PROLOGUE

The enemy aircraft couldn't escape her. It twisted and turned, rolled and yawed, leaping and tumbling about the sky, but she followed it, anticipating its every desperate manoeuvre. She opened fire at the machine with short bursts whenever she had a clear shot and watched the incandescent lines reaching out for it, however, time after time they passed harmlessly over or under it, close, but never quite intersecting their target. It was only a matter of time before she got a hit, though, so she persevered; her guns were powerful enough that even just a single strike in the right place would win the engagement for her.

She sensed it coming before it happened and grinned grimly, not at all taken by surprise, as the triplane rolled onto its back and dived vertically in a last ditch effort to get away, racing for the cover of the cloud a couple of miles below. Stick and pedals worked together in complete harmony as she threw her wonderfully responsive fighter on its nose and slotted in behind the tail of the Prussian machine, its body shining a brilliant red in the bright summer sunshine - red as the blood of the dozens of her fellow countrymen its pilot had spilled.

Even under such extreme circumstances, the pilot, a virtuoso of the air, still managed to evade her fire, and in frustration she held down the button on her stick, pouring stream after stream of lead at him as they dropped out of the sky, but then, with an ominous clunk, the juddering vibrations shaking her aircraft ceased and the guns fell silent, leaving her only with the hum of the airscrew and the rush of air flowing past the cockpit.

'What? Oh, come off it!'

She stabbed at the button a few times, hoping that it was only a jam and that the automatic systems in place to deal with just such eventualities would do their job, but of course there was no response; she had run out of ammunition.

She frowned. 'But I...'

She blinked, rendered speechless, her utter disbelief going unexpressed, as the aircraft in front of her jerked, twisting and slewing even more than it had previously, then swung around, disobeying every single one of the laws of aerodynamics that she knew so well and lived her life by, until finally, impossibly, it was pointing towards her, flying backwards while it continued to fall out of the sky.

She met the eyes of the enemy pilot, saw his mouth widen in its famous grin and shook her head in denial.

'This isn't how...'

Blinding white points of light flashed into being on the wings of the crimson triplane and her words were cut off by a scream of agony as her body was ripped apart by hot metal...

'... wake up!'

Gwen opened her eyes with a start, gulping for air and gazed up into the blue eyes of a concerned Kitty.

'Huh? Wha..? Kitty? What is it?'

In spite of the early hour and the fact that she had drunk a bucketful of champagne only hours before, the American looked awake and alert, fresh-faced. Her golden yellow hair was perfectly in place as well, pulled back into a ponytail which shone softly in the light of the gas lamp on the night stand beside the bed they were sharing. Gwen was positive that her own face would be blotchy and swollen and her hair would be a tangled mess, matted with the sweat that she could feel on her brow; it always was after even just five minutes in bed.

'You were shouting in your sleep, making an awful noise.' The beautiful young woman frowned in concern and reached out to brush several loose strands of hair out of Gwen's eyes.

Gwen blinked, trying to retain hold of the nightmare as it slipped away, illusive as the Prussian fighter that had prompted it. 'Too much cheese.'

Kitty chuckled softly. 'I did warn you about that Stilton, but I'm not buying it; I know you too well. Bad dream?'

'I guess... Sorry if I woke you.'

'No problem. I'm more worried about you.'

Because of the boisterous activities of a couple of their less well-behaved pilots the night before, the squadron had been restricted to a single suite of rooms in The Dorchester and had had to double or triple up on their sleeping arrangements, which was why the two of them had been stuck sharing a bed. However, since they were already roommates in their barracks back at Badger Base, they didn't mind one bit, especially seeing as the bed was so large that they still had more elbow room than they usually got in their standard issue Royal Aviator Corps beds.

Misfit Squadron were in London because they had been ordered to report to Buckingham Palace by King George VI after a scrap with the Crimson Barons which had seen one of their pilots, Lady Penelope Bagshot, injured and more than half of their aircraft destroyed. The Barons, the elite squadron which had been terrorising the enemies of the Prussian empire since before war had even been declared, had come off a lot worse from the fight, though. They had lost almost all of their aircraft and their leader, Hans Gruber, had been sent packing by Gwen, his triplane barely capable of staying in the air. His humiliation had been compounded by Gwen escorting him out over the Channel herself, making sure that nobody else attacked the crippled aircraft. Sir Douglas Pewtall, the commander of the RAC, and many of the ministers listening to the debriefing had been furious and ready to condemn her, but the King had seemed to understand and had accepted Gwen's decision to let Gruber escape as the correct one under the circumstances; not only was it the British thing to do, but Gruber himself had had Gwen in a similar position not long before and had let her go.

The battle with the Barons had been the culmination of a day of intense fighting that had seen nearly a thousand Prussian aircraft attack London in two huge raids. More than a hundred of the enemy machines had been shot down, but the cost had been high, not so much in RAC casualties, which had been commendably low, but rather in the damage that had been done to the city. It was civilians, not military personnel, who had borne the brunt of the attack, when bombers being harassed by RAC fighters dropped their payloads without a care for who or what was beneath them.

The Misfits had sustained one other loss that day aside from Lady Penelope - their home. Badger Base, successfully hidden until that day in the wilds of the Kent Downs, had been targeted by an entire wing of enemy bombers and been put out of commission. Thankfully, nobody had been killed, mainly because sufficient warning had been given by Badger Nine, Owen Llewellyn, the Misfits' second in command and their artificial eyes in the sky.

Once the Misfits had finished their report, the King invited them to stay at the Palace for a small reception. They had mingled with courtiers and fellow members of the armed forces, celebrating the victory won that day and attempting to emulate it by defeating as much of the Royal wine cellars as possible. They failed to make much of a dent in it, though, and after several hours of glorious fighting, they had beaten an honourable retreat and been conveyed by Royal autocars back to their lodgings at The Dorchester, the luxurious hotel on Airfield Lane by Hyde Airstrip. There they were met not only by doormen with mops and buckets at the ready in case the indiscretions of the previous night were repeated, but also by a message from the hospital in Folkestone, where Lady Penelope was being treated, informing them that their fellow pilot was out of the woods, conscious and expected to recover from her wounds.

This prompted fresh celebration and the Misfits immediately repaired to their suite, where they gathered there forces, renewed their determination and proceeded to attack the contents of the bar with far more success than they had the Royal stocks, carrying a resounding victory, largely due to the efforts of Badgers Three, Six and Twelve, Bruce, Mac and Scarlet, although Gwen and Kitty personally managed to vanquish two entire bottles of champagne.

The party had petered out around two, mostly because the room's alcohol supplies were exhausted and their leader, Abby Lennox, ordered everybody to bed, announcing that they were going to take some time off to visit Lady Penelope in hospital before returning to Badger Base to begin the rebuilding process.

Most of the Misfits had gone to bed happy and with a smile on their faces, but Gwen had been troubled and had tossed and turned for what felt like hours, wondering if she had been right to allow Gruber to escape. He was an ace many times over and would keep killing - it was possible, probable in fact, that she had condemned many of her fellow pilots to death via her actions, perhaps even some of the friends and colleagues sharing the suite with her that night.

When she had finally managed to fall asleep, that awful thought and the guilt it engendered had cast her straight into the alcohol-fuelled nightmare, where her subconscious mind had punished her for her honour.

'So, what was it?'

'Uh...' Kitty was still leaning over Gwen, staring into her eyes, her face only a foot or so from hers and Gwen was starting to find it slightly disconcerting. She couldn't help but remember the last time the two of them had been so close and her eyes flicked involuntarily to Kitty's lips, recalling the feel of them pressed against hers, how surprised she'd been, how excited...

She thought she saw those lips twitch upwards at the corners and tore her gaze away to look back into Kitty's eyes. There seemed to be a glint of amusement in them, but she couldn't be sure, since the only source of light in the room was directly behind the American and she dismissed it as her imagination; after all, the woman had been incredibly drunk and hadn't remembered the kiss afterwards. 'It was Gruber. I was dogfighting him again.'

'Oh? I would have thought you would enjoy dreaming about that; you did win after all!'

Gwen grimaced. 'Not in my twisted version I didn't.'

'Ah. You poor thing.' The American shook her head and smiled sympathetically her warm smile banishing the last of the cold left over from the nightmare.

'Will you two *please* shut up!' The usually gentle Irish-accented voice of Scarlet was rough with sleep, irritation and the aftermath of a night of heavy drinking as she lifted her head up to glare at them from the spare bed which had been set out for her at the foot of theirs. 'Do I have to pull rank to get you to let me sleep in peace?'

Kitty pulled back from Gwen and smiled sweetly at the red-haired woman who was their friend and roommate. 'No, ma'am!'

With a last wink at Gwen, the American went back to her own side of the bed.

With a grunt, Scarlet collapsed back down and replaced her sleeping mask. 'Bloody junior officers, no respect for their betters...'

Kitty raised an eyebrow at Gwen. Thinking the same thing they picked up pillows and threw them as hard as they could.

CHAPTER 1

Abby made the rounds of the bedrooms at eight the next morning, waking her pilots. In most cases it took only a knock at the door and a simple order for the pilots to grumblingly and grudgingly leave the comfort of the luxurious mattresses. However, in the case of Mac and Bruce, both of whom were dead to the world, snoring loud enough to rival Dreadnought's powerful steam engines and so firmly ensconced in sheets and blankets as to resist casual pokes prods and shakes, she was forced to gather reinforcements in order to assault their position.

Seven Misfits assembled in line-abreast formation along one side of the mattress that the two men were sharing, while Abby and Owen, as senior officers, took the high ground on the other side, standing on armchairs, armed and ready to pick off the stragglers as they retreated.

With a shouted order from their commander, the seven pilots heaved together, tipping the mattress on its side, sending the enemy tumbling from cover, while simultaneously the artillery opened fire. Streams of soda water hit the two thus-exposed targets and, amid much spluttering and coughing from the enemy and triumphant laughter from the victors, the day was carried.

At eight-twenty the Misfits trouped down to breakfast together in various states of wakefulness and with their day uniforms in wide variations of neatness.

Gwen sat at a small table with Kitty and Scarlet. She shared a pot of tea with the Irishwoman while Kitty ordered coffee, taking advantage of the supplies that The Dorchester had procured for its patrons at great expense.

She glanced around the room while she sipped at her tea and munched on a piece of toast. The Misfits were as boisterous as ever, even Mac and Bruce, who were obviously feeling the effects of the night before. She had expected nothing less, though; it was peculiarly British to be cheerful in the face of danger and death and it seemed that that attitude had rubbed off on their allies. That attitude apparently extended to the guests sharing the dining room with them as well; despite the heavy bombing of the day before, which admittedly had been heaviest on the eastern part of London and hadn't quite extended to the West End or the centre, they were showing no signs of fear or any desire to hurry their breakfasts and leave London in case there were further attacks. The British stiff upper lip was in full force, at least among the well-heeled, and the attitude was still one of resistance in the face of tyranny.

'Don't you agree, Gwen?'

Gwen blinked and glanced at Scarlet, who was watching her with an eyebrow raised and a smirk on her face. 'I'm sorry, what? I was miles away.'

'I was saying that perhaps I should ask for my old room back and leave you two alone.'

'What? Why would you...?' Gwen's brain eventually caught up with her mouth and she felt her face heat as she looked from the smirking Scarlet to Kitty, who was peering at her in exaggerated innocence while she forked scrambled eggs - real, not powdered - into her mouth.

'I... I don't think that's necessary.' Gwen stared down at her plate, but didn't miss the brief flash of disappointment in the young American's eyes that she instantly hid behind a smile.

The Irishwoman had picked up on an attraction that had been between Kitty and Gwen from almost the first moment that they had met and by the way Kitty had looked when Gwen had turned down Scarlet's idea, it seemed like she wouldn't be adverse to taking things a step further, but Gwen wasn't sure yet if that was the best idea.

It wasn't that she wasn't attracted to the American, because she was, very, and enjoyed her company immensely. Nor was it because Kitty was a woman - even though Gwen had never imagined being with a woman that didn't mean she rejected the idea completely and, while polite society frowned upon two people of the same gender being together, they didn't condemn it.

The reason was that she didn't know if she was ready for *any* kind of relationship.

After the death of her husband, Richard, she had completely cut herself off from all emotions except for her hatred for the Prussians. She had rejected ties to anyone and even gone so far as to not make friends with the pilots in her old squadron. It hadn't been until she had joined the Misfits that her resolve had started to weaken and then, after her fight with Gruber, she had come to a decision to finally let go of her husband and try to move on. She had been meaning to tell her friends, and especially Kitty, about it, but she hadn't been able to; either it hadn't been the right time, or they had all been too drunk.

She took a deep breath, then looked around, making sure that there was nobody within earshot before beginning. 'That's not necessary, thank you, but you never know what the future might bring; I took the photo frame out of my cockpit yesterday.'

Kitty beamed happily at Gwen before sharing a glance with Scarlet; there was no need for Gwen to explain any further because they both knew what the purpose of the frame was and what it meant that she had removed it from her cockpit - on missions Gwen placed a photo of her Richard in the frame and it was there not only as a symbol of her lost love, but also, they were fairly sure, of an unexpressed desire to join him as quickly as possible.

The two women reached out to put their hands on Gwen's where they rested nervously on the table. They didn't need to say anything; weeks of fighting and living together had given them an understanding that went well beyond normal friendship.

After a few seconds Gwen smiled and the women drew back their hands.

'Well, I for one am glad,' said Scarlet, going back to her thick Lincolnshire sausages and fried eggs, 'but if you two aren't going to get on with,' she waved a sausage at them, 'whatever this is, then Dougie has a couple of single friends in the ministry who he thinks would be perfect for you two.'

Kitty and Gwen rolled their eyes; the Irishwoman had been going out with Sir Douglas Pewtall, the Commander of the Royal Aviator Corps, and while the man was moderately handsome, somewhat dashing and very well thought of, he was also *old*, at least forty, possibly forty-five and nothing like the bubbly and vivacious Scarlet. Anybody he considered to be his friend was likely to be similar in temperament to him and not exactly someone they'd like to spend romantic time with, even if they had been in the market for boyfriends.

'I think I might tell him to bring them along next time the three of us come up to London, that way we can go on a triple date.' Scarlet smiled at them sweetly as she viciously stabbed a sausage with her fork, then used it to point at them one by one. 'I might even consider having him reassign you both to desk jobs as well. That would certainly teach you to assault a defenceless superior officer with down-filled weapons in the middle of the night.'

Abby managed to appropriate an aircraft for them from the authorities at Hyde Airstrip for the trip back to RAC Hawkinge on the south coast where they had left their surviving aircraft. It was a lumbering antique Lekker, a Prussian aircraft from the 1920's with three enormous steam engines. It had been discarded by its owner, a recently rich manufacturer of the fabric used in military uniforms, in a fit of patriotism at the beginning of the war. It had since been maintained by the crown as a pleasure craft and was perfectly serviceable, painted in royal livery and eminently comfortable, having been fitted with every luxury possible by its previous owner.

Abby flew them, not bothering to change into a flight suit for what was little more than a glorified autocar, and less than an hour later they landed at Hawkinge, then, after a quick check on their aircraft, or at least what remained of them, they took a couple of rather less comfortable RAC personnel carriers to the hospital in nearby Folkestone.

They were met on the steps of the hospital by Lord Bagshot, Penelope's husband. Lord Bagshot was a tall man in his early forties with a full head of well-coiffed hair. He was fifteen years his wife's senior and, aside from being a peer of the realm, had been an autocar racing driver until the war had broken out. According to Lady Penelope, their's had been very much a love match, which had grown out of their mutual need for ever-increasing velocity and excitement. However, a racing accident had left him with one leg slightly shorter than the other, which meant that he was ineligible for active service, so he compensated by doing what he could to support the war effort in other ways. Until recently that had included housing a Harridan squadron on his lands.

He greeted them with a smile, but Gwen could see that it was forced and there was a pain behind his eyes.

He shook their hands one by one before addressing Abby. 'Thank you for coming, I know how busy you must be.'

Abby shook her head. 'We are never too busy to take care of one of our own, Lord Bagshot.'

'Please, it's Basil, but call me Biffy, everybody does.'

'Biffy Bagshot? I'd rather not, thank you very much.' Mac's whisper thankfully only carried to the Misfits immediately around him and Scarlet's sharp elbow in his ribs put paid to any further comments.

'How is she, uh, Biffy?' asked Abby, not quite hiding a grimace at having to follow the Lord's instructions - she was of a like mind to Mac on the merits of the man's nickname.

'She is... well, you know her - she's putting on a brave face. Perhaps you will be able to get her to open up a bit more.'

Abby frowned. 'Why? What's wrong?'

Lord Bagshot forced another smile, much less successfully than before, though. 'You'll see.' He gestured for them to follow him inside. 'Shall we?'

They passed through reception then through a sparsely populated waiting area before entering the wards themselves. As they trouped along they couldn't help but notice that many of the people, - doctors, nurses, out and inpatients alike - stopped what they were doing to stare at them. At first they thought that it was something to do with their RAC uniforms and wings, which had come to be seen over the last few months as the mark of heroes, but they slowly came to realise that it was something more, as whispered conversations were carried out in their wake and people began to rush ahead of them. They began to gather something of a following, until finally they found their way blocked by a group of people, fronted by a small cluster of children who were all clutching newspapers.

'Excuse me, miss.' The smallest of the children, a thin waif of not more than five years, stood in the way of the diminutive Scarlet, picking the least intimidating of the Misfits to approach. 'Is this you?'

The child held out his paper, the *News of the Empire*, one of the more popular tabloids, in hands that were grubby from the print and Scarlet took it from the girl and the pilots gathered around to peer at it.

Taking up most of the space on the front page under the banner "Misfit Squadron Triumphant" was a reproduction of the photograph that they had taken over the summer to commemorate Gwen's incorporation into the squadron. It showed the twelve pilots lined up in two ranks in front of Wasp, which was parked in front of the hangar at Badger Base.

Scarlet frowned at Abby. 'I thought the papers were keeping our names out of things? Look!' She pointed at the bottom of the picture where their names were clearly printed as if it were some kind of team photo.

Abby took the paper from her and quickly scanned it. 'The Misfits, led by Wing Commander Abigail Lennox, today achieved a momentous victory...' Her eyes darted back and forth, scanning it like she did the sky. 'Special note must be made of the efforts of Aerial Officer Gwenevere Stone, pilot of Wasp, who managed to defeat the notorious leader of the Barons, Hans Gruber, in single combat and force him from British territory with his tail between his legs.' Abby looked up at Gwen with a wry smile. 'Looks like you're famous, Gwen.'

'We all bloody are,' grumbled Owen.

Mac and Bruce, however, rubbed their hands together and shared an eager look, already thinking of the drinks they were likely to get bought for them.

'Can I have me paper back, please?' Forgotten, the child had been watching his paper pass from hand to hand, growing more and more agitated.

Scarlet smiled down at him. 'Of course.'

She held it out to him, but he didn't take it, instead he held out a pen. 'Would you sign it first?'

Scarlet blinked at him for a second, nonplussed, but recovered quickly. 'Of course!'

On hearing her answer, the other children surged forwards as one, brandishing their own papers and pens, joined by many of the adults.

Chaos ensured, along with an awful racket that annoyed the doctors and nurses, until eventually Abby called for quiet and organised a kind of production line with the Misfits lined up along a wall, each armed with a pen, and the autograph hunters moving from one end of the line to the other in military precision. After about ten minutes, when everybody present was satisfied and it seemed that every newspaper in Folkestone had been signed, the Misfits were finally free to continue with their mission.

Lord Bagshot had left them and nipped ahead to prepare Penelope for their visit, so when they filed into her room and gathered around her bed, she was propped up on pillows and wide awake, with her hair presentable, if not decent.

She was deathly white with a waxy sheen to her skin and smiled weakly at them, waving regally with the hand that wasn't filled with needles leading to tubes. 'Hello, everybody.'

The Misfits were enthusiastic in returning her greeting and immediately bombarded her with comments on how pleased they were to see her and remarking on how they wanted her to be back with them as soon as possible, but Gwen didn't hear any of them, she just stared at the bed with her hands over her mouth and tears welling up. 'Oh no...'

The other pilots fell silent and looked at her, wondering what was wrong, but Gwen didn't look at anyone except Penelope who sadly smiled back at her.

'I'm so sorry, Penny.'

'Thank you, dear.'

'What? What is it? What's wrong?' Scarlet was frowning, looking back and forth from Gwen to Penelope.

It was Penelope herself who answered her and pointed out to the squadron what only Gwen had noticed. 'My legs, Ophelia, darling. I lost my legs.'

Everybody looked down at the bed, for the first time seeing what should have been obvious to all of them right away - that the sheets were flat where Penelope's feet and lower legs should have been.

There were gasps and tears sprang up in more than one eye, but Penelope instantly waved their concerns away, putting on the brave face that Lord Bagshot had told them about. 'Prussian lead did for one, but English soil did for the other - I shattered it when I landed, then all the manhandling and the trip to the hospital just made it worse, so they had to chop it off as well.'

Abby was the first to recover and spoke angrily into the shocked silence. 'I was told over the telephone that you were fine. This is not fine. I think your doctor and I need to have words.'

'I'd much rather you didn't, Abby, dear; they were only acting under my instructions.'

'Why?'

She shrugged. 'I simply didn't want you all to worry about me.'

'Oh, come off it, Penny,' Mac growled at her. 'You know damn well we'd want to know this kind of thing as soon as possible.' Of all of the Misfits, he was the one who had known her longest and had been flying on her wing since the inception of the squadron.

'A day or two makes no difference, Mac, and don't you worry; even though the doctors say I'll never fly again, I've already got Biffy contacting some people to make me some peg legs. We'll be flying together again soon enough!'

'Aye, we will, lass.' Mac huffed gruffly and turned away to stare out of the window, but too late to hide the moisture in his eyes.

There was another awkward silence and, being the practised socialite she was, Penelope filled it. 'I take it you've seen these? Biffy, would you be a darling and hand me those?'

She indicated a pile of newspapers on her bedside table and her husband did as he was asked. She fanned them out on the bed in front of her and they saw that the story had been given to each and every one of them and not just the national papers, either, but the smaller regional ones as well.

'I've read them all; it's not as if there's much else to do around here, and I must say I had no idea we were all such bloody heroes!'

The pilots laughed and, just as Penelope had intended, the conversation turned from her injuries to the story. Each publication told the story of the battle with the Barons in its own way, with more or less emphasis on the rest of the day's fighting and varying degrees of sensationalism. The only thing they had in common was the squadron photograph and the way they matched their names to the various aircraft whose exploits had become so well-known over the summer.

The Misfits remained distracted until a stern-looking nurse came in an hour later to kick them out, insisting that her patient needed rest. They would have protested, but they could see that Penelope was visibly drooping, so they said their farewells and promised to visit, even though they knew that they would most likely be kept far too busy by the war to do so.

They walked out of the hospital far more upset than they had been when they arrived, but were heartened only a short time later when Lord Bagshot caught up with them just as they were getting into the RAC wagons.

'I say! Wing Commander!'

Abby turned back at the man's shout and waited for him to jog down the stairs, limping only slightly from his old injury.

'Penny told me that your secret base isn't very secret anymore and I heard a rumour that it's likely to be out of commission for some time, is that right?'

Abby raised an eyebrow. 'It seems someone has been talking a little bit more than they should.'

'I have friends in Whitehall.' Lord Bagshot shrugged. 'Anyway, I wanted to offer you the use of my estate while you were rebuilding. The Harridan squadron that was in residence have moved back to their original base so I have plenty of room and full facilities and besides, I know that Penny would love to have you all there for moral support while she was recovering. It's not exactly secret, but it's right next to Windsor, which is bloody heavily defended and it's also within spitting distance of London, so the bigwigs can't complain about you being too far away from the fight if they need you.'

'I don't know...' Abby trailed off. Her initial reaction was to refuse, but the more she thought about it the more it struck her as a good idea. As the man said, it wouldn't be a secret because, thanks to the press, everyone now knew that Lady Penelope was one of them, but with the change in Prussian tactics it wasn't truly necessary to have a secret base anymore. It would make sense logistically as well; for a start they wouldn't need to waste time repairing the repair facilities before they could repair the aircraft. She smiled and gave him a grateful nod. 'Thank you. We accept.'

'Spiffing! I shall let Penny know! See you soon!' He reached out and pumped Abby's hand a few times then ran back up the stairs and disappeared back into the hospital.

The Hawkinge wagons took them to Folkestone station and from there the squadron caught a train to Canterbury, where they were met by three of Badger Base's steam autocars. They were the only three which had survived the raid and weren't entirely intact - one had a deep gash from shrapnel in its bonnet, another a missing door and the three machines had only a single windshield between them, meaning that they would be rather exposed for the journey. The weather was fine enough for that not to matter, though, and they treated the hour-long ride as if it were an outing in the country, shouting occasional comments back and forth between the vehicles and tilting their faces up to the late summer sun. However, the sight that greeted them at the base wiped away their smiles and quietened even the two most boisterous of the pilots.

The autocars dropped them off at the edge of the airfield in front of the officer's mess and mutely surveyed what was left of the beloved base that they had taken off from only a couple of days.

It was barely recognisable.

Almost nothing remained of the military installations on the far side of the airfield and the wreckage stood in a wide circle of devastation, the trees that had served to camouflage them all but gone. The lovely buildings which had formed part of the original holiday camp had fared slightly better, though, the officers mess and the administration buildings almost intact. More importantly, though, the landing field was pitted with huge craters and completely unserviceable. Crews were working to clear rubble and using shovels to fill in the holes in the airfield, but two days had not been nearly sufficient for them to make any real inroads on the repairs.

'Bastards...' muttered Bruce angrily. 'Look what they've done to my cricket pitch!'

The Misfits stared at him, momentarily lost for words.

Mac recovered first. 'Is that what's most important to you?'

The Australian shook his head. 'Well, no. Of course not.' He grinned. 'But we already know that the beer survived.'

The Misfits laughed, but the mood was still sombre when the man in charge of administration and the day to day running of the base, Squadron Leader Algernon Billingsworth, came out of the officer's mess and saluted Abby. He was a tall and painfully thin man who seemed to be compensating for his lack of corpulence with an overabundance of twirly moustache.

Abby returned his salute. 'What a bloody shambles, Algy.'

She said it with a wry smile, but the man evidently took it as a criticism and winced. 'Sorry, ma'am. We're doing what we can, but we're working with very few resources; all our heavy machinery was destroyed and replacements have been delayed, so as you can see...'

Abby held up her hand to stop him. 'None of that matters; we're abandoning the base. Just tell me about casualties, please. I've read your report and I know we didn't lose anybody, but I want to know why anybody was hurt at all if Owen warned you in time to get to the shelters.'

'We're abandoning...' The Squadron Leader's eyes widened and his moustache twitched in surprise, but he recovered quickly. 'Casualties, yes. Uh, well, most people *were* safely in the shelters before the first bombs fell, but the crew of Hummingbird were delayed getting Aviator Lieutenant Flynn off the ground and the staff of the officer's mess apparently felt it was their duty to rescue some of the more expensive wines.'

Abby sighed. 'Damn fools... And? What's the butcher's bill?'

The man racked his brains to come up with exact figures, twirling one of his handlebars absently as he did so. 'Um, two broken bones, a concussion, and a few minor cuts and scrapes. Oh, and a case of the Chateau Podreaux '89 was dropped down the stairs of the shelter when a bomb fell close by and jolted it from the hands of one of the stewards. It's a complete write-off, I'm afraid.'

'Oh, no, not the '89!'

Abby glanced towards the listening pilots and gave Derek, whose whine it was that interrupted them, a scathing look.

The tall, thin, balding, well-spoken and usually very serious Derek, was a true gentleman, from a family with old money, but no titles to go with it and had earned his nickname of "Twitcher" in the aviation community long before the Misfits were formed. He was not only a bird spotter, though, but also a wine connoisseur and had used his aircraft, Swift, to fly around the world, not just to see rare bird species, but also to visit vineyards, often killing two of his favourite subjects with one stone. While Bruce would drink anything you put in front of him, Derek was a true connoisseur and the loss of a case of extremely expensive wine was almost as painful to him as the loss of his aircraft would be.

Abby shook her head, then turned her full attention back to Billingsworth. 'I want orders in place that anything non-essential, which is *everything* except the aircraft themselves, is to be abandoned in the future. I don't want anybody dying over wine, not even a... a...'

'Chateau Podreaux '89.' Derek supplied in a stage whisper.

Abby gave him another look, causing him to wither under her gaze. 'Yes, not even that.'

Billingsworth nodded. 'Very well, ma'am.'

'Good. Right then, as I said, we're abandoning the base and I need you to organise the packing.'

The men and women nearby had paused in their duties to listen and Abby turned to address them as dismayed murmuring arose among them. 'I know that this is our home, but we can't fly from here, it's too damaged so we have to leave. We have been offered a new home by Lady Penelope Bagshot and her husband on their estate, so we will be moving there while we get back up to strength.'

'Back up to strength, ma'am?' asked a young servicewoman.

Abby only then realised that she had neglected to inform the men and women of the squadron how much the fight against the Barons had cost them. It hadn't occurred to her that they would only have read the reports in the papers, reports which strategically omitted the casualties sustained by the Misfits. She sighed. 'I'm sorry, you should have been told. We are down to less than half strength. Seven aircraft were damaged or destroyed and Lady Penelope has been injured and is not likely to be able to return to us. We're going to have enough work to do to get this squadron back into the air, without having to worry about rebuilding as well.'

She saw understanding, however reluctant, blooming in the eyes of the gathered servicemen and women and she turned back to Billingsworth. 'Halt all repairs and contact Whitehall, please, Squadron

Leader. Tell them that Badger Base is out of commission and no longer secret, so we are abandoning it.'

'Very good, ma'am.'

Abby began to turn away, but he stopped her. 'One last thing, ma'am. A few telegraphs have arrived for you over the last few hours.' He handed her more than a dozen small cards, saluted her smartly, then walked away, already barking orders that sent the watching personnel scurrying.

Abby glanced at the messages and laughed.

'What is it, skipper?' Bruce led the pilots as they gathered around her.

Abby wordlessly handed the cards to him.

'The Dorchester apologises for the recent misunderstanding and wishes to renew its invitation to Misfit Squadron to reside in its suites whenever it is in town,' read Bruce before turning to the next card. 'The Ritz Hotel wishes to extend its invitation to Misfit Squadron...' He flicked through the rest in quick succession. 'The Savoy Hotel wishes... The Royal Lodge... The Iron Tower Hotel... The Darwin Inn... The Brass Palace... Ooooh! This is nice!' He put on a high-pitched, nasal voice - his impression of an upper-class twit that had so entertained his fellow pilots in the past - and lifted his little finger from the cards as he read. 'Lady Wilberforce desires the presence of the *delightful* Misfit Squadron at a soirée to take place whenever it is convenient for the pilots to attend.' He kept flicking through the remaining cards. 'Bloody Norah, there's invitations to balls and dinners and all sorts of hoity-toity shindigs here! We won't have to pay for our own food and drink for ages!'

The Misfits cheered, but knew that they wouldn't be accepting any of the invitations anytime soon; all their energy needed to be directed towards getting the squadron back to operational status, no matter how tempting the prospect of free drinks was.

Abby clapped her hands to call their attention back to the matter at hand. 'Right, then, you lot! Go get your personal effects packed up. Bring one kit bag with whatever you're going to need for the next few days and leave the rest on your beds - I'll have them picked up and brought later with the rest of the equipment. We'll meet in the briefing hall in half an hour for a quick lunch before we go back to Hawkinge.'

She watched them as they started picking their way through the rubble that was strewn across the path down the side of the officer's mess, then turned to her fitter, Sergeant Potter, who had been hovering, waiting for a chance to speak to her. He had large scab in the middle of his forehead, from a deep-looking cut and she frowned at him.

'Why weren't you in the shelter in time, Henry?'

The man pushed his round glasses back on his nose before speaking. 'Well, ma'am, Hummingbird might not be my aircraft, but her fitters are my people and I had to make sure they were safe.'

'Very well.' Abby nodded her understanding. 'Now, please tell me you have some good news.'

Potter hadn't been able to tell her anything to lighten her mood, though, so Abby was feeling just as downcast when she reached the briefing hall after packing her own room up and her stomach only fell further when she caught sight of her son, Jimmy, sitting with her three junior pilots; there was a bandage around her head and his cheek was a mess of fresh scabs. The only thing stopping her from forsaking any dignity she might have left after having led the Misfits for so long and rushing to him was the promise she'd made both of them that she would let him make his own way and wouldn't keep checking up on him all the time. Also, by the animated way he was waving his hands about, he was probably telling the story of how he came about his injuries in an effort to impress the good-looking women surrounding him and really didn't need her butting in.

It was hard to believe that he was still only sixteen. War was making adults out of children long before their time.

She sighed and placed her kitbag with the others by the door, each with the name of one of her pilots stencilled on it in Indian ink, then made her way towards the serving tables at the back of the room. On the way she stopped at many of the tables to share reassuring words with the people under her command, so it was a while before she could make it back to the pilots. When she got there Jimmy was on the point of leaving and she grabbed him to keep him from rushing off. 'What the dickens happened to you, James?'

'Oh, wotcha, mum, didn't see you there!' He shrugged. 'I got caught in the bombing, no big deal.'

'What were you doing still outside? You should have been in the shelter.'

'I had to make sure Hummingbird got up alright, didn't I? Couldn't let Scarlet down!'

Abby glanced at Scarlet over Jimmy's shoulder, but the Irishwoman just shrugged; like all of them, she was helpless to get the boy to do what he was supposed to. Jimmy wasn't in the RAC, he was just there because of Abby, so he wasn't under military discipline and just drifted from one job to another as the mood took him. If he got it into his head that he was one of the fitters of a particular aircraft, there was nothing any of them could do to stop him. 'I suppose not. Thank you.'

'No problem, mum!' Jimmy gave her a big grin, then rushed off to join a group of airwomen, who had just joined the queue for lunch.

Abby watched him for a few seconds then shook her head. She placed her tray on the table and sat down next to Gwen. 'Didn't he have a girlfriend?'

Gwen smiled. 'Yes. But there's no stopping him. You know that.'

Abby sighed again. 'Only too well...'

As soon as the Misfits had all finished eating, Abby got them moving.

The plan was for Kitty and Wendy to stay at Badger Base to pack up their workshops, ready for transport, before joining them at Bagshot Hall later that evening and Abby gave them permission to use as many people as they needed for the task. Meanwhile, the rest of the pilots would travel back to Hawkinge, where those with intact aircraft would fly them to their new base escorting the Lekker which would carry the others. The damaged aircraft would be left behind for the fitters to dismantle for transport.

The Misfits said goodbye to Badger Base, probably for good, and piled into two autocars for the trip back to Canterbury train station.

A slight adjustment had to be made to their plans, though, because a large metal box, containing the remains of the Barons who had been shot down, was waiting for them at Hawkinge, along with a message from Whitehall, saying that arrangements had been made for Scarlet to deliver it to coordinates near the French coast that evening. So, while the other pilots prepared to go to their new home, Scarlet dressed in her flight suit and prepared to make a foray into enemy territory.

Hans Gruber stood stiffly at attention as he watched the camouflaged aircraft follow the trail of red smoke that they had laid out for it and slowly lower the green metal box to the ground. Its overhead rotors were at full power as it struggled with the task - the box was far larger and heavily laden than on previous occasions because it contained the twisted remains of twelve Prussian aircraft and what the British had been able to scrape together of seven Crimson Barons, men who had been proved unworthy of the name he had given them. Also inside were his trophies, parts from the paltry four Misfit aircraft that he and his squadron had managed to shoot down. He didn't know which shamed him more, that those few trophies were the first his squadron had ever obtained from their enemies, or that the cost had been almost his entire troupe.

It was fortunate that he was such a well-loved and public figure, otherwise such a defeat might have cost him his rank, if not his freedom or his life. As it was, it had taken some judicious bending of the truth for him to keep hold of his squadron and standing behind him were fifteen new pilots, men whose names he hadn't bothered to learn and who would remain nameless and faceless to him until they had distinguished themselves. Three pilots had made it home from the raid, but he had had the two who had run at the start of the fight executed for cowardice and sent the third to one of the MU9 squadrons; he didn't want any reminders of past failures.

He was the only one left from the original Crimson Barons, now. The only one remaining of the brave squadron that had spread such glorious carnage over Spain, Poland, Denmark, Belgium and France. It didn't matter, though; the squadron would rise from the ashes, better than ever before, with him leading them in the new aircraft that was almost ready for him.

And then the Misfits would pay for their crimes.

He saluted as the aircraft rose back into the air, once more remarking at how beautiful the pilot was and wondering at the stupidity and cowardice of the British that let such women fight and die for them. Then, when the silly machine had disappeared over the trees, he lazily dropped the salute and walked forward to open the box, eager to see his trophies.

He was intrigued to find a slightly soiled white envelope pasted to the top of the box where it had been protected from the elements underneath the aircraft's spring. Even more curiously it was addressed to him in a neat but ornate script, obviously a woman's writing, and he wondered if it was a message from his opposite number, Abigail Lennox.

He opened the envelope and pulled out the single sheet of paper within. It was lightly perfumed and the note was written in the same hand as the envelope.

My debt to you has been paid.
Until we meet again.
Gwen Stone.
Pilot of Wasp.

Gruber laughed when he saw the two thick lines carefully drawn underneath the name of the aircraft - a pink one over a black one.

As if he didn't know the name of the aircraft or the pilot that had humiliated him.

When they met again he would destroy both, but his revenge would have to wait for a while; with the invasion of Britain on hold he had been assigned another task.

CHAPTER 2

Early the next morning after a hearty breakfast in the spectacular dining room of Bagshot Hall, where they now found themselves billeted, the Misfits wandered out into the grounds of the mansion to inspect their new home.

Lord Bagshot had been quite the scandal of the British aristocracy in recent years. Not only had he married a commoner, and for *love* of all things, but he had also given over much of his estate to the construction of a racing track for himself and a private aerodrome with full construction facilities for his new wife. He didn't care one jot, but he had won back a good measure of his prestige when he had been among the first to invite a fighter squadron onto his lands after the RAC bases had been bombed out. He had even paid for many of the additional buildings and facilities necessary to the running of said squadron out of his own pocket. Until recently it had been the Harridans of 223 squadron who had had the pleasure of his hospitality, but with the Prussians changing the focus of their bombing from aerodromes to cities, the pressure had been relieved from the RAC and they'd been had time to rebuild and recover. 223 squadron had returned to their newly reopened home a couple of weeks previously, just in time for the Misfits to move in.

The pilots wandered around, familiarising themselves with the facilities.

The main hangar was large enough for a squadron of fighters, but wouldn't be able to accommodate something the size of Dreadnought or Bloodhound, which would have to have something built specially for them. Next to it was a ready room for the pilots, equipped with leather sofas and a brass tea urn that would keep them well-supplied while waiting to scramble. There were several paintings by well-known aviation artists on the walls, but there were also a few framed newspaper clippings scattered among them and Gwen paused as one in particular caught her eye.

'Mac, is this you?'

'What? Where?'

'Here.' Gwen pointed to the article and the Scotsman wandered over. The rest of the pilots gathered around and to peer at the photograph on the printed page.

'Och, aye! That's me there next to Penny. That was the first time she beat me for the Schnitzel Trophy.'

Gwen read the article aloud for the benefit of those pilots who couldn't get close enough. 'In her very first appearance at the Schnitzel Trophy, sixteen-year-old Penelope Doris Bader took first prize, pipping last year's winner, William MacShane, to the post by less than a second.' She looked around in surprise. 'Why didn't anybody tell me that Lady Penelope was Penny Bader? I was there that day! I remember cheering her to this victory when I was eight! What happened to her? She won again two years later, but then she just disappeared.'

Mac shrugged. 'She fell in love and got married. Her heart was never in it after that, I s'pose there were jus' too many other things to do. Damn shame it was; competing with her was the best thing that ever happened to me - we pushed each other to greater heights. I never entered another cup after she left; it wasnae fun no moa.'

Mac turned and left the room, followed by the rest of the pilots, all except for Gwen who leaned in close to take one last look at the young woman in the photo, before hurrying after them.

Behind the hangar were several workshops and Gwen was delighted to find a fully equipped design room with several large desks. Lastly, there were row after row of barrack houses and a large mess hall for the combined personnel of the base to eat together, all far more luxurious than anything that would be found on a standard RAC base.

After their brief tour, the pilots naturally ended up standing on the airfield and they gazed soberly into the shadows of the hangar, the doors of which were open to reveal the fitters working on the aircraft which had made the flight up the evening before.

Of the twelve aircraft that the Misfits had started the 15th September with, only five - Wasp, Hawk, Hummingbird, Bloodhound and Vulture - were in an airworthy condition. Of the other seven, two

- Swordfish and Cheetah - had been destroyed and the other five - Dragonfly, Swift, Ballerina, Devil and Dreadnought - were on their way to Bagshot Hall in crates and would need extensive repairs before they flew again.

Abby took a few paces towards the hangar, then turned to face them and looked at their long faces one by one. She didn't like what she saw; despite their victory and the apparent waning of the Prussians' enthusiasm for invasion, the cost had been high and none of them were in a mood for celebration, especially after finding out Lady Penelope's true condition. She had expected nothing less from them, though; they cared about what they did and felt the extra weight that had been placed upon their shoulders by the press and the British public. The best thing to do would be to keep them busy - she needed to put them to work immediately.

'The King gave me a task last night - he told me to get this squadron back into the air and ready for combat as soon as I could. He told me that if there was anything that I required, that I just had to ask and it would be given to me.'

'More Podreaux '89!'

The pilots laughed and Abby joined them, allowing the lightening of their mood, knowing that they were going to need every little boost of morale that they could scrape together for the hard times ahead. 'I'll put that on the list, Derek. After the Duralumin sheeting, but *before* the padding for your seat.'

Derek's face fell and he sighed. 'I think I can make do with the '95 Beaujolais...'

'That's what I thought.'

There was more laughter at Derek's expense and much thumping on his back.

'Anyway, as I was saying, the King told me to ask for whatever I needed to get this squadron in the air as quickly as possible and I told him that I already had everything I needed; I have all of you. You are the back bone of this squadron and between you we have the talent and the knowledge that we need to rebuild our aircraft and make this squadron better than it ever was. It also doesn't hurt that we have Gwen Stone, legendary aircraft designer, to help us.'

There were chuckles as Gwen blushed. She'd never been comfortable with their praise, despite the fact that she had earned it by not only improving Wasp, but also designing Bruce's aircraft, Devil, from scratch in just couple of hours. Not to mention that she had built her first aircraft at only seven years of age *and* helped with the creation of the Hawking Harridan, one of the most successful British fighters of the war.

Abby smiled at her. 'I know I for one will be asking her to help me realise Dragonfly's full potential.'

'Hear, hear!'

Abby nodded at Owen's outburst and the eager nods of agreement it drew. It said a lot about the people standing before her that there were no hard feelings, hurt pride, or reluctance on their part to take advantage of the woman's genius.

'So, we're going back to the drawing boards, at least with A and B flight. I don't care if the aircraft are damaged or undamaged, this is our chance to make them better and we *have* to make them better; the Prussians aren't going to stop improving their aircraft and we've certainly given the Barons an ideal excuse to improve on theirs by wrecking all their old ones for them.'

Abby waited for the jeers to die down before continuing, but this time seriously. 'We have to stay ahead of the game if we want to win this war and I believe that together we can do that.' She looked around the group of pilots one by one, meeting the eyes of each of them in turn before finally coming to rest on Gwen.

'Gwen. I'm putting you in charge of the rebuilding efforts. I know this is a bit sudden, but, have you got any thoughts?'

Gwen grinned in delight at the prospect of having free rein over Misfit Squadron's aircraft and began sorting through the multitude of plans and ideas that she'd come up with in the months she'd been with the squadron. 'How long have you got?'

Abby laughed. 'Can you just give us a brief overview of what you think we should be doing?'

'Ah, you mean dumb it down for them?' Gwen grinned and jerked her head in the direction of the rest of the pilots, who laughed.

'Well, I wasn't going to put it like that, but yes.'

'Speed.'

Abby waited for Gwen to say more, but when she didn't she chuckled again. 'Perhaps dumb it down a little *less*. After all they're not *all* Welsh.'

'Hey!'

Abby stuck her tongue out at her second in command to more laughter before turning back to Gwen. 'Elaborate please.'

'Well, I spoke to Mr Rentley and Mr Joyce at the Palace and they told me about the springs they have in development. They have a new model, which they call the Phoenix. It's a complete rebuild from the ground up, but they're having teething troubles with it, so in the interim they have a new model Ozzy for the RAC. They say that the new mark of Ozzy provides more than ten percent more power than the one we're using right now, but the Phoenix is projected to provide almost *twice* as much power.'

There were gasps from the pilots at that and she nodded as she continued. 'The question for us designers and pilots, then, is what to do with that power. How to use it best.'

It was Abby's turn to nod. 'More speed.'

'Indeed.' Gwen nodded. 'There are two things that can be done with increased power. One is to increase the weight of our machines, allowing us to add more armour and weapons while keeping performance the same. However, for our fighters, an increase in speed would be far more useful. That does mean that A flight are going to make a few fairly big changes.'

Abby frowned. 'Like what?'

'Well...' She looked at Bruce and Monty and shrugged apologetically. 'For a start, we can no longer fly biplanes.'

As she'd expected, there were protests from the two men, but she stuck to her guns, needing them to understand and accept what was patently obvious to her. 'Sorry, gentlemen, but when the Prussians increase their speed, which they will, your slower aircraft will become obsolete; their tighter turning circles will mean nothing if the enemy can just stay out of your reach, climb above you and make runs that you can't match.'

Gwen bit her lip as the two biplane pilots whispered together, wondering if they were going to challenge her. She glanced at the other Misfits, seeking some indication of whether they agreed with her, not sure if she could defend her point of view if some of the immensely experienced pilots, many of whom were designers themselves, decided to argue against her.

Her doubts were assuaged when Owen winked at her, then dispelled altogether when both Abby and Mac gave her an approving nod, but it was the proud smile from Kitty that really warmed her heart and stiffened her spine with resolve to fight for what she knew to be true if necessary.

It didn't take long for the men to come to a decision and Bruce spoke for both of them. 'We don't really like it, but if you say that's what we have to do, then that's what we'll do. We trust you.'

'Thank you.' Gwen nodded at the two men gratefully, relieved not to have to confront anyone, then turned back to Abby. 'We're going to have to adjust our tactics to suit this new emphasis on speed because our turning circles are going to get wider and we can't be pure turn fighters anymore. That doesn't mean that we should all be flying the same type of aircraft as B flight, though, it just means that the challenge, as both pilots and designers, will be to find the optimum balance between speed and manoeuvrability.'

Abby nodded. 'That sounds logical.' She looked around at the gathered pilots. 'If you think about it, this is just the next step in the progression that pilots have already made in the transition from steam to springs. Imagine what would happen if a Dromedary or an LE5a went up against one of our aircraft.'

There were nods of agreement; they could picture the outcome easily enough and were smart enough to work out why.

'Owen. Thoughts?'

When big decisions needed to be made, Abby always asked Owen to play devil's advocate, he could usually come up with a perspective on the discussion that nobody else had thought of, fruit of his training as a scientist. 'That all sounds good and everything, but shouldn't we wait until we actually get some of these new springs before we go about completely redesigning our aircraft and buggering around with our tactics? It might be weeks, or months, before we actually get issued any of the damn things.'

Gwen grinned at him. 'Actually, I was promised the very first batch and as long as Rentley-Joyce know where to send them they should be arriving in the next few days.'

There was stunned silence for a good few seconds before guffaws broke out.

Abby smiled as the pilots surrounded Gwen, thumping her on the back and congratulating her; it was good to see the smiles return to the faces of the people that she had come to love so much.

Work on designing the new aircraft that were needed by the squadron began immediately. However, while the design of Devil had been very much a solo effort by Gwen, this time she was aided in the task by the other Misfit designers - Abby, Kitty and Mac. The plan was for Mac and Kitty concentrated mostly on the B flight aircraft that were their speciality while Abby worked on the turn fighters, with Gwen working on both projects, moving freely between the two teams to discuss their ideas with them before incorporating them into the completed designs.

Gwen was looking forward to all of the design work and the engineering work that it entailed, but it was the prospect of making adjustments to Wasp, more than anything else, that excited her and she already knew exactly what needed to be done to bring out the best in her.

She also had a very good idea of how to improve Dragonfly as well. Unfortunately, though, in order to make true improvements, Abby's aircraft was going to have to lose its most distinctive feature - the wings that so gracefully tapered outwards so that they were wider at the tips than the roots. Those wings gave the aircraft the aspect of the creature it was named for and were an innovation that had been far ahead of their time, making Dragonfly's rate of turn almost as good as that of biplanes and rarer triplanes. However, the days where that was a primary consideration were fast disappearing and the wings would need to be sacrificed, like Monty and Bruce's biplanes, and replaced by something more streamline. Something more modern.

The designs of the new aircraft had to come first, though, so Gwen stored her plans for Wasp and Dragonfly out of the way at the back of her mind and turned her full attention to filling the blank page on her desk.

They were less than an hour into their work when Bruce and Monty came to see them, looking somewhat sheepish, caps in hand quite literally.

Abby straightened up from her drawing board and frowned at them. 'Gentlemen? Is something wrong?'

Monty glanced nervously at Bruce and received an encouraging nod. 'We have a request to make.'

'Alright. What is it?'

'Well, we were thinking that we'd like to have identical aircraft, please. If you don't mind.'

'Really?' Gwen was surprised; the Misfits prided themselves on being individuals and their aircraft were as much an expression of their personalities as they were functional war machines. For the two men to ask for identical aircraft seemed almost sacrilege.

Bruce chimed in. 'Ever since you switched the squadron round and put Monty on my wing things have been clicking.' He grinned shamefacedly. 'More than it ever seemed to when I was on your wing. Sorry, boss.'

'I concur.' Monty sprang to the defence of his section leader. 'We have a similar style of flying and we've been very effective with similar aircraft, but we believe that we'll be even better with machines that have identical performance.'

'Understood.' Abby nodded, then glanced at Gwen, who just shrugged, before smiling at her pilots. 'I think we can accommodate you. It'll certainly make things easier for us and the fitters having one less design to deal with.'

'Bonzer!' Bruce clapped his hands together. 'Well, we'll let you get to it, then! Come on Monty, chin up! If our new birds are half as good as Devil, you're in for a treat!'

As soon as the door closed behind them, the wing commander turned to Gwen. 'Sorry, looks like your fun has been cut down a bit.'

Gwen chuckled and shook her head. 'I don't mind one bit; I have enough fun for now and this way I'll get to Wasp and Dragonfly quicker.'

'That's the spirit! Back to work then.'

Gwen tapped her forehead with a grin. 'I never stopped.'

Abby rolled her eyes. 'Good for you... But your designs are no good to me in there, are they? Put them on the damn paper!'

While the designers were busy drawing up plans, the rest of the pilots were far from idle. They volunteered to help with the repairs to the three repairable aircraft - Dragonfly, Swift and Dreadnought, which had arrived by road shortly after the pilot's tour of the facilities. Dragonfly was only lightly damaged and it would only be a day or so before she was back to her former glory, but Swift would take at least three days; she was in a similar state to the way Gwen had found Wasp when she had joined the squadron. Dreadnought was a whole other matter, though; the extensive damage to her engines, fuselage, wings and weapons would take far longer to repair. Even with every able hand working on her, they were looking at several weeks of hard work to get her back in the air.

However, the pilots dropped everything the very next morning, when two large delivery vans with Rentley-Joyce's swan logo painted on the sides arrived, loaded down with Ozzymandias Mark 45 springs. Abby immediately ordered them put into the available spring-powered aircraft, Wasp, Hawk and Hummingbird, for testing and three pilots of the aircraft, Gwen, Scarlet and Kitty, gleefully ran off to get changed into their flightsuits.

The new springs went into place without a hitch; their cases exactly the same size as the old ones, but then the pilots had to wait around impatiently while they were wound - they were never transported or stored fully wound; not only was it too dangerous, but also being under full tension for too long wasn't good for them.

Finally, though, the three wildly different aircraft were ready to fly and final checks were made before fitters guided them out of the hangar and onto the airfield.

Gwen and Kitty had to taxi to the downwind end of the grass field, but Scarlet just waved away her fitters, saluted Abby ironically, then put on full power, making Hummingbird leap directly up into the air. She transferred power smoothly from her overhead rotors to her forward airscrew and the gyrodyne leaned forwards and accelerated away. She skimmed the perimeter fence of the airfield, then flew above the wide lawn towards the mansion more than a mile away. The pilots laughed as she dipped to pass through the spray of the ornamental fountain before rising once more and buzzing the house, making the flag flutter briskly as she went past. She banked behind the trees beyond and quickly disappeared from sight.

The watching Misfits transferred their full attention to the two aircraft that were only now reaching the edge of the airfield and turning into place.

'Mac.' Abby spoke the man's name without taking her eyes from the machines.

'Aye. Ready.'

The aircraft stopped and the sound of their airscrews built as the pilots pushed their springs to full unwind while keeping their brakes on, but it was only for a second before they released them and the machines surged forwards eagerly.

'Now!'

Abby's cry had Mac looking at his chronograph.

'Wasp. Hawk.' As the wheels of each aircraft lifted from the grass, Abby said their name.

'Five seconds Wasp. Seven Hawk.'

Both times were marked improvements over how long the aircraft usually took to get off the ground and the gathered pilots made noises of approval. Hummingbird reappeared, zooming along at top speed only a few feet from the top of the trees on the far side of the airfield before disappearing again, but they barely gave it a glance and just kept following the fighters as they went higher and higher into the bright September sky.

Wasp came unstuck from the ground with a satisfying swoop, giving Gwen that familiar, and very welcome, feeling of weight that told her she was back in the air where she was free. Where she belonged. More than anything she was a creature of the sky; on the ground she felt awkward, ungainly, and not just physically, but mentally and emotionally as well - her inability to sort out her feelings about Kitty was a perfect example of that. In the air, though, her mind sharpened and everything seemed clear and simple. Everything was in its place and everything worked as it should.

Hawk had a slightly longer takeoff run than Wasp, but the faster machine soon caught up and slipped into place on her wing. The two aircraft turned in a wide circle as they climbed so as to remain within sight of the watching pilots; the flight was not just for them, but for the Misfits as a whole.

Gwen glanced across at her friend and saw a wide grin on her face which she was sure was mirrored on her own.

'How does it feel, Kitty?'

'Bloody marvellous!'

Gwen laughed at the American's very English turn of phrase. 'It does, doesn't it?'

'I didn't think ten percent would be so noticeable.'

'Neither did I, to be honest, but I'm not going to complain. The Fleas are certainly in for a surprise when our pilots get a hold of these.'

They flew on in silence, both pilots getting a feel for their new machines but, after something less than a minute, Gwen glanced at her altimeter and realised with a start that they had been climbing a lot faster than she'd realised. They were already high enough for any manoeuvres to be safe, but not so high as to be out of sight of the pilots, who had grabbed their flight helmets and goggles while the women had been changing so that they could watch more closely - it was time to start.

'Is there anything you want me to do in particular, Gwen? You know, to help you make decisions with the designs?'

Gwen smiled. 'Well, if you don't mind, it would be really helpful to know exactly how much faster the new springs will make B flight.'

'You want me to see how fast I can go? Well, that's not exactly not my idea of fun, but I'll do it anyway. Just for you.'

Kitty's deadpan voice made Gwen chuckle. 'Just bugger off already so I can get on with doing something a bit more serious.'

'Roger, Leader. Your wish is my command!' Kitty laughed as she peeled off and went diving away.

The pilots watched the two aircraft split up. The twin-airscrew Hawk dived and accelerated, but Gwen threw Wasp into a breathtaking series of aerobatics, spinning about the sky. For the turn fighters of A flight, the biggest gain brought about by having more power would not only be in sheer speed, but also in acceleration, which would dictate the ease with which they could transition from one manoeuvre to another.

They briefly tore their eyes away from Wasp when Hawk dived towards them under full power, pulling up to scream past them at only twenty yards distance and less than five yards above the airfield. It tilted its nose to the sky just before it got to the trees surrounding the base and went into a steep climb that seemed to go on forever before standing on its wing to do a tight turn and coming straight back, repeating the exercise. It was a manoeuvre that approximated the runs B flight made on enemy bombers and there were appreciative noises from Mac and Derek, both remarking at how little speed it seemed Hawk was losing on successive runs when compared to the old springs.

After only fifteen minutes, both fighters came in to land, their testing done. They could have been up for far longer, but neither of them wanted to keep their fellow pilots waiting unnecessarily before giving their verdict. Scarlet, of course, had decided to take advantage of her freedom and there was no sign of her whatsoever.

Kitty's report was simple, but delivered with much enthusiasm and a wide grin that had even the more jaded pilots smiling with her. 'Twenty miles per hour increase on the flat and I got a hell of a lot more than that out of her in a dive! She could have gone much faster, but I could feel the airframe starting to protest and didn't want to risk it. I'll have to at least strengthen the wing roots before seeing what she can really do, but *boy* does she feel good!'

Gwen laughed with the others before giving her own report, but rather more seriously. 'I think the ten percent increase in power the Rentley-Joyce boys told me about is a conservative estimate because at three-quarter unwind it felt something like full throttle with the old springs. Pushing past three-quarters doesn't give as much gain as I would expect, though, because Wasp can't use the extra power she's being given. So...' She paused, considering, her mind racing and providing solutions as fast as it found problems. 'It's not just our airframes and aerodynamic properties that we need to change, but also the way the power is being handled and delivered. Like Kitty said, we're going to need stronger airframes to handle increased speed, especially for B flight, but we also need different airscrews to convert the extra power to more thrust. They can't just be bigger, because we'd need longer undercarriages to keep them from ploughing the field on landing and taking off, so maybe five bladed airscrews, or a slightly different shape blade, or a rougher pitch... I don't know, we'll have to work something out, but when we do we should have a handy increase in both speed and acceleration, which is already noticeable, by the way. Oh, and I wouldn't be surprised if we saw an increase in range, either.'

The pilots stared at her in silence, each trying to assimilate all the information she had thrown at them.

After a few seconds, Abby tutted and shook her head in disappointment. 'You had a full fifteen minutes in the air and that's all you could come up with?'

Gwen blinked. 'Well, I... uh... well...' She raked her brain, trying to think of something else so as to satisfy her commander, but stuttered to a halt when she saw that her fellow Misfits were all grinning at her behind their hands and that Abby herself was having a hard time keeping a straight face. She glared at her in mock anger. 'You should know better than to tease me like that! You know I'll just take you seriously.'

Abby shrugged and allowed her smile to show finally. 'Sorry, Gwen, but if you're going to be teasing Owen with the rest of us, you have to be able to take it too.'

'Sounds like you've got your work cut out for you, Gwen, darling. Not just redesigning all the aircraft, but also keeping these ungrateful sods happy.'

The voice came from behind them and the pilots turned to find Lady Penelope smiling up at them from an old-fashioned wooden wheelchair that had most likely been sitting in a storeroom in Bagshot Hall for fifty years or more. She had a tartan blanket over her lap, although Gwen at least wasn't sure whether it was to disguise her missing appendages or to keep her warm.

Lord Bagshot was behind her, holding tightly onto the handles of the chair as if frightened she would zoom off and try to jump into one of the aircraft. He was looking tired and dishevelled, but had a wide smile. 'Sorry to interrupt, but Penny wouldn't let me take her up to the house without popping by to see how you were settling in first.'

The pilots rushed to gather around her and began bombarding her with questions all at once until Abby raised her voice. 'Misfits! For goodness sake! Give her some room to breathe!'

The pilots fell silent sheepishly and backed off the minimum amount that they felt they could get away with before looking to Abby to speak first. She tutted and rolled her eyes, then raised her eyebrow at Penelope. 'Should you be out of hospital?'

'No.' Penelope shook her head with a mischievous grin. 'They wanted to keep me for a few weeks, but Biffy told them where to stick that. He's contracted a nurse and a doctor and bought enough of the latest equipment to turn my room into a bloody hospital ward! So I'll be far more comfortable here than I would be in that awful place, and besides, I'll be able to keep an eye on you lot. Which reminds me...' She squinted up at Abby, a hard look in her eyes. 'I hope you're not going to wait as long to find a replacement for me as you did for Cece.'

Abby flinched involuntarily at the thought of her younger sister, the first pilot of Wasp, who had died over France in the early weeks of the war, but she forced herself to hold Penelope's gaze and even gave her a half smile. 'It's already well in hand. Whitehall are sending me the files of likely candidates by courier - they should already be on their way.' She looked around the group, smiling at their shocked and surprised stares. 'I'm just obeying the King's orders. We'll be back to full strength in plenty of time to go back on active duty, so there's no need for any of you to worry about that. Worry about the jobs you've been assigned instead. Speaking of which.' She turned back to Penelope. 'When you're feeling up to it, we could use your expertise with the new B flight machines; the more ideas the better, as far as I'm concerned, and there's a good reason you won the Schnitzel Cup twice.'

'I'd be delighted. A few hours rest and I'll be right as rain.' Lady Penelope smiled, but her voice was weakening by the minute and when she coughed in an attempt to clear it she had to close her eyes against a sudden pain, her face going pale.

Abby took the opportunity given her by Penelope's attention being elsewhere to give a concerned glance to Lord Bagshot. She received a grimace and a reluctant nod in return; he would make sure his wife didn't do anything that she shouldn't, which included rushing her recovery and joining them in the design shed before she was strong enough.

Penelope recovered slightly after a few seconds, but her breathing was ragged, her voice was weaker than before and her eyelids were drooping as the effort of coming down to greet the Misfits took its toll. 'Well, my darlings. I would love to be able to welcome you properly to my humble home, but as you can see I am rather indisposed; the medications, don't you know? Please do avail yourself of the facilities, though, and if there is anything you need, please don't hesitate to ask Biffy or one of the servants. Now, if you'll forgive me...'

Her voice trailed off and she sagged against the side of her chair, unable to keep herself from exhausted sleep any longer.

The pilots stared at her sadly for a few seconds, but then Lord Bagshot spoke into the silence, his harsh words the more shocking for the softness and gentleness of his tone as he tried not to wake Lady Penelope. 'I'll get Penny up to the house, but first let me just first say one thing - don't you *dare* pity her. She was hurt doing something she adored and defending the country she loves and I am positive that this little injury of hers won't keep her down for very long. So, just bloody treat her as you always have. It's what she wants and what she bally well deserves.'

He didn't wait for an answer from them, but just nodded and wheeled his wife away around the ready room, back the way they had come.

The Misfits looked at each other, displaying various degrees of shame and thoughtfulness, but then Mac chuckled.

When the others looked at him in disbelief he shrugged. 'She whipped my arse in the Schnitzel Cup as a wee sixteen-year-old girlie, against all odds. Do ye really think not having any legs is going ter keep her down fer long?'

He shook his head and then turned to go back to the design shed, calling to them over his shoulder. 'Shake a leg, yer daft Sassenachs, we've got work to do!'

'This is good, this is very good.'

Gruber looked from the plans pinned on the table in the design room to the almost completed frame of the machine under construction in the workshop next door and back again, comparing the two. He tried to imagine the finished aircraft in his mind, but couldn't quite, so he just shot the man standing next to him a mild look. 'But will it be good enough to beat the Misfits?'

'Undoubtedly, sir.' The white-coated scientist, Walter Blume, bobbed his head nervously. Despite being a well-respected designer and decorated ace from the First Great War, he was still nervous around Gruber and with good reason.

'It had better be.'

Gruber stared at the man, enjoying the way he wilted under his gaze. He briefly considered letting him know the consequences of failure, but in the end decided against it; sometimes it was best to leave things to the imagination and besides, Blume knew perfectly well what had happened to his predecessor.

He finally broke eye contact when he turned to the table next to the board and picked up the models that had served as inspiration for the new design.

The two model aircraft, one pink and one yellow, had been bought relatively cheaply in the Hamleys toyshop in London by one of his agents, then smuggled out of England at ridiculous expense by unscrupulous Cornishmen.

It was incredibly stupid of the British to sell accurate models of their most advanced technology in a toyshop for all to see; it rendered industrial espionage completely unnecessary. For years the Empire had been buying aircraft, ships and even autocars and trains to study, and the war had not stopped that. The Americans were much smarter and kept their cards close to their chest - for instance, all attempts by Prussian intelligence to get their hands on the plans of old man Tesla's new electrical weapons had failed and agents had been lost, but that wouldn't stop them trying; those weapons could change the course of the war and make it so much easier for the right side to win.

'Have you thought of a name for your new aircraft, sir?'

Gruber pursed his lips, thoughtfully. 'What is that English saying? *Give them hell?* Well, let us indeed give them "Hell".'

He tossed the models back onto the table, not caring if they were damaged; they had served their purpose.

He gazed through the window at his new machine, *Hölle*. 'Will it be ready in time for my departure?'

'She will be ready in three days, sir.'

'You have two.' Gruber gave the man a last, meaningful look, then left.

CHAPTER 3

Penelope paid a short visit to the design shed first thing in the morning the next day, bringing along with her a servant, who was weighed down with a few dozen cardboard tubes. The tubes contained blueprints of many of the aircraft, including Mac's, which had taken part in the Schnitzel Cup during the last fifteen years before the competition ended at the outbreak off the war. Lady Penelope had drawn them up herself, so that she could study them and improve her own designs and while she herself couldn't work for very long because she tired too quickly, those designs immediately proved invaluable as a reference tool.

The fitters completed preliminary repairs on Dragonfly by mid-morning and all that was left to do was apply a fresh coat of paint to the new Duralumin panels, which didn't stop Abby immediately dropping her pencil and taking her up to do her own evaluation of the new springs. She concurred with Gwen's assessment of them and authorised her to begin looking into new airscrew configurations. As a temporary measure, while Gwen ran her own tests, she and Abby decided to run a five-bladed airscrew on their aircraft, quickly put together by their machinists using existing blades. The new configuration worked well enough and delivered a fair increase in thrust immediately, without needing any further adjustments to their airframes, so they declared themselves satisfied for the moment and put the problem of airscrews to one side so as to concentrate on more important things.

The days passed extremely quickly as everybody, pilots and support staff alike, worked flat out, often long hours into the night. They were desperate to get the squadron back to readiness as quickly as they could; without working aircraft they all knew the Misfits were wasted and everyone was keen to have the most effective squadron in the Kingdom of Britain back in the fight as soon as possible.

Abby and Gwen split their time between the design shed and testing, getting used to the different feel and tactics that were necessary with the increased power. They began flying mock dogfights and interceptions on the Lekker, which they had been gifted by the Royal Transport Department, who seemed very keen to get rid of it. Work on the designs of the new aircraft slowed slightly as a consequence, but it didn't matter very much; the fitters had enough to be getting on with repairing Swift and Dreadnought.

Gwen was run off her feet, but Abby was even busier; not only did she have to do the same designing and testing as her wingmate, but she also had to look through a couple of dozen files, searching for a new pilot, as well as send regular reports to Whitehall on the progress of repairs. She was often awake until midnight and up again at dawn the next morning trying to keep up. Then, to cap it all off, the bigwigs, on hearing that Wasp had been repaired and that the Misfits could scrape together a section, had immediately put them back on limited readiness, thinking that the appearance of at least a few of the famous aircraft in the sky might do wonders for the rest of the RAC.

The Prussian air force, *Die Fliegertruppe*, or the "Fleas" as the British liked to call them, were being strangely quiet, though, and there wasn't anything much for the Misfits to do apart from continue with their work.

While the pilots understood the necessity of repairing and rebuilding and were willing to stay on the ground to help the fitters as best they could, it was very much a case of all work and no play and tempers quickly began to get short. On the eighth day, after a fight almost broke out between Charles and Derek, two of the mildest mannered of the Misfits, Abby decided to do something about it. She didn't need to organise anything frivolous this time, though, like she had with the glidewing competition at Badger Base, because it was obvious that all they needed was to get back up into the air.

She drew up a schedule for the fighter pilots to use Dragonfly, Wasp and Hawk, with the permission of their respective owners and contacted Whitehall with a request that missions be given to Owen,

Scarlet and Charles. When Swift was repaired a few days later, she was added to the ready list, giving the Misfits a section from each flight to play with, which opened up many more options of what to do with them and they began going for training flights and practised dogfighting in pairs, with A flight taking on B flight.

One afternoon, after almost two weeks of solid work an urgent message arrived for Abby. Squadron Leader Billingsworth delivered it to the design shed personally, considering it important enough to require his personal attention and she stepped outside the building to read it, not wanting to distract the others from their work.

Officer i/c Misfit. Report BPal post-haste. Hyde expecting.

Abby looked up at the squadron leader, who was smiling at her from under his copious facial foliage. 'You've read this, I take it?'

He nodded. 'I relieved the operator and took it down personally once I heard the identifiers. It sounds like we're getting back into the show.'

Abby frowned. 'Probably. But it's too early, we're not back at full strength. We need at least a few more weeks.'

Billingsworth shrugged. 'Perhaps they are expecting the impossible from you; after all you have delivered it to them before.'

Abby huffed in amusement and shook her head. 'Well, they're going to be disappointed this time.'

Billingsworth raised an eyebrow. 'We shall see.' He gestured at the message. 'Any reply?'

'Acknowledge and say that I'm on my way, please.'

'Yes, ma'am.' Billingsworth saluted her, then marched back off to the communications shed.

Abby went back inside to tell the others that she was going to be away for the rest of the day.

She had to admit that the call couldn't have come at a much better time; they had just finished the design of the new A flight aircraft. It had taken far longer than it had taken Gwen to create Devil, partly because there wasn't the same desperate urgency to get the entire squadron back into the fight, but also because, due to the increased power of the new springs, some basic principles that had always been applied to fighter aircraft no longer applied and the philosophy behind the design had to be adjusted accordingly. It was ready now, though, and all that remained was to neatly draw up two copies, one each for the two construction teams, which could be left for the morning; a few hours wouldn't make a difference. When that was done and the plans had been given to the construction teams, she and Gwen would help Kitty and Mac finish off the two B flight aircraft, after which they would be free to start improving Wasp and Dragonfly.

Gwen, of course, hadn't wanted to wait until Abby got back, so she continued working long after Mac and Kitty were gone for the night, finally finishing around midnight.

She put her pencil down and stretched while she frowned down at the pair of identical blueprints.

She and Abby had created a wonderful design, working together well and complimenting each other perfectly, just as they did in the sky, but she wasn't at all happy with it; it was too functional, it had been designed with only its purpose in mind. There was nothing special about it, nothing that spoke to her as a person and there were no small touches of individuality that said that its designers had put some of their own personality into it.

War was making aviation too impersonal and she had produced a machine that owed more to and appeared more like the Harridan and Spitfire than any of the previous Misfit Squadron aircraft.

She picked up the pencil again and leant back over each of the two copies in turn to angrily scrawl the only names she felt that she could give them - Rapier and Sabre - naming them as the weapons they were. She threw the pencil back down again with a snarl, then turned the light off and left to start the long walk up to the mansion and her bed, leaving the blueprints where they were.

Abby landed at Hyde Airstrip just as the sun was going down and was escorted directly to the changing room where she got into her dress uniform - she had no idea what she had been called for, so had decided to play it safe and dress for court. The corseted jacket was slightly tighter than it should have been, the gold buttons running in diagonal lines from her shoulders to her waist even more difficult to do up than they usually were; it seemed that nervous energy on its own wasn't quite enough to burn through the excellent food that Lord Bagshot was providing and she would have to get back up into the air more often if she didn't want to be too big for Dragonfly's cockpit soon. Once dressed, she settled the brown silk sash and gold oval-shaped medallion of the Order of Darwin in place over her shoulder for the first time since she'd been awarded it. Lastly, she took her top hat from its box and made sure that the purple silk band was straight and unwrinkled. As always she lamented half-heartedly that, when she had been recruited, she had been given only the rank of wing commander; if she'd been made a group captain, just one rank higher, she would have had impressive gold braiding around the front of the brim.

She gave herself a quick once-over in the mirror and smiled in satisfaction; the golden medallion on the brown ribbon really did look rather distinguished, although Scarlet had been right the night at the party when she had been awarded it; a red sash would look so much better against RAC blue.

Feeling far more self-conscious in her uniform than she ever had, far more than should be warranted for the addition of a simple strip of brown silk, she left the safety of the changing room. The guards led her to the security gate nearest the Palace, opposite Wellington Arch where she found an enormous autocar, flying Royal colours on either side of its wide bonnet, waiting for her. The Royal Guard driver opened her door for her with a salute and saw her settled comfortably before climbing in and pulling out onto the almost deserted street for the short drive to Buckingham Palace.

The sustained bombing of London had finally brought home to its denizens that they were in fact at war. Despite the defeat of the army in France they had been pretty much ignoring the conflict, going about their lives as if people weren't actually dying to keep them safe, but the carnage in the skies above them and the indiscriminate destruction wrought by the Prussian bombs had opened their eyes to the hard reality of their situation. In some ways it was a good thing; now that the populace knew exactly what they were up against, the government were free to act without fear of undue criticism. Rationing had been imposed on many basic items as shortages were foreseen and strict, almost draconian, blackout rules had been imposed.

The people of Britain had reacted as they always had, though, with stoicism and a firmly stiffened upper lip, banding together as they had whenever their way of life had been threatened by a tyrant - they had laughed in the face of the Little Corporal Napoleon, scorned Kaiser Bill the second and would equally defy his son, Kaiser Bill the third. However, not since King Philip I of Spain's armada had been bearded, had there been such a direct threat to the British Isles. Not even Boney himself had ever quite posed the threat that the Prussians did now and for the first time the British people found themselves in real danger.

Nobody knew whether the British spirit would hold up under such circumstances and with privations and things would only get worse as the war progressed.

Only time would tell, but Abby suspected that they would.

The autocar turned through the Palace gates, receiving the salute of the guards there, quadrupled since the last time she had visited, and pulled up into the interior courtyard.

She was shown to a seat outside the same conference room where the Misfits had been debriefed and asked to wait. She didn't sit down, though, but instead took advantage of being left alone in the Palace for the first time (apart from the ever-present, ever-watchful guards and servants) to wander around the room looking at the artworks on display.

She had long enough to appreciate only a single painting, though - a fairly recent piece by the Spanish artist *Salvador Dalí*, depicting the birth of a drooping aircraft from an egg, as if it were a bird, which was somehow completely captivating despite the utter unairworthiness of the machine - because the door to the conference room swung open only minutes after she'd arrived to divulge Sir Douglas Pewtall.

'Dame Lennox.'

She gave him a warm smile as she marched over and took his offered hand, nodding in greeting. 'Sir Douglas.'

He returned her smile. 'How are your new accommodations working out?'

'Very well, thank you, sir. Are they close enough to London to suit you and Aviator Lieutenant Flynn?'

She fought to keep her expression neutral as the man's cheeks turned a comically dark red. Pewtall was an excellent administrator and had been an equally good pilot in the first Great War, but, like many British men (and men in general), he was absolutely dreadful at dealing with his feelings. He was obviously extremely embarrassed to find out that it wasn't as big a secret as he thought it was that Scarlet had been sneaking out each night to meet him at an inn half-way between London and Windsor.

'Yes... well... anyway... Come on, we don't want to keep His Majesty waiting.'

He turned away, trying to hide his face from her and she took a second to compose herself and make sure that her uniform was still perfectly in place before following him.

There were only five people in the room, far fewer than there had been for the debriefing. She had been expecting to see four of them:

King George VI, the newly elected Minister for War, the Marshal of the Court and Sir Douglas, but the fifth and last was a pleasant surprise - Dorothy Campbell, recently promoted to Sky Commodore and a long-time friend. She wasn't ranked high enough to be a regular attendee at meetings like this and her presence indicated that there was indeed something in the offing. Abby couldn't make enquiries of her or even greet her yet, though, because there was a protocol to be followed and she stood to attention just inside the door, facing the King, who was sitting in his customary place at the head of the table deep in conversation with the War Minister, waiting for him to notice her.

After only about ten seconds the King finished what he was doing and looked up at her with a smile. He immediately stood and walked around the table, seeming genuinely pleased to see her and she wondered briefly if he actually was or whether he was merely wearing his politician's face.

Her doubts were firmly banished when he grabbed her hand and shook it with quite some enthusiasm.

'Good job on getting our Misfits back in the air, Dame Lennox, good job!'

Abby fought hard not to frown at his words, but couldn't stop her smile from slipping slightly. 'Thank you, Your Majesty, but we're still a good three or four weeks away from being back to full strength.'

The King waved away her protests. 'I've read the reports and I'm aware that you're still short a few aircraft and a pilot, but that is of no consequence; even a single Misfit section in the air is better than none.'

'Yes, sir. Thank you, sir.'

'And while we're on the subject - how are you doing in your search for a new pilot? I know that not everybody can be a Gwenevere Hawking, but there must be at least a couple of likely candidates among our intrepid airmen and women.'

'I'm doing my best, sir, but as you say, it is hard to find someone who measures up to Aerial Officer Stone. I'm narrowing the search down as much as I can, though, and hope to find someone in the next few days.'

'Good, good.' The King nodded, then waved her to a chair before going back to his own.

She sat down, trying not to crease her uniform any more than she had to and glanced around the table, smiling at Dot before nodding respectfully at the two other men.

The Marshal of the Court, who was hovering by the wall unobtrusively, on hand if the King should need him, returned her greeting with a solemn nod, but the Minister for War, Regis Cummerbund, an ageing man in his late sixties in a coal-black suit, with a thin face, severely parted white hair and a permanently disapproving look frowned across the table at her. 'Really, Wing Commander, you've had *more* than long enough to choose a new pilot. Please do so by tomorrow morning at the very latest; we need you back to full strength for this mission and from what I've heard of you *Misfits* your new pilot is going to be required to make some, let us say, *adjustments* before you are happy with them.'

Abby was unsure of the intention behind the man's words, whether they were a criticism or merely an observation of how different the Misfits were, but the barely perceptible sneer when he said the name of the squadron made her suspect the former. She decided to ignore his apparent disrespect, though, and concentrated instead on the information he had let slip. 'What mission, sir?'

The King gave Cummerbund a scathing look. 'Well, the cat's out of the bag now, so I suppose we should just get straight down to business. We're sending you to Russia...' He grimaced, interrupting himself. 'Sorry, the *Tsardom of Muscovy*.' He glanced over at the Marshal. 'Damn, I keep doing that. It would be quite bad if I said that to the Russian ambassador, dammit, the *Muscovite* ambassador tomorrow, wouldn't it?'

The Marshal nodded. 'It would be something of a faux pas, Your Majesty, yes. Please try not to.'

The Tsar of Russia, Nicholas II, had only the week before followed Britain's lead in shrugging off any notions of Empire after the very concept had been tainted by the Prussians. The Tsar had also decided that the name "Russia" itself was a little too close to "Prussia" for comfort, even though when pronounced in their native tongues they sounded nothing alike, and the Russian Empire had reverted to its old name of the "Tsardom of Muscovy" to further distance themselves from the tyrannical aggressors.

'You know me - I can't promise anything.' The King chuckled, shaking his head, then frowned, obviously trying to recover the train of thought that he himself had derailed. 'Where was I?'

'Russia, sir.' Pewtall said.

The King grinned at him. 'Very droll, Sir Douglas... Remind me to have you demoted.'

'You can't, sir; that's my job.'

'No, but I can order you to demote yourself.'

Pewtall chuckled. 'Yes, sir. That you can.'

'Ha!' The King grinned in triumph before turning back to Abby. 'Right then, Dame Lennox. I'm sending you to the *Tsardom of Muscovy*.' The King put emphasis on the words while staring pointedly at the Marshal, who nodded seriously, either not knowing that he was having fun poked at him, or so used to it that it was just water off a ridiculously dressed duck's back. 'We have intelligence that Bill the younger is a bit miffed with us and is looking for an easy target elsewhere and since America is well and truly off the table for now there's only one way to go. He is pulling back many of his forces from here in the west and sending them east towards the Muscovite border.'

'I thought they had a non-aggression pact?'

'They did, but apparently it no longer suits Bill and he's tossed it out the window.'

Abby shrugged. 'Maybe he needs something to distract his armies with after we gave them the shock of their lives.'

'Quite.' The King nodded his agreement. 'However, because of that pact, Muscovy is not ready for war - Nicholas has just been sitting back, twiddling his thumbs and sipping vodka while he watches us do all the fighting. Now that the Prussians have turned on him, he realises that he has no army, no modern weapons and barely any air force to speak of and is scrambling to catch up.'

'Damn fool.'

Cummerbund muttered the comment under his breath and the King frowned at him, disapprovingly. 'Please refrain from expressing your personal opinions in my council chambers, Mr Cummerbund. Save them for your drawing room where they will undoubtedly be better received by your cronies.'

'As you wish, sir.' The Minister nodded, accepting the reprimand, but didn't seem at all repentant.

The King scowled at him for a few seconds, before turning back to Abby with a far milder expression on his face. 'Anyway, despite his error in judgement in not helping us against the Prussians from the start, Nicolas has always been a good friend to us. So, while he gets his defences in shape, I've promised him a bit of help in the form of some tanks and guns, mostly American stuff that we've bought recently. I'm also sending fifty or so Harridans with a few instructors to train up their fellows on them. Oh, and I'm loaning him the Misfits, of course.'

'But we're not at full strength, sir. Why not just send a Spitsteam squadron, or more Harridans?'

The King sighed. 'Because Nicholas told me in no uncertain terms that he either gets you for a while or he signs on with the Prussians.'

The King spoke softly, trying to soften the blow, but the Minister for War was blunt and to the point.

'You have your orders, Wing Commander, and you will obey them. You are to go to Russia and hold their northern border at *all* cost.'

He glared at Abby and she shifted uncomfortably under his gaze. She wasn't happy with the order, but it there didn't seem to be any other choice. She opened her mouth to convey her acceptance of the task, but was interrupted by a soft voice.

'Muscovy.'

All eyes shot to the King, who just smiled back at them amiably.

There was silence for a few seconds, but then first Sir Douglas then Dorothy Campbell broke out into fits of laughter, accompanied by Abby. After a few seconds the King joined them and Abby swore that even the Marshal almost smiled.

Cummerbund didn't.

When things had calmed down again the King continued. 'You worked well with Sky Commodore Campbell before and she seems to have a good understanding of how Misfit Squadron can be best employed so we decided to give her overall command of this mission. You'll form the nucleus of her task force and you'll aid the Muscovites in defending the area around Murmansk against the Prussian assault until winter sets in. At which time you will be free to come home.'

'And if the Prussians overwhelm the Muscovites, like they have everybody else so far?'

'Then feel free to run for your lives and get back here whatever way you can.'

Abby chuckled. 'Thank you, sir. Most kind.'

There was a disgusted grunt from Cummerbund, but he stayed silent, apparently not wanting to be the butt of any more jokes.

King George was no longer in a mood to joke, though. 'I'm sure I don't have to stress how important this mission actually is, do I, Abby? If we can hold back the Prussians in the east, then they will be stretched thin trying to fight on two fronts, which might just give us the chance to push them back. However, if they defeat the Muscovites and absorb their resources, then that will undoubtedly be the beginning of the end for us and perhaps the whole world. I know you don't like it and frankly neither do I, but at least a part of me is glad it's you and your people who are going; you're our best hope for a good result. Nobody is expecting you to defeat the Prussians single-handed, but delaying them until winter will be invaluable in allowing the Muscovites to mobilise.'

'We'll do our best, sir.'

'I can ask for nothing more.'

There was another grunt from the Minister, but again he was ignored.

'You leave in two weeks.' The King held up his hand to forestall her when Abby automatically began to protest. 'Yes, yes, I know that's not nearly enough time for you to rebuild, but that has been taken into consideration. You will be going on the carrier *Arturo*. It's a bit of a relic, left over from the Great War, but it's big enough and has full facilities. You'll be able to use them during the voyage to complete all necessary repairs and construction and it will be staying in Archangel until you leave Muscovy, so if you really need them they'll be available after you arrive as well.' The King gave her a stern look. 'Please note that I said "necessary repairs", Wing Commander, and I do mean *only* those that are absolutely *necessary*. You should leave any of the tinkering that I'm sure you and Gwen have in mind for after your return. For now, just concentrate on getting your full squadron in the air.'

Abby nodded acknowledgement; there was nothing else she could do. 'Very well, sir.'

'One last thing...'

Abby looked at the King in dismay; in her experience, when a superior, either in the military or a company, said those three words it usually meant that they had saved the worst news until last and she was dreading to think what would possibly be worse than being sent into the arctic circle with insufficient time to prepare.

The King saw her expression and chuckled. 'Don't worry, I'm not going to spoil your fun any more than I already have.'

Abby smiled wryly. 'Thank you, sir. That's most appreciated.'

He laughed. 'I thought it might be! But you should reserve your judgement until you know what it is. I assume you've seen the latest articles about the Misfits in the press?'

'Yes, sir.' Abby grimaced; the articles had only gotten more personal since the publication of the photograph, printing personal details of each of the pilots, like where they had come from and what their backgrounds were. While for most of the pilots that just meant their home towns becoming a little bit more well-known, for Gwen and Kitty it had meant a lot more - a big thing had been made of Gwen being the daughter of the Hawkings, something she'd tried to keep secret even from her fellow Misfits, and Kitty had been turned into some kind of unofficial figurehead for the drive to get America to enter the war. Surprisingly, though, the usually snobbish British broadsheets hadn't expressed much of an opinion on Scarlet's poor Irish origins.

It was all unwanted attention, but it hadn't been particularly intrusive into their private lives; none of the information was secret or especially personal and it was all readily available from anyone who knew the pilots. Abby got the feeling that was about to change, though.

'Yes, I'm sorry about that. We kept them off your back as long as we could, handing them official reports and such for them to write their stories from, but I'm afraid they are no longer satisfied with just that. They rightly say that the people deserve to know more about the pilots behind the aircraft which were so instrumental in... what was that bloody phrase that I couldn't for the life of me say, Sir Douglas? The one in that awful tabloid. Bashing Bill's something or other?'

'"Beating back Billy's bullying bombers", sir.'

The King mouthed the words, rehearsing them under his breath, but the man who had struggled with, and overcome, a speech impediment years before couldn't quite manage them and instead he just waved his hand in Pewtall's direction. 'Yes. *That,*' he said, rolling his eyes. 'The people were clamouring to know who you were, not just the names of your aircraft. We thought that if we gave the papers your service records it would keep them happy for a while, but all it's done is whet their appetite and they're demanding more. Fortunately, though, they are not unreasonable and realise that they cannot do anything to hinder your work, so they have reluctantly accepted our stipulation that only a single one of their members, accompanied by a photographer, be allowed to pester your squadron. To that end, a Mr Featherstonehaugh from The Times will be joining you at Bagshot Hall as you prepare. He will be looking to put a personality to the names that have appeared in the press, so many of his questions may be of a private nature and I would ask your pilots to answer them as best they can, even if they are not entirely comfortable with them. He has been told to stay within certain limits in his questioning, though, and, as he is one of the more honest examples of his profession, we trust him to do so, but his work will also be scrutinised before we allow it to be published, so you needn't worry about him writing anything that none of us want the public to read. When you leave, he will accompany you to Muscovy to continue his work, but he won't be with you the whole time because, in addition to your activities, he will also report on those of the Muscovite Air Service's new Harridan squadron and the situation in general.'

The King sighed. 'The glow of our recent victory will soon fade and the morale of the Kingdom will not remain as high as it is for very long. As the war drags on, and we inevitably face setbacks, the people will need *something*, a *symbol* on which to pin their hopes, and currently that is Misfit Squadron. I know this request is distasteful to you and you are disdainful of being in the public eye, but I hope you'll agree that it is necessary.'

Abby nodded reluctantly; unfortunately he was right on all accounts. 'Yes, sir, I do.'

'Excellent.' The King clapped his hands and stood up, causing the rest of the people in the room to scramble to their feet. 'Your orders will be made official and sent to you in good time by Sir Douglas and Mr Cummerbund, but count on leaving in the first week or two of October.'

'Very good, sir.'

The King began to make his way from the room, but stopped and turned back to her, very nearly causing the Marshal, who had been following him too closely, to bump into him. 'Will you stay to partake of a little refreshment? I know that Elizabeth in particular would be overjoyed to hear about your new aircraft and I believe Mr Joyce is here tonight, I'm sure he would like to know how you're finding his new springs.'

Abby smiled and nodded. 'I would be delighted, thank you, sir.'

'Excellent!'

Abby dropped back to let her superiors go first and Dorothy Campbell fell in by her side as they followed a respectful few yards behind the dignitaries.

'That ribbon looks good on you, *Dame* Lennox. Congratulations.'

Abby chuckled softly. 'Thank you. You know better than anyone that I've never done this for the medals and the accolades, but I have to admit it is rather fetching.'

'Don't let it go to your head; I've seen favourites come and go in this place, although you're lasting far longer than most.'

'I won't, don't worry.'

'Good.' Campbell gave Abby a warm smile before turning serious. 'It looks like we're going to be working together again, Abby. So, how are you really getting on with your repairs? Please tell me that you were exaggerating for the big men and that you're actually only a few days away from being ready.'

Abby shook her head. 'I'm afraid not, Dot. I was actually being truthful.'

'Drat. Oh well, what the King said about being able to complete the job on the way is true, but I would have liked you to have time to make at least some improvements, despite what he said.'

'So would I; we have to keep getting better if we're going to stay ahead of the Barons.'

'I know. But what I don't know is if you'll ever be given the chance.'

Abby frowned and looked at her. 'What do you mean?'

Campbell glanced meaningfully in the direction of the Minister for War. 'Ever since his promotion, Cummerbund has been very vocal in his opposition to Misfit Squadron and what he sees as the King's unwarranted and dangerous dependence on them. It's making him rather unpopular with the people, but he is gathering some support in the house.'

'Support for what?'

'To supply you with Harridans or Spitsteams, turn you into a regular squadron and stop wasting British funds and resources on something that he insists Britain doesn't need.'

'But that's... can't he see that...' Abby stumbled to a halt and Campbell stopped with her. 'Why is he doing that?'

The woman shrugged. 'Politics. He's much more powerful opposing the King than blindly following and since you're the King's pet project he's attacking him through you. A failure in Russia, or even just a perceived failure, will give him an excuse to shut you down and the King will be powerless to stop him.'

'But doesn't the King have the final say in this kind of thing?'

'Under normal circumstances, yes, but these aren't exactly normal circumstances are they?' Campbell smiled wryly and motioned for them to start walking again before the others got too far ahead. 'It was the King who insisted on sending the British Exploration Force to France and Parliament weren't exactly pleased as to how that turned out, so he's having to do things he wouldn't ordinarily, merely to keep them happy.'

'Second-guessing the King isn't going to help us win the war!' Abby hissed keeping half an eye on Cummerbund, to make sure he wasn't trying to overhear them.

'I agree.' The sky commodore nodded earnestly. 'But as I said - it's politics. Anyway, I'll be popping by to brief your squadron before we leave, we'll have a nice chat then. For now, try to enjoy your night and be nice to as many people as you can; you never know when you might need a friend.'

They had reached their destination and Campbell stopped just out of earshot of the guards at the door and leaned in to give Abby a peck on the cheek. 'Don't worry, we'll get through this.'

'Through what? The war? The mission to Muscovy? The War Minister's idiocy?' Abby glanced into the large reception room and grimaced; it was filled with people, soft and unobtrusive classical music, fake laughter and even faker smiles. 'Or just the evening?'

'All of it.' The sky commodore laughed gently and gave Abby a pat on the arm, then wandered into the room, already calling out a greeting to a group of people, who looked inordinately pleased to see her.

Abby watched her friend speaking to the courtiers for a few seconds, making them laugh, seeming totally at home and wondered how the awkward woman, who'd been assigned to help her put together Misfit Squadron because nobody else had wanted her, had become so comfortable in such a setting. The two of them had always looked on in horror as the officers around them had played the popularity game, but it seemed that it was a skill that she was going to have to develop, and as quickly as possible, if Misfit Squadron was going to survive the war.

Not for the first time did she wish that she was just a pilot again; things were much simpler in the air. That wasn't possible, though, so she sighed and plastered what she hoped wasn't too gormless a smile on her face, then went to follow her friend's example.

It was approaching midnight and the city was pitch black when Abby left the Palace, absolutely exhausted, heading for The Dorchester, where she was staying the night before flying back to Bagshot Hall in the morning.

The reception had turned out to be quite pleasant, not nearly as bad as she had feared it would be, and the conversations with Mr Joyce and Princess Elizabeth had indeed been enjoyable - the Princess had actually volunteered to fill the empty slot in the squadron and Abby had had to turn her down, not because she wouldn't have fit in or wasn't a fantastic pilot, but rather because she was only fourteen years old. She hadn't been able to fully enjoy herself, though, because of the shadow of the impossible mission in Russia, or rather Muscovy, that was now hanging over her squadron's heads.

It was thoughts of that which kept her awake well into the wee hours of the morning, despite her tiredness, and then, when she did finally get to sleep, her dreams were haunted by visions of a thin man in a black suit with severely parted hair and a disparaging scowl.

CHAPTER 4

It seemed to Gwen that she had only been asleep for minutes when she was rudely shaken awake.

She opened her eyes and looked up at the dim shape hovering over her. 'Wha... Kitty? What is it? Waddya want?'

There was a laugh, a very masculine, very melodious *Welsh* laugh. 'Sorry to disappoint you, Gwen, but it's me, Owen.'

Gwen didn't particularly enjoy being dragged abruptly from a deep sleep, but she had to admit that the man's lilting voice wasn't the worst way to be woken up. 'What is it? Is it Abby? Has something happened?'

'Nothing like that, don't you worry, it's just that there's been a request for our services.'

The thought of a mission, of getting up into the air and into combat, immediately brought Gwen to full consciousness and she sat up with a jerk. 'What is it?'

Owen pointedly looked away when the sheets fell away from Gwen, revealing her sheer silk nightie. 'Um... Get some clothes on and I'll fill you in on the way to the airfield. I've got an autocar waiting for us at the front door. Quick as you can, mind you.'

The light coming from the corridor outside the room briefly dazzled Gwen when Owen went out of the door and she blinked rapidly as she swung her legs out of the bed and started getting changed, but froze at Kitty's annoyed growl from across the room. 'Have fun, you lucky, lucky, b...'

'Go back to sleep and stop being so jealous,' Gwen said, cutting her off with a chuckle. 'I'll let you risk your life next time.'

She grabbed her shoes and padded towards the door, but stopped when a hand reached out to grab hers.

'Please be careful.'

Gwen stared down at the young woman. Gone was any pretence at envy and in its place was genuine worry that made Gwen's heart swell with affection.

Even though the two of them had spent hours working together in the design shed there hadn't been many opportunities for them to speak about their feelings, mostly because Gwen had engineered it that way. However, she'd seen the looks that Kitty continually shot her way, had noticed the excuses the woman found to be near her, or that she never lost any opportunity to make some kind of physical contact, no matter how insignificant, and Gwen was all too aware of how the American made her feel in return, often finding herself staring at her while she was supposed to be working. She still had serious doubts about whether she wanted another relationship, though, especially one where she might have to watch her partner die in battle. Her heart hadn't received the message her brain was sending, though, and it was pounding loudly in her ears as she looked down at the American.

'I will, don't worry.' Her voice cracked and she bit her lip as she was drawn into the blue skies of the woman's eyes.

Scarlet chose that very second to snort and roll over and Gwen started and guiltily looked over at her. The Irishwoman didn't wake and immediately went back to her snoring, but the moment was lost, so Gwen just smiled down at Kitty, gave her hand a squeeze, then left.

The autocar Owen had appropriated wasn't one of the squadron's boringly practical vehicles, but rather one of Lord Bagshot's collection, an open-topped two-seater spring-powered sports autocar, as responsive and agile as Wasp, and Owen sent it careening along the road towards the airfield without any headlamps, relying only on the light from the full moon to see by.

Gwen found the ride exhilarating, but she tried to keep her mind on the job at hand instead of just sitting back and enjoying herself. 'So, what's the flap about? Why did you wake me at this godawful awful hour of the morning?' She peered at the clock on the dashboard of the autocar. 'Bloody hell, Owen, did you know it's two in the morning?'

Owen laughed and spoke to her without taking his eyes from the road. 'Sorry to disturb your beauty sleep, Gwenevere, but early warning detected a raider heading towards the south coast ten minutes ago and they want us to have a crack at taking him down.'

'Don't they already have other squadrons flying night interceptions?'

The Prussians had all but abandoned their daylight bombing raids and were instead sending smaller groups, and in some cases isolated aircraft, against strategic targets during the night. The RAC in turn was trying to intercept these aircraft, but with wildly varying degrees of success.

'Of course and they've managed to bring down a few bombers, but this is one slippery Flea, apparently - he's been coming over for the last ten nights to bomb London, taking off from somewhere around Dieppe and crossing the coast over Eastbourne - he's arrogant enough that he takes the same route every time. Fighter Command have sent pilots up after him every time he's appeared, but either they fly around for hours unable to find him, or they do and he shoots them down. We've lost three Harrys and a Spit to him so far, apparently.'

'What? Really?' Gwen blinked, not sure she had heard correctly.

Owen nodded with a grimace. 'They think we might be dealing with someone flying a purpose-designed machine, something like Dreadnought - heavily armed and armoured and with an unusually large load.'

There was no time for Owen to say anything more because they had already reached the airfield. They went through the gate in the fence, which was held open for them by two Military Guards and straight across the grass field, ignoring the perimeter track. There was a slight chink in the blackout curtains on the hangar and a red light came through it, revealing the presence of fitters working to ready aircraft, but aside from that the base was deserted.

The early autumn night air was cold and Gwen was shivering slightly in the light clothing that was all that she had taken time to grab, so she hopped out and ran through the ready room, straight into the changing room as soon as the autocar stopped. She started getting into her flight suit as quickly as she could, joined seconds later by Owen, who began to do the same.

He grinned at her enquiring look and shrugged. 'You don't think you're the only one getting to have some fun tonight, do you? I'm going up with you to guide you onto the bomber.'

'Good. Anything that helps me take him down.' Gwen paused as something occurred to her. 'Oh, uh, by the way, I keep meaning to ask you - has this been cleared with Abby? And why me?'

Owen grinned. 'No need to bother her with something like this, right? And besides, I'm second in command, so I'm in charge when she's not here - if she didn't want me using my authority she shouldn't have given it to me.'

Gwen laughed. 'That's good enough for me.'

'And as for why I chose you, well, I thought you'd welcome a bit of excitement for a change.'

'Thank you, I think.'

Owen laughed at her doubtful expression and they both looked up as a sleepy steward, who Gwen recognised from the officer's mess at Badger Base, knocked then came straight in with some steaming mugs of tea and bacon sarnies.

Even with a few seconds wasted on wolfing down the food and drink, they were both ready in less than five minutes and they grabbed their gloves and helmets and went back out into the night, running blindly towards where they knew the hangar was, blinking furiously to try to get their night vision back.

They pushed through the curtains and came across a frantic scene as the fitters of both Wasp and Bloodhound raced through final preparations, one group loading ammunition into Wasp's guns and putting a last few turns on her spring, while a second group pushed the other aircraft to the side to make room for Owen's large radar-equipped machine to leave the hangar.

Abby's fitter, the grey-haired veteran Aviator Sergeant Jenkins, latched closed the trapdoor on the ammunition loading bay in Wasp's right wing and looked up as she ran over. 'You're fully loaded with armour piercing rounds and ready to go, ma'am.'

'Thank you, Sergeant.'

Gwen climbed up onto the wing then stepped into the cockpit and dropped onto her seat. She began to plug herself into her machine, placing the communications jack into its socket on the right side of her seat before reaching down to plug her suit into the combination heater and oxygen apparatus under her seat, adjusting the controls on the panel to her left and sending a warm flow of air around her suit to remove the chill that she was still feeling. She turned on her radio and as soon as it came alive she tuned it to the squadron frequency. While she tightened her straps and began running her final checks on the controls and instruments, she listened to Owen as he spoke to Fighter Command from his cockpit.

'...airborne in two minutes, report status of intruder, please.'

'Bandit is holding course three four zero at angels five, ten miles off Eastbourne, over.' Tophat was the sector station at RAC Kenley - the Misfits had been placed under their control when they'd moved.

'Acknowledged, Tophat. Badger Leader out.'

Gwen smirked at Owen's usurping of Abby's call sign as she did her checks, then looked over at Jenkins, who was waiting for her to finish. She gave him the thumbs up, which he immediately returned, then they both looked to Bloodhound, waiting for the order to go.

Owen finished his preparations just after her, his big engines roaring into life as the water within them reached the boiling point and excess pressure was released with a gout of steam that billowed upwards in a thick cloud that burst when it hit the roof of the hangar. His fitter gave the necessary signals and the red lights were dimmed to almost nothing as the curtains were drawn back and the two machines were pushed out into the night.

The wind was in their favour so Owen lost no time in turning onto the airfield and piling on full power, but Gwen held back, giving him a good head start before doing the same, not wanting to run into him in the dark.

In a surprisingly short time, the long wings of Bloodhound caught enough air to lift off, the four hugely powerful engines powering it rapidly to a speed that was only just shy of what the biplanes of A flight had been capable of, and it soared into the sky.

Wasp took off moments later, a hundred yards behind and Gwen had to slot mildly magnifying lenses in place to keep the machine in sight. Despite Bloodhound's light blue colouring and the full moon, it was almost invisible in the night sky and she wondered how she was ever going to spot the enemy aircraft, which presumably would be appropriately painted for nighttime activities. Gwen was able to drop back slightly to a safer distance, though, when Owen turned on his wingtip lights. Left over from before the war when Bloodhound was his own personal scientifically-orientated aircraft, the lights weren't exactly very tactical, but there was nothing else in the sky with them apart from the enemy bomber, which was still many miles away, well beyond visual range, so it didn't matter.

'Badger Leader to Badger Two.'

'Two here. Go ahead Leader.' Gwen put extra emphasis on the Owen's call sign, but didn't otherwise comment.

'I'm going to grab some height. Make Angels five, heading one three five, best speed, and we'll see about guiding you onto the target.'

'Roger, Leader.'

Gwen turned gently away from the red and green lights of Bloodhound and pointed her noise into the black, accelerating and quickly leaving the big machine behind as it continued to climb into the sky.

England was nigh on invisible beneath her; there were no lights of houses, no headlamps from passing cars, no street lights, there weren't even any running lights to be seen from the ever-present barges on the canals leading to London. The only sign that there was anything at all below her was the reflection of the moon on the occasional water surface as she flitted silently past.

Gwen felt strange. Not just because she was flying in the dark, something that she had only ever done a few times before during training, but because she was going into combat on her own, with only a single support aircraft. She never been as alone in the sky as she was at that moment - there was only her, the Prussian bomber and the watchers, Owen and Tophat, neither of whom would be able to help her if she got in trouble.

'Badger Leader, Tophat here. Bandit is holding steady on course three four zero, now at angels four. Speed two-fifty approx.'

'Roger, Tophat. I have him on scope. Moving to intercept. Keep this frequency clear until further notice, please.'

'Roger, Badger Leader. Happy hunting, out.'

There was a brief silence, then Owen came back over the radio. 'Badger Two, adjust course to one one five and make angels four. Target ten miles and closing, moving from right to left in front of you.'

'Roger, Leader.'

Gwen adjusted her course and height, hating the fact that she had to keep most of her attention on her red-lit instruments, but having to; with no external reference it was all too easy to become disorientated and confused and many a pilot had fallen out of the sky and crashed, not even realising they weren't flying straight and level.

'Target now four miles, turn five degrees left.'

'Roger.'

A nudge of the controls swung Wasp onto her new heading and Gwen slotted lenses in place and began to search the sky in front of her.

'Three miles.'

Gwen's eyes began to play tricks on her, blotches appearing at the corners of her vision, drawing her attention and she had to resist turning towards them every time.

'Two miles. Turn two degrees right.'

Owen had to be very close if his scope could pick out enough detail to give such accurate course corrections and Gwen relaxed slightly, knowing that, despite not having a wingman, she was at least better informed than her target, who would have no idea she was coming.

'One mile. Dead ahead.'

Gwen leaned forwards against her straps and squinted into the night, sure that she should be able to spot a large bomber at less than a mile. There had to be some glint of light off of its fuselage from the full moon, or some patch of darkness that was blacker than the surrounding...

Her heart leapt into her mouth and she jerked her stick back into her lap in a panic as a shape loomed large directly in front of her and the drone of huge steam engines filled her cockpit. Too late, she realised that the bomber was much further away than she had thought it was and tried to correct, but it flashed past beneath her before she could bring her guns to bear.

'That bloody thing is *huge!*'

It was only when Owen responded that Gwen realised that she had spoken aloud and that her radio was still open. 'Say again, please, Badger Two.'

'Repeat, I have made contact with the target, Leader.' She grinned to herself, even as she flung Wasp into a hard turn to bring her round to the left, putting her on a course that would slowly converge with the bomber's and threw the spring into full unwind, wanting to pull ahead of it and cut it off. She lifted her eyes from the instruments and searched for the enemy aircraft, but it had disappeared into the night.

'Understood, Two.'

Gwen could almost hear the smirk on Owen's face; he'd heard her the first time and was just teasing her about her lack of discipline.

'Um, Badger Two requesting directions, please; I seem to have lost him.'

'Target is half a mile off your left wing, recommend heading three five zero during twenty seconds then hard turn.'

'Roger, Leader.' Gwen stared into the night in the direction where the Flea should be, trying to spot him again, while keeping half an eye on her chronograph, but it was useless; there was no way to spot the intruder. She was going to have to trust in Owen's directions and rely on her own reactions to get in whatever shots she could.

Twenty seconds passed and she turned hard, simultaneously throttling back.

Owen saw her manoeuvre and gave her the information she needed. 'Turn to two one zero. Target half a mile, closing fast, almost head on.'

Gwen gritted her teeth, the numbers involved flashing through her head in an instant - the combined speed of the two machines was around six hundred miles an hour. That was ten miles every minute. A mile every six seconds. Half a mile would be covered in three, two...

Lines of incandescence reached out towards her, deceptively lazily, seemingly coming from nowhere, and she kicked her rudder and twisted her stick, jerking Wasp around while trying to line her reflector scope on their source. She squeezed the trigger, letting off less than half a second's burst, but then had to jerk the stick back to avoid the enormous machine as it flashed past her.

A quick glance at her altimeter told her that she was still safely at five thousand feet, so she throttled back, then rolled Wasp over and pulled the stick into her lap.

Wasp built up speed, going through the vertical, then slowly came back up to horizontal on a reverse course, now almost two thousand feet below and directly behind her target, although the only thing that told Gwen all of that was happening was the red illuminated gyroscopic attitude indicator directly in front of her.

The realisation of what had happened slowly came to her - just because she couldn't see the bomber, didn't mean it couldn't see her and while the bomber was evidently painted a dull dark colour, the top side of Wasp was a lovely pink colour.

She glanced out of the cockpit to confirm her theory and found that her wings were glowing beautifully in the moonlight. Gwen chuckled wryly; she had almost been killed by her favourite colour. Well, in her current position below the bomber, there was something she could do about that.

Gwen flipped Wasp on her back again and flew on into the night, upside down; while Wasp's topside was pink, her underside was painted black in honour of her previous pilot. It was a shiny black, polished to a high gloss, but it would hide her far better than the pink.

'Badger Two, this is Leader. Maintain heading - target is holding steady one mile ahead of you. Time to interception at current speed approximately forty-five seconds.'

'Roger, Leader. Give me a countdown to contact please.' Gwen's voice was slightly strained; she wasn't used to being upside down for so long and it was making her feel quite strange, but better the blood rushing to her head than a lump of lead, so she maintained her unconventional orientation.

Gwen kept an eye on her instruments as she pushed the stick forwards slightly and began a slight climb, aiming to come up under the enemy's belly, hopefully unseen until the last moment.

'Twenty seconds.'

The altimeter climbed through three thousand feet.

'Ten seconds.'

Knowing that there would be no way to see the bomber because it would be below her nose, Gwen kept her eyes glued firmly to the instruments. Three thousand five hundred feet came and went.

'Five.'

Three thousand eight hundred.

'Now!'

At Owen's shout Gwen flipped Wasp right-side up, pulling up to point her nose at the sky and there, a hundred feet almost directly above her, silhouetted against sparse silver clouds, was one of the biggest aircraft she had ever seen, almost twice as big as Dreadnought.

She lined her guns up on the target and opened fire, holding the button down.

The tracer rounds painted the way through the darkness, intercepting with the enemy bomber and she saw sparks fly as they hit metal. She nudged her rudder, walking the spray along the aircraft, spreading the damage from the heavy cannon shells as widely as she could.

Too late, the enemy reacted and swung guns towards her, tracer reaching out for her, spraying haphazardly across the night, but she had finished her run and was already banking past the big machine.

There was a flare in the darkness that illuminated her cockpit and she jumped, thinking that she had been hit, but there had been no corresponding thump from an impact and she swung around to bring the bomber back into view.

The sight she was confronted with was awesome in its majesty and yet terrifying - the huge aircraft was wreathed in flames. The hydrogen reserves in at least two of the engines must have exploded, causing the flash that she had seen and the flames were spreading along the feed lines, unchecked.

She allowed the bomber to pull away slightly, not wanting to be too close to it if the fire reached the main hydrogen tanks before the supply was cut off. The aircraft was completely out of control, its pilot either dead or no longer at the controls, and she watched as it went into a dive that started shallow, but swiftly accelerated until it was pointing almost directly downwards.

She dived smoothly after it, throttling right back and using flaps to fall back even further, easily following it as it fell from the sky until, with a crashing crump that was audible even from a thousand feet, it ploughed into the ground.

Burning pieces scattered everywhere, illuminating the surrounding farmland for miles around and Gwen nodded in grim satisfaction; tonight there would be fewer bombs falling on London.

Abby walked into the dining room of The Dorchester for breakfast and sat at one of the small tables. A waiter immediately brought her tea, toast and a copy of the morning edition of The Times. As she put sugar into her tea she glanced at the headlines to see if there was anything of interest and immediately waved for the waiter to come back.

She gave him instructions, then, as he went to follow them, she began buttering her toast.

She was tucking into scrambled eggs by the time the waiter returned, bringing with him a telephone.

Abby took the apparatus from him and spoke clearly into the receiver as she fluffed out the newspaper and gazed at the photo depicting the wreckage of a huge bomber, under the headline "The Return of Misfit Squadron."

'Hello, Owen? It's Abby. Is there anything you'd like to tell me?'

The British newspaper, The Times, didn't name the aircraft that the Misfits had shot down, but even in its mangled condition Gruber knew it by sight as the *Nachtfalter* and couldn't stop laughing.

The mess was silent apart from his laughter and the pilots of his squadron were eyeing him nervously from the other side of the room, but he couldn't care less; everything about the report was just too *delicious*.

Not only had the pompous, arrogant pilot - a pacifist scientist turned fanatic - been found dead in a machine that he had touted as invincible to whoever would listen and gotten exactly what he deserved, but he would also no longer be able to argue against Gruber and his squadron, or take any of the interest and praise of the public that should rightly be his. And then there was the stupidity of the British at sending a bright pink aircraft at night during an almost full moon and the novel and ingenious way that the pilot had removed that disadvantage.

It all conspired to have him almost rolling around in his seat as the journalist, one of his favourite war correspondents, Mr F. Featherstonehaugh, added his own special touch of humour to his description of the deadly duel.

Eventually, though, Gruber finished the article and managed to regain control of himself. He threw the paper to one side and wiped his eyes with a handkerchief, then waved for one of the waiters to bring him another drink.

While he waited for it, he gazed around the walls of the mess, taking in his numerous trophies. They were leaving for Norway in the morning, flying to the forward base in Denmark from where they would support the invasion, so it would be the last time he would see them in a while and had wanted to admire them one last time. His gaze lingered on the ones above the bar, the ones from Misfit aircraft, and he replayed the kills in his mind, his fists curling around an imaginary yoke as he sent a stream of death into the enemy machines, feeling the familiar surge of adrenaline and triumph. Unfortunately, it looked like it would be a long time before he would be able to add any more pieces of Misfit aircraft to his collection, but there should be at least a few kills to be made up north.

He smiled at the thought, then glanced across the room at his pilots and immediately started laughing again when they hastily looked away from him, avoiding his eyes - he had been hard on them during their training flights and they were nervous for the coming fight, fearful of him.

As they should be.

The waiter brought his drink and he grabbed it from the tray, swallowing half of it in one gulp to sooth a throat that was unaccustomed to such merriment, before staring back across the room, assessing.

His pilots had shown some of the skill he had chosen them for during those training flights, but he couldn't wait to properly test them in combat; then he would see exactly what kind of men he had allowed into his squadron.

CHAPTER 5

There were mixed reactions from the Misfits to the news of the mission to Muscovy. Some of the pilots were looking forward to getting back into the fighting, but others, like Owen, saw things much the same way as Abby had.

'It's a suicide mission! They're sacrificing us to keep the Tsar happy!'

Abby had gotten back to Bagshot Hall at midday, just in time for the brief meal the pilots allowed themselves, and thankfully it was just them, Lord Bagshot and Lady Penelope in the luncheon room to hear Owens outburst. She shook her head, trying to deny something that she suspected was true. 'Yes, it's going to be dangerous, but suicide? We've been in tough spots before and we always got out of them.'

Owen glared at her. 'Yes. Most of us, anyway.'

Abby glared at him, ready to bawl him out, but managed to stop just in time. She took a deep breath to calm herself; while she was hurt by Owen's callous and unnecessary reference to her sister, she wasn't going to bite back at him. The squadron couldn't afford any rifts when there was so much to be done; everybody had to be completely focused during the next two weeks if they were going to be ready for the trip to Muscovy and have the best odds of survival.

She looked around the table, meeting the eyes of her pilots. 'Like it or not, we're soldiers. We signed up for the war and promised to obey orders. And these are our orders.' She forced a smile. 'Ours not to reason why and all that.'

'We promised to obey orders that make *sense*, Abby. We signed up to be Misfits, not grunts to be thrown away...'

Abby glared at her second-in-command. 'So our lives are worth more than anyone else's? Than a Harridan driver's, for example?'

Owen blanched. 'No, of course not, but our training, our experience...'

'If it wasn't us going it would be someone else and *we* have a better chance of getting the job done and coming back alive precisely *because* of that training and experience, not to mention our skill and aircraft.'

'I know, but...' Owen gritted his teeth and shook his head in frustration. 'Look, I'm willing to give my life if need be, if it saves lives or takes us a step closer to winning the war, but I just don't see how trying to do the impossible in Muscovy and dying uselessly is going to do that!'

'You're not the only one who sees this as a bad idea, Owen, but as I said, we have no choice in the matter and besides, just think how famous we'll be if we succeed.' Abby forced a grin, changing the subject and hoping that everyone would forget about Muscovy for at least a while. 'Almost as famous as Gwen here, who has managed to put the squadron, but especially herself, firmly back into the spotlight. Front page news in all the papers and I particularly enjoyed the report in The Times... Speaking of which, we are going to be joined sometime today by a journalist: the King has allowed the press to send a writer to follow our daily routine and write about who we really are.'

Again, there were mixed reactions from the pilots. Most of them were wary, just as she was, and only a few, Scarlet and Bruce predictably among them, seemed genuinely enthusiastic at the chance to gain renown.

Mac was one of the sceptics. 'Well, if we have to be stuck with some nosey busybody then I at least hope they're from the New Aviator; they're the only ones who actually understand something about what we do, but even they, well...'

He left what he was accusing them of unsaid, but the pilots understood perfectly and there were nods of agreement and many a rolled eye at the thought of the technically inaccurate and often overly dramatised articles in what was supposed to be the foremost publication for aviation enthusiasts.

Abby shook her head. 'I'm afraid not, Mac, it's a Mr Featherstonehaugh from The Times.'

The Scotsman barked with laughter. '*Fanshaw*? What kind of silly stuck up snooty aristo English name is that?' He gave Lord Bagshot a cursory glance, and held up a hand in a feeble attempt at apology. 'No offence, my Lord.'

Lord Bagshot was smiling broadly at Mac's tirade, enjoying it just as much as everyone else, and he waved away the Scotsman's apology. 'None taken.'

'Most kind.' Mac barely acknowledged him, before launching straight back into his diatribe. 'He'll undoubtedly be some unsavoury type with no social skills, just like every other journalist I've ever met. Although he is from The Times, so he'll probably have airs and pretensions of grandeur and self-importance.'

There was laughter and Mac took the opportunity to grab a breath, but before he could continue he was interrupted by a cough and turned to find that the Bagshot's butler had just come through the door behind him. The painfully straight-backed man crossed the room carrying a silver tray at shoulder height, which he presented to Lord Bagshot, revealing that it had a single white calling card on it.

'Mr Featherstonehaugh of The Times, my Lord.'

Lord Bagshot took the card and frowned at it briefly. 'Show him in, please, Cuthbert.'

'Very good, sir.' The butler bowed and walked from the room, as stiffly and slowly as he'd entered it, glancing disapprovingly down his nose at Mac as he went past.

There was more laughter from the pilots as Mac made a face at the butler's back, but it quickly died down when the dour man returned, closely followed by the journalist.

'Mr Featherstonehaugh of The Times, my Lord.' The butler gave a short bow to his master, another very English sneer at the Scotsman, then left, closing the door firmly behind himself.

The man nodded at the group, meeting their eyes briefly one by one. 'My Lord, Lady Penelope, ladies, gentlemen, how do you do?'

He smiled at them, but his greeting was returned with silence as the group stared at him.

Prepared for the worst by their low expectations and Mac's joking, most of the Misfits had expected to be confronted with someone approximating the typical image of a journalist - a hunched and unkempt older man, with ink-stained fingers, wearing a cheap suit and with pale skin and thick spectacles from working too long in dark rooms, but the reality was far different. He turned out to be young, in his mid to late-twenties, impeccably, if not expensively dressed in a dark-grey suit with a matching cravat. The only sign of his chosen profession was the small notebook tucked in the breast pocket where a handkerchief would usually go. His blonde hair, fashionably long, framed a chiselled face and he carried himself with a bearing and assurance that spoke of good education and breeding.

Abby recovered first and glanced at Lord Bagshot, who, as the host, had the right to greet the man first, but he just waved his permission with a grin, still thoroughly entertained.

She stood and walked around the table. 'Mr Featherstonehaugh, my name is Abby Lennox, welcome to Misfit Squadron.'

The man shook her preferred hand with a smile. 'Wing Commander Lennox, it is a pleasure to meet you.' He glanced around the group again. 'As it is to meet all of you.'

The pilots belatedly made their greetings in an uncoordinated chorus, which Lord Bagshot let die down before calling out, gesturing to an empty chair next to Kitty near the far end of the table. 'Take a seat, young man, you must be hungry after your journey. Will you join us for a spot of lunch?'

'Thank you, my Lord, I would be delighted.'

'Wonderful, I'll have Cuthbert lay you a place. And please, call me Biffy.'

Featherstonehaugh gave him a small bow. 'I would be honoured, Biffy, but only if you,' he looked around the room at the pilots, smiling winningly, 'if all of you, call me Freddy.'

'Very well, uh, Freddy. And your photographer? I was told you were bringing a chap to take photographs, will he be joining us as well?'

Featherstonehaugh paused on his way down the table to the chair. 'My photographer, Mr Jones, is currently on assignment. He will join us in a couple of days.'

'Does Mr Jones have a first name?' asked Penelope. 'Perhaps I might have seen his work.'

'If you read The Times then you have, undoubtedly, Lady Penelope, but his work is only ever attributed to "Mr Jones"; he was given the name "Inigo" by his parents, who were admirers of the great man's work, and naturally insists on just being addressed as "Jones" or "Mr Jones".'

'That is perfectly understandable.' Penelope smiled. 'We will endeavour to do so.'

'Thank you, Lady Penelope.'

The journalist sat down and Lord Bagshot rang the small bell he had at hand.

The butler instantly appeared and, while he was busying about, Bruce leaned in to whisper to Mac. 'Unsavoury character, eh?'

'Mebbe not,' replied the Scotsman reluctantly. 'But "Freddy Fanshaw?" C'mon, really?'

The brief conversation, carried out in a stage whisper, carried easily to everybody in the room, including the journalist, but he was tactful enough to ignore it.

Abby joined the butler in glaring at them, then gestured at her pilots while she spoke to Featherstonehaugh. 'These are the Misfits. I'm sure you'll have plenty of time to get to know them, so I won't bother introducing them to you now, except to say that the young officer sitting on Lord Bagshot's left hand is Gwen Stone, who made such a stir this morning. I assume you'll be wanting to speak to her first?'

The journalist gave Gwen a small bow, nodding elegantly over the table with his upper body. 'Miss Stone. Congratulations on your victory.'

Gwen returned his nod with a smile. 'Thank you.'

'I look forward to hearing about it from your perspective some time; the official story that the Ministry has given us is rather hard to believe.' He smiled wryly at her, before turning his attention back to Abby. 'However, as interested as I am in the squadron's heroic exploits, I'd like to start at the very beginning, if I may, Wing Commander, and ask you to tell me in your own words how the Misfits came about.'

Abby nodded. 'Very well, we can sit down together later, once we're of duty.'

Gwen broke in. 'I'd quite like to hear that, actually; in all the time I've been a Misfit, I've never found out much about why the squadron was formed, or how you did it. Why don't you tell us now?'

Gwen's request was backed up by the rest of the pilots, most of whom didn't know the details.

Abby shrugged. 'There's not much to it. The King, well he was still Emperor George II back then, called me in to Whitehall one day and told me to form the squadron.'

'Oh, come off it, Abby, there has to be more to it than that.' Penelope said. 'Why don't you tell us the gory details?'

Abby looked around the table, seeing the enthusiastic faces, all willing her to tell her story and sighed. 'Oh, very well, but don't blame me if you fall asleep in your Boeuf Bourguignon.'

1937

Abigail Lennox consulted the small map attached to her thigh and wondered for the umpteenth time why it was her that had been called up to London and not Cecily. Her sister Cece was the charismatic one, the life of the party, she was the one that everybody liked and wanted to be with and she should be the one going to Whitehall for some secret assignment, not Abigail, the practical and frankly boring aircraft designer, the mechanic, who preferred to be left to her own devices and was usually to be found covered in grease or graphite.

The Emperor had sent the message to her, though, not Cece, so consequently it was Abigail flying from their home in Norfolk to the capital first thing in the morning. She was hoping that the Emperor was going to give them some kind of grant or commission to build or design aircraft for the burgeoning Aviation Corps, that way they would be able to afford to keep the Lennox Aviation Company going - something that had become increasingly difficult since their father had died three years before.

Navigation wasn't really her strong suit, so she sighed with relief when the elegant glass and iron tower of Buckingham Palace finally came into view, shining in the light of the spring morning. She adjusted course towards it, knowing that her destination, Hyde Airstrip, was right next to it, then took in the sight of the sprawling metropolis that stretched almost as far as she could see in all directions.

It was her first time seeing London from the air; permission to overfly the city was not given to just anybody and it was quicker and easier just to take a train down from Norfolk if she had business there. As usual, there was a haze over most of the city, especially in the east where most of the industry was concentrated, but it didn't stop the view from being spectacular.

She had very little time to enjoy it, though, because as soon as she passed into the city's airspace, the stern voice of the Hyde Airstrip tower filled her ears.

'Unidentified aircraft, this is London control, you are entering a restricted area, please state your business.'

'London control, this is, uh...' She glanced down at the map, in the corner of which she had scrawled the strange call sign she had been given. 'This is Badger, requesting permission to land.'

There was a short pause before the same voice came back on, sounding decidedly more friendly. 'Welcome, Badger, permission granted. Wind is ten knots from the south and we are landing from the north. Please join the holding pattern, you are number three. Once down, proceed directly to hangar one, where you are expected.'

'Acknowledged, control, and thank you, Badger out.'

Abigail swung her aircraft out towards the north, crossing the line of Oxford Street and search her left side for the two aircraft that were in front of her in the queue to land. She quickly spotted them - one, an enormous blue and gold zeppelin, was almost on the ground. It had dropped its guy ropes and was being towed into position by two heavy pilot wagons. The other was a gold-painted pleasure aircraft, a long fat thing with two large wings above and below its bulky fuselage, which had four huge engines sandwiched between them. She watched it come around onto its final approach a fair distance from the airstrip and winced; it could barely manoeuvre, dipping its wings less than twenty degrees to make the turn and even then looking like it was struggling to stay in the air. She pitied the poor pilot who had to land it on the tight runway; it wouldn't have much room to spare.

She turned onto her base leg and watched the golden aircraft as it dipped over the last buildings then the trees at the edge of the airstrip. It touched down just beyond the markers, sending puffs of grass and dirt rising from its wheels, then black smoke from its engines as it put them into reverse pitch. Surprisingly, it was barely half-way across the airstrip by the time it had slowed sufficiently to turn off towards its stand. Everything about the landing had been impressive and spoke of an expert pilot who was very familiar with his machine.

'Badger, this is London control, you are clear for landing.'

'Roger control.'

Abigail banked her aircraft onto final approach and throttled back, putting her aircraft easily on the glide path. She had done her homework so she knew that the hangar she had been assigned to, the Imperial hangar, was at the south end of the airstrip, so she didn't aim to hit the grass too soon, but instead flew along just above it, bleeding off speed, before finally settling to the ground almost exactly level with the big gold aircraft that had preceded her. She throttled back, but allowed her speed to stay up, coasting towards the big hangar at the end, where there was a man in a blue RAC uniform waving what looked like ping-pong bats at her, as if she didn't know that the big red-painted building with the bloody great golden lion on the side was the Imperial hangar. She obediently followed his directions, though, coming to a halt in front of the hangar and blocking her spring at his command.

She unplugged and grabbed her bag from the small storage compartment behind the seat, then climbed out, stepping onto the wing before jumping down to the ground.

The man with the bats came over with a few other fitters, who grabbed the wings of her aircraft and began pushing it inside.

'Beautiful machine.'

She blushed and glanced sideways at the man, expecting to see a sarcastic sneer; her aircraft was unpainted metal and was squat and admittedly quite ugly. It was the one that she and her sister used to test new ideas and had been the only one of their aircraft that had been airworthy to come at such short notice. She was surprised to see genuine admiration in the man's eyes, though.

'Oh, er, thank you.'

'What's her name?'

'Butterfly.'

The man raised an eyebrow, but still didn't scoff. 'Reminds me a bit of the old Lennox LE5a.' The aircraft disappeared into the shadows of the hangar and he turned to face her, sticking out his hand. 'Corporal Henry Potter, ma'am.'

'Abigail Lennox.'

The man chuckled on hearing her name. 'That would explain the aircraft, then.'

Abigail smiled at him. 'Yes, it would.'

He jerked his head in the direction of the hangar. 'Better get you inside, ma'am; there's an officer waiting for you.'

'Lead on, Corporal.'

There was a female wing commander standing by the wall just inside the hangar doors, making sure to stay out of everyone's way while she watched the fitters working on Butterfly. She was in her late forties, the curly brown hair poking out from under her uniform cap streaked with grey and there were deep lines around her eyes betraying endless hours spent squinting into the sky, searching for enemy aircraft.

Potter saluted her and the woman returned it smartly. 'Thank you, Corporal, I'll take her off your hands now.'

'Yes, ma'am.' The man nodded at Abigail. 'Don't you worry, ma'am, I'll keep a good eye on Butterfly.'

'Thank you, Henry.'

The fitter went to supervise the team working on Abigail's aircraft, leaving the two women alone.

The wing commander stuck out her hand. 'Dorothy Campbell, ma'am. Pleased to meet you. I've been assigned to escort you to Whitehall.'

'Abigail Lennox, but I suspect you already knew that.'

The woman nodded before looking at Abigail's black flightsuit. 'You'll be wanting to change, I suppose?'

'Yes, please; I don't want to meet the Emperor wearing skin tight leather if I can help it.'

The woman winked. 'Oh, I don't know, he might enjoy it.'

Abigail laughed and followed her towards the back of the hangar.

Ten minutes later, the two women were sitting in the back of a large black autocar flying the Imperial colours as it made its way past Buckingham Palace and up The Mall towards Whitehall.

The wing commander stroked the soft leather seats on either side of her legs with a smile. 'This is quite nice, isn't it? It's the first time I've ever been in one of these official autocars; I don't warrant one. What they have in mind for you must be important.'

'You don't have any idea what that is, then?'

'I'm afraid not, they just asked me to show you around and make sure you didn't get lost.'

'Never mind, it'll just have to be a surprise.' Abigail grinned and the woman returned it.

The autocar turned off The Mall before Admiralty Arch and headed up Horse Guards Road, past a group of guards exercising beautiful black horses and a squad of Artillerymen drilling in the large courtyard, who paused in what they were doing to salute the car. They bypassed both Downing Street, where the Emperor kept his office hours, and the Foreign and Empire Office and stopped in front of the large white building at the end of the road.

The Imperial Guard driver held Abigail's door for her and she stepped out and looked up at the building in puzzlement for a second before glancing sideways at the wing commander. 'Haven't they just moved the treasury in here? They're not going to make me the Emperor's accountant, are they? I mean, I do the company's books, but I'm not exactly equipped to run the entire Empire.'

The woman laughed. 'I think that's highly unlikely and anyway, we're not going in there, we're going round the side.'

She took Abigail to an unobtrusive door in the side of the building and pressed a buzzer.

The door immediately clicked open and the woman pushed it wide. 'I don't want to scare you or anything, but I'd advise not making any sudden movements and keeping your hands open and by your sides for the next few minutes.' She smiled, then led the way inside.

Abigail was taken through a rigorous security check, which included the contents of her bag, hygiene items included, being dumped on the table and rifled through and a thorough pat down by a very apologetic female Imperial Guard, before she was allowed any further than the bare concrete room just beyond the door. She found the search quite obtrusive, but was mollified somewhat when she saw that the same was being done to Campbell, in spite of her being a military officer and in spite of the fact that she had obviously been there before and knew them well enough to laugh and joke with them while they did their duty.

The search was carried out efficiently and they were soon cleared and passed through into the passages beyond. They went down a flight of stairs and turned a corner, but then came to an abrupt halt as they were confronted by a slim, clean-shaven man in his early forties, wearing a black suit and accompanied by two red uniformed Imperial Guards.

The wing commander immediately snapped to attention, but the man shook his head with a smile. 'At ease, Wing Commander. No need to stand on ceremony with me, you know that.'

'Thank you, Your Imperial Majesty.'

As soon as she relaxed, the Emperor turned to look at Abigail. 'Miss Lennox, welcome.'

Abigail was unsure whether to bow, curtsy, salute, wave or just faint away at being so close to the ruler of the British Empire and was relieved when he held his hand out to her, negating the necessity to choose.

She took his hand and shook it firmly. 'Thank you, your Imperial Majesty.'

'Please, just call me sir; all that Imperial Majesty stuff is a bit of a mouthful and once per day is enough, don't you think?'

'I, uh, I suppose so, Your, uh, sir.'

'Excellent! By the way you sound a bit like me, there, would you like me to refer you to my doctor? He'll sort you right out.'

The two women laughed, delighted that the Emperor could so easily joke with them about something that had caused him so much trouble and embarrassment in the past.

He smiled, pleased, and Abigail mused that he was probably surrounded with people who laughed at any joke he made, whether it was funny or not, and probably appreciated their honest amusement.

'I hope you will forgive me if we get straight down to business, Miss Lennox; much as I would like to spend a pleasant afternoon in your company, I have too many duties to attend to.'

'Of course, sir.'

'Thank you.' He nodded, making her feel as if it had mattered whether she had said yes or no. 'I arranged to meet you here to show you how serious the situation really is. While we will do everything we can to prevent it, I, and my ministers, believe that war is most likely inevitable and we are rushing to prepare for it before it is too late.' He turned and led them down the corridor, deeper into the complex. 'This facility is only one of the many preparations we are making.'

As they went, the Emperor pointed out various rooms and their uses, from bathrooms, kitchens and dormitories, to the communications and map rooms. They finished the tour in a small meeting room where the Emperor showed Abigail to a chair before taking one himself.

'While I will continue to make most of the decisions of running the country from the Palace and Downing Street, the war can be run from here if London is ever threatened. We are under several dozen yards of concrete, with dedicated telephone lines running to all the major installations around the country, both military and civilian and I am assured that there is, or at least there will be enough supplies to last for a year or so locked down here. I shudder to think of the quality of the food if it keeps for that amount of time, but as long as there is enough tea, I think I can make do.

'However, while a place like this is undoubtedly essential, it is not the most important of the preparations that we have to make. That would be the expansion and training of our armed forces and that it why I have brought you here today.'

He picked a newspaper up from the table in front of him and pushed it towards her. 'Have you seen the reports from Spain?'

Abigail took the paper and looked at the story that had been highlighted in red marker. It was a report of the air battle over North-Eastern Spain and dealt with a Prussian Squadron that was fighting on the side of the Spanish Rebels in the Iberian Civil War. They were an elite squadron that called themselves *die Karmesinroten Barone* - the Crimson Barons - and had apparently knocked the Republican Air Force out of the sky without losing a single pilot or machine.

'My ministers insist that I do not have to worry about the Crimson Barons, that the Imperial Aviator Corps with their new Harridans and Spitsteams will be perfectly capable of taking care of them, but I'm not so certain.' He looked at Campbell. 'That's not to say I have any doubts about the RAC, wing commander; I am sure they will handle themselves very well when faced with Die Fliegertruppe, I am merely saying that they do not have the resources that that Prussian squadron in particular have behind them. Which brings me to you, Miss Lennox. I want you to form a squadron to counter them, to do the same to the Prussians as they are doing to the poor Republicans. I want you to find our best minds and pilots and make something out of them to defend this realm against *that.*' He stabbed his finger at the article in punctuation.

'Why me, sir? Surely one of those minds or pilots would serve you better?'

'I looked at them all, believe me, but you are the one that stood out above all the rest; you've been holding together your father's company, whilst simultaneously bringing up a son, designing and building new aircraft, keeping your sister's impulsiveness in check and, to top it all off, I'm told that you are a brilliant pilot! As far as I can see, you're the best person for the job.'

Abigail shook her head. 'But I'm not really a military kind of person, sir.'

The Emperor laughed. 'Good! Because I don't want a military kind of squadron! I want you to find the men and women that wouldn't necessarily flourish in the military, but who have lived and breathed our proud British aviation tradition their whole lives, who wouldn't necessarily fit in with RAC discipline and would work best if they didn't *have* to fit in. A squadron of misfits, if you will. Do you think you can do that, Miss Lennox? Are there people out there like you - brilliant pilots and designers - who would fight for their country in the difficult times to come?'

Abigail thought about all the men and women she'd met at the various conferences or heard good things about. If she could gather them together she knew that they would form something special, something that would easily counter anything the Prussians, with their functional but unimaginative aviation techniques, could put into the air. The only trouble would be persuading them.

She nodded. 'I think there are, sir and I will do my utmost to get them for you.'

The Emperor beamed happily. 'Excellent! Thank you.'

'You're welcome, sir.' She grinned. 'And thank *you* for giving us our name.'

Ten minutes later, Abigail was slumped in the chair in the meeting room in a daze.

Somehow, not only had she agreed to put together the squadron, but she had been commissioned in the RAC as a wing commander, had her sister commissioned as a squadron leader and also somehow sold the Lennox Aviation Company to Hawking Aircraft Manufacturers. The Emperor had pointed out, and she had reluctantly agreed, that neither she nor her sister would have the time to keep it going and that it was failing anyway. He had said something about it being a very good offer from some honourable people, that the Lennox name would live on in the squadron, but by that point Abigail had been too stunned to listen properly and had just signed the thick sheaf of papers that a colourfully-dressed aide from the Emperor's court had placed in front of her one by one.

Once that had been done, the Emperor had stood, shaken her hand, then made his excuses and hurried off to Downing Street, leaving her staring into space and wondering what she had done.

She blinked and glanced to one side, meeting the eyes of the wing commander. 'What just happened?'

The woman smiled, barely holding back a laugh. 'The Emperor just got everything that he wanted and the British Empire just got its best hope of survival. Come on, let's get you back to Hyde, we have a lot to do.'

'We?'

This time the woman did laugh. 'Did you miss the part where I was assigned as your liaison with the government?'

Abigail grimaced. 'I think I must have done, but I'm glad; I really don't want to have another meeting with that man any time soon - I might end up signing away my firstborn. Or a lung.'

The two women made their way back through the underground complex towards the exit, but before they got there, a grey-haired man in a dark-grey suit stepped out of one of the dormitories and stopped them.

'Miss Lennox, if you wouldn't mind?' He gestured for Abigail to go into the room.

The wing commander frowned at him. 'Minister Peterson? What's going on?'

'Nothing for you to worry about. We just want to have a quick word with Miss Lennox. It'll just be a couple of minutes and then you can whisk her away, back where she came from.'

'Please?' The man gestured again, insisting, and Abigail nodded and moved past him. The wing commander made to follow her, but the minister blocked her way. 'Not you, Campbell, just her.'

He herded Abigail into the room and closed the door firmly behind her, then walked past her to sit with his fellows.

Abigail had to cover her mouth and fake a cough to stop herself from laughing when she was confronted by the strange sight of four dark-suited men, who she recognised as forming part of the Emperor's inner circle of ministers, the most powerful people in the country, squeezed together facing her on a low metal military-type bed like sparrows on a fence.

'Gentlemen. What can I do for you?'

'We wanted to get a look at you personally.'

'And warn you.'

'War is coming and we can't afford to waste this country's resources, not even on one of the Emperor's pet projects.'

'At the first sign that your efforts are not worth the cost to the country, we will shut you down.'

'Is that understood?'

The men took it in turns to speak, bombarding her, almost as if they'd rehearsed it, which she supposed they might have.

She nodded. 'Perfectly.'

'Good.'

'Very good.'

'Then we are done here, but remember you are now a member of the Imperial armed forces and therefore under the orders of the government and not just the Emperor, *Wing Commander*.'

'Dismissed.'

They looked at her expectantly and she gave them a small, extremely ironic bow, then turned on her heels smartly, pulled open the door and marched out.

Campbell was waiting for her a little way down the corridor so that she couldn't be accused of eavesdropping and she raised an eyebrow at Abigail's stormy expression.

'I have just been warned to make sure that our efforts are worthwhile, Wing Commander Campbell.'

The woman rolled her eyes. 'Take no notice; they're just jealous old men who don't want women having any power whatsoever and have never liked us being in the military. The Emperor will take care of you and stop them from interfering.' She began to lead the way towards the exit. 'By the way, if we're going to be working together, you should call me Dot. Unless you want me to call you Wing Commander Lennox all the bloody time?'

'God no!' Abigail laughed then considered for a second. 'And call me Abby.'

For a long time after Abby finished the only sound was the furious scribbling of the journalist as the pilots absorbed the piece of their history that their commander had hinted at, but never fully shared with any of them.

Gwen eventually broke the silence. 'How did your sister take my parents buying your company? And you signing her up for the RAC? Was she upset?'

Abby shook her head. 'She was pretty happy, actually; she'd been trying to get me to sell for a while and it turned out that she'd actually been thinking about joining the RAC anyway.'

'That's pretty lucky.'

Abby shrugged. 'I always got the sneaky suspicion that I was the King's second choice, that he'd already sounded Cece out for the job and that she turned it down and pointed him in my direction. If so, then he would have known how she would react.'

'Don't sell yourself short, Abby, darling,' said Lady Penelope. 'I can't imagine anyone accomplishing what you have over the last three years. None of us could have.'

Abby began to protest, but she was immediately drowned out when the Misfits started showing their agreement with Penelope's statement, variously stomping their feet or banging teacups and cutlery on the table as they called out their support. She blushed, meeting the eyes of her pilots one by one and settled for nodding her thanks.

The noise eventually died down and was replaced by the sound of silver spoons against fine china as the pilots polished off their desserts and resumed their conversations.

'Was the Minister for War one of the men in the war rooms?'

Owen's softly-voiced question plunged the room back into silence and all eyes turned to Abby.

She tried to picture the four men on the beds in her mind. She had still been in a bit of a daze after her meeting with the Emperor and hadn't paid them much attention as individuals, only really remembering them as a group of unsmiling and unfriendly old men. Cummerbund was only a junior member of the council of ministers at the time and had been virtually unknown until his appointment as Minister for War, so she hadn't taken particular notice of him at the time, but she seemed to remember him being one of them. 'I think so, yes.'

There was a sharp sound as the journalist snapped his notebook closed, causing a few of the people around the table to jump, startled, and all eyes shot to him. He looked up and saw everybody staring at him and gave them an apologetic grin. 'Pardon me.' He looked at Abby. 'That was wonderful, thank you.'

Abby was only able to give him a slight smile in return; the realisation that their problems with the War Minister may have been going on for far longer than they had realised had put something of a dampener on the mood. 'You're welcome. What are your plans for us, Freddy? Who will you want to question next?'

'Actually, I'd like to hear how you recruited your pilots first before delving into their pasts and such.'

Abby nodded. 'Very well, whenever I have time. Perhaps in the evenings when we are all done, over a pint or two.'

'That would be delightful, thank you.'

'Mr Featherstonehaugh!' Lord Bagshot called from his place at the head of the table. 'You haven't had a chance to eat.'

'Indeed I have not, my Lord, but no matter; I have been nourished in another manner. However, if you'll permit me, I will dig in now.'

He began to eat, but stopped again almost immediately when Abby stood up.

She nodded to him. 'Unfortunately we can't keep you company, Freddy.' She glanced around the table. 'Fun's over, time to get back to work, Misfits.'

CHAPTER 6

Despite Abby's absence, construction had begun that morning on the two new A flight aircraft. There was a slight delay, though, because when Gwen arrived at the hangar to go over the designs with the fitters she found that there were different names on the plans. The ones she had angrily scribbled, "Rapier" and "Sabre", had been rubbed out and in their place had been written "Raptor" and "Sable" in an elegant script. When she confronted Bruce and Monty about it, the stunt pilot just grinned, while the Australian shrugged, smiling just as cheekily as his wingman, and answered 'couldn't bloody read your writing, sorry Gwen, isn't that what it says?'

Gwen had stared at them for a few seconds, speechless; the two men had seen the anger in her scrawled writing, had known her well enough to suspect what she had been thinking at the time, and done what they could to defuse her frustration by immediately giving the machines a personal touch.

In the end all she could do was smile. 'Yes, Bruce. Now come on, let's get these aircraft built.'

With the added incentive of new aircraft to work on and the flush of Gwen's recent success in the air, there was an air of true excitement around the base that had been somewhat lacking before and the fitters and pilots redoubled their efforts with new energy.

Since the two new A flight machines were identical it meant that the pieces for them could just be duplicated, saving a lot of time, and they were completed after only four days, well ahead of schedule. The fitters then immediately moved on to the two B flight aircraft, plans for which had been completed shortly after those of Sable and Raptor. With every able-bodied man and woman in Misfit Squadron working on them they took just four days to build.

When the aircraft were presented to the squadron, there was a surprise for Gwen which quite literally brought her to tears - each of the aircraft had some part of them painted pink.

Mac's machine, which he named Jaguar in honour of Lady Penelope's lost Cheetah, was twin-springed and had long, sharp, triangular wings. It was painted gold with black spots and had pink nose cones on the airscrews.

Monty had chosen to make his machine bright orange in tribute to Ballerina, but with a pink vertical stabiliser.

Bruce's Sable was a lush deep brown except for pink gun ports along the leading edge of the wings.

The unnamed aircraft, an elegant, twin-springed machine with wings that had gently-curving trailing edges, had been left unpainted, though. That way the new pilot could not only name their own aircraft, but also chose its colourings and feel that it was really theirs.

Finally, in early October, about three weeks after the fight with the Barons, the Misfits once more had a full complement of fighters.

They were still a pilot down, though, and there was less than a week before they were due to leave for Muscovy.

Abby had still been unable to find a replacement who satisfied all her criteria, but in the end she had had to bow to pressure from the King and the War Minister and had made her choice of the best of who was available. A couple of days after the last aircraft was completed, an Aviator Sergeant from a Spitsteam squadron arrived at the local train station and Abby went to bring her to the airfield in one of the squadron autocars.

The pilots had been to and told to be on the airfield to greet their new colleague and were standing in a loose line in front of the ready room, watching the autocar being admitted through the base gates before making its way around the perimeter road towards them.

Owen gave a theatrical sigh. 'I really hope she hasn't found us another Gwen Stone; one's enough.

Gwen grinned and glanced along the line at him. 'Would you prefer another Scarlet?'

The diminutive Irishwoman put her hands on her hips and turned to peer up at the tall Welshman.

He laughed and shook his head. 'Nope! Not that either. I just want someone who's not going to show me up and steal all my credit on a night mission...'

Gwen tutted and rolled her eyes exaggeratedly 'You're never going to forgive me for that, are you? It's not my fault the papers don't find you interesting enough to write about, or even mention. Be thankful; even if they did, they probably wouldn't spell your name right, Squadron Leader Fle... Fffew... Phlegm.'

Owen glowered at her. 'It's Llewellyn and I'm fairly sure even the English know how to spell that.'

Derek smiled at him mildly. 'Not the way you pronounce it they don't. Although we could always just tell them your name is Sheepish; I'm pretty sure they can spell that.'

The Misfits had stopped laughing by the time Abby got out of the autocar, but she could still tell that something had been going on. She gave them a puzzled look, but didn't comment and just stood waiting for her passenger to join her.

The new pilot turned out to be a slim woman in her early twenties, with dark hair done neatly up in a bun under her day uniform cap. She marched to Abby's side and put her kitbag on the floor, then snapped smartly to attention.

'As you were, Aviator Sergeant.' Abby's wince was barely perceptible, but the Misfits didn't miss it and there were a few exchanged glances and raised eyebrows as the woman relaxed only slightly to stand at parade rest.

'Boys and girls, meet Chastity Arrowsmith. She will be joining us on a temporary basis, to be made permanent after our mission if she proves good enough.' Abby looked at the woman. 'Which, if her report is to be believed, she will.'

The woman, Chastity, nodded. 'I won't let you down, ma'am.'

Again there was a minute twitch from Abby, only noticeable to the Misfits, who knew her well, and which spoke volumes about her opinion of the new pilot's stiffly formal behaviour.

'Alright then, I think the best thing to do is get into the air. Do you feel like meeting your new aircraft?'

For the first time the woman showed a hint of emotion, a slight upward turn of her lips that almost approximated a smile and there was the barest touch of enthusiasm in her voice as she replied. 'Yes, ma'am.'

'Good.' Abby jerked her thumb over her shoulder in the direction of the ready room. 'There's a dressing room inside, go get your flightsuit on - we have time for a flight before lunch.'

'Yes, ma'am.' The woman picked up her kitbag and threw it on her shoulder before drawing herself up to attention again. She executed a smart quarter turn to the right and marched a couple of paces - a perfect parade manoeuvre - then fell out and hurried into the ready room.

The Misfits were already dressed from a training flight that morning, so they stayed where they were and watched her go, then turned to throw sceptical looks at their leader, who had wandered over to join them.

Abby shrugged. 'So she's a bit military. I'm sure she'll lighten up after a few pints. Give her a chance - at least see how she flies first before judging her.'

There was a soft rattling sound from behind them and they turned, just catching a glimpse of the rear wheels of Lady Penelope's wheelchair, disappearing around the back of the ready room towards the perimeter road where she must have left her autocar. She had obviously been silently watching them from the shadows under the eaves where they hadn't been able to see her.

The pilots looked at each other, their hearts breaking. Nobody said anything, there was no need to; they all know how their friend must be feeling, seeing her replacement arrive and knowing that she was one step further away from the squadron she loved.

Lady Penelope was much healthier and had almost fully gotten over the shock of the loss of so much blood and the amputations. Aside from her doctors, she had been working with a man, Nicholas Park, who the Misfits suspected was a therapist of some kind, and had become a lot stronger. She no longer needed her husband to push her everywhere which meant she had been free to visit the design shed whenever she wanted, but hadn't been able to work the long hours that the other designers had and so had acted more as a consultant, popping in whenever the designs were being discussed.

She had also been smiling a lot more the last week or so, but the pilots knew that deep down inside she couldn't be happy cut off from the sky, none of them would be, and the few trips that she'd been on in the Lekker with Wendy were not a substitute for the freedom of flying her own aircraft.

Fortunately, they weren't left alone with such depressing thoughts for too long, because the woman reappeared after only a couple of minutes, dressed in a standard issue RAC flightsuit and helmet, and joined them on the grass.

Abby nodded at her, then addressed the whole group. 'First off, with Penelope leaving us we have to change the battle order of B flight. Derek is now B flight leader, Badger Five. Kitty will stay on his wing and will become Badger Six. Mac, congratulations, you're now Badger Seven, leading the second section and Chastity, you're on his wing as Badger Eight.'

She looked at the pilots one by one, making sure they understood, before continuing. 'Right then, since this is our first time in the air together for a while, we'll run through some basic squadron manoeuvres, both for ourselves and to get our new pilot used to working with us. Then we'll have a few practice dogfights with the sections of each flight going up against each other, and we'll finish off by running some interceptions on Wendy in the Lekker.' She looked at Wendy. 'It would be good if you could do that for us until we leave, actually. If you don't mind taking some time off causing explosions.'

The big woman grinned. 'I don't mind at all; the army boys are getting a bit fed up with me blowing bloody great holes in targets their tanks can barely scratch anyway. It'll give their egos a chance to heal a bit.' Wendy had appropriated the Lekker as her own and had bolted racks to its wings so that she could use it as a testbed for her weapons. When she wasn't working on Dreadnought, she could be found flying around over the army's firing range.

Abby smiled at her. 'Thank you.' She turned to face the rest of C flight's pilots. 'As for you three, Charles, Owen, observation duty as always and Scarlet, you're free to carry out your own exercises as you see fit. Any questions?'

There were none so Abby continued. 'Mac, give Chastity a quick walk around of her aircraft before we take off, please, just to familiarise her with her new machine, but don't worry too much about her; she's had experience on twin-spring fighters.'

'Nae problem, Abby. Come on, you.' Mac motioned for Chastity to follow him and began to speak to her as they walked towards the aircraft, followed closely by the other pilots.

For a long time the Misfits had barely had a chance to think or even feel, spending all of their waking hours working themselves almost to the point of exhaustion, apart from short breaks to eat, but with the fighters finished they at last they were able to set aside their extra duties as mechanics and designers and had room to breathe. They also had energy left at the end of the day to socialise and, more importantly, at least for Mac and Bruce, to drink.

In the evenings, while the service personnel enjoyed themselves in the fully stocked mess on the base or caught up on their sleep, the pilots retired to the sitting room in the mansion to listen to Abby telling the journalist how she had recruited the pilots and those hours spent sitting in the overstuffed armchairs and sofas in front of a roaring fire which banished the cool of the autumn nights, quickly became the highlight of the day for them and brought them even closer together than they had been before. It also allowed Chastity to learn a bit more about what she was getting herself in for and served to introduce her to the kind of behaviour that was more normal for the squadron. As Abby had predicted, she had slowly begun to lose her stiff military bearing and even started calling the pilots by their first names instead of "sir" and "ma'am."

Most of the Misfits had been recruited in relatively conventional ways, like Owen, who had approached Abby when he'd finished his radar project with the government, or Lady Penelope, who Abby had met previously and personally asked to join, or Charles, Derek, Bruce and Monty, who had been recommended by the newly appointed Sir Douglas Pewtall.

Other stories were a bit more interesting.

Wendy had been languishing in a Defence Ministry think tank, developing conventional weapons, having her decidedly unconventional ideas ignored and Abby had initially approached her just to provide interesting weapons for the squadron. However, when they got into talking and the big woman revealed her plans for a combination bomber and gun platform, Abby had leapt on the idea and immediately secured the funds from the Emperor.

Abby had found Kitty in France after the American had fled Spain in Hawk, the only survivor of the foreign pilots who had gone to fight for freedom in the Iberian Civil War.

Curiously enough, Abby had spotted Scarlet in a newsreel at the cinema, during a light-hearted segment which showed the "Irish Sheep Herder" who used an aircraft instead of a dog.

It was the story that Abby told of how she had recruited Mac that had them alternately on the edges of their seats with excitement and rolling around in laughter, though.

Scotland 1937

William "Mad Mac" MacShane wasn't really mad, he just liked people to think he was.

Abby knew that, but she was still nervous when she flew Butterfly up to the west of Scotland and landed in a field just outside Taynuilt, the tiny town where Mac had his workshop. There was nobody to meet her as she would have expected if she had landed at a proper airfield, mostly because there wasn't a proper airfield to be had - the nearest airfield was actually in Oban, ten miles away, which was where she would have to go to get her spring rewound if Mac couldn't do it, or wouldn't for some reason. Mac himself had his workshop right on the loch, Loch Etive, and used it to land his aircraft, which were all float aircraft.

It was about a mile from the field to his workshop, along a dirt road through the woods, but she hadn't made it more than a hundred yards before an ancient buggy, not much more than four wheels, two seats and an engine, came bouncing towards her down the road.

It screeched to a halt, causing her to skip to the side out of its way when its squealing brakes stopped functioning for a few seconds, and sat idling noisily, the engine making ominous popping noises and leaking steam from its joints.

The driver glared at her over the steering wheel. He was in his early thirties wearing goggles and a battered brown leather flying helmet from under which poked an unruly mop of shockingly ginger hair. He was filthy, his hands, his overalls and his face, where they weren't protected by the goggles, all covered in grease. 'Whaddya want?' He growled at her, his words barely intelligible.

Abby smiled in the face of his hostility. 'William MacShane?'

'Aye.' The man said cautiously. 'Who's askin'?'

'My name is Abigail Lennox, I'm from...'

'Lennox?' The man interrupted with another growl. 'As in Lennox Aviation?' He grunted and waved a hand at her dismissively. 'Be gone withya! I've told yer once and I'll tell yer again - I'm not selling to some bloody Sassenach company, no matter how good the offer or good their aircraft.'

'I'm not here about...'

He ignored her and stood up to peer over her shoulder towards Butterfly. 'That's a nice machine, though, I wouldn't mind tekkin a wee looksie at her afore yer go.'

He didn't wait for her to answer before sitting back down and slamming the buggy into gear, making an awful crunching noise, then lurching forwards, sending Abby scrambling to get out of his way once more.

She rolled her eyes and took a deep breath, searching for patience, before jogging after the man.

When she caught up with him he was already running his hands, wiped "clean" on a rag in his pocket, over the aircraft, grinning and muttering happily to himself. 'Verra nice, verra nice...' He eyed her as she approached. 'It's not one o' yer da's, though, is it?'

Abby shook her head. 'No, it's one of mine.'

Mac grunted. 'It's good.' He continued his inspection while he spoke to her. 'I was sorry to hear about yer da. He was a good man was Clifford, but as I told him back in thirty-five, I'm not selling to anyone. Not even to Lennox.'

'I understand that, but I'm not here to buy your company. I don't even own Lennox Aviation anymore; we sold to Hawking.'

'Hawking?!?' Mac almost spat the word at her and she blinked in shock. 'Hell's bells, what did ye go and do a stupid thing like that fer? Have ye seen their bloody Harridan? I've never seen a more boring aircraft! Yer da mus' be spinnin' in his grave!'

He stormed away, heading back to his buggy.

She followed on his heels, not wanting to lose him. 'I sold Lennox because I was given something more important to do.'

He rounded on her angrily. 'What could possibly be more important than honouring yer father's legacy?'

Abby met his angry stare without flinching and spoke quietly, her words barely audible over the chugging of the steam buggy. 'The Emperor himself charged me with forming a squadron of elite pilots to counter the Prussian threat. I want to make sure that Britain survives long enough to honour the legacy of everyone who lives in this country, not just my father.'

Mac stared at her and for a long moment Abby thought he was still going to storm away, but then he deflated with a sigh. 'Aye. It's coming ter that, isn't it?'

'It looks that way.'

'And ye want me to join this new squadron?'

'You as well as your fastest and best aircraft.'

He squinted at her suspiciously. 'Ye promise I won't ever have to fly a bloody Harridan?'

Abby laughed. 'I promise! That would defeat the whole object of the squadron.'

'And yer going to be leading this, what, "band of merry men" or something equally British?'

'Misfit Squadron, actually. And yes, I'll be leading it.'

'Misfits... I quite like that.' He grinned. 'But I'm not going to join up unless ye do one thing.'

'What's that?'

Mac pointed at Butterfly. 'Prove to me ye can fly that thing; I'm not following a worse pilot than me!'

Abby grinned. 'Can't say fairer than that, I suppose. Have you got something to rewind her with?'

Mac did of course have a rewinding machine for his own aircraft, one that he had hand-built himself, and he took Abby to his workshop in the buggy to fetch it.

It proved to be as bone-shattering and hair-raising a ride as she'd feared it would be; unlike the driver's seat, the passenger seat was just bare metal and unpadded and, despite the brakes being unreliable at best, Mac drove fully in accordance with his nickname.

His workshop turned out to be a series of low, wooden huts, five of which were hangars, sitting directly on the waterfront with ramps leading down into the water. The sixth and largest, his actual workshop, was set back from them and there was also a small, but well-built bungalow a little further along the road among the trees where the man obviously lived.

The five hangars were identical, open-fronted and backed, allowing Abby a brief view of the machines housed within as Mac zoomed past. They were of all types, all shapes and all colours. The only thing that they had in common were the floats underneath them that permitted them to launch from the placid Loch.

Mac saw her craning her neck to try to get a better look and smiled. 'Dinna fash yerself; yer'll get a better look later. If ye can fly as good as yer aircraft looks, that is.'

He backed up to a small lean-to behind the main workshop and when he hopped out to hook a small trailer to the back of the buggy Abby groaned; she had hoped that the winding machine would be in another vehicle, one that was a bit more comfortable.

Once the trailer was secured, Mac climbed back in and they started back towards Butterfly, going just as fast and wildly, even with the extra weight and unwieldiness of the machine.

Half an hour later Abby was back in the air and circling over the Loch at a thousand feet. She shifted in her seat and winced; it definitely felt like she had bruised something, which meant that it was going to be a very long, very uncomfortable flight back to Norfolk. She was seriously considering stopping off somewhere for the night - she was going to have to rewind somewhere anyway, so she might as well get a bit of a rest.

The state of her posterior was completely put out of her mind, though, when below her an aircraft slid slowly down the ramp from its hangar and splashed into the Loch. She frowned slightly; it was a single spring aircraft with straight wings that looked like tongue depressors and a stubby body - it didn't look anything special and she wondered if she had somehow been wrong about Mac's talent, or whether perhaps he'd lost his creative edge after retiring from the Schnitzel Cup competitions.

She watched as the aircraft moved forwards, gliding smoothly across the water towards the open Loch, then, without stopping, it turned into the wind and accelerated and in only a few seconds the white trails from its floats disappeared as it got airborne.

Abby had given Mac her radio frequency and the headset built into her helmet crackled as his voice filled the airwaves. 'Alrighty, then. Here's the rules. Ye follow me wherever I go. If ye get more than a quarter of a mile behind, ye lose. If ye get more than fifty feet above me, ye lose. If ye can't take the heat, ye lose. If ye crash, ye lose. Weeeell... That last one's a wee bit obvious, but I just thought it would be nice to let ye know anyway.'

His laughter filled her ears and she couldn't help but chuckle along with him, even though she was becoming increasingly worried about what he was getting her into and how mad he was going to turn out to be in the end.

'Fall in behind me, then, and let's do this!'

Mac led her into the hills and valleys to the north of his workshop. At first he took it easy, undoubtedly assessing the capabilities of her aircraft, but when he had done that, the gloves came off and he increased speed at the same time as he decreased height.

What followed was an exhilarating and often terrifying flight of almost two hundred miles through the Highlands of Scotland. Mac obviously knew the terrain, or at least the route they were taking, like the back of his hand. He knew exactly how fast he could go down each valley and how late he could pull up before crashing into the hills or mountains at the end of them, he knew the air currents and the thermals and used them to his advantage, testing to see whether Abby was good enough to spot what he was doing, and he skimmed the Lochs and fields low enough to scare the sheep. And he did it all while laughing he head off with the excitement of it.

He led her almost as far north as Inverness before swinging back around. On their way back south he detoured to Ben Nevis and took her on a swooping ride around the collapsed crater and through the gullies and ridges before once again turning for home. However, when they were once again nearing Taynuilt, he surprised her when he straightened out and began to climb, but she quickly caught up and fell in next to him, wingtip to wingtip and looked over.

He grinned at her. 'How're ye doing there, Abby? Filled yer trews yet?'

'Afraid not, Mac. Looks like I win.'

He laughed again, throwing his head back. 'Not yet ye haven't!' By now they had reached eight thousand feet, just above a solid layer of cloud. 'Here's a last wee test for yer, lassie!'

No sooner had he spoken than he pushed his stick forwards, nosing his aircraft into a dive.

Abby followed suit, her stomach hitting her chin and her eyes filling briefly with red as the G forces surged far into negative numbers. She remained on his wing and slightly behind him, not wanting to collide with him if he throttled back, but he didn't, instead, he kept the power on as they dived, pointing almost directly downwards.

They were through the clouds in scant seconds and they burst back into clear air, the ground appearing once more, shocking in its closeness as it filled Abby's vision. Her hand twitched as her instincts screamed at her to pull back on the stick and she barely managed to stop herself, gritting her teeth and clenching her muscles as the needle on her airspeed indicator went up and up, at the same time as the dark blue of Loch Etive loomed ever nearer.

'So, Abby, this squadron of yers, will I have to do all that salutin' and marchin' and stuff?'

Abby blinked, unable to quite believe that he was trying to carry out a normal conversation when they were less than fifteen seconds away from ploughing into the waters of a loch. 'You might have to salute the Emperor occasionally, but apart from that, no. And no marching whatsoever.'

'That's a shame, I quite like a bit of marching occasionally; it's quite stimulating.' He laughed.

Abby glanced across at him, then looked at the ground, so close below them and coming a lot closer with every passing second. She looked back at him and tensed, her hand tightening on the stick, preparing to pull it back, not willing to kill herself just to convince a pilot, who was obviously suicidal, to join her.

'Hold on to yer hat!' With a primal howl, the Scotsman pulled out of the dive and Abby instantly followed suit, yelling to keep the G forces from causing her to black out.

The nose of the two aircraft came up together, but painfully slowly, too slowly, and Gwen's scream took on a note of panic as she assessed the manoeuvre and saw that she wasn't going to make it. She fought to pull the stick further back, putting every ounce of her strength into it, knowing that Butterfly could take it. Her weight increased minimally as the aircraft pulled up ever so slightly more, but it was enough.

She came out of the dive less than ten yards above the water and watched in amazement as Mac did the same... nine and a half yards below her, his floats sending up a light mist of water. She glanced at her air speed indicator and winced; even though the needle was falling rapidly it was still showing over three hundred miles an hour. At that speed, if the floats had touched the water any more firmly the man's aircraft would have nosed in from the friction and been torn to shreds.

The white plume of water disappeared as the madman gained a couple of yards more height and she put Butterfly back on his wing.

'I thought I had ye at the end there.'

'You almost did,' Abby admitted.

The Scotsman's laughter came over the radio, obviously delighted with the afternoon's fun. 'Well, if ye still want me, I'm yers and so are me bairns. Set yerself down and we'll have a wee chinwag.'

'Roger that, Mac, and welcome to Misfit Squadron.' Abby grinned and banked steeply away from him. She permitted herself a smart barrel roll to celebrate, before heading back to the field she'd landed on.

CHAPTER 7

With only Dreadnought left to repair and a few days remaining before they left for Muscovy, Gwen wanted to begin making modifications to Wasp and Dragonfly. Abby vetoed the idea, though, saying that the squadron needed the time for training. They were crossing the ocean on an aircraft carrier and to make their embarkation as quick as possible, A and B flights were going to land on the carrier and needed to learn how to do so. Of C flight, only scarlet would fly to the carrier, the rest would land at a nearby airfield and have their aircraft dismantled for the journey.

A naval airman was sent to teach them about carrier landings and he had an area the size of the Arturo painted on the landing field, along with four lines near one end that represented the four "arrester wires" that stretched across the carrier's deck, which helped to stop aircraft that landed on it.

The setup wasn't ideal because the airfield wasn't moving forwards or pitching up and down like an aircraft carrier would do, but it was the best they had. Over the space of an afternoon of continuous flying, the pilots got used to aiming at a target that was far smaller than the one they usually did and touching down on a precise point. The Navy man had them landing as close to the third "wire" as possible, then putting on full power to take off again, simulating a failed attempt. They easily got the hang of it and after only a few tries, they were all doing it pretty much perfectly every time.

It seemed that landing was going to be no problem for any of the aircraft of A or B flight making the trip directly to the Arturo, but taking off again was going to be a very different prospect.

The eight aircraft took it in turns to sit at the end of the painted out flight deck, run their airscrews to full power, then release their brakes, trying to take off in the space that was allotted to them.

A flight had no real problems in carrying out the manoeuvre, but it soon became clear that none of B flight's machines could get even close and at the end of the day they had to face the fact that those aircraft would be unable to fly for the duration of the journey.

When flying had finished for the day, the naval airman had actual arrester wires installed on the airfield for the pilots so that they could get the feel of making the landing and they were ready in the morning for when the Misfits turned up.

After a few trial runs they, of course, made a game of it.

Points were awarded for hitting the third wire, less for the second and fourth and even less for the first. No points were awarded for someone landing past the wires without hooking at all and all accumulated points were taken away from anybody who missed the deck entirely.

Hooks had been installed in the aircraft of A and B flight during the previous week in preparation for the mission and, despite Hummingbird not needing a hook, Scarlet had insisted on getting one "just in case" and she joined in the fun, but only after Abby had banned her from cheating and using her overhead rotor.

The competition turned into quite an event and the support personnel made their way to the airfield to watch whenever they found themselves off duty. They sat on the grass in front of the buildings, bringing food and drink with them and Squadron Leader Billingsworth gave them permission to patch a radio into the tannoy system so that they could play music, turning the occasion into a bit of a picnic. Throughout it all, the photographer that Freddy Featherstonehaugh had brought with him, Mr Jones, a small weaselly-looking man in his forties with an intense gaze but a very nervous nature, scurried around, taking candid photographs as unobtrusively as he could.

A flight had the best overall results because of their manoeuvrability and lower landing speeds, but once again Chastity showed how good a pilot she was.

The newest Misfit had named her aircraft "Dove" and painted it completely white, except for thin brown highlights on the wings and tail that were reminiscent of feathers and pink blades on the airscrew, and she landed perfectly, catching the three wire time after time. In the end, though, she was pipped to the post by Abby when a gust of wind made her overshoot the mark on her final attempt and catch the four wire.

The Misfits wanted there to be some kind of trophy for Abby, like the airscrew that that Gwen had been made to wear after the glidewing contest and Owen proposed that she perhaps be cocooned in arrester wire for the day. However, Abby wouldn't let them do anything silly, simply because they couldn't afford to waste any flying time and the pilots accepted, grumbling, but as soon as she was out of earshot they began discussing what they could do to her on the journey, or in Muscovy.

The day before the Misfits were due to leave, Lord Bagshot decided to throw a farewell party in the evening. A pavilion was set up in the grounds, food and drink brought in, guests invited and musicians organised, but before everybody could enjoy themselves, the preparations for the journey had to be completely finished and that included briefing those people that were going.

None of the squadron, except for the pilots, who had been sworn to secrecy, knew exactly where they were going yet, although, thanks to the carrier landing exercises, everybody now knew they were going by sea. Not everybody in the squadron was making the journey to Muscovy either - the administration staff wasn't needed because Dorothy Campbell and her staff were going to be taking care of the admin for the entire mission, nor were most of the mechanics and other support staff needed for the same reason. Those people that were being left behind were to be scattered among other RAC squadrons, wherever they were most needed, but would be recovered when the Misfits returned. Not even Jimmy was coming with them; Abby had told him in no uncertain terms that he was to stay behind and had arranged for him to join a Spitsteam squadron for the duration - the same one that his current girlfriend, Rebecca, was going to, which mollified him slightly.

In the end, then, it was a little more than a hundred people, the pilots, their fitters and a few other essential personnel, who filed into the ballroom of Bagshot Hall to be briefed by Dorothy Campbell on the details of their mission.

Three of the boards from the briefing room at Badger Base had been set up at the front of the room, but they were covered in white sheets to hide what was pinned to them and drew many a curious look from the men and women as they took their seats.

Abby and Dot Campbell were sitting behind a desk at the front of the room next to the boards and as soon as everybody was settled Abby stood up to start things off.

'Morning, everybody. As you've probably guessed, Whitehall has a job for us to do, so tomorrow we get back into the war.'

There was some cheering at this from the support staff, but it died down quickly; they were eager to hear what Abby had to say. The pilots stayed silent throughout, though; they knew that there was no cause for celebration.

Abby waited for silence to fall again before continuing. 'The mission is not what any of us were expecting, though. With the bombing in Britain moving more towards small night raids there is no longer any need for us here, so we are being sent to help in another theatre of the war.' She nodded to a couple of airmen and they pulled the sheets off of the boards to reveal several large scale maps.

The leftmost board had a map of Northern England pinned to it, the one in the middle had one showing the northern oceans, with a route marked on it in red, but it was the third board, showing their destination, that everybody's eyes shot to.

Abby picked up a wooden pointed from the desk and went over to the huge map, which showed the whole of the eastern end of Europe from Finland to the Ukraine.

The geography of the east was not one of the subjects widely taught at schools in the former British Empire and the countries pictured on it was unfamiliar to many of the people present, but there was no need for them to ask as she immediately tapped their destination with the pointer and named it for them.

'We are being sent here, to Murmansk, in the north of the Kingdom of Muscovy, what most of you will know better as the Russian Empire. There we will join with the Muscovite air force in trying to hold back the Prussian armies that are even now on their way east.'

There were surprised murmurs and the support staff whispered among themselves, but silence fell again rapidly as the men and women turned their attention back to their commander.

Abby went to the map of England and once again used the pointer to illustrate her words. 'The squadron will take off tomorrow morning at dawn. The aircraft of A and B flights, along with Hummingbird, will fly directly to the HMS Arturo, which is waiting for us at Gourock, about ten miles downriver from Glasgow. The remainder of C flight, along with the rest of the support staff in the Lekker and a few other transports procured for us by Sky Commodore Campbell will go to an aerodrome near the port of Glasgow. There they will remove the wings of Bloodhound and Vulture and pack the two aircraft up for transport before being brought downriver and transferred to the carrier along with Dreadnought, which is already there. The taskforce, comprising the Arturo, three destroyers and attending supply and support ships will depart as soon as everything is aboard.'

She stood in front of the middle board and faced her audience. 'From then on and until we reach Muscovy we will essentially be guests of His Majesty's Navy, although the aircraft of A flight may be called upon to defend the convoy if we find ourselves under attack. Conditions will undoubtedly be different to the ones that you are used to, more cramped and with worse food, but I expect you to behave in as exemplary a fashion as you would anywhere else when in uniform.'

There were some chuckles at this and a few knowing looks thrown in the direction of the pilots; the support staff were well aware of how well-behaved Bruce and Mac were and had all heard the story of them befouling the steps of The Dorchester the night of the fight with the Barons.

Abby rolled her eyes. 'Alright, I'd like you to behave better than that, but it would probably be too much to ask. Just don't get into any fights and make me have to throw you overboard.' She shook her head in exasperation and glanced over at the sky commodore. 'They're all yours.'

Campbell stood up, a broad smile on her face, and took the pointer from Abby as the latter sat down.

'Good morning, Misfits.'

Abby raised her eyebrows at the chorus of replies that the sky commodore elicited; she herself hadn't warranted, or even expected, such a courtesy, but it seemed that a guest did. She met Owen's eyes, but the Welshman just grinned at her and pointedly turned away to look at the woman giving the briefing.

'First of all I want to tell you how important this mission is. As most of you may know, at the beginning of this little shindig people are already calling the Second Great War, the Prussian Empire signed a non-aggression pact with the Russian Empire, what is now the Kingdom of Muscovy which essentially let the Prussians do what they wanted with Europe and Africa as long as they didn't do anything the Muscovites didn't want them to do. However, now that we've stopped them here in the west, they're looking for something else to do and it seems that they've turned their eyes on this big fat prize to the east.'

She went to the map of Eastern Europe and pointed out places as she named them. 'They have already broken the pact by invading neutral Ukraine and the Muscovite Baltic territories and are now looking to push on into the heart of Muscovy itself. If they manage to defeat the Muscovites, they will be given access to untold resources and will most likely swarm back west and overrun us. Tsar Nicholas has specifically asked for the Misfits to help prevent that from happening. Our task is to hold back the invading armies in the north and keep the arctic supply lines open for more convoys like ours, while the Muscovite army tries to hold the centre and south of the line.'

She held up her hand as murmurs started. 'Now, that doesn't mean we have to defeat the Prussians all by ourselves, although knowing this squadron you'll give it a damn good try.'

As she had expected, her audience laughed and the tension that had been building dissipated. She turned back to the maps and pointed at the one in the middle with the red line on it that threaded its way through the arctic. 'The Arturo and its convoy will steam north to Iceland. There it will join up with another convoy that left days earlier, comprising more escort ships and supply ships with the rest of the armaments that we are taking to the Muscovites, among them ammunition, tanks, artillery pieces and the Harridan fighters that will form the backbone of the Muscovite air force.'

Campbell glanced at Abby. 'There are three RAC instructors going with us to train the Muscovites on the Harridans and they'll be billeting with your pilots on the Arturo. Try not to be too bad an influence on them; they have a serious job to do when they get there.'

Abby blinked at her, feigning shock. 'Us? Bad influences? We would never do anything to corrupt any of the King's men and women or tarnish the reputation of the Royal Aviation Corps!'

'Of course you wouldn't...' Campbell shook her head and sighed, to more laughter from the Misfits, then turned back to the board. 'From Iceland the entire convoy will head north-east, giving the Scandinavian countries a fairly wide berth, before darting in to the Muscovite coast and making landfall near Murmansk. Misfit Squadron will then be transferred to Vaenga airfield, some miles from the city, along with the Harridans and the instructors.'

She pointed out the map of the area around the north of Muscovy. 'The main threat you'll be facing will come from Finland. They're allied with the Prussians and are providing them with a way to move directly against the north of Muscovy. We're expecting heavy fighting because, as I've said, they're in a bit of a hurry for some reason. That's in our favour, though, because unless they have this whole area conquered before the winter sets in they'll have to leave it until spring, which means their flanks will be open if their forces in the south push too far forwards. So, if we can hold the Prussian assault in the north back until the depths of winter - early December at the latest - then the weather will do our job for us and we'll be able to come home.

'Do not be under any illusions, though, this is going to be a *very* tough fight and it may well not be winnable. Be warned, if we can't hold back the Prussians we might find that we have to pull out in a hurry, so take nothing with you that you wouldn't want to lose.'

She gazed around the room, taking in the faces of men and women who, far from looking scared at the thought of the battle ahead, seemed keen get back into the war and make a difference. She nodded, satisfied. 'Having said that, the King and I have every confidence that if *anyone* can pull off the impossible, it's Misfit Squadron.'

The raising of the pavilion proved the highlight of the morning and, with nothing else left to do, most of the squadron turned out to watch it being put up.

It was delivered in four long thick canvas-wrapped sections, so big that each needed its own vehicle and were unloaded one by one by twenty straining and sweating men. The watching squadron offered to help, but the workers refused; apparently the pavilion in its broken-down form was delicately prepared and even a single misstep in unwrapping them could delay the erection process by hours.

The fat, sausage-shaped sections were laid one by one on the grass of the lawn at very specific places that were marked out by a man with a theodolite. They were then unfolded lengthwise until the ends were touching, forming a giant rectangle. The resulting long thin tubes were then unrolled towards the centre of the rectangle, revealing that they were in fact isosceles triangles and the men rushed about connecting each triangle to its neighbour until the result was a solid white sheet of canvas, reinforced with a polymer coating on its upper side to protect the occupants from the elements.

Next, four small steam engines were wheeled down ramps from the backs of the vehicles and the men attached them to four six-inch-thick metal disks which they fixed to the corners of the rectangular canvas. The engines were checked over quickly, then ignited and when they were all whistling happily, with a full head of steam, the foreman gave a signal, levers were thrown and they began to chug.

At first there was no noticeable change, but then the tight sheet shivered and ever so slowly began to rise above the ground as columns telescoped from the disks.

When questioned, the workers revealed that the full process of the pavilion's raising was going to take close to an hour, longer if one of the columns stuck and the process had to be halted while the problem was sorted. So, while the spectacle was still interesting, it was too slow to hold the interest of the squadron. That problem was solved very quickly, though, when Lord Bagshot himself came out of the mansion and called for volunteers to help to set up several tables on the patio and his cooking staff began to bring out snacks and drinks.

The Misfit jazz band, the "Individualists", had been rather upset when they had found out that Lord Bagshot had contracted a twenty-piece swing dance band that was visiting from America for the party, until someone pointed out that they would be free to drink and dance. Now, though, they saw their chance and ran off to get their instruments. However, instead of their usual upbeat dance music, they played lighter tunes that were more suitable for an afternoon of socialising.

Rank was set aside, as the Misfits always did on such occasions, and the pilots mixed with the support staff, to eat and drink. They showed much more restraint and drank far less than they usually did, though, knowing that they had a long night ahead of them and not wanting to miss the real party or a minute or the little remaining time they had together before going their separate ways.

Gwen noticed Kitty wandering off towards the pavilion, the engineer in her curious as to how the telescoping support poles worked, just as she was, and she realised that it was perhaps her last chance to speak to the American before they left.

She started to follow, but stopped after only a couple of steps and hurried back to the bar. She grabbed half a pint of bitter, downed it in a single long draught, then wiped her mouth with the back of her hand, took a deep breath and started walking before she thought better of it.

Kitty smiled as Gwen approached, slowly and elegantly unfolding herself from where she had crouched down to peer at the mechanism connected to one of the small steam engines. 'Hi, Gwen.'

Gwen nodded and returned the smile. 'Hello.' She stood by the tall American's side, her mind racing as she tried to think of something to say. In desperation, she pointed at the growing column. 'It appears fairly straightforward. Is it?'

'It is.'

Gwen bent and watched the process, seeing how the shaft from the steam engine turned a bolt on the side of the thick metal disk, which made the dozens of concentric rings of the column rise one by one above their fellows, before locking into place with a loud and solid sounding clunk.

She watched it for a while, trying to gather courage that the alcohol hadn't been sufficient to give her, then, not nearly ready, but realising that she had to do something before things got truly awkward. She stood and met Kitty's frank gaze, her cheeks heating at the way the beautiful American's piercing blue eyes bored into her, as if she knew what was going through Gwen's mind, which, she mused, was entirely likely.

'Um... Fancy going for a walk?'

'I'd love to.'

Kitty's genuinely pleased smile warmed Gwen and banished all doubts from her that she was doing the right thing. She turned and Kitty fell into step with her as they wandered away from the mansion towards the air base, deserted now except for a few military guards and some of the more dedicated fitters, who were in the hangar, making sure that the Misfit aircraft were ready to fly at dawn the next day.

The walked in silence along the lawn, past the ostentatious marble fountain depicting Poseidon in his chariot, being drawn along by the beasts of the sea, which had built by a Bagshot ancestor with pretensions of being a naval man, and they were almost all the way to the perimeter fence of the base before Gwen worked up the courage to start speaking.

'There's something I've been meaning to ask you for a while now.'

'And what's that?'

'The night of the party on Badger Base, when we got back to the barracks...'

Gwen hesitated, still not sure quite how to ask, but Kitty just laughed.

'Took you long enough!'

Gwen blinked at her. 'What? So you *do* remember kissing me?'

'Of course! How could I ever forget something like that?'

'But you were so drunk, I thought...'

Kitty shook her head. 'I was drunk, yes, but I'm never *that* drunk.' She winked. 'From one scientist to another, let's say I was carrying out an experiment.'

Gwen frowned. 'I'm not sure that's entirely ethical.'

Kitty shrugged and gave her a cheeky smile. 'Maybe that's something we can debate over a few drinks sometime?'

'Maybe.' Gwen smiled. 'So, what was your grand experiment anyway? You kissed me to see how I would react?'

'Only in part. I also just really wanted to.'

'Oh, well, that makes it alright then...' Gwen laughed.

They reached the end of the long lawn and looked through the chain links of the fence at the hangars where their aircraft waited patiently for them to come and bring them back to life in the air.

Gwen started slightly when she felt Kitty's arm go around her, but then relaxed, slipping her own arm around the woman and resting her head against her, glad for the comfort and the physical contact that she'd denied herself for so long.

They stood there for a while, just enjoying each other's company and listening to the distant sounds of the party, floating to them on the light breeze, the laughter of their friends mixing with the music of the band, who were playing a jazz version of one of Elgar's ever-popular *Pomp and Circumstance* marches.

Gwen couldn't believe how comfortable she felt, as if it were the most natural thing in the world for the two of them to be there, with their arms around each other, but she couldn't stay like that for too long otherwise she might not be able to say what she needed to.

She turned to face Kitty and hesitantly reached up to cup her cheek with her free hand.

At five foot seven, Gwen wasn't short by any means, but the American was a good four inches taller than her and she saw the big blue eyes widen in surprise as she stood on tiptoes and leaned forwards to kiss her.

She felt Kitty relax with a sigh, her soft lips parting as Gwen pressed forward, but then it was Gwen's turn to melt when the woman took all control of the kiss away from her, deepening it and pulling the two of them closer together, her strong body pressing against hers, her breath sweet with just a hint of the bourbon she'd been drinking.

All of her concerns, all of her worries faded away as Gwen's focus centred on woman holding her, the lips pressed against hers, the tongue that flicked maddeningly, teasing her own, and she wished she could stay that way forever, but she forced herself to come back to the world.

She gently broke the kiss and took a small step back, pulling out of Kitty's arms, wincing slightly at her heartbreaking whine of protest.

She reached out to take the woman's hands. 'I know I've been avoiding you and I'm sorry; it's because I didn't know how to tell you that I'm not ready to take this further. But I want you to know that I like you a lot and sometime soon, when I've sorted out the mess in my head, I hope we can explore what we mean to each other. Will that be alright?'

'Well, I'm not going to pretend I wouldn't like to take you into the trees over there and do a heck of a lot more kissing, but I guess I can wait a bit longer.'

Gwen glanced in the direction of the trees and her mouth went dry as images of what the two of them could get up to in the cool shadows, hidden from view, flashed through her mind. She cleared her throat, then met Kitty's mischievous, assessing eyes and smiled. 'Thank you for being so understanding. And while we're being honest with each other, I must say that I have a few experiments of my own that I'm quite tempted to carry out.'

She laughed at Kitty's delighted face, then squeezed her hands. 'Come on, I really need a drink!'

Still laughing, she dragged Kitty back to the party.

The columns holding up the canvas of the pavilion finally reached their full height and the workmen turned off the engines and wheeled them away, leaving only one behind. They then began laying a wooden floor across the whole of the giant space, which snapped together with dovetail joints, much like a jigsaw puzzle, before constructing a small stage at the narrow end of the rectangle furthest from the mansion.

The sun was going down when the pavilion was finally finished, but the Misfits still weren't allowed into the pavilion, because now it was the turn of the serving staff to begin setting up. The Bagshot Hall kitchen workers had been supplemented by the squadron's cooks in order to produce enough food for several hundred people, but Lord Bagshot had hired an outside company to provide serving staff so that the Misfits could join in the festivities. Those staff now began setting up, lining the short side of the pavilion nearest the mansion with tables and filling them with the food and drink streaming out of the kitchens.

Finally, everything was ready. The swing band had arrived and were in place on the stage, the food and drink was waiting and the guests had arrived, including notables from Whitehall, dozens of the support staff's family members, local aristocrats such as Lady Bracknell and

Lord Augustus and his new wife, and numerous others who couldn't *possibly* have been left off the list.

The only thing left to do before starting the party was for Lord Bagshot to give his welcome speech and the Misfits were herded into position on the lawn in front of the mansion ready for him to appear.

Three people came through the door of the mansion, though, instead of the two that had been expected and a shocked hush spread throughout the entire squadron as Lady Penelope *walked* out onto the patio, supported between Lord Bagshot and the King.

They watched her stumping, only slightly awkwardly, across the patio until she came to a halt at the top of the three stairs leading down onto the lawn and smiled down at them.

She opened her mouth to speak, but before she could, the silence was broken and replaced by thunderous applause. She laughed, her eyes welling up as the noise washed over her, meeting the eyes of the many people in the crowd who she had gotten to know during her time with the squadron.

The applause went on and on and seemed like it would never stop, the squadron delighted that this woman, one of their beloved pilots, was looking so well after an accident that could easily have killed her, but finally the King held up his free hand for quiet.

He was obeyed almost immediately and he chuckled. 'Plenty of time for all that later, some of us are thirsty!'

The Misfits laughed, but only briefly before they turned their attention to Lady Penelope, who gazed down at her friends, valiantly fighting back tears. 'Thank you, thank you all. I... I had prepared something to say, but I'm afraid you have left me speechless. I...'

Lord Bagshot handed her a handkerchief and she dabbed at her eyes, before clearing her throat and raising her voice. 'I do apologise. I don't actually have much to say, beyond to welcome you all and hope you enjoy yourself this evening. However, His Majesty would like to say a few words before we begin.' She nodded at the King. 'Your Majesty.'

The King smiled warmly at her. 'Thank you, Penny.'

He looked out over the men and women gathered below who stilled completely, waiting for him to speak. 'Well, I don't know if you've noticed, but things have been a little bit quieter over England lately - in a fit of pique, Kaiser Wilhelm has announced to the world that the Kingdom of Britain will be defeated by siege and he's buggered off to bother someone else, knowing that he can't defeat us!'

The King's words engendered rather rude comments, mostly about Kaiser Bill's parentage, or the rumours that he only had one of a certain unmentionable part of his anatomy instead of a pair. They all knew that the Kaiser was just trying to give an excuse for giving up on the invasion; there was no way the Prussians would ever win like that - the British Isles and the stoic British people could hold out for an extremely long time and were already using the breathing room to consolidate their forces.

The King indulged the jeering for a while, but then held up his hand for quiet again. 'We're not safe yet, though, not by a long shot, but the Prussians have made their first great mistake. We will rebuild and rearm and when *we* are ready, *we* will take the fight to *them* and with this squadron leading the way we cannot help but be victorious and crush the threat of tyranny into the dirt once and for all!'

The Misfits broke out into cheering and the swing band struck up the national anthem as the King and Lord Bagshot helped Lady Penelope down the stairs and led the party into the pavilion.

The foreman who had overseen the raising of the pavilion waited until they had taken their first step onto the wooden floor, then flicked a switch on the last remaining engine. Tiny white lights, delicate, cool-burning electrical filaments on fine wires hanging from the roof, sprang into life overhead, creating a soft fairytale atmosphere under the pristine canvas.

The national anthem ended and the band immediately launched into their signature tune "In The Mood" which had the men and women immediately grabbing partners and rushing to fill the dance floor, straight past the King with barely any deference to his rank.

Well and truly started, the party was soon in full swing, but the pilots didn't join in straight away. Instead, they followed their hosts to the drinks table and surrounded them, demanding explanations with their expectant silence.

The King gave them a grin, then tactfully wandered off to see what the hovering and anxious-looking Marshal of the Court wanted.

Lord Bagshot looked around the semicircle of pilots and laughed. 'As you can see, my wife and I have been hiding something from you.'

Owen snapped his fingers. 'Nicholas Park! I knew there was a reason I knew that name! He was the one developing walking tanks like the Prussians have for the army in the warehouse next to mine.'

Lady Penelope nodded. 'He wasn't very successful with the tanks, but as you can see, his ideas weren't all bad.' She lifted her skirts to reveal gleaming steel ankles and brass shins. 'At least now I have an excuse if I wear the wrong trousers to a dinner party.'

As one, the pilots leaned forward to get a closer look and Gwen was amused to note that the more interested they were in engineering, the further they bent.

'I'm not quite as proficient with my new legs as I was with my original ones, but I did promise that one day I would fly again and, thanks to Mr Park, who has designed and built these for me, I am confident that I will very soon.'

'How do they work?'

This question came from behind the Misfits and they turned as one to find the Princess Elizabeth with a single Royal Guard escort looming behind her. The pilots bowed, but she waved the courtesy away with a smile and stepped forward to join them, showing a composure in the face of such august company well in advance of her years.

'Well, Your Royal Highness...'

The young girl smiled. 'I've told you Misfits before and the order still stands, it's Liz. Or Elizabeth, if you must. At least while we are discussing matters scientific.'

Penny returned her smile. 'As you wish.' She pulled the skirts higher on her right side to reveal the joints at the knees of the metal leg. It was a gesture that would have scandalised most of the society that she moved in, but none of the pilots batted an eye at it; not only were they used to seeing their friend in a skin tight leather flightsuit, but it wasn't as if she were revealing her *own* legs anymore.

'Well, I'm a bit lopsided. The left one's fairly simple, just a glorified peg-leg really with an articulated ankle, but the right one is the real demonstration of Nick's genius. It's clockwork and moves somewhat like the wheels of a locomotive. Just think of the knees being the wheels and the legs being the drivers.' She raised her leg in front of herself, demonstrating how the enclosed disks which formed her new knee rotated.

The princess leaned in to inspect it, her nose only inches away from it, far closer than any of the pilots had - able to get away with such a breach of decorum because of her rank and age. 'How do you control it?'

Penny smiled down at her. 'It controls itself. There is a gyroscope in the knee which detects when I lift it and put it down, keeping my lower leg vertical without it just hanging uselessly, which means that it stays firm if I'm stepping up on something.'

'And how is it attached?'

'I hope you'll forgive me if I don't show everyone that part!' Penny laughed as she smoothed her skirts back into place. 'My thigh inserts into a padded brass cup. Small Duralumin tubes, much like the frame of an aircraft, run up my leg from that and are attached to what amounts to a suspender belt, which spreads the weight on my hips. All told, it weighs only slightly more than my old one.'

The princess stood up and gave her a smile and a nod. 'Thank you.'

'You're welcome, Elizabeth.'

The young girl turned to look at the pilots standing behind her and quickly honed in on Abby. 'Dame Lennox, I see you have found someone to fill that spot I desperately wanted to take in your squadron.'

Abby smiled; the princess had tried to join the squadron several times since its inception and it looked like she wasn't going to stop any time soon, despite the King and Abby insisting that she had to be eighteen before she could even be considered. 'I'm afraid so. May I present Aviation Sergeant Chastity Arrowsmith.'

Chastity drew herself up to attention and stood stiffly as the princess stepped over to her.

'As you were, Sergeant.' Liz smiled and stuck her hand out. 'It's a pleasure to meet you.'

Chastity blinked at the hand in shock, as if she couldn't believe that she was going to shake the hand of royalty, but recovered quickly and accepted it.

'The pleasure is all mine, Your Royal Highness.'

The princess raised an eyebrow and didn't release Chastity's hand until the woman had corrected herself and called her Elizabeth, but then she nodded with another smile and turned back to Abby. 'I'm dying with curiosity to see your new aircraft, but I won't take anyone away from your celebration tonight. Perhaps when you return?'

Abby nodded. 'You're welcome any time, you know that.'

'Thank you.' Liz sighed. 'Well, thank you for your time, but I must leave you and see to my duty.' She looked around the pilots, meeting their eyes one by one. 'Safe journey and happy hunting.' She moved away, following in the wake of her father as he made the rounds of the guests.

The Misfits watched her go, but then once again their full attention turned back to Lady Penelope.

'Why did you keep this from us?' Abby's gentle voice was only just audible over the music and sounds of revelry.

'I'd like to say I did it so that I could see the looks on your faces when I walked out,' she grinned. 'Priceless by the way, but I didn't. I didn't tell you about it because I didn't want to get everybody's hopes up; we didn't know if this was going to work, whether I would be able to use these legs or not.' She slapped her right thigh, making the brass ring dully. 'But, as you can see, I can and I'll be back in the air soon enough!' The smile dropped from her face suddenly and she sighed. 'However, I doubt that the RAC will ever let me back into combat and the odds of me rejoining the squadron, at least as a pilot, are very long indeed.'

Scarlet laughed. 'If you want back into the RAC, I'll have a word with Dougie. He won't say no to me, don't you worry!'

Lady Penelope smiled at her. 'Thank you, Ophelia, and I may take you up on that if the King doesn't beat you to it; he has already promised to have a quiet word with Sir Douglas if he is obstinate when the time comes.'

'You'll be welcome back in Misfit Squadron anytime, you know that,' said Abby.

Penny sighed. 'Ah, but you don't need any more pilots now, do you?'

Abby shrugged. 'We'll just knock together a new aircraft for you - we've had a bit of practice recently so it'll only take a week or so. And I was thinking of kicking Owen out anyway.'

'Hey!'

There was laughter at Owen's typical response to Abby poking fun at him, but none of them missed it when Lady Penelope turned away, ostensibly to order a drink, but in reality to hide her face, using her husband's handkerchief to wipe her eyes once more.

When she was herself again she turned back around and clapped her hands. 'Right! What the hell are we all just standing around here for? There's dancing to be done!'

She signalled a passing waiter carrying a tray filled with champagne flutes and gestured for him to serve the pilots, then turned to pick up her own drink from the bar. It was only water, which betrayed to a few of the more observant Misfits that she was still under some kind of chemical regime for pain.

When everybody had a glass, she raised hers. 'A toast! To Britain, her allies and Misfit Squadron.'

Hans Gruber watched as the last of the so-called *Norwegian Freedom Flight* aircraft struck the ground and cartwheeled, pieces breaking off and flying in all directions as it tore itself apart.

The small squadron, formed and equipped by the noted engineer and inventor Bror Wyth, had proved a thorn in the side of the Prussians until the Kaiser himself had sent Gruber north to deal with them. In two swift and brutal engagements the Barons had first broken, then slaughtered them and now all their pilots were either dead or in chains awaiting transport to Bertha.

Hölle had been a joy to fly, much better than Flamme, and he had to admit that his pilots had also performed adequately, but in the end it hadn't been enough of a test for them to distinguish themselves and they remained merely numbers to him. He hoped that the Russians, who their fool of a Tsar insisted on calling the Muscovites, would present more of a challenge, but he doubted it.

Still, despite the ease with which they had been defeated, it had been a valiant effort on the part of the Norwegians and he could respect the courage of the men and women who had tried to hold back the inevitable, but there was nothing a single squadron of twelve aircraft could do against the Crimson Barons, no matter their passion or motivation.

It was a lesson that he would enjoy teaching to the Misfits when next he met them in the sky.

PART 2

RELOCATE

CHAPTER 8

In spite of the almost universal presence of fierce hangovers, the entire squadron was up and running before dawn and the move went ahead on schedule.

The pilots had held back from drinking very much for once, knowing that they had to be flying again before the alcohol would be fully out of their system and knowing that the landing on the aircraft carrier was going to be hard enough as it was sober. The support staff, though, had pulled out all the stops, trying to make up for the weeks of hard work during which they hadn't been able to enjoy themselves. Many of them hadn't slept and their eyes had dark circles under them, but they still carried out their jobs with ruthless efficiency and had the aircraft in the air an hour and a half before dawn, exactly on time.

The larger aircraft - the Lekker, the transport aircraft carrying the support staff, Bloodhound and Vulture - had no trouble making the three hundred and fifty mile journey to Scotland from Bagshot Hall, but it was only just within the range of the fighters and trying to do it in one go wouldn't have left them much tension to make the landing on the Arturo. For safety, then, the air ministry arranged for them to be rewound at a deserted airfield in the Lake District, which was occupied by a team of RAC fitters for the day in utmost secrecy.

While their aircraft were being seen to, the Misfits took the opportunity to stretch their legs. The airfield supplied an abandoned holiday camp that was reminiscent of the one that they had occupied for Badger Base, but this one was on the top of a small hill with spectacular views of the lush green fields of Britain on all sides.

The pilots sat on the grass and silently watched the sunrise, with all its purples and reds and yellows, the fluffy clouds in the autumn sky catching the colours, and, while it remained unsaid, it crossed the mind of every single one of them at some point or another that it was possibly the last time that they would see the sun rising over the country that they had sworn to defend.

Too soon, though, the fitters were finished and the nine Misfits stood slowly, reluctant to take their eyes from the spectacle, but eventually tore themselves away and trudged back to their aircraft.

From the Lake District it was only a short hop to Gourock and less than half an hour later they were in a holding pattern over the Arturo.

The town was a moderately popular seaside resort and there was the usual line of boarding houses and small hotels along the waterfront. It even boasted its own yachting club, but the small white boats in the shallow bay were dwarfed by the immense flat-topped grey ship sitting half a mile offshore.

Usually an aircraft carrier would steam into the wind to help an aircraft land, but the Arturo wasn't going to be able to do that, so the conditions the Misfits had to cope with were actually quite similar to the ones they had practised at Bagshot. Scarlet went first because she could just land directly in the position the crew wanted her in and she was followed by B flight, then A flight in reverse order with Abby landing last. It was a time consuming process because, for safety, each aircraft had to be taken down below in the hydraulic lift near the bow before the next one could land. Eventually, though, they were all safely below in the hangar deck, which occupied about two-thirds of the space immediately below the flight deck, where they joined three RAC Harridans, already wingless and pushed against a bulkhead. Navy mechanics set about removing the wings of B flight's aircraft under the worried gaze of their pilots, who were reluctant that anyone should touch them except their own fitters, but aware that time and space were at a premium.

A young Naval officer, short, spotty and barely out of his teens, approached and stood in front of the pilots, gaping at them in something like awe.

Abby watched him for a few seconds with an amused smile, then called out over the racket of the work going on. 'Something we can do for you, Midshipman?'

He looked to her and there was a moment of almost panic as he recognised her, but then he drew himself up to attention and gave a speech that he had obviously been rehearsing in his head, but that still came out quite hesitantly when faced with the reality of giving it to people who were living heroes. 'Midshipman Simkin, ma'am, with the C-C-Captain's c-c-compliments. He, uh, he apologises for not being here to welcome you in person, but says he'll meet you later, once we're underway and out to sea. He asked me to show you to your quarters in the meantime and see you s-s-settled.'

'Very good.' Abby nodded. 'Lead the way, please.'

The young man took them through a door in the side bulkhead and into a stairwell that led down into the depths of the ship. They went down one flight of metal stairs, then through another door and a short distance along a corridor towards the stern. One last door took them into a small ready room, which was packed with leather sofas and armchairs that looked like they had once been expensive, but had seen far better days. Three people were there already, two women and one man dressed in RAC day uniforms and as the Misfits entered they leapt to their feet and stood at attention.

Abby went to greet them, waving at them to relax. 'You must be the flight instructors. Abby Lennox, pleased to meet you.'

The shorter of the two women stepped forward to take Abby's offered hand. 'Squadron Leader Rosaline Pemberton, ma'am, and these are Aviator Lieutenants Howard and Drake.' The other two instructors nodded when they were introduced, first the woman, then the man, and Abby returned their nods with a smile.

More handshakes were exchanged when the other pilots were introduced to Pemberton, but before they could make further conversation, a polite cough from the young Midshipman interrupted them.

Abby turned to him. 'Yes, Mr Simkin?'

'The head and your berth are through the door over there.' He pointed to the back of the room, then indicated a table to one side. 'And there are tea and refreshments. If there is anything else you need, please use the radio next to the door to call for a steward. And I've been ordered to tell you that you should stay here until someone comes to get you, ma'am. Please don't wander around outside, at least until you've been given an orientation or the captain gives the say-so.'

Abby smiled warmly to assuage his worries at having to tell the fabled Misfit Squadron what they could and couldn't do. 'Very well, Mr Simkin, we will do as we are told.'

'Thank you, ma'am.' The young man gave her a nervous smile, then left, shutting the door firmly behind himself.

Abby turned back to her pilots. 'Right then, lets stow our gear or whatever they say in the navy, then I'm dying for a cup of tea.' She nodded at the instructors. 'Be right back!'

Their "berth" proved to be just two barracks rooms with ten bunk beds in each and four extremely small single rooms, one of which had already been claimed by Squadron Leader Pemberton. There was no kitchen area and only very basic washing facilities which included a single shower with a sign on it forbidding people from leaving the water running. There was no space for entertainment or relaxation beyond the ready room that the instructors were in and to the dismay of many of the pilots there was no sign of alcohol anywhere either. Neither was there a single window to the outside world. It was all a very dull grey metal - floor, ceiling and furniture alike - and the only decoration was a small oil painting on the wall of the corridor depicting a stormy sea and an old sailing ship in the process of being broken apart on a rocky shore, but that had probably been put there by some wag to scare people who were nervous about going to sea.

The pilots glanced at each other, but nobody said anything, they just took the opportunity to change out of their flightsuits and use the very basic facilities before going back to the ready room.

'Right, then! Kitty, Gwen, you're on tea duty. Chastity, start handing out those sandwiches, please, and I'll have a slice of that Battenberg as well.'

While the three junior pilots went off to obey Abby's commands, the rest of them took seats with the instructors around the large coffee table in the centre of the room.

Scarlet smirked at Kitty and Gwen as they filled the tin mugs with steaming hot tea from the large copper urn and started handing them round. She was very pleased that she was no longer one of the three most junior pilots, but they took a measure of revenge on her by putting salt in her tea instead of sugar, making sure to be busy and look innocent when she spat it out all over Derek. Chastity, meanwhile, gave out tin plates and lugged the large tray of sandwiches over to the table, before going back for the two cakes that were with them, a Victoria sponge and the previously mentioned Battenberg.

The pilots didn't stand on ceremony and dug in without delay; it had been a good few hours since they'd had breakfast.

While she was eating, Gwen realised that the instructor, who had been introduced as Drake, wouldn't stop staring at her. He was a rakishly handsome young man with light brown hair, only a few years older than herself, with a permanent half smile and an amused glint in dark blue eyes that were somehow very familiar. She frowned at him, wondering why he was being so rude, while at the same time becoming more and more paranoid as to whether she might have something on her face, like a piece of cake or butter from the sandwiches.

Drake...

She started when she realised why he was looking at her as if they had been properly introduced, it was because they had been. Many years before. 'Digger? Is that you?'

All sound stopped as the Misfits paused in their eating to listen in.

He smiled at her. 'Hello, Goosy.'

Gwen pointedly ignored the raised eyebrows and amused looks of her colleagues and tried hard not to react to his use of his private nickname for her, but it was to no avail; they had heard and would be sure to use it against her whenever they could.

Abby smiled at Gwen. 'You know each other, then?'

'We've met.' Gwen shrugged, before winking at the man.

She had first been introduced to Lord Rudyard Sebastian Augustus Cholmondeley Drake the fourth, son of an Earl and heir to a fortune, when she was six. He had been a mature and worldly-wise eight-year-old who was sulking because he had been lumped with taking care of a young girl by his parents when the Hawkings came to visit instead of having his daily flying lesson. Making the best of a bad situation he had dragged her along to the estate's airfield, hoping to bore her, while at least getting some use of the time he had been allocated with the family pilot. When Gwen had impressed the pilot and shown him up with an understanding of mechanics that, try as he might, he couldn't quite get his head around, he had sulked at first, but then when the pilot had offered to take them both up he had seen his opportunity to get his lesson after all and forgiven her.

That had been the start of a friendship that had lasted until he was eleven and had been sent to board at Eton, however, those three years had been enough for him to spark in her a love of flying that she hadn't had before, having previously only been interested in engineering in general.

'It was years ago. I taught Gwen to fly.'

'Oooh, Rudy, you liar! You did not!

'Did too!'

'It was Manfred who taught me.'

'At first, but when he left I took over.'

Gwen conceded the point with a nod. 'Yes, but I'd already solo'd by then. You only taught me aerobatics.'

Drake, or Rudy as he'd been, when she hadn't been calling him "Digger" (for the unfortunate tendency he had of landing his fortunately forgiving aircraft too hard while he was learning and carving divots out of the airfield) nodded. 'I'll give you that, but there's a big difference between flying a circuit and actually *flying* and that was due to me.'

Gwen snorted and prepared to give a scathing reply, but fell silent and blushed when she heard the sniggers that were coming from all around her. Too late she realised that the two of them had picked up where they'd left off and returned to the childish bickering that had formed a large part of their conversations in the past.

'Oh, please, don't stop on our account; this is absolutely fascinating.' Abby smiled at them before popping the last few crumbs of her cake into her mouth and licking marzipan from her fingers.

Gwen could feel her cheeks growing even warmer and she took refuge in a sandwich while she stared at her tea, but Drake just laughed. 'I apologise, Wing Commander.'

Abby nodded graciously. 'No need to apologise; we're used to this kind of behaviour from Goosy.'

The pilots broke out into laughter, no longer able to contain themselves and Gwen shrank as all eyes turned to her, wishing the inadequately padded sofa she was sharing with Kitty and Scarlet would swallow her.

Abby waited for the laughter to die down before leaning forwards to get another slice of cake. 'What is the story behind that name anyway?'

'There isn't one.' Gwen mumbled, then thrust a finger at Rudy, her eyes wide with alarm, when he grinned and opened his mouth to speak. 'Don't you dare! Or I'll tell them about the nuns.'

It was Rudy's turn to cringe and he eyed his fellow instructors nervously, prompting a fresh round of laughter, which only died down when the door opened and Dorothy Campbell came in, accompanied by a Naval officer and Midshipman Simkin.

Chastity jumped to her feet at the sight of the superior officers, quickly followed by the instructors. The other Misfits stared at them for a few seconds, before groaning and slowly following their example, but Campbell just laughed and waved them down again. 'Oh, don't bother.' She wandered over and took a spare armchair in the ring around the coffee table and looked up at the still-standing Chastity. 'I could murder a cup of tea, please.'

'Right away, ma'am. Gentlemen?'

When both Naval officers shook their heads, the Aviator Sergeant hurried over to the table at the side of the room and poured just one mug which she brought back to Campbell.

'Ah, that's the ticket, thank you.' Campbell nodded at Chastity before smiling at the group. 'Morning, everyone and thank you for coming. I hope you enjoyed your flight, because odds are you aren't going to get back into the air for a week or so, conditions and the Prussians permitting.'

The Misfits had known this, but they still groaned and she chuckled before continuing. 'Don't worry, you'll have plenty of work to do when we get to where we're going, so take the opportunity to have a good rest and try to think of this as a pleasure cruise.'

Bruce blew a raspberry, provoking laughter from everyone, including Campbell. 'Seriously, though, there isn't going to be much to do on the journey, so try to think of ways to stay sane. Because we're under Navy rules you'll get a rum ration every day, so that should help a bit, but it won't be enough for some of you people.' She looked pointedly at Bruce and Mac; obviously the story of their disgracing the steps of The Dorchester had made the rounds even at Whitehall. 'Just try to stay out of trouble and be ready to go straight into action when we get to Muscovy, please.'

She turned in her seat to nod at the naval officer, who had moved to stand behind her. 'This is Lieutenant Commander Bush, he's our liaison with the captain. Mr Bush?'

The commander nodded to the group. 'Pleased to meet you. Anything you need, just let me or Midshipman Simkin know and we'll try to sort you out. Just don't ask for more rum, because you won't get it.'

Mac scowled and turned to Abby. 'I don't like this boat. Where do I get off?'

Abby smiled sweetly at him. 'Shut up, Mac. Sorry, Commander, please go on.'

'Sounds like it's going to be an interesting passage...' The commander chuckled and shook his head. 'Anyway, I came to let you know that the rest of your people are on their way - their ship just left Glasgow and they'll be transferred as soon as they arrive. When they're safely aboard we'll get on our way and once we're out to sea I'll come and get you and take you to see the captain, then around the ship for a quick tour. After that, you'll have free rein of the flight deck, the hangar and this level, which is where the mess halls are, but I'm sorry, the rest of the Arturo will be out of bounds to you; we don't want you getting hurt.'

Abby grinned. 'Or getting in the way?'

He smiled at her. 'Well, I wasn't going to say it, but that either.'

'Don't worry, Commander, as I told Mister Simkin, we'll behave ourselves.'

'Thank you. Well, that's all I came to say. As I said, I'll be back when we're out to sea.' He looked at Dorothy Campbell. 'The jolly boat is standing by to take you to the flagship when you're ready, ma'am.

'Thank you, Commander, I'll be right there.' Campbell nodded to him and he returned it, then left, taking the midshipman with him.

Once the door had closed, Campbell looked around, taking in the metal walls and the battered seats. 'Well, it's not Bagshot Hall, but I'll wager we've all had worse.' She held up her mug. 'At least there's tea, eh?'

'Are you not staying with us, Dot?' Abby asked.

'No, I have to be in the flagship with the rest of the task force commanders, which means I won't be seeing a lot of you during the voyage and I'm also going to be staying with the fleet until we get to Archangel so I won't be around to see you settle in to Vaenga. I assume I can trust you not to get into too much trouble without me during all that time?'

She gazed around the group questioningly, but received only innocent expressions in return and groaned. 'Lord help us all...' She drained her tea and grabbed a slice of cake before standing and going to the door.

'Happy hunting, Misfits.' She smiled, gave Abby a wink, then left.

CHAPTER 9

The fitters and the rest of the pilots, along with the crates holding the larger aircraft, came on board less than an hour later and the ship got under way. It wallowed slightly as it turned, betraying how top-heavy it was, but it was not too alarming and when it had settled on its course the only thing that betrayed the fact that it was moving was the constant vibration of its massive engines; there was no up and down or side to side movement at all, which was a good sign for if they had to fly from it during the journey to provide air cover. This was the first convoy taking the northern passage to Muscovy and they had to pass Norway, recently occupied by Prussia, and Finland, one of its allies, to do so and had no idea what kind of resistance they were going to encounter, if any. The ships were of course armed with ship to air weapons, but they were ineffectual at best and if they were attacked the convoy would rely on A flight for defence, along with Hummingbird and the two Navy fighters that the Arturo carried.

There was plenty of tea left over for the three C flight pilots and they helped themselves as soon as they joined their companions, wrapping their hands around their mugs to take away the chill of the brief, but brisk, trip along the river. The sandwiches and cakes had taken quite a beating, but that didn't bother them much; they had had plenty of time to stuff their faces at the aerodrome while their aircraft were being dismantled.

Abby filled them in on what Dot Campbell and Lieutenant Commander Bush had said, but that didn't take long and the conversation naturally turned to speculation about Gwen's childhood nickname. Fortunately, though, she was spared too much embarrassment by the appearance of Midshipman Simkin who seemed to have completely lost his nervousness around them after seeing them joking around with the senior officers before. He informed them that the captain would be delighted to receive them on the bridge before their brief familiarisation tour.

The corridor outside their room ran all the way along the side of the ship from stem to stern and they followed Simkin along it towards the bow, passing dozens of closed doors, identical to the one leading to their rooms, and the occasional sailor, each of whom gave them curious looks.

The bridge occupied the entire width of the ship, fifty yards or so back from the pointed bow, and was on two levels. The level that they entered was the lower of the two, the support deck, and it was filled with gauges and wheels and indicators, with more than a dozen men and women rushing back and forth between them, seemingly at random.

An ornate brass spiral staircase, wide enough for three people to ascend side by side, was in the corner of the room immediately to their left and Simkin took them up it to the command deck above.

The contrast between the two areas of the bridge couldn't have been greater. While the room below had been airless, enclosed and cave-like, lit by electric lanterns and soft indicator lights, the command deck was airy, spacious and bright, with plenty of room to move around. It had huge windows on three sides which provided plenty of natural light, a brisk breeze and a spectacular view of the Scottish coast sliding slowly past on both sides. Curiously, though, because the ship had a completely flat top to give aircraft as much room as possible, the bridge was actually underneath the flight deck and the thick metal slab jutted out in front of it, blocking any sight of the sky.

In contrast to the crowded room below, there were very few crew members here and there was an air of quiet preparedness, rather than the chaos below.

A couple of sailors were standing by a single bank of instruments which lined one wall under the port side windows, an officer was at the ready at the tables covered with charts beneath the starboard ones and another officer along with a third sailor manned a large old-fashioned wooden wheel, which looked as if it had come off of a Napoleonic war vessel, in front of the forwards windows.

Dominating the room, though, was a huge wooden chair on a plinth, with dials on one arm and what looked like an antique speaking horn built into the other. A large man with an equally large beard, shot with white, and impressively bushy eyebrows occupied the chair and he turned to look as the pilots appeared at the top of the stairs behind him. He all but leapt out of his seat, bouncing down to the floor, and rushed over to meet them.

'Our distinguished guests! Come aboard, come aboard!'

The captain, Johnathan Hewer, shook everybody's hand as they stepped onto the wooden deck, giving each of them a warm smile, but when he had greeted the last of the pilots he leaned over the brass rail to peer down the spiral staircase. 'Is that the lot of you?'

'Yes, sir.' Abby nodded. 'Were you not informed how many of us you'd be accommodating?'

'Of course, but I didn't think it possible that so few of you had managed to do so much to turn the tide of this war.'

'We weren't alone in our efforts, Captain.'

'Of course, of course,' he nodded at Pemberton and the other instructors. 'One cannot overstate the sacrifice that the rest of our noble aviators have made, but the way the press paint it the Misfits were alone in the skies against the entirety of Die Fliegertruppe!'

Abby sighed. 'Yes, we're not exactly happy about that.'

The big man nodded, a knowing look in his eye. 'I'm very glad to hear that; the last thing that Britain needs right now are heroes who believe that their work is done and they can rest on their laurels.' He waved a hand vaguely at his bridge. 'I wanted to welcome you in person, but I'm afraid you're going to have to excuse me now; my officers need orders. I will see you later at dinner.'

'We look forward to it, sir.'

'Excellent! Good day, then, Wing Commander.' He nodded at Simkin. 'Take good care of them, Midshipman.'

'Aye aye, sir.' The young man saluted then went and opened the door in the back of the bridge. 'This way, please.'

The pilots were herded out of the door and into the bare metal corridor that ran the width of the ship behind the bridge. There were doors some yards to either side and the Midshipman led them towards the one on the left, speaking over his shoulder to them as he did. 'I don't know if you've been told yet, but there are certain doors on this ship that have to be kept closed at *all* times when not in use. You'll know which doors they are because they'll have one of these instead of a handle.' He patted the wheel on the door. It was a yard across and the spokes were several inches thick. 'The ones in this corridor are the most important, because this space serves to isolate the bridge from explosions in the hangar, but there are other spaces just like this one protecting the engines and the hydrogen stores. If you leave *any* of these doors open, then expect the wrath of the first officer to come down on you like a tonne of bricks.'

Owen raised an eyebrow. 'The first officer? Not the captain?'

Simkin smiled pleasantly. 'If the captain ever has to step in and deal with a matter of discipline personally, sir, then you'd better know how to swim.'

The young man turned the wheel with some difficulty and swung the door open, revealing that it was almost a foot thick.

The noise of heavy machinery hit them immediately, along with the smell of grease and hot metal, and they stepped through into the hive of activity that was the hangar.

Despite Simkin's protestations and calls for them to stay together and that it was dangerous, every single one of the A and B flight pilots immediately rushed to their aircraft to make sure that it was being taken care of; even though they knew that the naval mechanics were perfectly capable, they were universally relieved to find their own fitters had taken over.

Dragonfly was sitting closest to them, just in front of the depression in the deck that the hydraulic lift went into when it was down. Wasp, Sable, Raptor and Hummingbird were lined up behind her. They were airscrew to rudder, because the hangar was only just wide enough to accommodate a single aircraft. Beyond them, B flight's aircraft were still in the process of being dismantled, but Dove and Jaguar were already pushed against the far wall along with the crates holding Dreadnought, Vulture and Bloodhound and the three Harridans of the instructors.

The huge space was essentially just the area immediately under the solid slab of metal that comprised the flight deck. It was extremely draughty because, while bulkheads lined both sides and thick columns held up the ceiling, there were large holes open in the sides of the ship, through which could be seen the shorelines. It looked like bulkheads could be slid into place over the openings when necessary, though.

Gwen found Sergeant Jenkins supervising the rewinding and cleaning of Wasp. His forehead under his grey hair was even more creased than usual as he watched the men and women under his command.

'What's the matter, Sergeant?'

'It's all this bloody salt and damp, it's going to play havoc with her, ma'am.'

Gwen chuckled as she eyed the man rubbing an already spotless pink wing with a chamois leather cloth. 'We've been at sea for all of five minutes, I'm not sure she's rusty yet.'

Jenkins grumbled. 'Has a way of sneaking up on you, does rust. Gotta keep ahead of it.'

'Well ahead, apparently.' Something occurred to her and she frowned. 'Do you have any idea what the cold in Muscovy will do to her? If we're supposed to keep flying until conditions become too bad for the Prussians to invade, then it's going to get pretty bad.'

The fitter shrugged. 'I have no idea.'

Gwen looked at Wasp, assessing her. 'Well, I think that our main problems are going to be with moving parts and possibly ice on the wings.'

'The guns too, ma'am; they already get a bit dodgy with an English winter, but Murmansk is within the Arctic Circle - I'd hate to think what would happen to them up there.'

Gwen nodded thoughtfully. 'I suppose Wendy might know something about that and Mac must have dealt with snow and ice in Scotland, I'll have to ask them and I'll see if Abby can get someone to give everyone a briefing.'

'That would be helpful, ma'am, but don't worry; we'll keep you flying, no matter the conditions.'

'Thank you, Sergeant.'

Gwen smiled, then wandered away, leaving him to his work. She briefly admired Sable and Raptor as she went past, noting the proud looks that Bruce and Monty were giving their machines, and found Scarlet gazing out of the hole in the bulkhead next to Hummingbird, staring at a flock of sheep on the land going by only a few hundred yards away, her flaming red hair streaming sideways in the wind.

Gwen leaned against the railing next to her. 'Thinking of home? Or are you going to swim for it while you still can?'

'What? Oh, no; I can't swim.' The Irishwoman turned away from the sea and looked up at Gwen. 'Besides, I couldn't leave Hummingbird behind, I'd miss her too much.'

'Just Hummingbird? Nothing else?'

Scarlet grinned. 'What, like junior officers who keep me awake at night? Nah. Wouldn't miss them one bit.'

They looked up at a whistle that filled the hangar, reverberating from the metal walls and saw Abby standing with Simkin by Sable, taking her fingers out of her mouth and waving for everyone to go to her.

Gwen waited while Scarlet gave Hummingbird a loving caress, then they walked over, collecting a dejected-looking Kitty on the way.

'And what's wrong with you?' Instead of showing sympathy, Scarlet just tutted.

'I don't like to see Hawk like that, like a bird with clipped wings.'

Scarlet shook her head. 'Chin up, for goodness sake! It's only for a week or so and then by all accounts you'll get more flying than you know what to do with!'

'I know, but still...' The American shrugged and Gwen put her arm around the woman's shoulder.

Simkin waited for everyone to arrive before opening a door in the starboard bulkhead and taking them out into a small stairwell, which was open to the elements and had one of the ship's six large anti-aircraft guns on a platform to one side. They went up the four short flights of stairs and stepped up onto the flight deck.

There were dozens of Navy personnel on the flat landing platform that formed the very top of the ship, but not all of them were working. It seemed that, in good weather at least, it was a favoured place to spend time off. There at least half a dozen men and women sitting with their legs dangling perilously off the edge over the water next to the stairwell, a few others were kicking a football around in the very middle, away from anything dangerous, and another dozen or so were lying down, enjoying a bit of a kip in what would probably be the last warmth that any of them were likely to see in a while. The pilots took this in quickly, but the gaze of every single one of them were drawn inexorably towards the rear of the ship where there were two dark blue aircraft.

The Arturo's fighters, Hammond "Martinets", had been circling when the Misfits had arrived, to give them room with which to land, but they were present now, tied securely to the rear of the deck and ready for takeoff at a moment's notice.

At the start of the war, Britain had no carriers. The ones left over from the Great War were all in mothballs or scrapped, and when a few were hurriedly recommissioned there were no aircraft to fly from them, so the British had bought some from the only source available. The American-built and designed Martinets were equipped with equally American "Full and Houston" springs which were powerful, so as to get them off the carrier safely, but very short ranged, although that didn't matter so much since they were purely for convoy defence and didn't have to travel far. However, in order to keep weight down to a minimum, they were very lightly armed, with only four machine guns. That would be enough to take down a lightly armoured scout aircraft, but they wouldn't have much hope against even a single Hoffmann HO111 or Funkel FU88.

Once again, without waiting for Simkin to tell them it was alright, the Misfits made a beeline for the aircraft.

Two Naval aviators in dark blue flightsuits were supervising the rewinding and securing of their aircraft, but it was a third man, standing unobtrusively to one side observing the work that caught Scarlet's eye and made her pull Gwen and Kitty to a halt.

'Look at that! Doesn't he look dreamy!'

Gwen frowned, not quite knowing who her friend was talking about. 'You mean the pilot? The tall one? He's... alright I suppose.'

'No, not him, dummy! Freddy!' She jerked her head in the direction of the journalist. He was writing in his notebook, but every so often he had to stop and brush his hair from his face, pouting in annoyance as he did so.

Gwen took in the sight of the journalist. She had to admit he did cut quite a dashing figure, especially because he was the only person not in military uniform on the entire deck. It was alright for her to notice and appreciate that, but Scarlet on the other hand... 'I thought you were with Sir Dougie?'

Scarlet grinned and shrugged. 'I am, yes, but that doesn't mean I'm blind. Besides, when the cat's away...'

Kitty broke in. 'Well, if you wanted to play then I'm afraid you've got competition.'

The three women watched as Chastity broke away from the group of Misfits that had gathered around the two pilots and wandered over to the journalist.

Scarlet scowled. 'That...'

The rest of her sentence was lost in the deafening sound of the ship's horn blowing, a warning to a passing sailing boat that had gotten a just a little bit too close, but their meaning had been perfectly clear and Kitty and Gwen laughed as they dragged their friend over to join the rest of the squadron in inspecting the aircraft.

Gwen spotted Rudy Drake bending down to inspect the heavily reinforced undercarriage of one of the fighters and she left her friends and crept over to stand behind him. She bent down until her lips were only inches from his ear.

'You could have used something that strong when you were learning.'

Drake started. He tried to twist, stand and look up at the same time and only succeeded in overbalancing and landing on his arse.

'Bloody hell, Goosy, what did you want to go and do a thing like that for! You frightened the life out of me!'

Gwen laughed and offered him her hand.

He allowed her to help him up then brushed his trousers down.

She jerked her chin at the undercarriage. 'Why are they so strong? Do you know?'

'One of the pilots said that it's because the American carriers have shorter decks with ramps at the ends to give fighters a boost into the air.'

Gwen nodded. 'So a normal undercarriage would just buckle if it wasn't reinforced.'

'Exactly.' Drake grinned. He looked her up and down, taking in her officer's uniform and nodding in approval. 'So, they promoted you and made you a Misfit, did they? I had no idea. It suits you, though; you never did like to do what you were told.'

Gwen gasped and feigned a shocked expression. 'Whatever do you mean?'

Drake laughed, then shook his head. 'You haven't changed one bit, Gwen.'

He smiled warmly at her and she smiled back, gazing into deep blue eyes that were so different from Kitty's, but just as inviting...

She caught herself when she realised the direction her thoughts were going and flinched back slightly.

He frowned. 'What's wrong?'

'I...' Gwen searched for the words to tell him about Richard and Kitty, to tell him about the feelings that she was only just coming to terms with, but couldn't find them, so instead she forced a smile and turned back to the aircraft, doing what she always did when things got too intense. 'Do you think they'll let us go for a joyride if we ask nicely?'

She pretended that she didn't see Drake's puzzled expression and wandered away to rejoin the other Misfits.

The two naval aviators, Lieutenant Chalmers and Sub Lieutenant Rossiter were more than happy to show off their machines to the Misfits and swap stories with them, but Simkin pointed out that, not only were the two pilots theoretically on duty and had work to do, but there was the whole voyage ahead of them during which to socialise.

The Misfits reluctantly said goodbye to the aviators and the midshipman led them towards the nearest stairwell, but before they'd gone a dozen paces Bruce tapped Abby on shoulder and stopped her.

'Erm, don'tcha think we're missing someone boss?'

He pointed towards the bow, where Chastity and Featherstonehaugh were wandering down the middle of the deck, more than a hundred yards away, as if they were taking a romantic turn around the park together.

Abby rolled her eyes. 'Mac. If you can't keep Badger Eight under control then maybe it should be you that Penelope replaces when she returns and not Owen.'

Mac growled in annoyance and stomped away towards his errant wingmate.

Chastity's instincts served her well and, before Mac had even got half-way to her, she sensed the incoming threat. She looked up, saw the approaching enemy, then hurriedly disengaged from her target and headed full speed for the shelter of the rest of her squadron.

Mac glared at her as she bustled past her, then gave the journalist the evil eye, before stalking back towards the waiting pilots who just laughed and followed Simkin down the stairs.

The rest of the tour wasn't nearly as interesting, although the engine room held at least some fascination for the engineers among them, being filled as it was with immense steam engines that were as antiquated as the rest of the ship, which had been built in 1917, then retired, then refitted and brought back into service when the powers that be saw that war was inevitable. The three storey high engines had been modernised and converted to burn hydrogen, but they retained the over-decoration and useless embellishments that had become all the rage in the late nineteenth and early twentieth centuries - the steel shells of the machines were covered with brass pipes, kept polished to within an inch of their lives and adorned with fins and whorls and cogs that served no discernible purpose. Their hydrogen was supplied by rows of tanks built into the very centre of the ship, armoured so that if any one of them blew up it wouldn't set off a chain reaction that would destroy the vessel, and the smoke that they exhaled, already far less than when they had been fuelled by coal, was passed through filters before it was expelled under the waterline, to minimise the chances of giving away the ship's position.

The Misfits and instructors finished their tour at the officer's mess, just in time for lunch, and they joined the naval aviators, who still had Freddy Featherstonehaugh with them, at one of the tables.

The mess was panelled in dark wood and hung about with trophies, much like the officer's mess at Badger Base, although there were more photographs and less pieces of enemy vessels - understandable since most things destroyed at sea tended to sink without leaving behind much in the way of mementos. There was, however, one item that drew the interest of the Misfits - one of the walls was divided diagonally by four yards-long pieces of wood in the shape of an X which many of the pilots took to be oars at first, but on closer inspection proved to be an enormous airscrew.

Lieutenant Chalmers saw the direction of their gaze. 'That's off one of the big Italian flying boats, a Q501. Rossiter shot it down in the Med off Malta in August. Huge ruddy great beast it was. Made a bloody great splash when it went in and the wings tore right off, but the airscrew's above the fuselage on those things so it survived intact. What was left of it floated long enough for us to rescue the crew and take a few souvenirs. We got that, the non-com mess got the tailplane and the enlisted men's mess uses the two floats as buffet tables.' He grinned. 'If you ask me we're getting more use out of it than the Eyeties ever did in the air.'

The pilots laughed, but then conversation was momentarily suspended when stewards appeared with the soup course.

When everybody had had a chance to sample some of the delicious cock-a-leekie soup, Abby raised her voice to be heard across the table. 'Mr Featherstonehaugh!'

The journalist looked up and raised an eyebrow with a smile. 'Who?'

Abby chuckled. 'Sorry, *Freddy*. I was under the impression that Mr Jones would be accompanying us.'

Featherstonehaugh nodded. 'He is.'

'Then where is he?'

'I'm not quite sure exactly. The last I saw him he was embracing a porcelain bowl and giving his breakfast a second chance at life, but he might have made it to his bunk by now.'

Chalmers guffawed. 'Seasick? In port? That is a feat unheard of except in literature. What will he do when we hit the North Sea?'

'He assured me that it was just the haggis he ate last night.'

'Ah.' Mac nodded sagely. 'If he got it in Glasgow then there's no tellin' what was in it. Ye cannae get a decent haggis in toon, ye got ter get it fresh.'

'So I have heard,' said Featherstonehaugh. 'And that might well be the cause, but I rather suspect that the amount of whisky he washed it down with might have aided matters.'

Abby chuckled. 'Well, we can only hope that he recovers enough to have a steady hand for his camera, otherwise the British press will not be getting very much from him until we reach Muscovy. Speaking of which - when can we expect your articles to start appearing?'

'I managed to finish my series of articles about the formation of the squadron last night before bed and cabled them to the ministry this morning. As soon as they give their approval they will go to the papers, who will run one each day. I was instructed to divide the story up into as many parts as I could, while still keeping each individual article as interesting as possible and I'm happy to say that, with the quality and quantity of material you all gave me, I have been able to put together a sizeable amount of them. At least enough to keep Misfit Squadron in the papers until they come back from the frozen north, which is what the Ministry wanted.'

Abby chuckled. 'Out if sight, but not out of mind?'

'Or heart.' Featherstonehaugh looked around the group, perfectly seriously. 'Or must I remind you all once again of your importance to the morale of the country?'

CHAPTER 10

It was a two day journey to Iceland to rendezvous with the rest of the convoy and then, depending on the weather, another five or six around Norway to Murmansk where the Misfits would disembark and fly to the nearby Vaenga airfield, while the rest of the convoy went on to Archangel.

Knowing that they weren't going to be able to fly whenever they wanted, the Misfits had already agreed that they would use their time to help Wendy and the fitters with Dreadnought - repairs were almost finished and there were only four or five days of work left at the most. It wasn't what most of them would prefer to be doing, but it would get them out of their quarters and keep them from getting bored.

They began straight after lunch, but almost immediately Gwen found another distraction for them all.

She had been working with a couple of Wasp's fitters, fixing armour plating to the fuselage, when she happened to look through one of the plate glass windows. Instead of an empty space, she found crates of all shapes and sizes with the Misfit Squadron crest on them. She called Abby over from where she was bolting Duralumin to a wing and pointed them out.

The rest of the pilots needed very little excuse to put down their tools and they gathered around the fuselage.

'Wendy?' Abby raised an eyebrow at the big woman, who just shrugged innocently.

Owen took in the sight of the crates in his wife's aircraft and laughed. 'Please tell me you smuggled the contents of Badger Base's wine cellar aboard!'

Quite a few eyes lit up at that thought and Abby gave Wendy a mock stern look. 'Do you have illegal alcohol that we are going to have to dispose of?'

Wendy chuckled cheekily. 'Sorry, no - I packed the contents of my workshop in there to save room, I must have um, *forgotten* to leave it all at Bagshot Hall.'

Abby groaned. 'I wonder what Captain Hewer would say if he knew we've smuggled experimental weapons on board his ship.'

Owen laughed. 'And our aircraft? What are they? Hell, Misfit Squadron itself is one big experimental weapon!'

Abby laughed and nodded. 'You're right. Although, I think we're going to keep this between ourselves for now.' She bent and took another look at the crates, a slow smile spreading across her face. 'What the captain doesn't know about can't hurt him, but it might hurt the Prussians...'

Dinner that night was to be a formal affair to properly welcome them on board, so the Misfits put on their dress uniforms, complete with silk sash for Abby and numerous medals for all, except for Chastity who had yet to win any and Gwen, who only had one.

The dinner didn't take place in the officer's mess, as they had expected, but instead in the captain's state room which was a leftover, like the engines, of another time.

The captain claimed that it was designed to be a replica of the Dining Cabin in the *HMS Victory*, which was preserved in Portsmouth, only on a slightly larger scale.

The walls were painted a light blue and covered with paintings, all portraits of famous captains, except for one, which covered almost the entire wall behind the captain's seat and depicted the Victory at *Trafalgar*. The floor was tiled in a black and white check and the ceiling, thankfully higher than the room it was based on, was made entirely of wood with the thick support beams painted white. The long wooden table, solid English oak, was bolted to the floor and seated forty, although that evening there were only thirty diners, including the Misfits, the RAC instructors, Freddy Featherstonehaugh, and the captain and senior staff, who were wearing tail coats the dark blue of the water outside the portholes over breeches and stockings the pure white of sea spray - Napoleonic War era uniforms that were perfectly suitable for their surroundings.

The Misfits were introduced to various Naval traditions during the meal, like remaining seated when they toasted the King and immediately following the Royal toast with the traditional one for a Saturday "our husbands, wives and sweethearts" which was given quietly and rather timidly by Simkin, as the junior Navy officer present, and which was replied to with far more enthusiasm and relish by the rest of the officers, who cried out "may they never meet!" in unison.

After dessert, while the stewards were offering around tea and an assortment of liquors from the captain's personal stock, the captain pushed his chair back from the table and smiled, raising his voice into a break in the conversations. 'How about a game of cards? I know my officers prefer that awful American game, poker, but I don't suppose any of you *Wreckers* fancy a rubber or two of whist?'

Gwen smiled, not just at the captain's use of the Navy's nickname for the RAC, but also because it seemed anachronistic for them to play whist after a meal, but it was entirely appropriate for the Napoleonic setting. She herself had learnt to play at an early age, part of her mother's attempts to broaden her horizons beyond mechanics and she eagerly volunteered as did Abby, but it seemed that none of their fellow Misfits played.

She had to hide her grin behind her hand when the Navy officers saw that there were only three players and tried to make themselves as unobtrusive as possible, desperately looking anywhere but at the captain, obviously having struggled through games with him before.

Her eyes briefly met those of Drake, but she instantly looked away, not wanting to give the impression that she wanted him to play - she had been avoiding him all afternoon and the things that had been left unsaid between them would make the game very awkward indeed.

Out of the corner of her eye she thought she saw him shifting in his seat, preparing to offer himself, but she was saved by Freddy Featherstonehaugh.

The journalist held up his hand, to all appearances an angelic schoolboy in his black tail coat, winged shirt collar and bow tie, which made him seem more like a prefect at Eton than a worldly-wise journalist. 'It seems you need a fourth, Captain, will I suffice?'

'Indeed, sir, indeed!' The captain stood and offered his hand to Abby, sitting in the place of honour at his right hand. 'Come, Dame Lennox, let us repair to somewhere more quiet and let my men attempt to deprive your squadron of their rum rations.'

Abby accepted his hand and allowed him to help her to her feet. 'I have a feeling your men will be ruing the day they met my pilots and will most likely be sober for the rest of the journey.' She winked at Kitty, who was literally rubbing her hands with glee at the prospect of playing a game that she had been weaned on and had taught to the men and women at Badger Base during the long days after the Battle for France, before the Battle over Britain had fully gotten under way.

Gwen smiled up at Featherstonehaugh when the journalist offered her his hand, following the lead of the captain, and the four of them filed from the room while behind them the dining room erupted into shouts and scrapes as chairs were rearranged and variants discussed.

The four whist players sat in cushioned wooden, high-backed chairs around a small table in the captain's lounge. It was a cosy place, hung with velvet curtains and wallpapered to resemble a similar room in a modest country manor. Two leather armchairs flanked a hearth, which was laid, but not lit. There were a couple of matching sofas behind them under a row of brass portholes and bookcases filled with thick leather-bound tomes were along one wall. A thick rug was spread on the floor underneath the baize-covered card table.

The noise coming from the adjacent dining room was muffled by the thick wooden door, but occasionally the volume would rise so much that it was clearly audible. It didn't disturb them, though, such was their concentration on the game.

Gwen found herself partnered with Abby for the first rubber and she proved to be a competent, but somewhat mediocre player. They won, thanks to a good run of cards, but only barely and, to her shame, Gwen was glad when they drew for new partners for the second rubber and she got Featherstonehaugh.

The journalist proved to be a brilliant player, understanding her every lead and responding in kind. The two of them thoroughly trounced the captain and Abby and the latter conceded defeat with a wry smile, pushing her chair back from the table with a sigh and picking up her freshly refilled brandy.

'I think I'm rather spoiling this for all of you. Perhaps you should just play with a dummy.'

The captain shook his head. 'Of course you are not, Dame Lennox! Please don't sell yourself short! You at least know to lead the king from a sequence of king, queen, knave, and *not* to lead an ace when you have one - lessons which have escaped my officers, many of whom continue to ask what trumps are half-way through a hand. And besides, even though the two of us were completely outclassed by our opponents, there is as much to be learnt in defeat as in victory and it has been an honour to fall victim to two players such as they. I'm just glad we weren't playing for money! Although, I feel that I owe you something at least.' He looked from Gwen to Featherstonehaugh and back again.

'The game and the company have been reward enough for me, sir.' Gwen shook her head and smiled warmly, receiving a grateful nod from the captain, but the journalist brought his notebook out from where it had been concealed in an inner pocket of his jacket and laid it on the table. 'Perhaps I might ask you to share a little background on yourself, sir, for my article?'

The captain laughed. 'You may ask, but I doubt you will find much in my story to interest your readers.'

'I am sure there is, sir. Please. Indulge me.'

'Very well.' Despite his protests, Gwen could see the captain was pleased that the journalist wanted to know more about him. 'My family has been fishing the North Sea out of Hull for generations. Cod mostly, but some sole and plaice. I was the youngest of four brothers so there was no chance of me ever getting my hands on the company, but I'd always loved the sea and had worked on the boats since I was eight, so when I was seventeen and the Prussians started playing silly buggers the first time around, I spoke to my father and he agreed to pay my way into the Navy's school at Dartmouth - HMS Britannia. War broke out just before I graduated and I was assigned to a battleship in the North Sea fleet. I...'

The captain stopped and looked up as his first officer, Commander Twining stepped into the room.

'Excuse me ladies, Mr Featherstonehaugh.' The officer nodded at the group before looking at his captain. 'Sir, you're wanted on the bridge.'

'Can't it wait for...?' The captain broke off at a look from Twining. 'Oh, very well.' He downed the rest of his brandy and stood up. 'I'm sorry, but I'm afraid we shall have to take this up some other time; it seems that duty calls.' He smiled apologetically at Featherstonehaugh then bowed to Abby and Gwen in turn. 'Dame Lennox, Officer Stone, it has been an absolute pleasure. Please feel free to enjoy my lounge for as long as you like.'

After the door had clicked softly closed behind the captain, Featherstonehaugh closed his notebook and put it away, then smiled at the Misfits. 'Well, it is quite pleasant in here, but I rather think I'd like to see what all the ruckus is about in the other room; if Navy officers are to be made paupers at the hands of a Misfit pilot, then I want to witness it firsthand.'

Abby and Gwen laughed and accompanied him into the din of the dining room.

Fortunately, the stakes in the poker game had only been matchsticks, because otherwise there might well have been some very upset naval officers and Misfits, as Kitty did indeed manage to take everyone to the cleaners. The only people who did even passably well were Bruce, her best student, who managed to bag about a fifth of the pot and Simkin, who held even, proving himself to be a very good bluffer, if not so astute at playing the cards themselves.

The party ended just before midnight, mostly because many of the officers had to go on watch at eight bells and the pilots were escorted back to their rooms by the midshipman, who reminded them not to wander around the ship on their own, then bid them goodnight.

Most of the Misfits collapsed directly on their beds, only pausing to strip the outer layers of their dress uniforms off so as not to wrinkle them, but a few went to use the bathrooms, Gwen among them. After she'd gotten rid of the huge amount of alcohol she'd imbibed and cleaned the prodigious amount of fur off her teeth she wandered back to the women's bunk room, bouncing off the corridor rooms as the ship pitched and reeled beneath her. She had her hand on the handle of the door when she heard her name being called and she turned to find Drake coming towards her down the corridor.

She leaned against the wall while she waited for him, using it to prop herself up; with no flying to be done she'd let herself drink far more than she usually did and was decidedly unsteady on her feet. He, on the other hand, looked far too sober and for some reason that annoyed her so she frowned at him.

He hesitated, suddenly uncertain at her angry look, his long stride faltering slightly, but didn't stop until he was standing right in front of her, looming over her.

She squinted up at him, trying to focus on him, but wasn't quite able to; the corridor was spinning slightly and her eyes kept slipping sideways as if the Arturo were changing course.

'Gwen.'

Her frown faded into a smile; she liked it when he used her proper name and not the silly one. 'Yes, Rudy?'

'What was that about on the flight deck? For a minute I thought there was something happening between us, but then... Did I say something wrong?'

'No, Rudy, you didn't.' She reached up to stroke his face and smiled; she liked tall men. And women. Kitty was tall. Richard had been tall as well.

She shook her head, trying to get the image of her dead husband out of her mind, not wanting to return to the bad times she was trying to move on from, and reeled when a wave of dizziness hit her at the sudden movement. She squeezed her eyes shut and reached out for something to steady herself and found the handle of the open door as well as something much softer and clung to them both, waiting for the ship to steady under her feet. 'Bloody hell, I think I'm a bit drunk.'

'Gwen, please. Just tell me what's going on with you. With us. Can there be an "us?"'

She opened her eyes again and peered up at him. 'I'm just a bit confused right now, with Richard and... and... just give me time, alright?'

She stood on tiptoes, using the hand that was already conveniently twined in his jacket to pull herself up, and kissed him on the cheek.

'G'night, Rudy.'

She patted his cheek once more, smiling at his shocked face, then staggered into the bunk room and closed the door on him. She tottered over to her small metal wardrobe and began stripping off her dress uniform, not noticing the hurt look Kitty gave her.

CHAPTER 11

The Arturo passed Iceland after dark the next day, but didn't stop, instead it just steamed straight past, collecting the rest of its convoy as it went, not losing any more time than was necessary as it headed steadily north into colder climes and passed into the Arctic Circle.

At dawn the day after, the Misfits were rudely awakened by klaxons sounding battle stations and the thump of pounding feet on the decks above and around them. They'd been briefed as to what the noise meant and what they had to do if they ever heard it, but they hadn't been expecting it so early in the morning and it caught them all in a deep sleep brought on by another late night filled with poker, this time in their own rooms.

Gwen had never been a graceful waker and the continuing noise didn't help improve either her mood or her cognitive abilities and she had stumbled out of the bunk room and half-way down the corridor before realising that she was still barefoot and in her nightshirt. She swore and ran back to her bunk, pointedly ignoring the smirk of a detestably wide-awake Kitty, who was almost dressed, and struggled to put on underwear and her flightsuit before grabbing her flotation jacket. The other pilots had already gone by the time she left the ready room and the stairwell was deserted as she pelted full speed up to the hangar deck. She tripped over the door sill in her haste to make it to her station by Wasp and would have fallen if it weren't for the fact that Derek and Owen were standing just inside. She careened into them sending them reeling, but they managed to grab her before she could fall.

Owen raised an eyebrow and chuckled. 'Drunk again, Gwen?'

'What is it? What's happening? Why have we stopped?' Gwen peered around with bleary eyes, only now realising that the ship was silent around her except for the constant thrum of the powerful engines and the rush of the sea past the open bulkheads. She stood on tiptoes to look over the group of pilots and saw that there were dozens of big sailors forming a solid ring around them, hemming them in, preventing them from getting to their aircraft.

She flinched and cried out in surprise as the big metal door slammed shut behind her with an almighty clang. She span around to find a huge man dressed in work trousers standing in front of it, grinning down at her, his tattooed arms crossed over his bare chest.

'Um, what's going...?'

Before she could complete her question a booming voice filled the cavernous hangar. 'WHO DARES COME INTO MY FROZEN DOMAIN?'

The sailors, the men bare-chested and the women in loose white tunic shirts, seized the pilots and dragged them to the side of the hangar, then up the stairwells and into the dawn light on the flight deck. They were pushed and shoved into a rough line facing the bow, along with their fitters, who had obviously been similarly accosted, and a few men and women in navy uniforms who looked as unsure of what was going on as they were.

Several hundred sailors, almost the entire crew, were also waiting for them there. They stood silently, all dressed like the brutes from the hangar and all seemingly unaffected by the chill that was in the early morning air, encircling the Misfits, hemming them in with the curious item that had been set up on the deck and the even curiouser figure that occupied it.

Sitting on the hydraulic lift that was supposed to be for the aircraft was a huge throne on an iron dais. It was at least fifteen feet tall all told, its frame formed by curving brass piping and two large crossed anchors. The whole thing was crowned with a golden trident and hung with fishing nets, rope and strips of sail canvas.

Occupying the thrown was a glowering figure who was barely recognisable as the captain. He was dressed in long, dark-blue and white robes, like foam on the ocean, and his face and beard were painted white. A long white wig, threaded with seaweed, covered his shoulders and fell to his waist from underneath a tall crown of brass which was formed by telescopes held together by sextants. He was holding a heavy-looking silver trident, as tall as his throne, and he brandished it above his head imperiously. The crew roared as he pumped it in the air three times, but then immediately fell silent when he thrust it viciously at the gathered pilots and fitters.

The executive officer, Twining, stepped out of the crowd. He was dressed the same as the other naval men and women, but his shoulders were draped with fishing nets as if they were some sign of high office. He stalked up and down the line of men and women who were still being held in place by the large sailors, meeting their eyes one by one, making a show of sniffing at them and showing his disdain. 'The Lord of the Winter Sea demands to know if any of you scurvy bilge rats have passed within his domain, the great circle of ice, before.'

One of the sailors who had been corralled with the pilots, a young man still in his teens, piped up, his voice squeaking in his nervousness. 'What's that, sir?'

Twining instantly scuttled forward, all but pouncing on the boy. 'The great circle of ice that you mortals call the Arctic Circle, boy!' He rolled his eyes theatrically and turned to look at the Lord in his throne, raising his voice. 'This one is obviously not a seaman! Please, my Lord, let me save time and just throw him to the sharks already.'

The captain laughed cruelly. 'Maybe later.'

Twining bowed low to show his consent, but then immediately spun back to the boy and hissed directly in his face. 'Well, have you, you dockyard oyster?'

'Have I what, sir?'

'Been through the Arctic Circle before, you leg iron!' he roared.

The young man cringed back. 'N-n-no, sir!'

Twining maintained eye contact for a long second, then turned to scowl at the rest of the men and women in the line. 'What about the rest of yers?'

Gwen took a deep breath, then put up her hand, knowing that it would call Twining's immediate ire and hoping that she would be able to keep a straight face when he came for her.

There were gasps from the audience, overly theatrical on the most part - they had obviously been through the pantomime before and were enjoying themselves immensely.

Gwen bit her lower lip to stop herself from laughing as Twining capered grotesquely towards her and thrust his face in front of hers, their noses only an inch apart.

'Have we imprisoned some worthy incorrectly?' He asked her in a stage whisper before stepping back and gesturing imperiously and raising his voice. 'Speak, woman! When you passed this way before, did you make proper obeisance, petition for safe passage, pass the test and receive my Lord's token?'

He turned sideways to show her his left arm and pointed to one of his many tattoos, one that showed a circle, pierced by a trident. Every single man and woman on the flight deck followed suit, all showing that they were likewise marked.

Gwen stared at the symbol in shock, no longer worried about laughing, but instead wondering whether the captain and his first officer intended to tattoo the pilots. She shook her head nervously. 'I flew over the circle to go to Japan with my parents as a child, but I didn't...'

He cut her off with a roar, throwing his arms wide and turning to face the audience. 'Then you stay where you are and face the test!'

There were cheers, jeers and laughter from the watching men and women, happy that they weren't going to be deprived of a victim.

'What test?' Abby called out, taking the lead for her squadron.

Absolute silence fell as Captain Hewer stepped down from his throne, the heavy deep-sea diving boots he was wearing under his robes making an impressive noise on the deck as he stomped forwards. 'A test of stamina and endurance. A test to see whether you can survive here in the north.'

Silence reigned once more, except for the passage of the sea against the hull and the thrum of the engines as he walked along the line, taking the measure of each of them one by one before going back to his throne. He mounted the dais then turned to face them. 'Will you take my test and prove yourselves worthy?'

'Um, my Lord?' Twining put his hand up meekly. 'They don't have any choice; they're already here.'

'Ah yes.' Hewer grinned evilly, then raised his voice in the commanding bellow that had deafened them in the hangar. 'PREPARE THEM!'

The large sailors tightened their grips and frogmarched them back down to the hangar where they were given a pair of white trousers and a white shirt. They were also provided with a pair of the same soft-soled plimsolls that the navy personnel wore about the ship that gave grip on the often-wet floors.

It was easy enough for most of the pilots, fitters and sailors to change, but A flight and Scarlet had to struggle out of their flightsuits, having only just struggled into them. Finally, they were done, though, and they were taken back up to the flight deck. However, this time, instead of dragged out into the middle, they were kept at the side, near the rail.

Twining looked them over, wrinkling his nose in disgust once more. 'Right then, you sorry lot. To complete the test and prove yourselves worthy all you have to do is make a single circuit of this deck. Running, mind you.'

Gwen did some quick calculations - Arturo was five hundred and fifty feet long and seventy feet wide, even if they ran around the very edge of the flight deck that would be less than a quarter of a mile in total, an easy run for even the least fit and oldest of their fitters. She pursed her lips and looked at Twining. 'What's the catch?'

A surprised look crossed Twining's face for an instant, as if he hadn't been expecting the question from any of them, but he hid it quickly with a wide grin. 'Well, there might be a few difficulties to surmount along the way...' He laughed, then raised his voice. 'Places!'

The sailors spread out around the deck, creating a wide corridor all the way around the outside.

Twining raised an eyebrow at the men and women around him. 'Well? What are you waiting for?'

The sailors immediately took off towards the stern at a sprint, like frightened rabbits and were closely followed by the three RAC instructors and the fitters, each of them worrying about only themselves. However, the Misfit pilots stayed together as a pack, as a squadron, knowing that they were stronger together when facing the enemy

At first they were just jeered at by the surrounding sailors and Gwen began to wonder if that was the worst that was going to happen to them, whether it was about putting up with humiliation, or providing a spectacle, but then, just as they were settling into their rhythm, the hoses turned on.

Gwen gasped in shock when the ice cold sea water hit her and she faltered, spluttering and gasping for breath, holding her hands up in a futile effort to block it, but after a few seconds the stream moved to Kitty, running beside her and she had a brief respite to look around.

There were multiple streams of water coming from all around them, coming from hoses of all sizes, from ones that were only a couple of inches of thickness which were used for cleaning, up to ones that were almost a foot thick, which needed a dozen sailors to lift and direct.

Gwen saw that the men and women who had run ahead were having a bad time of it. Because they were strung out and running singly, the hoses were able to concentrate on them and they were being battered almost constantly by the water, in fact it seemed that the hoses were deliberately seeking out anybody who was on their own. She laughed in delight when Rudy Drake was knocked off his feet, but she received her comeuppance when the next big hose ahead of them turned towards her and she took the full force of it on her chest. It submerged her as effectively as if she had dived into the ocean and stopped her dead in her tracks.

However, no matter how difficult she was finding it, Scarlet had it worse; as the smallest and lightest of them, she was being knocked around like an airship in a hurricane. Gwen wasn't the only one to see her difficulty, though, and Abby's shout of "close formation!" had the Misfits bunching up together around the woman, protecting their most vulnerable member as much as they could, just as they would do in the air.

The streams from several hoses were turned their way and remained on them, trying to split them up, but they stayed together and ran on, taking strength from each other.

As a group, the force of the water was lessened, but there was no way to avoid the cold, though. It began sapping their will and they slowed as they rounded the first corner at the stern of the ship.

It was Mac who first started shouting, mostly roaring incoherently, but occasionally yelling out a recognisable swearword. Bruce laughed and joined in, using colourful antipodean language, which Gwen resolved to learn as soon as she could. One by one the others began calling out as well, each doing what they had to in order to get their blood flowing and clear their heads, just as they would when they were pulling heavy G's in the air. As they went they collected their fitters, pulling each struggling man and woman under their wings for protection and drawing them, sometimes forcibly, along with them.

They rounded the next bend and headed back towards the bow along the long corridor between the sailors and the sea.

By this time, they had caught up with the men and women who had sprinted ahead, many of who were already completely exhausted because of the constant persecution of the hoses, but now they saw the example of the Misfits and began to band together. Some of them, including the instructors, joined the massed ranks of the squadron, but most sought out friends and colleagues first, seeking to help them and be helped in turn.

The water didn't let up, but with everybody moving in groups, progress was much easier and they covered the length of the deck quickly.

They rounded the bow, going around the massive throne on the lift, with the white figure on it watching them impassively and before they knew what was happening, they found themselves back where they started and blocked by a solid wall of sailors.

The water cut off and the men and women collapsed to the deck, shattered, but they were there for barely a second before they found themselves picked up and wrapped in blankets. They were then lifted by cheering sailors and carried on their shoulders back to the centre of the deck, where they were held aloft while silence fell once more and all eyes looked to the Lord of the Winter Sea.

The silence dragged on for long seconds as the white-painted man surveyed them solemnly, but then a wide grin spread across his face and he leapt to his feet, spreading his arms wide. 'Give them my mark and make it known to them that they will be forever welcome in my realm!'

Amid more cheering, the exhausted pilots, fitters and sailors were gently lowered to the ground, handed mugs of steaming tea and led over to where several men and women were sitting on stools, already holding tattoo needles.

Gwen eyed the buzzing machines warily, watching the first of the newly-initiated sailors grin happily while she got her mark.

One of the sailors standing by Gwen, a woman in her thirties with heavily muscled arms and oil-saturated pores, saw her hesitation. 'Don't worry, miss; passengers only get the symbol drawn on in pen and even us sailors get a choice as to whether we want it permanent-like or not.'

Gwen eyed the symbol on the woman's arm, it was flanked by a couple of similar marks, perhaps for other notable crossings, but a fair few other tattoos, some far larger, were scattered around what could be seen of her upper body. 'Do many sailors choose the pen instead of the tattoo?'

The woman chuckled and shook her head. 'Nope, none.'

'I want one!' Scarlet called out, bouncing across the deck enthusiastically to take the place of a newly marked young man.

The assembled crew cheered in delight, but the other Misfits just looked at her in shock and watched her sitting patiently while the old man operating the machine cleaned the needle, expecting at any moment that she would change her mind and leap out of the seat. However, in the end it wasn't just Scarlet who opted to get the tattoo, but a surprising number of fitters as well and, to the pilots' continuing surprise, Owen and Wendy too, and they gazed into each other's eyes and held hands as two grizzled veterans set the black ink into the meat of their upper arms.

Finally it was done and as one the crew gave three cheers, led by the captain himself, then began to disperse, some going about the job of swabbing the decks, but most disappearing below to have breakfast or to get ready for duty.

Captain Hewer had already handed his crown and trident off to attendants, who were riding the hydraulic lift down to the hangar with the throne, taking it to wherever they kept it until it was needed for the next time, and he removed his long wig and ran his hand through his hair as he approached the Misfits, who were gathered by the starboard rail.

'Damn fine showing, Wing Commander, damn fine.' He reached out and took Abby's hand and pumped it vigorously. 'We have a similar ritual for crossing the equator, but that one's just a bit of a lark, this one's much more serious and has a purpose to it, you know, and a lesson.'

Abby smiled wryly. 'And what might that lesson be? Beyond not to get on a Navy vessel passing through the Arctic Circle unless you like being wet and cold.'

The captain laughed. 'That's part of it, yes - we all need to appreciate how cold the water is here and how little time anyone who ends up in it would survive. However, the main thing that we hope our sailors take away from the exercise is that if they and their friends are going to have a chance at surviving, it's going to be by working together. And that is a lesson you Misfits have apparently already learnt and learnt well.' He waved his hand at the sailors who were still hanging around, comparing tattoos, reluctant to leave, much like the Misfits themselves. 'At the very least it gives them a bond they will share for the rest of their lives.' He smiled avuncularly at the men and women of his crew as they skylarked in the middle of the deck before turning back to the pilots.

'Congratulations. All of you.' He nodded, then marched off towards the stairway, pointedly ignoring the sniggers that arose from behind him as he tripped over his costume. He steadied himself on the rail, then, with all the dignity he could muster, lifted his skirts and clomped down the stairs towards the lower decks.

Gwen watched him go, then pulled back her blanket to reveal the symbol on her arm. She had chosen the temporary option, but she could understand why some people would want to have a reminder of the ordeal that they had just gone through, it had been very memorable and it seemed that the Misfits had been brought even closer together, if that was possible.

She just couldn't imagine marking her body permanently, though, but maybe that was because she just hadn't found something that she believed in enough to want to commemorate it that way.

'It looks good on you. Maybe you should have got it done permanently.'

Gwen looked up to find Kitty standing in front of her. The American had wrapped her blanket around herself like a toga, leaving her arms and hands free. It was very fetching.

Gwen shook her head. 'No way! I couldn't...' Something occurred to her and she looked at her friend's arm. 'You didn't...?'

Kitty laughed. 'No! Of course not!' She used a finger to demonstrate the temporary nature of her mark, rubbing away the tail end of the trident. 'When I get a tattoo it'll have to be for a very good reason, not just crossing an imaginary line.'

'*When* you get a tattoo?'

Kitty shrugged. 'You never know where life is going to take you.'

'Indeed not.' Gwen gestured pointedly at the mighty metal beast that they were standing on, which was steaming its way through the waters at the top of the world.

They took a moment to look out over the rail and appreciate the view of the dozens of ships that surrounded them. The lumbering cargo ships and the sleek naval hunters that protected them.

'So...' started Kitty, hesitantly. 'You and Lord Drake go back a long way, then.'

Gwen peered up at her, squinting against the biting wind of their passage. 'Yes. We were friends many years ago.' She saw the anxiety in her friend's eyes and reached out to lay a hand over hers on the railing and smiled in reassurance. 'He's just that, though, no more. Yes, he and I have a lot of catching up to do, but he's not going to get between us.'

'Really? It's just that you told him the same thing that you told me - that you needed more time.'

Gwen blinked. 'Did I? When?'

'A couple of nights ago, after the captain's dinner party.'

'Really?' Gwen frowned, trying to remember, but the night was hazy and she didn't recall much after the whist game. She had a vague impression of being alone with Rudy at some point, but not much more than that.

She shook her head. 'I'm sorry, I can barely even remember speaking to him, but I suppose I must have meant that I wasn't ready to tell him about my feelings for you and my decision to move on from Richard.'

'Oh, OK, that makes sense. I suppose.' Kitty's expression lightened slightly, but she still seemed doubtful.

Gwen gazed up into Kitty's eyes. She briefly wondered if she could get away with giving her a kiss to reassure her, but then frowned when she became aware of a clicking noise coming from close by. She turned her head to see Freddy Featherstonehaugh standing only a few yards away, writing furiously in his notebook, while Mr Jones, who had apparently finally released his death grip on a toilet bowl, scuttled around, taking photographs. Gwen released Kitty's hand and put all thoughts of kissing out of her mind, not quite ready to be caught so intimately on film. She gave the woman a last smile, then went and called Abby's attention to the two men.

Abby blinked and raised her voice to be heard over the conversations going on around them. 'Mr Featherstonehaugh!'

The journalist looked up, startled at hearing his name, then smiled and wander over to join the pilots, who were all scowling at him in his warm and dry condition.

'Wing Commander,' he inclined his head to her in greeting, then gazed around at the other pilots. 'Ladies, Gentlemen. It seems that congratulations are in order.'

'Thank you, but how is it that you escaped the clutches of the Lord of the Winter Sea?'

He laughed. 'I didn't, I fell foul of him several years ago, as did Mr Jones. We did a piece together for Imperial Geographic Magazine on the whaling industry around the North Pole and had the pleasure of going through a similar ceremony to today's, although we didn't do nearly so well as you did.'

'Does that mean you have a tattoo?' Chastity asked coyly, stepping forward and stroking his arm where the mark would be if he had one.

The Misfits shared looks, rolling their eyes at her shameless flirting, but Featherstonehaugh just raised an eyebrow and smiled at her. 'Maybe one day I'll show you them.'

'Them?' She asked in surprise, but the journalist had already wandered off, chuckling.

<h1 style="text-align:center">CHAPTER 12</h1>

A storm settled in over the next few days, with gale-force winds driving towering waves against the ships of the convoy. The smaller ships tossed and plunged, but the Arturo remained as steady as a rock in the face of this demonstration of the Lord of the Winter Sea's power, something which Mr Jones especially appreciated.

Work continued on Dreadnought, but the holes in the bulkheads of the hangar now remained tightly closed to block the worst of the weather. The winds still found gaps, though, and chilled the air in the metal space in a way that made teeth chatter and gloves a necessity, simply to avoid damage when touching anything metal.

Drake and the other instructors had volunteered to help with Dreadnought and he somehow managed to arrange to work on whatever task Gwen had been assigned to and they used the time to catch each other up on what had happened in their lives in the decade or so since they had lost contact with each other. They didn't have much in the way of privacy, but that was fine with Gwen; it meant that the conversation couldn't turn to personal and also that Kitty wouldn't have any reason to be jealous or hurt.

After Drake had been sent to boarding school they had exchanged a few letters, but they had quickly drifted apart, as children were wont to do and they had dried up as they had both moved on to new and more exciting things.

From Eton, Drake had gone to Cambridge University, where he had read "Mechanics in Literature". He had joined the University Air Squadron, just like Richard had, which meant that when the war broke out he was already in the RAC and had been in one of the first squadrons sent to France. Then, after that debacle, he had been posted to Scotland to train new pilots, but he had caught the first waves of bombers to come over.

He laughed and spoke widely about his stint in Scotland, regaling her with anecdote after anecdote, obviously seeing it as quite a happy time, when bombers were escorted only by lumbering MU10's and RAC casualties were virtually nil, but he barely talked about France except to say that it was best left forgotten.

Gwen in turn filled him in on her journeys around the world with her parents for conferences, describing the wonderful things she had seen. She told him about her aircraft, her studies and her ideas. One evening, after screwing her courage up all day, she even managed to tell him about Richard without too many tears.

The storm soon blew itself out, but left behind heavy clouds that hid whatever daylight there was to be had so far north. The metal of the passageways and aircraft no longer burned to the touch, but it was still cold enough to require extra blankets on their beds and the addition of layers of thermal underwear beneath their work clothes.

They were now four days past Iceland and that put them firmly into enemy controlled waters. That didn't mean that there was more chance of attack, though; nobody was expecting them to be there and the Prussians had better things to do than send resources into the far north, away from the battlefronts.

Everybody was on edge, waiting for an attack that seemed like it was never coming and when the klaxon did finally bray, the Misfits were unsure for a second what was going on, thinking that perhaps it heralded another joke at their expense, but when the navy personnel in the hangar began rushing round in organised chaos, grabbing flotation jackets and metal helmets, they dropped their tools, abandoned the repairs on Dreadnought and ran for their stations. While Scarlet and the pilots of A flight rushed to change into their flightsuits and the fitters readied their aircraft, the rest of the pilots joined the damage control teams they'd been assigned to. Their job would be to stay in the hangar, standing ready to try to prevent the destruction of the precious aircraft if the carrier was hit and fire broke out.

Gwen was first back, followed closely by Scarlet and they both paused at the unmistakable sound of an airscrew at full power passing directly over their heads, going rapidly towards the bow, immediately followed by another.

Gwen grinned. 'Has to be something up there if they launched the Martinets. Wonder if we'll get to have a crack at it?'

Scarlet rubbed her hands together. 'Well, I don't know about A flight, but I'm definitely going to go and have a look to see what's what.'

Gwen frowned. 'How? You're last in line!'

Her question went unanswered, though, because Scarlet was already sprinting towards Hummingbird.

'Come on, Gwen, get a move on!'

Abby appeared through the door behind her and Gwen sprang into action at her shout and together they ran to their aircraft. She climbed into Wasp and went through final checks while her fitters put the last few turns on the spring. She plugged herself in and tightened her straps, then, with everything ready, she looked up, watching impatiently as Dragonfly was pushed forward onto the lift, but something in the mirror above her caught her eye and she frowned. She leaned to the side and looked out of her cockpit, craning her neck to try to see behind her.

Hummingbird's overhead rotors were turning, approaching full speed and her fitters were being buffeted by the downforce as they pushed her backwards. They turned the aircraft to face the side bulkhead just as a group of sailors opened one of the large openings in the side of the ship and Gwen watched, open-mouthed, as Hummingbird lifted a couple of inches from the floor and sailed majestically through it.

Gwen couldn't help but laugh; the Irishwoman must have been planning her disappearing act from the very first day, when she had caught her looking out one of the holes in the bulkheads. She had indeed been thinking about escaping through it and had even worked out that she could take her beloved gyrodyne with her by simply having the safety railings in the gap removed. She briefly wondered if the captain knew what the Irishwoman had done, but quickly realised that Captain Hewer wasn't the kind of officer who would let anything happen on his ship without his knowledge.

She couldn't afford to spend any more time wondering how Scarlet had managed to gain permission, though, because she was being waved forward by a Navy technician and her fitters were pushing her onto the lift.

The metal platform jerked into motion, then began to rise smoothly into daylight and, as soon as she could see over the deck, she was looking around, searching for friendly and not so friendly aircraft, but not finding any anywhere in sight.

The radio in her ears had been ridden with static because of the thick metal deck, but now it sprang to life as she rose into clear air and she listened in as she began taxiing towards the stern of the ship.

'...see him. Hunter Two, do you have eyes on?'

'Negative, Hunter One.'

'Damn these clouds!'

The two naval aviators, Chalmers and Rossiter were obviously not having any luck with whatever they were pursuing and their conversation didn't give Gwen much in the way of information, but obviously someone had reported that she was on deck, because the next call over the radio was for her.

'Badger Two, this is Tinman, do you copy?'

'Tinman, this is Badger Two, I copy.'

'Badger Two, radar has incoming enemy aircraft at ten thousand feet, heading one five zero, thirty miles. No visual contact.'

By this time Gwen had reached the stern of the ship and deck hands had grabbed her wings with practised hands and were turning her into position. 'Roger, Tinman. Badger Two ready for takeoff.'

'Roger, Badger Two, go and get him.'

'Thank you, Tinman.'

Gwen smiled in anticipation, gave the sailors on either side of her a wave, then opened her throttle wide and released her brakes.

She was pushed back into her seat by the acceleration, but her whoop of joy at finally being back in Wasp was cut short as the end of the ship rushed towards her in a highly disconcerting manner, like sprinting towards a cliff with nothing beyond except a fatal plunge.

Her every muscle clenched as she quickly began running out of room and she glanced nervously at her air speed indicator, but in the end Wasp reached takeoff speed and leapt into the air with almost fifty yards to spare and she exhaled in relief. Her conscious mind had known that the deck was much longer than her takeoff run, but her every instinct had still tried to convince her that she wouldn't make it and that she should slam on the brakes before it was too late. It was an instinct that would have undoubtedly killed her.

'Thank you, Mr Rentley and Mr Joyce!' She resolved to give the two men a big kiss when she got home and thank them for the extra power that had made the takeoff far safer than it would have been, then banked sharply to put Wasp on an intercept course for the enemy aircraft.

Even though Tinman, the radar controller in the Arturo, had told her there was only one enemy aircraft, she kept up her scan of the sky;

old habits died hard and British pilots died all too easily if they stopped looking around for even a second. She completed her first scan in seconds and after a quick check of her instruments began on the next, never pausing in the endless task, but there was nothing in the sky with her and with the thick clouds she couldn't even see her fellow Misfits or the two Hammonds.

In her rear view mirror she caught sight of the hydraulic lift coming back up with Bruce in Sable, continuing the horribly inefficient process of lifting and launching each aircraft individually and she sighed; it was just as well they weren't under a determined attack because they would present easy targets, flying out to meet them one by one.

The enemy aircraft was likely only a scout aircraft, one of several that would be sent out on a daily basis from the coast of Norway, just as they were from England into the Atlantic and the North Sea, looking for passing convoys that they could direct bombers or undersea boats onto. Typically they would be long-range spotters, much like Vulture or Bloodhound, that would fly a straight line directly out to sea, then head parallel to the coast for a set distance, before returning home along another straight course, describing a thin triangle. With only three or four aircraft you could cover an immense amount of sea, but the odds of finding anything were still incredibly low. The fact that one of the enemy aircraft was heading directly for them was either extremely bad luck, or meant that the Prussians knew that they were there. However, the clouds that were preventing them from finding the aircraft might also work in their favour and hide the convoy, unless, of course, the enemy had some kind of radar, in which case it would undoubtedly spot the ships, or the British aircraft, which would amount to the same thing, because they had to have come from somewhere.

'Enemy aircraft now at ten miles. He's gone past you, Hunter flight. Badger Twelve, he should be right on top of you.'

Gwen swore. Ten miles out was too close; the convoy was in plain sight of the aircraft and all it would need was a break in the clouds for them to be discovered. Thankfully, though, the enemy wouldn't be able to report immediately; they were well out of radio range of Norway and they would have to fly most of the way home first.

'Tinman, Badger Twelve here, I don't see him.'

Owen had been to see the radar in the carrier and had reported that it was one of the original models that he had worked on many years ago before the war. It was not nearly as sophisticated as the one in Bloodhound, or even the ones on the British coast and wouldn't be able to do much more than alert them to the presence of hostiles. It certainly wouldn't be able to effectively guide the fighters onto their target like he had been able to direct Gwen against the night bomber only weeks before.

'Tinman to all aircraft, enemy has reversed course. He's running for home. He must have seen us.'

Gwen swore even louder and willed Wasp to increase speed, even though she knew the aircraft was already going as fast as it could. They had to catch the enemy before it got out of radar range and into radio range of home, otherwise the convoy might not survive, at least not intact. Not only would lives be lost, but the Arturo was the juiciest target of all for the Prussians and if they damaged or destroyed it then, not only would the mission to Muscovy be a failure, but the Misfits might well be put out of the war permanently - an accidental encounter in the frozen northern oceans might tip the balance so far that the British wouldn't be able to recover.

'I see him! I'm going to try to cut him off.' A surge of hope sped Gwen's heart at Scarlet's excited shout, the same time as it made her ears ring, but those hopes were dashed again almost immediately. 'Damn! Lost him again. He must have changed course.'

Gwen gritted her teeth angrily. A game of hide and seek like this could last for hours, much longer than the British aircraft, especially the Hammonds, could safely stay in the air.

There was one thing she could do, though.

She lifted Wasp's nose and began to climb, reaching under her seat to turn the heating up as the temperature in the cockpit dropped steadily.

At twenty thousand feet she reached the top of the cloud cover and burst out into bright sunshine, but she didn't stop there. She went up another ten thousand feet before levelling off, then slotted lenses over her goggles and began scanning the clouds below, watching the many gaps for signs of activity.

Movement directly in front of her drew her eyes, but the object turned out to be the bright yellow cross of Dragonfly. Another two specks on her left, darker ones, turned out to be the Hammonds on parallel courses, half a mile apart. There was nothing else for a long minute and she was beginning to despair of ever finding the enemy when a dark shadow come out of the bright white of a cloud far off to her right.

'Tinman, this is Badger Two. Enemy in sight. Eight miles from my position bearing...' Gwen lined up the compass on her wrist to take a bearing. 'Three one zero. Distance approximately six miles. Hunter One and Two, turn to heading two four zero, he's ten miles from you. Badger Leader, adjust heading to two seven zero, bandit at five miles.'

She swung Wasp towards the aircraft just as it went into a cloud bank and disappeared again, but even from the short glimpse she'd gotten she could tell that she was rapidly overhauling it.

She searched the clouds, looking for the next break that it should appear in and found one about two miles ahead of its position. She didn't dive to try to intercept it, though, because she knew that she was too far away and wouldn't get to it in time, but rather stayed where she was so that she could guide the others.

Two miles at approximately two hundred and forty miles an hour, that was four miles every minute. So it was thirty seconds, more or less, until the enemy would cross the next gap, unless he changed course again. Which she wouldn't put past him; it's what she would do after every time she was exposed.

The hands on the Frobisher chronograph that her parents had given her for her last birthday seemed to slow as she split her attention between it and the break in the cloud, waiting, willing the pilot of the enemy aircraft to think he was safe and fly a straight course.

There! Once again the enemy broke into the open. This time she was more than a mile closer and could make it out much better at full magnification. It was a twin steam-engined aircraft with long, fragile-looking wings, obviously built to have an extremely long range, and there were what looked like iron rods sticking out of its nose that were likely antennae for a radar system. It was painted a dark blue, at least on top, which blended very well with the ocean below, and there were iron crosses on its wings, like the Prussians, but bright blue, not black, which Gwen figured were the Finnish variant.

Gwen grinned gleefully when she saw Dragonfly go through the previous gap in the clouds - they were slowly closing the net on the intruder. She clicked the radio transmit button, about to report in, but stopped, rendered speechless with surprise; for some reason the enemy aircraft had just spouted a plume of dirty black smoke from its right engine as the hydrogen tanks were hit. She watched, incredulous, when seconds later a huge explosion ripped most of the Finn's right wing off and it lurched to the side and began to spiral sharply out of the sky.

'What the...?'

Gwen's puzzlement lasted only a brief moment, though, as Hummingbird burst into the open in the aircraft's wake and she watched Scarlet bank hard to follow the stricken enemy machine in its final moments.

'Hello, Badger Two. Say again, please?'

Tinman's voice brought Gwen out of her trance and she sheepishly released the transmit button and laughed, shaking her head and resuming her customary scan of the sky.

She'd completely forgotten about Scarlet and, while she had been trying to guide the other aircraft, the Irishwoman had been quietly doing what she did best.

'Don't worry, Tinman, Badger Two's just a bit upset that I took the kill away from her.'

'Tinman here, who is this please?'

'Oh, right, yes, sorry.' Scarlet tittered, her melodious voice filling the airwaves. 'Badger Twelve reporting enemy aircraft destroyed. It's gone into the drink, no survivors I'm afraid.'

'Good show, Badger Twelve. All aircraft, this is Tinman. We have no more intruders on our screens, come on home, job well done.'

The Misfits were brought in to land in the same order that they had been in Scotland, meaning that Scarlet was first down. While they were on approach, Gwen thought for one awful moment that the Irishwoman was going to be crazy enough to try to land back through the gap in the hangar bulkhead. She had visions of her rotors shattering and ripping through the hangar, tearing apart the machines and people within, while Hummingbird plunged into the icy water, but thankfully she didn't.

Recovering the aircraft didn't take nearly as long as taking off because they could just taxi straight onto the lift once their hooks had been detached from the cables, but it was still a good ten minutes before all the Badgers were safely below and the Hammonds were back on board.

Scarlet was swamped as soon as she stepped out of Hummingbird's cockpit, not only by the Misfits and their fitters, but by all nearby naval personnel as well. The captain himself even turned up after a few minutes and he shook her hand, congratulating her enthusiastically, before going to speak to Abby.

'Well, Wing Commander, every day your pilots seem to find something to surprise me. Who would have thought a scout aircraft of Hummingbird's peculiar characteristics would be able to take down an enemy aircraft that size.'

Abby smiled. 'Hummingbird carries two cannon and Scarlet has claimed several kills with her. If she had her way, she'd join us on sorties!'

'I can well imagine that firebrand going up again a flight of MU9's solo!' Hewer gazed in admiration at Scarlet, who was describing her kill to a rapt audience. 'Well, because of your pilots this convoy is much safer than it otherwise would have been. Which isn't to say that our two Hammond pilots don't acquit themselves exceedingly well whenever they are called upon to defend us, it's just that, with us being allocated only two of them, they are rather limited in what they can achieve.' The captain shrugged, giving her a look that spoke volumes about his thoughts on the allocation of funds and resources by the War Ministry. 'I must get back to the bridge, but I just wanted to say well done. Again.' He smiled, then made his way back across the hangar to the doors that led to the bridge.

The sailors were on duty, so the celebrations soon petered out and the Misfits wandered off, the pilots going to change out of their flightsuits while the rest went back to work on Dreadnought.

Abby caught up with Gwen at the door to the stairway down to their rooms. 'Good thinking out there, Gwen.'

Gwen smiled. 'Thank you, but I was just following Owen's example.'

'If you don't mind, I won't tell him that.'

'Of course not, I wouldn't want him to think he was useful.'

Gwen winked and Abby laughed, delighted to have a partner in the torment of her second-in-command.

'Wing Commander!'

They turned as someone called out from across the hangar and found Lieutenant Commander Bush striding towards them. He came to a halt by their side and gave Gwen a polite nod before addressing Abby. 'I wanted to add my own congratulations to those of the captain's and invite you and your fellow pilots to dine with the officers tonight. We should be making landfall in a day or so, weather permitting, and this might be our last chance to properly host you.'

'We would love to, thank you, Commander.'

'Excellent! And there's no need to stand on ceremony with us, day uniforms will do, that way if things get a bit messy it doesn't matter.' The big man smiled and gave them a nod, then started away, but stopped when something occurred to him. 'Oh, by the way, I'm not sure if you realise, but, even though you destroyed the aircraft, the Prussians are going to know something is up, simply because it didn't make it home. They'll have no idea where we are exactly and we'll be a long way away from here before they realise their aircraft is missing, but they'll know there's someone lurking around out here and that might have a bearing on your mission.'

Abby nodded. 'Thank you, I'll bear that in mind.'

The dinner party with the officers was far less formal than the one with the captain had been and the commander's comment about it getting messy was fully explained when at various times during the evening food was thrown at certain people, including Mac and Gwen herself, for some faux pas or another.

The rum rations were supplemented by the addition of beer, several kegs of which had been bought for the mess last time they'd been in port and the party got merrier as the evening went on.

There was one serious note to the evening when, at seven forty six precisely, during dessert, Owen met Abby's eyes and tapped his watch. In reply she simply nodded and silently raised her glass.

Owen immediately joined her and as each Misfit caught sight of them they did the same.

The naval officers watched them, puzzled, as did Gwen, who looked a question at Scarlet, sitting opposite her. In reply, the Irishwoman mouthed a single word - *Cece.*

Gwen nodded in understanding and joined her colleagues in raising a glass to the woman who she had never known, but whose aircraft she had been flying for months.

The pilots drank, each using the moment to remember in their own way the woman who had given her life for others, then returned to their meals as if nothing had happened.

It took a few moments for conversation to return to normal and, while the naval officers were reluctant to ask about something that was so obviously very private, the journalist in Freddy Featherstonehaugh had no such qualms and he leaned forwards to speak to Abby across the table.

'Excuse me, but would you mind my asking what the meaning behind that rather emotional gesture was?'

Silence fell as everybody wondered how Abby would take the question and several of the more drunken naval officers prepared handfuls of spotted dick to fling if needed, but she smiled, somewhat sadly, and nodded, to the disappointment of the aforementioned officers.

'Today is my younger sister's birthday. She died in France.' She looked at the executive officer, Twining, sitting at the head of the table. 'I apologise for bringing down the mood of the party.'

'Please,' Twining shook his head, 'if we do not take time to remember those who have died, then we are in danger of forgetting what we are truly fighting for.'

'Thank you.' Abby nodded her gratitude then turned back to the journalist. 'Cece died of injuries sustained during a fight against overwhelming numbers. We were sent up against a bomber raid with a heavy escort along with a squadron of Harridans. At one point Cece spotted two Harridans in a dogfight with eight Prussian fighters, MU9's. She didn't hesitate and ordered Monty to stay with the squadron while she went to the rescue.'

Abby's voice cracked and she paused, taking a sip of her drink while she fought to control her emotions. 'She managed to shoot down five of them and drove the rest away, saving one of the two Harridans.'

She took a deep breath, once more struggling with the tears trying to force their way out. 'But that was when the Crimson Barons showed up. She...'

She faltered again, but this time she lost her fight and was forced to stop, covering her eyes.

Owen came to her rescue, continuing the story. 'None of us were there to see it, we had to hear it from the Harry pilot afterwards, but apparently she was jumped by Gruber and three of his pilots. Going up against MU9's is one thing, going up against Flamme and three Blutsaugers is quite another, but even so she managed to shoot down one of them before Gruber got the upper hand.'

He stopped and looked at Abby, wondering if she wanted to continue herself, but she nodded and forced a smile, silently giving him permission to continue.

Owen grimaced, but returned her nod and went on with the story. 'Gruber hit her with multiple shots and according to the Harry pilot she just stopped manoeuvring and started flying in a straight line. The remaining Blutsaugers flew away, but Gruber stayed. He flew with her, on her wing for ten seconds or so, then just broke off. That was the last the pilot saw of her, because he had to return to the fight.'

Owen paused. If Abby was going to stop him it would be now, when all that was left to tell was the tragic finale, but she just stared into her glass, not meeting his eyes, so he took a deep breath and finished the story.

'Her aircraft, Wasp, was riddled with holes, missing its tail and barely capable of staying in the air, but somehow she got home, bringing it back to us so that it could fly again. She, however, was beyond repair and died of her wounds in the cockpit, less than a minute after she landed, as if with her aircraft safe she could let go. Wasp is in the hangar above us as we speak and has helped this squadron shoot down countless Prussians.'

Owen finished and there was a respectful silence as those people who hadn't known the full story, including Gwen herself, took the time to fully assimilate it.

Then, one by one, the Navy officers lifted their glasses and mirrored the gesture that the Misfits had made before.

CHAPTER 13

Despite Lieutenant Commander Bush's ominous words, there were no further incidents during the rest of the voyage; either the Prussians just hadn't been expecting anybody to send a convoy round the North, it being so close to winter, and weren't prepared to follow up on the loss of their scout, or they were too busy elsewhere. Whatever the reason, the convoy arrived safe and sound off the coast of the Kingdom of Muscovy just after dawn three days after the incident with the scout plane.

The Misfits had been ordered not to show themselves until it was absolutely necessary and had been instructed to rendezvous with a Muscovite aircraft over a deserted stretch of the Muscovite coast which would guide them to Vaenga. That meant that, despite the fact that none of B flight's machines or Bloodhound could take off from the carrier on their own, they had to find a way for them all to do so.

Most of the sailors said that it was impossible and indeed there were several enterprising souls running a book for those people who wanted to wager on the outcome, but the squadron had put their heads together during the voyage and, between the lot of them, had come up with a uniquely unconventional solution to the problem.

Dreadnought had been fully repaired and the fitters had spent the previous day reassembling her on the flight deck, along with Vulture, Bloodhound, and all four B flight aircraft. They had been taking a big risk to do so because if they were attacked the only aircraft that would be able to take off would be Hummingbird, but it had been necessary for the next part of the plan.

The A flight pilots and Scarlet carried out their final checks in the hangar. They were supervised by Naval fitters because their own had been sent ahead the night before in two destroyers, along with a supply ship carrying the dismantled Harridans, in order to set things up at Vaenga and be on hand to take care of the aircraft when they arrived. Then, when they were ready for takeoff, they made their way up to the flight deck to watch the rest of the squadron.

Everything had to be done in a precise order and there was no room for mistakes. Dreadnought had been placed furthest forward on the deck, almost blocking the hangar lift and the first move was hers to make. Her engines coughed and began to turn as a compartment in the roof of her fuselage opened and a dark grey balloon quickly began to inflate. Once the balloon was fully inflated, her engines rotated, pointing the airscrews almost directly upwards, and roared as they were put into full emergency power.

As the huge, eye-achingly painted machine lifted gracefully from the deck, a signal was given and the thrum from the Arturo's engines deepened as the captain put her into full power, accelerating ahead to compensate for the slight forward motion that Dreadnought had when taking off in such a fashion and keeping underneath her as much as possible.

Dove had been placed in a sling attached to the winches in Dreadnought's wings, much like the old comical drawings of a baby in a stork's mouth, and as Wendy delicately slowed her ascent, Chastity was gently lifted into the air.

This manoeuvre in itself was nothing unusual for the Misfits; it had been employed many times at Badger Base with Bloodhound, which had a takeoff run longer than the runway, but they had never tried it with multiple aircraft before and in order to get all of the aircraft off the carrier, Jaguar and Hawk had been put in similar slings - Jaguar fixed to the bottom of Dove using the attachment point where a second spring would go and Hawk similarly attached to Jaguar.

It seemed that everybody on the ship held their breath when Jaguar lifted into the air, but it was when the sling became taut around Hawk that hearts really missed beats; Dreadnought had more than enough lifting power for all three B flight machines, their combined weight was comparable to Bloodhound's, but the system that they were using meant that the weight of two aircraft was on Dove. She had been chosen as the newest of the machines and as the one that theoretically had the strongest fuselage, but there had been no way of testing whether she would be able to cope and if she couldn't then it would likely result in the death of at least two pilots, if not three.

Thankfully, Dove did cope with the weight and the ungainly four-headed creature steadily gained altitude, soaring up into the blessedly clear skies, doing so more and more rapidly, the interceptor aircraft swinging sickeningly from side to side, looking more like dead fish than the elegant predators they were.

The audience on the carrier knew what was coming, but it was still a shock to them when Dreadnought reached a safe height and Hawk suddenly dropped away and plummeted from the sky. The twin-boomed aircraft spun lazily, showing that she hadn't been properly centred in the sling, but as soon as she had gained enough speed and her wings bit into the air, Kitty expertly righted her and put full power on to climb away. The sling dropped from her to fall harmlessly into the sea, where it bobbed, buoyed by floats, to be recovered once the Misfits were away.

The process was repeated by Jaguar and Dove, much less dramatically, and finally the watchers were able to draw a breath as the four aircraft went into a holding pattern over the carrier.

Compared to the drama of Dreadnought's departure, that of the rest of the aircraft was almost normal. Bloodhound was helped aloft by Vulture which had a similar balloon system to Dreadnought and then it was time for Hummingbird to fly from the side of the carrier and land on deck to pick up Swift, the last remaining B flight machine, in its sling.

Finally, all that remained was for A flight and the Harridan instructors to get aloft one by one and, only an hour after Dreadnought's engines had powered up, all fifteen aircraft had formed up at twelve thousand feet and were speeding towards the rendezvous point.

It was just as well they had Owen in Bloodhound with its radar, otherwise they would never have found their escort.

Not only was he circling the wrong coordinates, but he was at twenty thousand feet and not the twelve that they had been told to expect him at. They were also unable to contact him over the radio because the frequency they had been given only filled their ears with static and they couldn't try other channels for fear of giving their presence away to any listening enemies that close to the border. Then, when they formed up on him, he was obviously so startled that his aircraft, a silver three-engined leisure craft much like their Lekker, lurched in the sky as its pilot jerked on the controls in shock. When he finally regained control and was no longer a risk to them, Abby formed on his wing and waved, receiving, bizarrely, a salute with a shot glass from the pilot in return, before he began a shallow turn towards the coast, a few miles away.

Their destination, Vaenga, was only twenty miles inland, some fifteen miles north of Murmansk and not far from the river that fed the city. Thankfully, despite not having gotten anything else right, the pilot didn't manage to get lost, although the airfield was almost as well-camouflaged as Badger Base had been and it would have been easy enough to do.

Half a dozen large, but squat, hangars nestled among thick forests of silver birch trees. They flanked an oval landing field made of sand that had been flattened and compressed by machinery and that was long enough for even the larger aircraft to operate comfortably. Smaller brick buildings, barracks and mess halls and such, were separated from the hangars by what looked like a security gate and a gap in the trees leading from the gate showed where a single narrow access road winded its way towards the city, which could be just about made out in the distance.

As the British landed, familiar figures came out of the buildings to meet them - the support staff had evidently arrived safely, which was a relief, given the generally shoddy organisation the Misfits had encountered up until then.

The Muscovite machine landed first, but Abby and Gwen were hot on its heels and were directed to one of the low hangars by soldiers in greeny-grey uniform. Abby jumped out of her cockpit as soon as she could to speak to Sergeant Potter and Gwen hurried after her, not wanting to miss the conversation.

'Well, Sergeant?' Abby spoke quietly so that the nearby Muscovites wouldn't be able to hear.

'It's adequate, ma'am, but no more than that. Their repair facilities are dreadful, they have scant stocks of ammunition or Duralumin, beyond what we brought with us and I wouldn't be surprised if most of that weren't half-inched before long. And as for the base - there are very little in the way of creature comforts, although there is plenty of grub and a whole bloody warehouse full of vodka.'

'I'll talk to Sky Commodore Campbell about having a reliable guard posted on the stores. Anything else?'

'The airfield.'

'What about it?'

'Well, it's alright if it's dry and it'll probably be better when the ground freezes, but there's no drainage and if we get any heavy rain then it's probably going to turn to mush. We might want to see if we can't reinforce the undercarriages on A and B flight.'

Abby looked at Gwen. 'That's your department, Gwen. Assess the situation, please and make a decision on how feasible it'll be.'

Gwen smiled, pleased to be given such an important task. 'I'll see if we can pump some water from the river, we can pour it on the side of the field and see what happens.'

Abby nodded. 'Do that if you can. Anything else, Henry?'

The fitter sighed. 'Well, there is one thing, ma'am...'

'What do you mean you don't bloody like them?'

Sergeant Potter had taken them to the hangar where the crated Harridans were being assembled one by one. There he had introduced them to the commander of the squadron who were going to be trained up on the British fighters, Captain Sergei Baryshnikov, a short and swarthy, but colourful character with a long thin black moustache. He was wearing a light blue uniform which would have been more appropriate on a cavalry officer in the nineteenth century, with a tall black busby, shiny black riding boots and an immense amount of gold braid on his jacket. He and his squadron had evidently put on their dress uniforms to greet the Misfits, but then gotten so sidetracked at the sight of the aircraft they were being forced to fly that they had completely forgotten to do so.

'Just look at them! They're so... so... *boring*!' The Muscovite waved dismissively at the two Harridans that had already been assembled and exclaimed in excellent English that was only slightly tainted by an accent. 'Where are the bright colours to taunt the enemy? The brass pipes to add flair...? There is not even a single cog in sight! Come!'

He gestured for them to accompany him and, followed by the rest of his pilots, they went back out of the hangar and along to the next one in line. He stood in front of the open hangar doors and opened his arms wide, beaming at a group of stubby fighters sitting inside. 'Now, *that* is what a fighter should look like! Yours...' he bowed apologetically, '...they are not bad, they are very pretty... but these are *Russian* machines and would run rings around them. We don't need those, those... *Harried Dames* or whatever you call them, we have our own *wonderful* aircraft.' He looked lovingly at the machines, which gleamed in the cold morning light.

Gwen gave the aircraft a once over, assessing them, trying to look beyond the bright colours, which put even the Misfit machines to shame - compared to the drab camouflage of the Harridans, which in their factory form didn't even have the splash of colour usually provided by roundels, they looked like peacocks next to chickens. They were identical, factory-constructed aircraft, with thick, stubby fuselages that ended in blunt noses and short wings which would provide plenty of lift and allow them to roll quickly. They were quite obviously turn fighters and would probably have been very effective, if it weren't for the unnecessary decorations strewn all over them - brass pipes that led to nowhere and did nothing, golden cogs that weren't actually attached to anything. There were even lines of semi-precious stones ringing the canopies of a few of the aircraft, which had to ring the pilot with a soft halo when the sun shone on them. She had to admit that they looked lovely and each of the machines was very distinct and individual, but the embellishments only really served to add weight and ruin their aerodynamics.

Russians had always liked to decorate their technology as much as they could, often adding impractical touches that had no discernible purpose, almost as if they were seeking to disguise its function and turn it into a work of art instead, like their famous Fabergé eggs which hid mechanical delights within a beautiful shell.

The British on the other hand had always focused on practicality and function foremost, but they were especially austere now that resources were being conserved as much as possible. While some decoration was certainly allowed, and encouraged as long as it didn't affect the proper working of the machine in question, it was kept to a minimum. Only the very vulgar, or those seeking to highlight how rich they were, ornamented their property or inventions, but even then, they never went to the same lengths as the Russians.

The British were like the Prussians in that regard, but while British technology was always elegant and pleasing to the eye, Prussian solutions to the same problems were invariably stark and almost brutal in their efficiency.

In this case, though, the function of the aircraft hadn't only been disguised by the Russians, it had also been impaired and the Misfit machines, even those of B flight, would absolutely annihilate them. The Harridans, despite being stock aircraft, would undoubtedly do the same.

Abby rolled her eyes at Gwen and smirked, obviously having come to the same conclusion as she had. 'Fancy jumping back into a Harridan?'

She hadn't thought she would, but as she sat in the cockpit of the Harridan, waiting for Abby to give the signal to takeoff, she found herself enjoying herself, smiling widely as she reacquainted herself with the machine she had flown before joining the Misfits, the machine she had helped design and test.

It was one of the new marks of Harridans that her parents had brought out only recently, armed with twelve machine guns and equipped with the new Rentley-Joyce spring. It had been easier to ship new Harridans straight from the factory rather than send any of the older models, so the Muscovites were being supplied with them even before some of the British squadrons got their hands on them.

'Ready, Badger Two?'

'Rodger, Leader.'

'How about you, Wolfpack Leader?'

Gwen glanced across Abby's Harridan at the two Muscovite aircraft lined up next to them. The Muscovites, or Russians as they still insisted on being called, were part of a squadron that were called the "Wolfpack". They had performed very well in the Great War and were considered to be the best squadron in Muscovy, which was probably why the Tsar had chosen them to convert to the Harridans.

'We Russians were born ready, Badger Leader.'

Gwen could almost hear Abby's eyes rolling and fought hard to keep a straight face as Abby replied. 'Roger. Take the lead, then, Wolfpack.'

The two Muscovites, Russians, exchanged a few words in their own language, before Baryshnikov shouted 'let's go!' immediately following it with a wolf howl, breaking almost all the rules of radio discipline in a single exchange, and the two aircraft surged forwards.

Gwen exchanged a look with Abby, who grinned. 'You heard the man, Badger Two. "Let's go."'

'Roger, Leader.'

Gwen opened up the throttle at the same time as Abby and the Harridans accelerated. The difference between the performance of Wasp and the Harridan was immediately noticeable, but not nearly as exaggerated as she had feared - her parents had done a good job in converting the potency of the new spring to thrust and she resolved to take a good look at the airscrews after the flight to see what they had done.

She waved to the rest of Misfits, who had all found places to sit on the cement path in front of the hangars and were lifting their feet off the ground to the bemusement of the Russians, then turned back to the job at hand.

Even though the Russian aircraft had a good few seconds head start, the Misfits caught up with them easily and were off the ground first. They had arranged to meet at six thousand feet and they were there well before them, circling the airfield and using the time to get used to their aircraft and take a better look at the surrounding countryside.

Gwen spotted dozens of encampments in small clearings in the forest surrounding the airfield, all with what looked like artillery or anti-aircraft guns. It seemed that they were going to be well defended, which was a relief seeing as the front lines were only ninety or so miles away and there were only two thin rivers in the way and not the twenty-mile English channel. She just hoped that the gunners had been informed of their arrival and wouldn't be taking potshots at the two strange aircraft in the sky.

It took almost a minute for the Russian aircraft to reach them, but the commander didn't seem at all phased by this demonstration of the Harridan's superiority and continued to be cheerful over the radio. 'Why are you in so much of a hurry to be beaten by us? You should slow down and enjoy the day! Perhaps we should call this off; it's not too late to concede defeat and admit that our machines are better and prettier than yours. We could go back down and have some vodka while we talk about how we can improve your aircraft for you.'

Gwen saw Abby shake her head in exasperation before answering. 'That is a very generous offer, but no, thank you, Wolfpack Leader; we have found out that there is as much, if not more, to learn in a loss as there is in a victory.'

Gwen grinned grimly as Abby echoed Captain Hewer's words after the whist game, but wondered if the Russian would be capable of learning anything from his coming experience.

'An admirable sentiment, but we Russians never lose!'

Baryshnikov laughed, but neither Abby nor Gwen did, instead they shared another look, this time the dismay evident on both their faces; the man's conceit would get him and his friends killed very quickly when the Prussians arrived - it was the kind of attitude that was left over from the times before the Great War when conflict was seen almost as fun and not many people died. Until then, Gwen had almost been thinking of suggesting to Abby that they go easy on the Russians, so as not to hurt their feelings, but she completely dismissed the idea; it was time to wake them up to the harsh reality of the war they were going to be fighting, before their commander's foolishness got the Misfits killed.

'We break on three and may the best man win!' The Russian laughed once more, then began to count. 'One. Two. Three.'

Despite the fact that the Russians broke off just after Baryshnikov counted two, the Misfits were ready for them and Gwen followed Abby into a steep turn that took them away from their opponents, before gathering speed in a shallow dive.

Gwen watched the fighters in her rear view mirror and grinned in satisfaction; she'd been right about their performance - they'd managed to get the manoeuvrability of a biplane into a single winged fighter, but the cost had been speed.

Unsurprisingly, the Russians had taken the direct approach and swung immediately to follow the Misfits, using their tighter turning circles to try to get on their tails. However, the difference in speed between the machines had allowed the British to open up a good lead and, even when they sacrificed some of that for height, turning back towards their opponents, their higher rate of climb took them up above the Russians, well out of reach of their guns.

The Russians were essentially forced to circle below the British and wait for them to come back down and Baryshnikov's laugh was rather more forced than before. 'Those machines certainly run away very well! Is this the fighting style that you British want to teach us? It is as dull as your *Hurried Ants* look.'

Gwen glanced across at Abby, taking note of her clenched jaw, which had nothing to do with the G forces they were pulling and knew that she was thinking the same as she, that this was no way to teach the Russians a lesson. They were going to have to throw their newly developed tactics out of the window and get their hands dirty like they used to.

She was ready, then, when Abby threw her Harridan on its back and dove directly at the two colourful machines.

They closed the gap with the pair in less than a couple of seconds, taking them completely by surprise with the suddenness of their manoeuvre, and Gwen was amused to hear Abby muttering "rat a tat a tat" under her breath as they screamed between them, scattering them in panic.

There wasn't a single protest from the sturdy Harridan as Gwen pulled the stick into her lap, staying with Abby as she pulled out of the dive and following her into a quick Immelmman which put them behind the lead Russian's aircraft.

'I've got this one, Badger Two, you take the other.'

'Roger, Leader.'

A quick glance in the direction she'd seen the other Russian break showed him slightly below them half a mile away and she turned sharply, leaving Abby to stay with Baryshnikov, who had begun to throw his machine into a creditable series of aerobatic manoeuvres.

The second Russian was not nearly as good as his leader and it only took a few turns for Gwen to get behind him and she was able to stay there during his clumsy attempts to shake her off. He wasn't a bad pilot by any means, but he needed practice and lacked the experience she'd had over a summer of hard fighting against the best the Prussians had to offer.

'Enough!' Baryshnikov called out, stopping the duels. 'You took us by surprise there, it wasn't fair. We will fight one more and this time we will be ready for your tricks.'

They met up again at six thousand feet, this time starting the dogfight by going head to head, but, to the Russian commander's dismay, the result was exactly the same. This time he didn't call it off or acknowledge defeat, he just dived below the two thousand feet hard limit they had agreed upon for safety and landed back at Vaenga, leaving his wingman to escort the British home.

There was no sign of Baryshnikov when the three aircraft landed and it was the pilot of the second Russian aircraft, Staff-Captain Nikolai Polikasparov, who parked his aircraft next to theirs, then marched over to meet them. He turned out to be a young man with piercing blue eyes, fair skin and hair that was so blonde it was almost white, in stark contrast to the rest of the squadron, who were on the main part darker skinned and dark-haired, the men invariably with moustaches like Baryshnikov's and in some cases beards. He was wearing a very expensive-looking leather flight suit, with liquid pockets around legs and abdomen, which fit him like a glove, accentuating his slender, but well-proportioned form. He snapped a smart bow before flashing brilliant white teeth at them. 'I apologise for the commander - he is not a good loser.' His accent was much thicker than Baryshnikov's was and his English not as precise, but he was still perfectly understandable. 'To tell the truth, none of us are; we have been taught of the glory of the Empire and the impossibility of its defeat for so long that it is hard to us to even contemplate the possibility that we may lose a single fight, let alone a war.'

Abby shook her head. 'There's no need to apologise; there were harder heads than his in the British government at the start of the war. Let us just hope it doesn't take as many lives being lost to open his eyes, and those of others like him.'

'I don't think it will; he is an intelligent man and he will see this for what it is. After he has blown off some steam, he will be back and you won't be able to stop him from demanding to be taught everything you know.'

Abby smiled. 'We brought instructors with us who will be doing that, but it would be our pleasure to show you a few tricks to kill the Prussians with.'

'Thank you.' Polikasparov gave another of his sharply formal nods, then gestured for the Misfits to go with him. 'You must be hungry, please, allow us to show you to our officer's mess where we have refreshments prepared for you.' He gestured to where the rest of the pilots, Russian and British alike - who had been watching the combats together with vastly different feelings - were waiting for them in front of the hangar containing the newly arrived aircraft of A and B flights.

The men and women of the Wolfpack had changed out of their dress uniforms and were now wearing their day uniforms, which were cut very much like the British ones, but in a quite fetching dark grey, the colour of storm clouds. They escorted the Misfits and the instructors to the mess, where their youngest female member was waiting for them on the steps of the hall with a loaf of bread and a pot of salt on a white cloth. She bowed and offered it to them with a smile.

Polikasparov gestured to the bread. 'This is the traditional Russian welcome. You take some bread, dip it in the salt and eat.'

After Abby had eaten some of the bread, he escorted her inside the mess hall, closely followed by the rest of the Misfits, who were each escorted into the hut by one of the Russians after sampling the bread.

While the outside of the mess hall had been plain, just exposed brick and tile, the inside was anything but. There was not a single patch of wall that was not covered with a shawl, a tapestry or a trophy. There were even numerous banners hanging from the low ceiling, just above head height. The overall effect was of a kind of Aladdin's cave, with treasures in every corner.

The space in the middle of the room was filled with long wooden tables, piled with food and lined by benches, and it was to these that the Misfits were being led, but Gwen held back. She paused just inside the door, taking in the riot of colours that rivalled the machines that the Russians flew and her eyes naturally went first to the trophies on the wall nearest to her. The most recent of the ones in the room, they were from Great War aircraft - a long two-bladed wooden airscrew competed for space with a couple of Prussian tailplanes and numerous small bits and bobs that included things like instruments and gunsights. However, these aviation trophies were almost lost among the chaos of the dozens upon dozens of trophies which came from when the squadron had been a cavalry unit, some of which looked truly ancient, with markings on them that dated from hundreds of years ago. One in particular of the banners hanging from the rafters caught Gwen's eye, though; it was recognisably British and by its tattered state it had been taken in the heat of battle.

'My family's shame.'

Gwen looked to the side and found Rudy Drake gazing up at the banner while he munched on a slice of bread. 'Sorry?'

He gestured at the banner with the bread while he chewed and swallowed his mouthful. 'That thing was lost by one of my great great something or others in the Crimean conflict. It's the only stain on my family's reputation in an otherwise glorious contribution to building and keeping the Empire the King has suddenly decided isn't an Empire anymore.' He laughed bitterly and shook his head, real resentment in his eyes. 'It's funny how, whenever my family is being talked about at court, the loss of those colours is what unfailingly comes up, not any of our numerous victories, which, as you know, date back to Good Queen Bess.'

'I think you may have mentioned that, oh... once or twice when we were growing up.'

Drake saw her mocking expression and laughed, his mood lightening in the face of her gentle teasing. He gestured with the bread. 'You should have some of this, it's delicious.'

The bread was covered with some black substance that looked thoroughly unappetising and she wrinkled her nose at it. 'Is that caviar? Does it taste as bad as it smells?'

'My word, Goosy, have you never had caviar before? I thought you said your parents brought you to Russia?'

'They did, when I was fourteen. We were at a symposium in St. Petersburg and I made friends with this Italian boy my age. His family lived on their airship, travelling the world...'

'And you bewitched him, he took you home to his mama and you ate home-cooked Italian food every day you were here and didn't get to sample the local cuisine. Oh, Goosy, you always were a bit of a man-eater, weren't you?'

Drake grinned and sauntered away before Gwen could do more than scowl.

She watched him go, shaking her head and smiling wryly.

'Captain.'

With a start, Gwen realised that the Russian man who had escorted her inside was still with her, standing unobtrusively just behind her shoulder, and she turned at his greeting and found that Baryshnikov had returned.

The Russian captain was smiling, all sign of his earlier annoyance completely gone, as his young wingman had predicted and he stepped forward to offer Gwen his hand. 'Well flown, Officer Stone, I can see why Wing Commander Lennox wants you on her wing to protect her.'

'Thank you, sir.'

Abby had seen the captain come in and she came over to them. 'Captain Baryshnikov! Have you changed your opinion of the Harridans?'

The Russian nodded enthusiastically. 'Yes. They are very good machines, but you were lucky to win because you made some very basic mistakes. We will fly them much better.'

CHAPTER 14

Baryshnikov hadn't just come to tell them that he'd changed his mind about the Harridans, he also brought with him a message from the Tsar, requesting the presence of Misfit Squadron at the Winter Palace in St. Petersburg as soon as was convenient - a command dressed up as an invitation.

The captain further informed them that, in order to keep their presence secret for longer, they weren't permitted to fly, but a special train with sleeper, lounge and restaurant cars had been provided for them and had been waiting for them to arrive in a siding not far away for several days.

The Misfits as a whole were loath to leave behind their aircraft, but they couldn't refuse, especially seeing as a second message had come from Dorothy Campbell saying that they had to go whether they liked it or not. So, just a couple of hours after they'd arrived and before they could make themselves at home, the Misfits found themselves on a train, speeding through the Muscovite countryside, heading south towards the capital city, St. Petersburg, at just over fifty miles an hour. They had left the instructors behind, not only because the invitation was just for them, but because they had to start training the Russians immediately, whereas the Misfits didn't have much to do until the Prussians started to make their move.

St. Petersburg was only about six hundred miles from Murmansk as the raven flew and the Misfits were expecting the journey to take a little over twelve hours, but they were told by one of the stewards on board that it was going to take more than twenty-four because the train would be taking a very roundabout route to get there, winding its way around the multitude of lakes that were in the way and also avoiding some of the more direct tracks that ran too close to the border for comfort.

The Misfits were very glad, therefore, that the Tsar had seen fit to send what, judging from the Imperial crests on the decorations, plates and cutlery, must have been his own personal train, or one of them at least.

It was extremely comfortable, in an old style much like the Orient Express, with velvet curtains and wood panelling. There was even proper furniture in place of the thinly padded benches that were becoming more and more usual in Britain, with the drive for efficiency packing as many passengers into each car as possible like so much cattle. There was a full staff on board, including stewards, cooks and soldiers to guard them, and they saw to the pilots' every need, supplying snacks and champagne as soon as they were on board, before serving lunch, the menu of which had obviously been prepared carefully and especially for them, consisting as it did of typically British food. However, the cooks obviously weren't used to the menu and had gotten things a bit mixed up - the Yorkshire Pudding was served as a dessert instead of with the roast beef and the jam roly-poly was cold and brought along with the main course, as if it were an accompaniment. The Misfits didn't mind one bit, though, and still gorged themselves, laughing when Bruce unrolled the roly-poly, then wrapped it around a piece of beef as an "experiment", declaring it a resounding success and trying to convince the stewards that that was how it should have been served.

It had been a long day and most of the pilots decided to take a nap after lunch, curling up on sofas in the lounge or retiring to a bunk in the sleeping car, but Gwen wasn't very tired, so she went to the observation deck, a metal and glass covered sitting room on the roof of the lounge car, to watch the countryside going by.

She was immediately taken by surprise by the sheer amount of machinery she could see in the fields - it seemed that every village they passed by was surrounded by fields, but instead of men and women working them there were large iron and brass contraptions with multiple arms and legs, all unceasingly digging or harvesting.

She wasn't an expert on Russian history, but she remembered reading somewhere that automated farming machinery had been invented by a group of scientists in Moscow, then introduced throughout the country in the late nineteenth century. It had been paid for in large part by the Tsar himself, in return for a meagre ten percent of the produce, which was then sold to neighbouring countries. Not only had the Tsar become one of the richest monarchs in the world, but production had increased, hunger had decreased and the people were left with more time to actually enjoy their lives. As a consequence, Russia had become incredibly stable, with one of the highest standards of living of any country and a level of art and culture, even among the common people, that was unparalleled. Many scholars expounded that that was why the Tsar could get away with being a one man show and not have the Parliament that the King had been forced to accept.

The countryside itself was beautiful, with endless forests and pristine lakes that were invariably surrounded by beautiful wooden buildings and had colourful fishing boats bobbing up and down on them - the automation of work apparently only extended to agriculture and not fishing.

The gentle swaying of the train and the way the scenery moved sedately past the windows had a very soporific effect, much like counting sheep and, before she knew it, Gwen found her eyelids drooping and she curled up in the armchair and stopped fighting the exhaustion that had been building for so long.

Just before noon the next day, the train pulled into a station secreted underneath the Winter Palace, which, like the train itself, was for the Tsar's personal use.

The Misfits, dressed in their best uniforms, with the matching floor-length ceremonial dress coats they had been issued for colder weather and their top hats tucked firmly under their arms, were met by Dorothy Campbell. She was accompanied by Freddy Featherstonehaugh, Mr Jones and a delegation of Palace Guards, wearing white uniforms with breeches under knee-length coats that flared out from the waist and which were covered with even more gold braid than Baryshnikov had sported on his jacket. They were led by a handsome young captain, blonde and barely more than twenty-five years of age, who introduced himself as Pyotr Mussorgsky, a surname which drew more than a few raised eyebrows, although nobody commented.

Campbell and her staff had been flown to the capital from Archangel in a Muscovite transport aircraft the day before. They had spent all afternoon and late into the night, organising the distribution of the weapons they had brought with them with the army commanders and the sky commodore was looking very tired, but she nonetheless had a wide grin for them.

The guard captain, Mussorgsky, took them to a large lift which had room for all of them and while they were clanking their way up to the palace, Campbell took the opportunity to speak to Abby and the rest of the Misfits in turn took the opportunity provided by the confined space to listen in on their conversation.

Campbell got straight down to business, knowing that they didn't have much time before the lift doors opened again. 'Muscovite reconnaissance aircraft report that Prussians aren't making their move yet, they still seem to be consolidating their forces, bringing up artillery and mechanised battalions. They look like they're going to open up at least three fronts, one in the south, one in the Baltic and the last up north where we are. At the moment the forces deployed in the north are relatively small compared to the other fronts, but we expect that to change when you show your faces.' She grinned. 'Actually, we're hoping that they commit a lot more forces to the north, because it'll take the pressure off the other fronts and then when winter comes they'll be effectively rendered useless until spring.'

Abby didn't have time to tell her friend exactly what she thought of that because the doors slid open and they were hustled out by the Royal Guards.

A short corridor led to another door which opened into a long thin rectangular gallery, which Mussorgsky called the "Military Gallery," the walls of which were covered with hundreds of portraits, row after regimented row of them, each the exact same size, of what looked like military commanders. Like the Wolfpack aircraft and the Tsar's train, they were so covered in gold and jewels that barely an inch of bare wood was left exposed on the frames. The cogwheel symbol, that Muscovites seemed to like so much, was prevalent on all of them, but they were joined by other items, like horseshoes, compasses and sextants, that probably related to the branch of the military the men and women belonged to. It should have looked tacky in the extreme, but it was so expertly done that the portraits seemed to glow from within as they caught the illumination coming from the skylights.

The Misfits had no time to appreciate the magnificent sight, though, as they were all but chivvied along to stand in front of a pair of double doors situated half-way down the gallery. White and heavily decorated by what looked like solid gold, the doors were almost fifteen feet tall and flanked by two guards in ceremonial uniforms, complete with burnished bronze breastplates and, of all things, pikestaffs. With them was a master of ceremonies, dressed in a deep red calf-length coat, also heavily embroidered with gold thread, with boots to match and carrying a long silver staff.

Captain Mussorgsky and his fellow guards arranged the Misfits in pairs in order of rank, with Abby and Owen in the front and Chastity next to Gwen at the back, showing a knowledge of the visitors that was surprising to say the least.

Since it was only the Misfits that were going to be presented, Featherstonehaugh, Mr Jones and Dorothy Campbell weren't included in the group and were told to enter the room afterwards, following them, but not with them.

When everything was in order, the master of ceremonies banged on the floor with his staff, three heavy blows that resounded through the chamber. The doors swung open and a fanfare filled the air before the echoes of the staff had even died away.

Flanked by the Royal Guards, who marched in lockstep, the Misfits entered the room. The pilots didn't try to emulate the guards; they would have just looked and felt silly, but Gwen noted with a smile from her vantage point at the back of the group that every single one of them stood up just a little bit straighter, even Bruce, who had barely straightened from his habitual slouch for the King.

Gwen's first impression of Buckingham Palace had been of opulence, but the Winter Palace made it seem almost a hovel in comparison. However, while the seat of Britain's power had been rich but elegant, the Tsars of Russia seemed to have been wanting to make a statement with their home, and as far as Gwen was concerned, that statement was overt wealth.

The room that they entered was huge, much bigger than the throne room in Buckingham Palace, but while that had been warm, welcoming and very grounded, this was airy and light and somehow called to the aviator in Gwen. It was predominantly white, but there was gold everywhere - on the columns, the massive chandeliers, inlaid into the floor and even around the frames of the large windows on either side.

The room was also filled to capacity with people, all of whom were turned their way, and not just on the floor, but looking down at them from the balconies that ringed the room and Gwen had to stifle a laugh when she heard Mac's muttered comment of 'I thought our being here was supposed to be a bloody secret?'

The crowd parted to make way for them and the Royal Guards marched them smartly down the centre of the room towards the dais at the far end, where a huge red canopy with the Imperial Russian crest hung over a golden throne.

Tsar Nicholas II was waiting for them there, standing at the top of the steps in front of his throne and he watched impassively as the pilots arranged themselves in front of him, each pair smartly breaking off in turn, as if they were performing a manoeuvre in the air, and joining the end of a line as it formed in front of the dais, with Abby and Owen in the centre and Gwen and Chastity on opposite sides.

Suspecting that they were going to be made a spectacle of, Abby had insisted they spend a few minutes on the train rehearsing and thankfully it went much better than it had, mostly because none of the participants were drunk.

Once the Misfits were all in place, Abby gave a sharp order and they gave a small bow, creditably together, the only sound the clicking of Mr Jones' camera as he immortalised the moment.

Finally, the Tsar smiled. He brought his hands together delicately and suddenly the whole room was filled by thunderous applause. The clapping went on and on while the Tsar descended the steps and greeted each and every one of the pilots with a firm handshake and only ceased when he had returned to his place in front of his throne.

'So, Commander Campbell, these are your famous Misfit Squadron.'

The Tsar looked at them one by one, meeting each pilot's gaze in turn and Gwen took the opportunity afforded by the short pause to inspect him in return. He was old, over seventy, his hair and short beard long ago turned white, but his resemblance to the old Emperor George I, the current King's father, was uncanny, which wasn't surprising seeing as they had been cousins. He was also cousin to Kaiser Bill, but then again all of the Royal Families of Europe were related in some way or other.

He nodded to them, almost imperceptibly. 'Thank you for volunteering to aid us in our fight against the Prussian Invaders.'

'It is a pleasure and our duty, Your Majesty,' Campbell hurriedly replied before any of the more impulsive Misfits could comment on the way in which they had "volunteered" for the mission.

Another thing the Tsar had in common with both King George VI and his father was the mischievous glint in his eye and that brightened as he acknowledged the sky commodore's tact with a smile. 'I have a gift for you.'

At the master of ceremonies' clap, servants stepped forwards and helped the Misfits out of their woollen overcoats. Others then came forward and helped them on with new ones - long, black fur coats with silver-grey fur trim and gold-plated buttons with badgers on them, identical to the one on the squadron's crest.

'They are sable fur, made by our finest craftsmen, lined with wolf fur to keep you warm while you are here, although perhaps my cousin will grant you special dispensation to make them a permanent part of your uniform, like the bearskin hats of your Grenadier Guards? If so it will be my pleasure to supply you with them whenever you need them.'

There was applause from the audience at the Tsar's gesture and he let it go on for quite a while, smiling in appreciation of his courtiers' approval, before holding up his hand for silence.

'I wish you every success in the coming weeks. As you Misfits say - "happy hunting" - and welcome to the Kingdom of Muscovy!'

As more applause rang out around the room, the Royal Guards ushered the pilots across the hall and marched them right out of the room and back into the Military Gallery.

The big double doors banged closed behind them, shutting them off from view of the throne room and the Misfits, almost as one, sighed in relief and relaxed tensed muscles and stretched backs that weren't used to being held so straight.

Owen shook his head. 'Well that was short and sweet.'

Mac barked a laugh. 'We've come all this way for that? What was the point?'

Campbell came through the doors just in time to hear him. 'The Tsar is treading a very fine line where you are concerned. He has to play down your importance in public because if the Prussians got wind of how vulnerable Muscovy really is they wouldn't bother spending time to consolidate their forces and would invade straight away. On the other hand, though, he has to show his people that he is doing all he can to protect them.'

Abby frowned. 'Is the situation that bad?'

The sky commodore grimaced. 'Let's just say that the weapons we brought with us are going to *greatly* increase the effectiveness of the Muscovite army and, by the way Mac, it's not a secret that you're *here*, just where you're based. We actually want the Prussians to know you're here as a deterrent - we're here to show our faces and make the Prussians just that little bit more nervous about invading. So, with that in mind, Abby, darling, I'm sorry, but you and Owen are staying here with me; we're going to press the flesh for a few hours and then there's a lovely twenty-course state dinner that's been set up in our honour.'

'Oh great.' Owen groaned.

Wendy grinned at him. 'Enjoy yourself darling.'

Owen looked daggers at her, then turned to Campbell. 'I really think my wife should be with me for the dinner. For propriety's sake.'

The big woman growled at him. 'Don't you dare...'

Campbell sighed exaggeratedly. 'Where *is* my head at? Sorry, Owen, I had of course meant to say that you had a plus one on your invitation - they know you're married, so of course they took that into account.'

Wendy glared at her. 'What? Dammit, I'm a pilot not a diplomat! When are we going to fly?'

'Soon enough, don't worry.'

Knowing that there was nothing she could do or say to avoid her fate, the big woman turned her ire on her husband. 'Wait until I get you alone.'

Owen smiled at her innocently. 'Now now, darling, don't blame me. You heard the lovely sky commodore, you were already invited. If you're going to blame anyone it should be the Tsar.'

Wendy growled, letting her husband know in no uncertain terms that he hadn't gotten off the hook.

Campbell chuckled as Owen blanched, then looked at the other Misfits. 'As for the rest of you, Captain Mussorgsky is going to take you around the city so that the civilians can see the famous British pilots. I understand he's taking you to a special matinée in your honour at the ballet.'

Mac groaned. 'Ballet? Ach, if I put on a dress can I swap places with Wendy as Owen's plus one? Please?'

Campbell smiled sweetly at him. 'You will go to the ballet and look like you are a cultured person who is enjoying himself, Mac, that's an order, otherwise I *will* put you in that dress, but it won't be as Owen's plus one, it will be to go on stage as a member of the chorus.'

Mac grumbled, but took the sky commodore's order in the humorous way that it had been intended and nodded with a laugh. 'Yes'm!'

'Good.' Campbell took a deep breath and glanced at the door, where the master of ceremonies was waiting to take the four RAC officers back in. 'Right then, play nice all of you and remember that we're here to "help", not to save the Muscovite's arses, and it's only us and our machines - there are *no* Harridans and *no* armaments. Got that?'

She glanced around the group, making sure everybody understood then nodded. 'Good. Quarters have been arranged for tonight in a town house nearby used for distinguished guests. Enjoy your evening and make sure you're all on the train tomorrow morning - it leaves at eight sharp.' She lifted her head to look at Captain Mussorgsky, who had been hovering at a discrete distance. 'They're all yours, Captain.'

She nodded at the master of ceremonies and, as he opened the doors again, she plastered a smile on her face and winked at Abby. 'Once more unto the breach, dear friends...'

CHAPTER 15

As soon as the senior officers had disappeared back into the throne room, Captain Mussorgsky led the rest of the Misfits through the palace towards the main entrance.

They went fairly slowly, taking what seemed to be quite a roundabout route, through rooms where there were visitors and courtiers, and Gwen couldn't help feel that they were being put on display, like the trophies on a mess wall. That impression only intensified when they got out into the streets and found that the large black spring-powered autocars waiting to take them to the theatre had been parked in plain sight in the square outside the palace and had naturally drawn a lot of attention. Policemen in green uniforms and peaked caps were struggling to hold back more than a hundred cheering people, all straining to get a glimpse of them as they came down the steps and any debate as to whether they had gathered just out of curiosity as to who would get into the vehicles was dispelled instantly when many of them started waving very homemade-looking British flags.

Those crowds were replicated outside the *Imperial Mariinsky* theatre and it didn't stop there, because inside they were welcomed by the directors of the ballet company and themselves and fed caviar and champagne, before being taken to the Imperial Box, where they were announced as if they were royalty and given a standing ovation by not only the entire audience, but the orchestra as well.

Just as they had felt awkward being lauded as heroes by the people in the hospital where Lady Penelope had been treated, most of the

Misfits were very uncomfortable with all the attention they were getting. They didn't enjoy receiving such praise and recognition for doing what they thought of as their duty and they took their seats quickly after politely acknowledging the applause. All except for Scarlet, who shamelessly stood at the front of the box to wave and blow kisses and had to be tugged backwards into her seat by Kitty.

After the audience had finally retaken their seats, an usher handed out souvenir programmes and Gwen smiled as she read the name of the ballet that was going to be performed - Coppélia, one of her favourites. It wasn't one of the big and ever-popular Tchaikovsky ballets that seemed to be all that many companies ever did, instead it was a fairly short comic ballet, which, she reflected, would please Mac, as he wouldn't have to sit through almost three hours of romance. She had seen Coppélia a few times with her parents - they were patrons of the Royal Opera House and had taken her there every time they were in London after they had collected her from Hamleys - but that evening's performance was special, combining as it did the splendour and classical repertoire of ballet with the most modern of technology.

The ballet told the story of an inventor who makes very lifelike doll, capable of dancing, which a young man somehow falls in love with. The young man's girlfriend sees this and dresses up as the doll to mock him, pretending to make it come to life. Usually the parts of the dancing doll and several others that the inventor has made were played by dancers, who then have to dance as if they were mechanical beings, but in the production that night, those dolls were played by actual clockwork automatons, created specially for the ballet company.

Afterwards, Gwen wasn't sure what had been more magical about the ballet. Her engineering mind said the automatons, with how superbly they had been crafted, but the girl in her, that still remembered those nights in London, insisted that it had been the dancing itself, which had been every bit as good, if not better than what she had seen in Covent Garden.

Mac had complained at having to go to the ballet, but she was sure she had seen him laughing at the antics of the inventor and he had clapped just as loudly as everybody else during the curtain calls. Bruce had also been very reluctant, but when Mussorgsky took them backstage and introduced them to the ballerinas he was very enthusiastic in his praise. Freddy Featherstonehaugh had stayed at the palace to fulfil his journalistic duties in reporting on the far more important state dinner, but he had sent Mr Jones along and the photographer took dozens of pictures of the pilots backstage with the company, making sure that the world would see that they weren't just killers, but had an appreciation of culture as well.

Gwen congratulated the dancers, many of which spoke excellent English and had danced on the London stage during tours, and got as many of them as she could to sign her programme, intending to keep it and put it with the rest of her collection at home. However, at the first opportunity, she slipped away to examine the automatons, wondering if they had some kind of mechanical brain, but was disappointed to find that they were merely incredibly complicated clockwork dolls, like in the libretto of the ballet.

In the end, the pilots stayed so long that Mussorgsky had to round them up and usher them out so that the dancers could prepare for the evening's performance.

It was dark by the time they came out of the theatre and, while Mr Jones went to rejoin his partner at the palace, the Misfits piled back into the autocars to go to dinner.

The place that he took them to was only a few streets away from the palace and was a cross between a pub and a mess hall. It was dimly lit and decorated as if it were a wooden hut in the forest somewhere, with wooden beams overhead, wooden panelling on the walls and wooden furniture. A bar ran the length of one side of the room, behind which several men and women were kept busy fetching drinks, usually vodka, for the patrons, most of whom wore some uniform or other, the dark grey of the Air Service mixing freely with the dark blue of the Navy and the dull green of the Army. The rest of the space was taken up by long tables lined with cushioned benches, only about half of which were full.

The Misfits attracted a fair amount of attention as Mussorgsky led them across the room towards an empty table, but, unlike in the streets, nobody made much of a fuss of them, although the captain was greeted by many of the people as he went past, quite a few of whom shot curious glances at the pilots and asked him questions, obviously about them. He didn't stop to talk to them, though, but just shouted out answers to them, loudly so that the whole room could hear, and kept moving.

The table he took them to was one of the smaller ones in the room, seating only a dozen or so and it had apparently been reserved for them because there was a sign on it in Cyrillic writing. As soon as they sat down, a waiter appeared and whisked the sign away and, after a short discussion with Mussorgsky, the food and drink started to arrive.

The bottles of vodka were immediately attacked by Mac, Bruce and the captain, but the rest of the pilots filled their glasses from the jugs with a tasty beer-like drink called "kvass" made from bread which, they were assured, was only lightly alcoholic.

'A toast!' Mussorgsky stood, holding his glass aloft. 'To the Russian Empire and the British Empire, may they last forever! Za nashu druzjbu! To our friendship!'

'To our friendship!' The Misfits stood and clinked glasses with him.

The Muscovite threw back his head and downed his vodka in one gulp, followed by Mac and Bruce, but the others just settled for large gulps of their kvass.

The captain smacked his lips and smiled at the Misfits. 'Well, my friends. I was tasked with bringing you here tonight so that you could meet some of our fighting men and women.' He gestured around the bar. 'As you can see, this is where many of our soldiers come when they are off duty. Here you will find Royal Guards like me and aviators like yourselves, general officers and common privates. In this hall rank does not matter, regiment does not matter; here we are all united by a single purpose - to defend our home. We do not stand on ceremony, we mix, we make friends. Sometimes we even find lovers.' He winked at Scarlet, who he had obviously already pegged as someone who enjoyed life to the full. 'Do not feel that you have to stay at this table to eat; all the food is paid for by the Tsar and nobody will mind if you join them and sample what they have.'

He looked at Bruce and Mac. 'There are a couple of women at the bar who have been looking at you two since we came in, perhaps you might satisfy their curiosity as to who you are?'

Bruce laughed. 'You don't have to tell me twice, mate!' He slapped Mac on the shoulder. 'Come on! On your feet soldier!'

Mac chuckled and picked up his glass as he stood. He gave the table a bow. 'See yous in the mornin'!'

Scarlet stood up as well. 'I see some likely looking lads over there, I'm going to see if I can get them to teach me some Russian!'

Mussorgsky turned to the few Misfits that remained. 'And you, ladies? Gentlemen?'

Derek, Charles and Monty shared glances. None of them were heavy drinkers so that was off the table and they weren't the most sociable of people, preferring more intellectual pursuits to romance. After a few seconds of silence Derek shrugged. 'I think I saw some people playing with military figurines near the door.'

Mussorgsky chuckled. 'Those would be our amateur tacticians, they like to recreate famous battles and discuss how the generals got things wrong, while showing how they would do things better if only they had the chance.'

Monty laughed. 'That sounds like a discussion I could enjoy.'

'Me too,' said Chastity. 'Mind if I join you?'

Monty smiled. 'Of course not!'

The four stood and wandered off to the other end of the room.

The captain looked back and forth between Kitty and Gwen, the last two pilots left, and nodded as if they had answered an unspoken question. 'Perhaps you would like me to leave you alone?'

Gwen raised an eyebrow at his perceptiveness, but after a quick glance at Kitty she shook her head. 'Actually, I wondered if I could ask you a question.'

'My name, correct?'

'How did you know?'

He shrugged. 'It is the first thing that everyone asks, and yes, I am the great-grandson of Modest Petrovich Mussorgsky.'

'Did you know him?'

The captain laughed. 'No! He died thirty years before I was born!'

Gwen chuckled wryly. 'Sorry, I know the music, but not much about the man.'

'That is fine. To tell the truth, neither do I!'

The three of them laughed and the captain turned to Kitty, about to ask her something, but, before he could, a woman arrived at their table and he immediately fell silent, giving her a nod.

The woman was in a grey Air Service officer's uniform, but she was wearing a similarly coloured greatcoat over the top which hid the rank boards on her shoulders. However, by Mussorgsky's respectful gesture the two Misfits could tell that she was a very high rank, one which required deference despite the captain's assertion that everyone was equal in the hall.

She was a rather plain woman, in her late thirties or early forties, but there was an air about her of quiet confidence that spoke of giving orders and having them obeyed without question.

She smiled at the captain then spoke in excellent English as she offered her hand to the two Misfits in turn. 'Good evening, Captain, ladies. My name is Ana, how do you do?'

'Gwen.'

'Kitty.'

After the pilots had shaken her hand, the woman she sat down opposite them, squeezing in next to a suddenly very nervous-looking Mussorgsky. She nodded in the direction of Scarlet, who was in the centre of one of the noisier groups in the hall. 'Your friend there told me that you had flown against one of our Polikasparov fighters.'

'If they are what the "Wolfpack" squadron fly, then yes,' said Gwen.

'They are. And what did you think?'

Gwen thought carefully before replying, not wanting to offend. 'They're not bad at all. They're very agile and should do well against most Prussian aircraft, but the MU9's and HH190's will pose a real problem for them.'

Gwen was surprised when the woman considered her words seriously instead of just dismissing them out of hand and insisting on the invincibility of Russian aircraft.

'And what would you do to improve them?'

'Well, for a start they would perform much better if they weren't so covered in unnecessary decoration that spoils the airflow around them.'

The woman, Ana laughed. 'True, true, but you try telling a Muscovite that he cannot express his individuality! What else?'

Gwen thought back to what she had seen of the fighter and how it had handled, picturing its design in her mind, seeing its thick wings with the four machine guns on each side, the wide fuselage. There was no point telling the woman that the design itself needed changing, though; the Muscovite war machine couldn't afford to change existing machines, instead it had to use what it had the most effectively. 'The faster Prussian fighters are going to want to use their superior speed to make passes at them rather than getting into a turn fight and the only thing your pilots can do is to try to use their manoeuvrability to always present their front to them. To capitalise on that you should equip them with heavy cannon instead of their eight machine guns and put more armour on them - you need to make the Prussians fear going head to head with them.'

The woman nodded. 'Interesting idea and that would also help them to destroy the bombers when they come.' She stood up. 'I will see what I can do. Thank you and happy hunting.' She gave them all a nod and a smile, which the Misfits returned, then patted Captain Mussorgsky on the shoulder, said something in Russian to him, then walked away to disappear into the crowd.

Kitty frowned at Gwen. 'What was that about? Who was she?'

Gwen jerked her chin at the captain, whose hand was shaking as he poured himself a vodka then downed it in one go. 'No idea, but I'm sure he knows.'

'I'm not sure if he's up to telling us; the poor guy looks like he's seen a ghost.'

'Or run out of vodka.'

Kitty laughed with Gwen and the two women smiled at Mussorgsky, waiting for him to recover, but the man just continued to stare into his empty glass.

'Captain?' Gwen called out softly after several long seconds.

Mussorgsky came out of his trance and blinked at them, his eyes wide. 'What? Sorry?'

Gwen raised an eyebrow at the haunted look on his face. 'Who was that? Your wife? You look like she told you not to stay out too late or you'll be sleeping on the sofa.'

Kitty joined in the teasing of the poor captain. 'Or warned you against getting too close to us.'

He shook his head. 'No, I'm not married. That was Grand Duchess Anastasia.'

Gwen's jaw dropped. 'Oh, wow. You really weren't kidding about the rank thing...'

Mussorgsky shook his head mutely.

'So, what did she say to you before she left?'

'I shouldn't...'

'Oh, come on, it's just us. We won't tell anyone else.' The two women smiled, trying to put him back at ease and leaned forward over the table so that he didn't have to raise his voice as much.

The captain took a deep breath then looked them in the eyes. 'She said that if anything happened to any of you tonight then I would be executed in the morning.'

Kitty craned her head to peer into the crowd, trying to spot the Grand Duchess. 'Wow, and she seemed so nice...'

'To us, maybe.' Gwen huffed then looked back at Mussorgsky. 'She wouldn't really do that, would she?'

The captain refused to meet her eyes and poured himself more vodka.

Gwen saw that the man was extremely uncomfortable with the subject, but found the perfect excuse to change it when something the woman had said came back to her. 'Polikasparov. She said that they were Polikasparov fighters. Isn't that the staff-captain's name?'

The captain smiled weakly, grateful for her thoughtfulness. 'The second in command of the Wolfpack is the son of the designer and manufacturer of the aircraft.'

Gwen rolled her eyes and laughed, trying to return the mood to what it had been before Anastasia's visit. 'Is there anybody in this country who isn't related to someone famous?'

Mussorgsky nodded. 'I'm sure there are a few people, yes. I just don't know any'

Despite being sure that Anastasia wouldn't carry out her threat, even if something happened to one of the Misfits, the mood had been spoiled and not even the sight of Scarlet joining in with some traditional singing and dancing then regaling the hall with a rather bawdy Irish folk song could restore them to the carefree attitude of before. In the end Gwen and Kitty decided to call it a night and go off to get some sleep after an hour of food and conversation with the captain. Mussorgsky had to stay to keep an eye on the rest of the squadron, and while he went to find a soldier to escort them to their assigned quarters, the two Misfits wandered over to the bar where Bruce and Mac were still drinking with the women, both junior army officers, who the captain had pointed out.

Bruce introduced his partner as Natasha, a good looking dark-haired woman in her early twenties and Mac introduced his as Katerina, who was slightly older than her friend, but stunningly beautiful, with blonde hair that was a shade lighter than Kitty's and almost as fair as Polikasparov's. The women nodded politely to Gwen and Kitty, but it was clear that Gwen and Kitty were interrupting something and they were relieved when Mussorgsky came back with a young army officer in tow to take them to their billets. They said goodnight to Mac and Bruce, who barely heard them, then went to tell the others that they were leaving. Chastity decided to accompany them, but Charles, Monty and Derek were caught up in recreating the Battle of Waterloo, so it was just the three of them who followed the soldier out into the night.

Their new coats were surprisingly effective against the chill air and it was only a short distance, less than half a mile, so they elected to walk instead of going by autocar so that they could better appreciate the city, which was even more beautiful by night than it had been during the day.

The air was crisp and very clean, with none of the particulates or pollutants from steam engines in the air that plagued most other major cities, mainly because there were virtually no such engines in regular use in Muscovy. In the past, Russia had always been a big proponent of clockwork, using it for everything that they could and only consenting to use steam when they absolutely had to. They had never been satisfied, though, and had always sought an alternative to the dirty and inefficient technology.

Early attempts to harness electricity as an effective replacement failed, but then, in 1881, Fyodor Blinov, one of the scientists who had been instrumental in the invention and introduction of farming machinery throughout the country, had come up with a spring powerful enough for a small vehicle - the precursor of the ones that were now in universal use in things like the Misfit's fighter aircraft. His idea was developed and expanded and in the space of only a few years, steam power had become almost extinct, the only remnants being the long-distance trains like the one they had come to the city in and the larger vehicles used by the army and for transporting heavy goods. So, the few autocars that passed them on the streets were naturally all spring-powered and silent, as were the clockwork trams that went by, hissing along shining brass tracks inlaid into the streets, providing public transport for free to the populace. The trams were strangely-proportioned iron and glass boxes, which were tall and double-decked, but thin and quite short and looked like a stiff breeze would topple them easily. They were painted in gay colours and with gold leaf on their sides proclaiming their destination and moved along on rubber wheels with metal strips attached that slotted into the tracks in the streets. The pilots followed a couple with their eyes as they went past, curious to the mechanisms that ran them and the officer offered to flag one of them down for them. The pilots were tempted, wanting a closer look, but in the end they refused, just like they had the autocars and instead continued their leisurely stroll through the almost deserted streets.

The Prussian bombardments that had plunged nighttime London into darkness hadn't reached St. Petersburg yet and all of the major buildings they could see were brightly illuminated by electrical arc lamps, giving them a pale white glow and making them seem to float above the ground.

Immediately outside the dining hall was St. Isaac's Cathedral and they wandered arm in arm around it, taking in its huge golden dome, shining to rival the sun in the artificial light. The rest of the white stone building was liberally embellished and highlighted with an abundance of gold leaf, but they were surprised to see that there wasn't a single cogwheel in sight and, when questioned, the soldier explained that the only symbols allowed on churches in Muscovy were ones that pertained to religion.

Past the cathedral was a wide boulevard that ran alongside a park with twinkling lights in its trees, which fronted the large building that was the Navy Headquarters. This building, despite being military in nature, was also brightly illuminated and, unlike the cathedral, its designers had felt no compunction against plastering it with symbols of a less esoteric nature and gold sextants warred with bronze compasses, which fought with brass telescopes that contested silver anchors for space on its walls. All surrounded by the ubiquitous cogs.

A few minutes later, they passed into the marble-paved square in front of the Winter Palace, where they had met the Tsar. They weren't staying there, though, and they left its brightly-lit, but remarkably unadorned, green and white façade behind as they turned right into the smaller streets that surrounded it.

Their quarters were only a few streets away in a building that overlooked one of the smaller rivers running through the city. A couple of guards had been posted on the street door and there were several others inside, playing chess just inside the entrance.

The Misfits had been allocated the top floor in its entirety and a clanking clockwork lift took the three pilots and the soldier up to where another guard was waiting in front of a large wooden door. He opened it for them and saluted as they went past.

Their guide followed them inside. 'Your bags in bedrooms. Captain Mussorgsky come get you at seven and a half for go to train.'

The women smiled, thanking him for the escort and he grinned, saluted them and left.

As soon as the man had gone, Gwen deflated, or at least tried to in the painfully tight corset. 'I don't know about you gals, but I need to get out of this damn uniform.'

Kitty laughed. 'You still haven't gotten used to it?'

'Not one bit and I don't think I ever will. I think, instead of asking the King to let us wear these, admittedly rather fabulous, fur coats we should get him to let us wear our flightsuits as dress uniforms.'

Chastity wrinkled her nose. 'You mean go out in *public* wearing form-fitting leather? Don't you think that would be rather indecent? Besides I rather like these uniforms and we don't get nearly enough chances to wear them in my opinion.' She turned to admire herself in one of the several floor-length mirrors next to the exterior door, fluffing up her skirts and the white petticoats beneath them until the outer ones stuck out almost horizontally.

Gwen gave herself a brief glance and couldn't help but cringe; apart from the coat, which was truly spectacular and she hoped would be added to the Misfits' uniform, she wouldn't normally have been caught dead in anything like the getup which comprised the RAC's dress uniform, no matter how fashionable; the corset didn't look bad and gave her a nice figure, which she didn't actually have, but the skirts and the voluminous and far too numerous matching petticoats underneath gave her the aspect of some kind of cake decoration.

Kitty came and stood beside Gwen. Her eyes travelled up and down Gwen's body appreciatively, lingering momentarily on her bosom. 'You look lovely, Gwen, but I do have to admit I like you better in a flightsuit as well.' She grabbed Gwen's hand and made a show of trying to pull her away. 'Now come on, let's get you out of these clothes!'

Gwen laughed as Kitty started playfully tugging at her clothing, batting at her hands but not making too much of an effort to stop her, but then blushed and froze when she caught Chastity staring at them - it seemed that the new Misfit pilot either hadn't quite realised where the American's interests lay or was even more innocent than she looked. She cleared her throat and waved vaguely in the direction of the bedrooms. 'Why don't we go and see where our stuff is.'

After having a quick bath and getting changed for bed, the three women went and sat in the small sitting room that was just beyond the reception room to wait for the others.

Abby, Owen and Wendy arrived an hour or so later, shortly after eleven, all three looking exhausted and not a little bit green after having sat through such a long dinner, but it was well past midnight when the rest of the Misfits showed up, Derek and Monty all but carrying an almost comatose Bruce between them.

'What the hell happened to him?' Abby laughed, but then frowned when she saw that they were missing a Misfit. 'Where's Mac? Wasn't he with you?'

Charles grinned and spoke up in his soft voice. 'Mac has apparently fallen in love. He's gone for a midnight walk along the river with Katerina. He's not nearly as drunk as this daft bugger,' he patted Bruce fondly on the head, 'and he promised he'd be waiting for us at the Palace before eight tomorrow.'

Abby sighed. 'I certainly bloody hope so otherwise there'll be hell to pay.'

Gwen shared a glance with Kitty and by the American's wide-eyed expression saw that the same thing had occurred to her and that they had to hope that if Mac did indeed miss the train, it wouldn't be enough to bring down the Grand Duchesses ire on Captain Mussorgsky.

To the relief of everybody, Mac was waiting for them when Captain Mussorgsky delivered them to the palace the next morning at eight. Bleary eyed and hungover and still in his dress uniform, now quite dishevelled, he nonetheless had a huge smile on his face.

'Good night, Mac?' asked Abby with a raised eyebrow.

'Best ever. Thanks for not sending the Ruskies out looking for me, Abby.'

'You haven't betrayed my trust yet, Mac,' she looked around the group. 'None of you have. And that means you all get the benefit of the doubt.' She smiled sweetly at them. 'But I will be *very* disappointed if you ever do.'

Campbell, along with Featherstonehaugh and Mr Jones were also on the platform waiting for them, the sky commodore looking almost as bad as Mac. She didn't smile when she approached Abby, though. 'Safe journey back, Abby.'

'Thank you. You're not coming with us?'

Campbell shook her head then grimaced and put a hand to her temple. 'I wish, but I've got too much to do here; Sir Robert Swollocks, the Ambassador was supposed to have been taking care of negotiations for the alliance between Britain and Muscovy, but he's gone missing, so I'm stuck doing it.'

Abby frowned. 'Gone missing? What does that mean?'

'Just that - that nobody knows where the hell he is. Nobody's seen hide nor hair of him for a few days.'

'How is that even possible?'

Campbell shrugged. 'No idea. What it does mean, though, is that I can't go to Vaenga to take command, so you're going to have to do it. You're going to have to run the whole show up north until I can get away, which, by the way it looks now, might not be until it's all over. The people in Archangel and Murmansk are going to include you in their planning sessions, so I'm afraid you're going to be very busy the next few weeks and not just flying. However, and I know it's scant compensation, but I have spoken to Whitehall and managed to arrange for you to have a field promotion to group captain, so at least you'll be the same rank as any of the Muscovite pilots and won't have any problems there.'

Abby opened and closed her mouth like a fish, for once not quite knowing what to say, either about her sudden promotion, or the responsibilities that had been unexpectedly thrust upon her.

Campbell laughed and stepped forward into the silence to give her friend a hug. 'You take care of yourself, Abby, alright? And take care of our boys and girls. Get them all home safely.'

Dot gave Abby a last squeeze then stepped back and looked around the squadron. 'I have to get upstairs; today we're discussing canned vegetables. It promises to be very exciting.'

The pilots laughed sympathetically, not wishing for one moment to be in her shoes.

Campbell drew herself up and fixed her eyes on Abby. 'Happy hunting, *Group Captain*.'

Abby stood to attention and saluted smartly. 'Thank you, ma'am.'

After they had said goodbye to Captain Mussorgsky and thanked him for taking care of them, the Misfits climbed onto the train.

Freddy Featherstonehaugh and Mr Jones weren't going with them, they were staying in St. Petersburg for a few days to cover the negotiations and Chastity again tried Abby's patience by saying a prolonged farewell to the journalist. Finally, though, blushing furiously, she joined the rest of the squadron and they waved to Campbell through the lounge windows as the train pulled out of the station. However, as soon as they had been swallowed by the tunnel that would take it out of the city to the north, they surrounded their commander and bombarded her with congratulations.

Abby wasn't very happy, though. 'Thank you, everyone.'

'What's wrong?' Owen asked. 'You've finally gotten that scrambled egg for your hat you've always wanted!'

Instead of smiling happily like the rest of her pilots, Abby just sighed. 'That's nice, yes, but I can't help feeling that it's just a consolation prize.'

CHAPTER 16

A waiter informed the Misfits that breakfast was ready for them and they eagerly made their way to the dining car, but Mac said he wasn't hungry and headed straight to bed, telling everyone in no uncertain terms that he wasn't to be woken until they arrived at Vaenga.

The pilots had a slap-up English breakfast, which had been specially prepared for them from fresh supplies obtained from the palace, and then, when they were all stuffed, they trouped up to the glass observation deck to talk, feel the sun on their faces and gaze out at the scenery in comfort while their food went down.

St. Petersburg had disappeared behind them by that time and the sun was well and truly up, although it was still low to the horizon because of how far north they were. The weather had been fine, as the Indian summer that they had been experiencing in England seemed to have followed them, but there had been a bite to the air as they had walked to the palace that morning which presaged the winter to come and made them wrap their new coats more firmly around themselves.

The morning passed very pleasantly, with tea and hot chocolate whenever they wanted it and elevenses actually served at eleven with an assortment of pastries and a very nice traditional Russian layered honey cake which Gwen remembered having eaten quite a lot of when she'd been in St. Petersburg with her parents. But then, at twelve, just as some of the pilots were considering going to the sleeping car to join Mac in a nap, a shadow flickered across the train.

Every single one of the Misfits immediately squinted up into the cloudless sky, wondering what had passed over, expecting it to be a

Muscovite aircraft, on patrol. They had been shown a map of the route the train was taking on the way to St. Petersburg and the Finnish border was only thirty or forty miles from the tracks at some points of the journey, so it was entirely possible that Muscovite squadrons were posted nearby, safely out of bombardment range but within scouting distance.

'There!' Kitty had the sharpest eyes of the lot of them and it was she who managed to first pick the black speck out of the blinding glare of the low sun. The other pilots followed her arm and encountered it with ease.

Gwen frowned. 'That's...'

'Down! Everybody down!'

Abby's shout had the pilots diving for cover behind the sofas just in time as the HH190 opened fire and the train rocked from the impact of its guns.

The Prussian fighter streaked past with a roar, only yards over the top of the train and climbed back into the sky.

'It's coming around for another run!'

Charles' panicked cry had them scrambling around the opposite side of the sofas to put them in the way again, but Gwen knew that they would be scant protection against the twin cannon that the fighter had mounted under its nose and she called at Abby. 'We have to get downstairs and find some proper cover, maybe get off the train and into the woods; we're sitting ducks here.'

Abby nodded. 'I know, but it's too late now. After this pass.'

'Here it comes.'

Derek's voice was calm and Gwen lifted her head to stare; he was standing with his hands on his hips looking up at the fighter with interest, having come to the same conclusion she had, that the sofas wouldn't protect them from the guns. However, she knew that the bullets weren't the only threat - if the fighter hit the observation deck it wouldn't just be a direct hit that the people sheltering inside would have to contend with, but razor sharp glass shards as well. She opened her mouth to tell him exactly that, prepared to physically tackle him and get him behind a piece of furniture if he didn't heed her words, but his gleeful laugh and exultant cry stopped her in her tracks.

'Go on! Get the bastard!'

Gwen peered over the top of the sofa and looked up at the Prussian fighter. There were two other aircraft honing in on it and as she watched it broke off its run and turned sharply, diving away, heading back towards friendlier skies, pursued by the Muscovites, but it was obvious straight away that they were never going to catch it; it was much faster than they were.

The aircraft disappeared behind the trees and the Misfits slowly got to their feet and looked around.

'Is everybody alright?' Abby looked around, searching for injuries.

Bruce had a small trickle of blood coming from below his hairline and he shrugged when everyone looked at him. 'Bloody teapot fell on my head. Hurts like hell. Just as well it wasn't full.'

It was Monty who started laughing first, but it only took a few seconds for everyone else to join in and soon tears were pouring down their cheeks.

They weren't just laughing at the stupidity of the injury Bruce had suffered, though, they were laughing in relief at their close call.

When everybody had calmed down a bit, Abby craned her head to see through the windows. 'Can anyone see where we got hit? The locomotive has to be alright otherwise we would have stopped.'

Owen pointed forwards. 'It looks like the sleeping car took the brunt of things...' He trailed off and his face went white.

The same thought occurred to everybody at the same time and they rushed together for the winding staircase, knocking aside the soldier who had been sent to find out if they were safe.

They rushed through the lounge car and into the dining car, past several waiters who were picking up broken plates and glasses that had been smashed to smithereens by a few stray machine gun rounds, and kept going towards the door at the front of the carriage. Abby led the charge through it and into the sleeping car where she came to a halt with a shocked gasp.

The curtains were closed over the windows and the bunk-lined room would have been dark if it weren't for the hundreds of holes letting in the sunlight from outside. They were mostly small, coin sized ones from the HH190's four wing-mounted machine guns, but there were at least half a dozen far larger ones, dinner plate sized, from its cannon. Correspondingly huge holes in the floor showed where the heavy rounds had gone straight through the carriage and they could clearly see the sleepers of the track through them, passing in a blur as the train kept going, fleeing the scene of the crime.

'Mac!'

There was a snort at Bruce's desperate shout and the Scotsman bleary-eyed face appeared in one of the larger streams of light coming through a gaping hole, not three inches from his head. 'Wha... What is it? Are we there?'

'No, but...'

'Then leave me alone, damn ye and stop making so much bloody noise!' He growled and rolled over, pulling the blankets up over his head. They flapped in the wind coming through the gaping hole. 'All that thumping around, it's a wonder I can sleep at all... And someone close the damn window, it's chuffin' freezin' in here!'

The Misfits could do nothing except stare at him as the sound of snoring filled the carriage once more.

To everyone's astonishment, Mac slept through the hasty repairs that were carried out on the sleeping car to cover up the worst of the holes on the floor and walls and it was only when the dinner bell went and the Misfits came in to change that he actually woke up. He sat up in bed, rubbing his eyes and gazing around in amazement. 'What the hell happened here?'

Bruce paused in doing his shirt up to look at him. 'Woodworm.'

Just after dawn the next morning, a waiter came to wake them up and informed them that they would arrive at the siding near Vaenga where they had caught the train from in a little over half an hour. They were puzzled, therefore, when only a few minutes later it screeched to a halt, almost throwing them from their feet as they dressed.

'Gwen,' Abby said, 'you're decent, go and see what's going on.'

'I don't think I need to; listen.' Gwen could feel the deck quivering under their feet, in spite of the train being stopped, and that, added to the faint rumbling, which was more a vibration in her chest cavity than an actual sound, could mean only one thing.

The pilots quickly finished dressing then climbed up to the observation deck.

Miles away, in the direction they were travelling, smoke was rising into the clear morning air, staining the bright blue with blacks and greys.

'Is that coming from Murmansk, do you think?' asked Scarlet.

Abby shook her head. 'I don't know, I just hope it isn't our airfield.'

A waiter came up the stairs and they looked at him. He managed to remain impassive in the face of their unasked questions, which wasn't surprising seeing as he had most likely waited on the Muscovite Royal Family many times.

'There is an air raid over Murmansk. We are waiting for it to finish before moving on. In the meantime, breakfast is served.' He bowed, then turned and went back down the stairs.

The Misfits were far more interested in the enemies in the sky than the food, though, and they stared out of the windows, every single one of them wishing that they were up, having a crack at the bombers attacking the city they'd been tasked with defending.

In the end, Abby sighed and turned away. 'Well, there's nothing we can do about this raid stuck here, but I'm sure there'll be more. We might as well go and eat.'

The wagon ferrying the Misfits from the train arrived at the airfield just in time for them to see the Harridans land.

Three of the Harridans had RAC markings and were in the factory camouflage, but none of the twelve with red and white Muscovite roundels had been left alone and "boring" as the Wolfpack leader had put it. Most only had a few splashes of colour to make them stand out, but somehow they had found time to completely repaint two of them - Baryshnikov's with a yellow top and a black belly and Polikasparov's with a distinctive combination of large bright pink and dark purple checks, apparently choosing to emulate the colours of the Misfits somewhat. However, surprisingly, there was no sign of any unnecessary pipes or cogs having been added to the aircraft.

The Wolfpack pilots demonstrated a widely varying proficiency with their new machines, from Baryshnikov and Polikasparov, who did perfect three point landings, to the couple who landed so heavily they bounced almost twenty feet back in the air. The Harridan was very forgiving, though and none of them quite managed to do any damage, no matter how hard they seemed to try.

Abby had left Sergeant Potter in command of both the British and Muscovite fitters while she'd been away and he met the wagon as it arrived.

'Good work putting the Harridans together, Sergeant.'

'Thank you, ma'am.'

'How did you stop them from putting their awful decorations all over them, though?'

'I didn't, ma'am. They had this bloody great box full of pipes and cogs and allsorts ready to stick on them and I was working myself up to try to stop them, but then a message came through early yesterday and it was like they all went into mourning. They packed away the decorations and went into a sulk. I'd give anything to know what was in that message so I can use it the next time they try to do something stupid with my machines.'

'Well, I think Gwen can fill you in on that, but you have to remember that they're not your machines anymore, Sergeant; they have been bought and paid for by the Tsar.'

Potter grumbled. 'They're mine until I'm satisfied their fitters can take care of them.'

Abby laughed. 'Very well, but you'd better certify them soon because you're going to be more than busy taking care of our aircraft.'

Potter nodded. 'Right you are, ma'am.'

Further conversation was rendered impossible by the arrival of the taxiing aircraft and Sergeant Potter hurried off to do his job.

Almost before her aircraft had come to a halt, though, Pemberton, jumped out and stomped over to Abby, her face like thunder.

'These damned Russians! They won't bloody do as they're told!'

Abby raised an eyebrow. 'What has happened?'

'This was their first flight as a complete squadron so I gave them orders not to engage the enemy; we can't have them charging in on the Prussians until they know how to use their aircraft properly. It would just be a waste of machines and pilots.'

'Of course not. And I take it they disobeyed those orders?'

'Too bloody right!' Pemberton spluttered, her face going through several interesting shades of red until it reached purple as she watched the Russian pilots come together outside of the mess hall and begin jumping around in celebration, doing some kind of extremely athletic dancing involving lots of shouting and clapping. 'There was some chat in Russian between Baryshnikov and some fool on the ground and they just abandoned the exercises and headed straight for the raid, without even a by your leave!'

'Did they have any success?'

'Well... yes.' Pemberton grumbled reluctantly. 'They bagged five or six and the three of us got another four... but that's not the point! They disobeyed orders and gave away that we're here on the first bloody raid over! I want the blighters court-martialled!'

Drake and Aviator Lieutenant Howard had come with Pemberton and had been watching her rant with expressions that could only be described as "amused", but at the Squadron Leader's insistence on punishment they both frowned.

Abby looked at them. 'What's your impression of them?'

The two exchanged a glance, then looked at their commander, obviously reluctant to contradict her.

'Speak freely.'

'They're damn good pilots.' Howard said.

'Just as good as any of our chaps.' Drake nodded agreement, then grinned cheekily. 'Although, they're not up to Misfit standards, obviously.'

Abby chuckled. 'Sucking up will get you nowhere with me, Lord Drake... But you're right of course.'

While the Misfits laughed, Abby turned to Pemberton. 'I think it's safe to say that the Prussians know that the Muscovites have Harridans now, correct?'

'Thanks to the damn Wolfpack, yes.'

'Then we need as many aircraft in the air as possible and it would counter-productive for us to ground them, wouldn't it?'

Pemberton stared long and hard at Abby, but she had enough sense not to try to continue the argument and eventually she just nodded, then stomped away to the ready room to get changed.

Abby watched her go, shaking her head, then turned to address the other instructors. 'My people know that I don't condone disobeying orders in the air - it's the one thing that will get them kicked out of the squadron, but I can see we're going to have to give the Muscovites a little leeway. I fully expect them to do their own thing most of the time and chase after kills whenever the opportunity presents itself.'

'As long as it doesn't get any of us killed.'

Abby nodded at Owen. 'Indeed.' She looked around the group of British pilots. 'We have to look after ourselves here, because our allies aren't going to. Let's do our job as best as we can, shoot down a few Prussians, and then make sure we all get home safely.'

Ah, that explains everything, thought Gruber as he read his spy's report of Misfit Squadron's activities in St. Petersburg. It explained the missing Norwegian scout aircraft in the Arctic Circle and it explained the report from the day before of colourful aircraft in the skies over Murmansk - the Misfits had taken the northern passage into Russia and were lending themselves to the resistance there. It seemed that the murder of their ambassador had come too late to delay the British in their relief efforts.

He pulled a fresh sheet of paper towards him and wrote out a formal request for the Barons to be sent back north to deal with them. Even though they had only just arrived in the Ukraine and were supposed to be helping with the push into southern Russia, he doubted there would be much resistance to his request on the part of high command, especially once they started losing aircraft to the Misfits. They would have to leave Bertha behind again, of course; it was too cold for her, but that was no real hardship and they would make do, just as they had in Norway.

He signed the paper with a flourish and grinned, happy at the prospect of facing Misfit Squadron again, far earlier than he had expected.

Life was about to become interesting again.

PART 3

RESIST

CHAPTER 17

The Muscovites had no radar system in the north, but the Misfits had the one in Owen's Bloodhound as well as Charles' Vulture to scout for them visually and over the next two days the two men took it in turns to keep an eye out for incoming raids. It wasn't a perfect system and it meant the two men were in the air for hours on end, but it worked.

During those two days, the bombers came in small raids without a fighter escort, apparently confident that they would meet little resistance and, wanting to keep the presence of the Misfits secret a little while longer, Abby ordered the Wolfpack intercept them on their own.

The Muscovite squadron did better than anyone had expected, even themselves, revelling in their new aircraft and getting nine kills over three engagements. They had two pilots shot down in return, but both bailed out and made it home and there were plenty of replacement Harridans to get them back into the air with.

However, on the morning of the third day, Charles spotted a much larger raid of almost thirty incoming bombers at twenty thousand feet, this time with a fighter escort, so Abby decided it was time the Misfits got into the fight.

The Misfits scrambled with the Wolfpack, but while the Muscovites flew directly at the bombers, the British climbed up to thirty thousand feet, out of sight in the sun. Then, once the Wolfpack had engaged (with howls over the radio that had half the Misfits laughing and the other half cringing in shame that they had to fight with such people) and had gotten their complete attention, the Misfits dived on the enemy formation.

The Prussians were taken completely by surprise and lost half a dozen aircraft in the initial pass and another eight in the subsequent fighting before turning for home in a panic.

It seemed that the Wolfpack needed less excuse to throw a party than the Misfits did and that evening they insisted on celebrating the first success of the two squadrons together. There didn't seem to be much difference between a normal evening meal and a party, though; there was perhaps a bit more singing and certainly more dancing, but the food was the same and there were the same prodigious quantities of vodka imbibed by the Muscovites.

Scarlet showed off the things that she had learnt in the hall in St. Petersburg, joining in some of the songs and dances and swearing with the best of the Muscovites, astounding and delighting them in equal measures, but the rest of the Misfits were far more subdued, knowing that they were only at the start of the campaign and the Prussians were only getting started.

They left the party at ten to go to their barracks building and sat on their beds to analyse the day's fight before sleep. It was something that Abby had liked to do in France, shortly after the squadron had formed when they were still getting used to their tactics and machines, but it hadn't been necessary in Britain with the squadron firmly established. However, with all the changes they'd made before travelling to Muscovy, she felt that it had become necessary again.

Abby started things off. 'Well, I'm loving the extra speed and acceleration I'm getting out of the new springs and the change in tactics is good against the bombers, but the MU9's are a damn sight easier to deal with as well. Not to mention that Wendy's cannon are pretty effective against everything the Prussians put up against us. Any thoughts, Gwen?'

'I'd dearly love the chance to tweak my airscrew a bit and the profile of Wasp's wings needs changing slightly to take full advantage of the extra power, but I agree that the new springs are really making a difference.'

Abby nodded, then looked at the next Misfits in the squadron order. 'Bruce, Monty, how were Sable and Raptor?'

The two men looked at each other briefly, then Monty nodded and Bruce turned to Abby to answer for them both. 'They're brilliant machines, Boss, but we're still not using them a hundred percent because we keep trying to slip back into our old tactics. We'll get the hang of them soon enough and then we'll show the Fleas what for!'

There were murmurs of agreement from the Misfits, who were all very eager to make up for several weeks of activity by taking the fight to the Prussians and Abby gave him a nod of thanks, before grinning at the new leader of B flight. 'Derek? Had any backchat from your flight yet?'

Derek chuckled. 'Not yet, but I know it's coming.'

'Too right it is, chum!'

There were laughs at Mac's comment but everyone quieted again quickly, knowing how important it was for the squadron as a whole to sort potential problems out while they were on the ground, not in the air.

'Kitty? Anything?'

The American shook her head at Abby's question. 'Nothing. All good.'

Abby nodded. 'Mac. How's your wingmate doing?'

Mac smiled at Chastity before answering. 'Fine and dandy. She's an excellent pilot, an excellent wingman and an excellent shot.'

'Good. Give her a few more sorties to get settled in, then let her take the lead a couple of times, please.'

'Right you are, Group Captain Lennox, ma'am!' Mac flashed her a grin and a sloppy salute, causing more laughter.

'Yes, thank you, Mac.' Abby looked at the last member of B flight. 'Chastity, how are you doing?'

The woman smiled. 'Good, thank you, ma'am.'

Abby waited for a second to see if she would add more, but when she didn't she nodded. 'Right then. Well, if C flight doesn't have anything to add...?'

Abby's tone of voice told them that she wasn't expecting there to be anything, but Wendy immediately spoke up. 'When am I going to get a crack at the Fleas, Abby? I'm itching to try out my new toys and you owe me a bit of excitement after that bloody state dinner.'

Abby had grounded Dreadnought, maintaining that there would be far better ways to use the big aircraft further down the line than just intercepting raids. Wendy hadn't been twiddling her thumbs in the meantime; Kitty, the squadron's expert on all things electrical, had helped her iron out all the kinks in the systems needed for her rockets, like remote ignition and release, and she had been busy fitting racks for them to the underside of her aircraft. That didn't mean she had enjoyed watching everyone else going off to fight that morning without her, though.

Abby laughed, not unkindly. 'I'm sure you'll get your chance; the Prussians will undoubtedly be moving troops up to try to cross the border into Muscovy and we'll undoubtedly take part in the attacks on them.'

'I hope they come soon.' The big woman grumbled.

'Patience, Wendy. And the same goes for you Scarlet; take the opportunity to get as much rest as you can because you'll probably have a lot of sleepless nights scouting around in Finland.'

The Irishwoman nodded. 'I'll be ready; I'm already studying maps of the ground over there.'

'Good.' Abby gazed around the group, meeting their eyes one by one, assessing their mood. They were confident, cheerful and very eager, just as they had been before France. She just hoped that the outcome wasn't the same. 'Right, let's get to bed, then; you know how the Prussians like their early starts and we need to be rested if we don't want to be shown up by the Russkies!'

Monty and Bruce simultaneously blew raspberries at that notion, then laughed and pointed at each other.

The meeting broke up and the pilots wandered around getting ready for bed. They had been assigned a single barracks block with just one bedroom and bathroom for both sexes, not just because it was the only one available, but because that was what the Muscovites were used to - they made no distinction between their soldiers and saw no need to provide much in the way of special arrangements for them. Abby had worked out a system which gave them some measure of privacy, though and the men went off to use the bathroom while the women undressed, before swapping over.

The men and women of the squadron had been separated for the sake of decency before, but the Misfits hadn't really *needed* such considerations and whenever it had been necessary they had been set aside; the group had always been very close and it wasn't as if their flight suits left much to the imagination. However, with a new member, adjustments had to be made, at least to start with.

It still remained to be seen whether Chastity would adapt to the squadron as well as Gwen had, though; being "excellent" in the air wasn't the only quality needed to make someone a Misfit.

Another Prussian raid was spotted building up just after dawn the next day and again the Misfits scrambled with the Wolfpack. This time they didn't get to engage, though, as the bombers dropped their payloads on the Muscovite forces on the border, almost a hundred miles away, rather than striking Murmansk as they had the previous days, then immediately turned back and raced for safety.

In the afternoon, Abby was called to a meeting with the local commanders and she was taken to Murmansk as a passenger in the sidecar of a swift, spring-powered motorcycle.

The city had been struck by several raids, but the small numbers of bombers hadn't done much damage and Abby was shocked by how the people seemed to be continuing with their everyday lives; in France, the civilian population had fled at the first sign of the Prussian advance, before the first bombs had fallen, but the Muscovites showed no sign of going anywhere.

It was almost as big a surprise to find that the military commanders hadn't set up their control room in some hidden location in the forest somewhere, but rather in a room that looked like it had once been a wine cellar or something similar, underneath one of the larger municipal buildings in the very centre of the city.

A huge table with a map of the surrounding country took up most of the damp and dark, low-ceilinged room which was so long that the far wall was lost in darkness. The rest of the space was taken up by a row of telephonists sitting behind a row of narrow desks against the side wall, standing by to relay the orders of the dozen or so generals who were gazing down at the table and sipping from glasses of vodka, a glass of which Abby was offered as soon as she came in, but refused.

The map extended from Murmansk in the north as far south as Moscow and from Archangel in the east to the far border of Finland in the west. The forces arrayed against each other were represented by beautifully carved figures of men with outmoded uniforms and muskets, artillery pieces that had gone out of date more than a century ago, and cavalry officers on rearing horses. The ones in Norway, Finland and the Baltic region in the south, representing the enemy forces, were carved from a lovely deep red wood whereas the ones arrayed against them were much lighter, almost golden in colour. She had no way of telling how many men and machines the figurines represented, nor what the Cyrillic written on the standards that each carried meant, but it was clear just by the fact that there were almost twice as many red figures as yellow that the Muscovites were heavily outnumbered.

She searched out Murmansk while she waited for the generals to notice her, wondering what her squadron was facing, and her mouth went dry when she saw exactly what the situation was.

The Muscovites had naturally concentrated most of their forces around the main population and industrial areas that were Moscow and St. Petersburg, leaving only a thin line guarding the border and very limited forces in the north. Either they didn't think that the Prussians would send much against Murmansk or they had an inflated opinion of what the Misfits would be capable of doing. Whatever the case, the Muscovites on the northern border were already outnumbered by the advance forces of cavalry and infantry markers and there were perhaps ten times more Prussians on the way.

'Group Captain Lennox?' Abby looked up to find one of the generals hobbling towards her, leaning heavily on a stick with his right hand. He was an older gentleman, in his seventies or perhaps eighties, thin, but sprightly, with a short white beard and sparse white hair. He came to a halt in front of her and changed his stick to his left side so that he could offer her his hand. 'Welcome to Northern Command. My name is Markian Mikhaylovich Popov and I have the dubious pleasure of being in charge of this fiasco.'

'Pleased to meet you, sir.' Abby nodded to him, then gestured at the table. 'When do you expect reinforcements to arrive?'

The general laughed. 'I don't! There aren't any coming.'

Abby blinked. 'I'm sorry?'

'The Tsar has made it very clear that he expects us to hold the line in the north with what we have.' The old man smiled widely. 'He has great confidence in you and after hearing what you did over the summer I don't think it should be too much trouble for you!'

A knot started to twist itself in Abby's stomach as she glanced at the map, staring in dismay at the advancing red pieces and the all too few yellow ones facing them. If it had been a game of chess she would have been contemplating tipping her king over, but it wasn't, it was all too real. However, if they made a mistake, they could be just as easily swept off the board as if they *were* just wooden pieces.

'In Britain we had the channel, a twenty-mile moat to defend. Here...' She gestured at the open country all around with only the thin line of the river at Murmansk and the even thinner one at the border providing any natural defensive line.

The general nodded his understanding. 'Yes, we are exposed, but we need only hold out until the ground freezes.'

'And how long will that be, exactly?'

'Ah, well, the old men who know about these things say the ice will come late this year.'

'Late? How late?'

'Mid-November at the latest. Perhaps sooner.'

'That leaves almost a month!'

The general smiled. 'Yes it does!'

'But...' Abby gestured wordlessly at horde of red markers that would swamp them when they arrived.

'Oh, they will be at the border long before winter fully sets in.'

Abby stared at him. He seemed cheerful, almost delighted at the prospect of facing such overwhelming odds.

He saw her expression and chuckled. 'Oh, do not think me bloodthirsty or foolish, madam. I know exactly how difficult the task ahead of us is going to be. However, the Prussians have no idea what they are getting into. This is not France or Belgium or even Norway, this is Russia and the people of Russia are not as soft and easily cowed.' He shrugged. 'Well, we're Muscovites right now, I suppose, but that will only last until the war is won.'

'Is that why the civilians haven't been evacuated?'

He nodded. 'They would not go.'

'But they'll be slaughtered!'

'Maybe. Maybe not. But it is their choice to make and would you deny them the chance to defend their homes?'

Abby wanted to say yes and tell him that they should be moving the civilians as far east as they could go, tell him that if they stayed, the red wave approaching wouldn't differentiate between civilian and soldier and would wash them all away, leaving nothing behind. She held her tongue, though; this was after all akin to the spirit that the British people had shown over the summer, just taken to the extreme.

She shook her head. 'No, I wouldn't.' She gestured at the table. 'So, what can we do to make sure that grandmothers do not die trying to kill Prussians with mothballs and handbags?'

The general laughed then turned to the table. 'If we are going to stop the Prussians before they get to us, then obviously we must find a way to strike at them.'

'Obviously.'

'Thanks to you, or rather thanks to your pilot, Charles Isaacs, we have been able to accurately pinpoint not only the enemy advance, but their aerodromes.' He pointed at the four red artillery markers that were a few dozen miles over the border into Finland. 'At the moment they have only four airfields. One is occupied by two fighter squadrons with perhaps sixteen small fighters and a similar number of twin-spring fighters, the other three hold their bombers, maybe one hundred in total.'

He turned to Abby. 'While you have had undoubted success these last few days, we will not win the war in the air by shooting down half a dozen aircraft at a time. That does not stop their advance and they will only send replacements. We need to strike their airfields and destroy *all* of their machines on the ground.'

He pointed at the map. There was a yellow Muscovite artillery piece about fifty miles to the south-east of the one that sat at Vaenga. 'We have two bomber groups there. They are old biplanes, barely able to carry a usable payload, but they are all we have. They would never make it on their own, but with the Misfits and the Wolfpack working together to escort them they have a chance.'

There was a bloodthirsty glint in the old man's eyes as he began to lay out his plan and Abby felt a shiver run through her body. She had met too many command-level officers in France who had that look - they were the ones who were far too eager to send their men to die and didn't care how many of them died.

'Tomorrow you will do as you usually do and fly to intercept the bombers. If they come to attack Murmansk then you will engage them, but if they attack the troops on the border, as they have done this morning, you will break off when they turn for home. When you land you are to rewind with all haste, then be back in the air in time to rendezvous with our own bombers.'

He grinned and again there was that flash in his eyes which transformed his face into something much more predatory. 'We have taught them that they need a fighter escort and now we will take it away from them by attacking their fighter base. Not only is it the closest, only thirty miles the other side of the border, but if we can destroy them, then their bombers will be sitting ducks during subsequent raids. And, once we have air superiority, we can attack their columns at will and delay their advance until winter.'

Abby looked down at the board while she sorted her thoughts and feelings. The general's plan, if you could call it that, was simple and direct and sounded very easy. However, she couldn't help but think that it wouldn't work; the British had been in a very similar situation in France and had tried similar things, but hadn't been able to stop the Prussians. She saw no reason why the outcome would be any different this time.

'I see your doubts, Group Captain Lennox and I recognise their validity.' The old man spoke quietly, seriously. 'If we fail, we will lose, but if we wait for them to come, we lose as well. So, unless you have a better plan, I see no other choice. Better to do our best and lose, than cower here and wait for the sky to fall. That is the Russian way.'

Abby nodded and gave him a wry smile. 'It's the Misfit way as well.'

Wendy, of course, was over the moon about the plan and clapped her hands in delight. 'That sounds like just the kind of mission to see what my babies can really do!'

Abby frowned at her. 'What makes you think you're taking part in the mission?'

Wendy blinked at her in surprise, but then her expression darkened with anger.

Before she could say anything, though, Abby laughed. 'Only joking! Of course you are!'

Wendy growled and smacked her big right fist into her left palm. 'If you weren't my senior officer...'

'Or your friend?'

Wendy stared at her coldly. 'Would a friend have teased me like that?'

'No... I suppose they wouldn't...' Abby's face fell as she looked into the big woman's eyes and saw the hurt behind the anger. 'I'm sorry, Wendy.'

Wendy held the glare for a second more, then laughed and pulled Abby into a bone-crushing hug. She growled as she jerking Abby into the air, drawing a squawk of protest, then threw her words back at her. 'Only joking! Of course you're my friend!'

The Misfits laughed, more in relief that there wasn't going to be a rift in the squadron, than at the joke, but the tension that had been building during the briefing was dissipated somewhat. None of them liked the plan, not because it was dangerous, but because it smelled of desperation and desperation usually got people killed. They had taken part in one such attack only too recently and it had cost a lot of British bomber crews their lives, not to mention that Dreadnought had barely gotten home.

'Right,' Abby said once the big woman had put her down. 'Let's go over the damn plan one more time, then try to get some sleep.'

CHAPTER 18

At first light the next day, the Misfits were milling around outside the mess hall in the cold morning air, drinking tea and munching on thick bread while they waited for the call that the Prussians had been spotted.

The Russians had finally finished painting the rest of their machines and the two squadrons made an extremely colourful display, lined up on the airfield, ready for the go. Unlike the Misfits, not a single one of the Russians had opted for a practical or sober colour, instead each seemed to be trying to outdo the next for garishness with all the colours of the rainbow represented, sometimes all at once. The only Harridans that were still in the factory camouflage were the spares still in their crates and the three being used by the instructors, who weren't accompanying them on the mission. The Misfits quietly and privately agreed that Dreadnought was still the most eye-aching of the lot, though, not only due to its dazzle camouflage, but also because of the sheer amount of paint it was able to display - some of the Russians had indeed tried to emulate its patterning, but because of the smaller size of the Harridans the effect was not nearly as nauseating. Vulture and Bloodhound were already up in the air, but Dreadnought and Hummingbird were on the flight line. Dreadnought had of course been fully loaded with ordnance and would be joining the Russian bombers in the attack, but even Scarlet had a job to do. She would land a few miles behind the border, ready to race in and rescue anyone who had to bail out.

Gwen sat hunched over on the mess hall steps, half-asleep still, sipping at her tea and watching the Wolfpack. The Misfits never took things very seriously, not even missions, and made jokes of just about anything, but they seemed almost dour when compared to the Wolfpack, who were laughing and joking loudly, even wrestling and dancing in some cases. Gwen had no idea where they got the energy and enthusiasm from so early in the morning, especially seeing as most of them were falling down drunk every night, and she wished she could absorb some of it.

Something caught her eye along the row of barracks buildings and she groaned as Rudy Drake came out of the small hut the instructors were using as a barracks and sauntered jauntily towards the mess hall. His lop-sided grin was firmly in place, his eyes were bright and his uniform and hair were absolutely perfect - he was just as annoying a morning person as Kitty.

'Looks like a bloody Labrador,' she muttered to herself. 'All he needs it to stick his tongue out and wag his tail...'

He spotted her and she felt her cheeks warm ever so slightly as his already wide smile widened further and, despite her tiredness and general state of grumpiness, she found herself returning his smile, albeit a lot weaker.

'Morning, Goosy!'

He came to a halt right in front of her forcing her to squint up at him.

'Mornin',' she grunted at him. 'What the hell are you doing up so early? You're not flying today.'

'I know, but I wanted to see you lot off.' He took a few seconds to glance around the group of Misfits, giving those of them who met his gaze a brief nod or wave, before turning back to Gwen. 'I wish I was going with you, but it seems that the generals and illustrious leader have the misguided opinion that the three of us are worth more as live instructors than dead heroes.'

She shook her head. 'No, they just don't want you spoiling the parade with your boring machines.'

Drake turned to look at the Russian aircraft and winced. 'The last thing you could accuse those poor Harridans of being is boring. I much prefer mine as it is.'

'Really? You're not jealous?' Gwen smirked at him. 'You're telling me that you wouldn't paint it if they let you? I can have a word with Abby; there's no reason why the three of you can't paint your aircraft as well and I know the Russians have got plenty of pink paint you could use.'

He laughed. 'It's a tempting offer, but no thank you; it's dangerous enough up there as it is and I prefer not to call too much attention to myself.'

Gwen nodded, feigning understanding. 'Because you're not a very good pilot.'

Drake didn't rise to the bait. Instead he turned deadly serious. 'No. Because I don't want to make myself a bigger target than I already am.'

She frowned at him. 'I can handle myself, Rudy.'

'I know you can and I'm not implying that! It's just...' He sighed and shook his head. 'Look, all I'm trying to say is take care up there, Gwen, and make sure you come back. I couldn't stand it if...'

He broke off and looked up over Gwen's shoulder as Kitty emerged from the shadows of the mess hall.

She sat down next to Gwen and smiled up at Drake, a cup of the strong coffee imported from the Ottoman Empire in her hand. 'Don't worry, we'll take care of her up there. The Misfits watch out for each other.' The American put her arm around Gwen and squeezed her shoulder as she sipped her drink.

Drake took in how close they were sitting, then smiled and nodded. 'That's good to know.' He bounced up the stairs past them and went into the mess hall.

Gwen turned to frown at Kitty, but before she could say a word a Muscovite soldier poked his head out of the communications shed. He shouted something in Russian which the Misfits had come to recognise as the Muscovite equivalent to "scramble" just as the klaxon started to sound.

'About bloody time!' Mac growled as he tossed his tea to the ground and broke into a run towards Jaguar, followed closely by the rest of the Misfits.

Gwen placed her empty mug rather more carefully to one side before standing up and sprinting after them.

Kitty fell in next to her, her long legs allowing her to keep up effortlessly. 'I have a really bad feeling about this mission.'

Gwen looked up at her. The American's brow was heavily creased and there was a look in her eyes that she had never seen before.

'We've faced far worse odds than this before.'

'I know! It's just...' Kitty growled, annoyed with herself, sounding much like Mac had just moments before. 'I don't know, maybe I'm just being paranoid, but like Drake said, watch out for yourself, OK?'

'I will, I promise.' Gwen reached out to give Kitty's arm a squeeze, then veered off, heading for Wasp, while her friend continued down the line of aircraft towards where Hawk was parked.

'Is Kitty alright?' called Abby from Dragonfly's wing.

Gwen nodded and raised her voice to reply. 'She's just nervous.'

'Ha!' Abby barked, tossing her head. 'So am I! But we have to play the cards we're dealt with.' She gave Gwen a grin, then stepped into her cockpit and slid down into her seat.

Gwen turned away and gave Wasp a quick glance. They had all done their pre-flight checks immediately after breakfast so as to be ready, but it was better to be safe than sorry. Once she was done, she nodded at Sergeant Jenkins. 'All set, sergeant?'

'All set, ma'am.'

'Good, thank you. Let's get this show on the road, then, shall we?'

The eighteen fighters, eight Misfits and twelve Wolfpack Harridans rendezvoused west of Murmansk and vectored towards the incoming raid.

The night before, Chastity had asked why they didn't just lurk around near the border so that they were in place when the Prussians came for their raid, regular as clockwork and the answer was simple - if the Prussians saw them waiting, either they wouldn't show at all or they would just turn back. So, just like the day before, the combined fighter forces were still more than fifty miles away when the Prussians dropped their bombs on the border, making a long run from north to south along the river before turning back towards home.

The general had assured Abby that the forces along the border were well dug in and were taking very little in the way of casualties, so it didn't really matter that they were allowing the Prussians to bomb unmolested, but it was still quite frustrating for the Misfits.

As soon as it was clear what the Prussians were doing, the allies broke off and raced back towards Vaenga. Because rewinding facilities were somewhat limited they split up into groups, with the faster fighters of B flight racing ahead, closely followed by Sable and Raptor with Dragonfly and Wasp lagging only slightly behind. The Harridans were not much slower, but even so the Misfits were almost rewound by the time they taxied into place.

The fitters were only topping off what little tension the fighters had used so it didn't take long and less than an hour after they had turned back from the interception, the allied squadrons were back in the air and climbing hard. Dreadnought and Hummingbird were already in the air, having taken off while the two fighter squadrons were on their way home and they formed on them as they sped for the coordinates they had been given south-west of Murmansk, looking to make their rendezvous with the rest of their forces.

'Wolverine Leader, this is Beetroot. Come in please.'

Gwen couldn't help but smile when the call from the air traffic controllers at Murmansk came in, not just because "Beetroot" was such an appropriate name for them, considering the Muscovites' obsession with putting the vegetable in just about everything, but also because area command had chosen a name for the combined squadrons that was as close to "Wolfpack" as they could get without actually using it.

'Wolverine Leader here, go ahead Beetroot.'

'Wolverine Leader, Hammer Squadron is twenty miles from you, heading two five zero, altitude five thousand feet.'

'Say again please?'

Gwen frowned as Beetroot repeated the message; five thousand feet was very low, the Muscovite bombers should be at twenty thousand feet at least, otherwise they would be easy targets for any anti-aircraft guns that they passed. They would even have been better off at five hundred feet, at least that way they would have cut down the amount of time they were visible to each gun position.

'Thank you, Beetroot.'

There was a few seconds of silence then the radio came back on. 'Leader to Nine.'

'Nine here, Leader.'

'Would you mind checking in on the bombers, please; I think I'm losing something in translation.'

'One moment, coming about.'

There was a short silence during which Gwen could almost picture Owen banking Bloodhound around, the long-winged machine making a stately turn to point its radar in another direction.

'Wolverine Leader, I have thirty plus aircraft on screen. They... They're at angels five! What the hell are they doing so low?'

'Leader, I see them, eleven o'clock low.' As usual, Kitty's sharp eyes had picked out the aircraft before the rest of the pilots and there was a pause as the Misfits slotted lenses in place over their goggles.

'What the...?'

Gwen would have laughed at Bruce's typical breach in protocol if it wasn't for the sight of the Muscovite aircraft.

The reason for their low altitude was immediately apparent - they just weren't capable of climbing any higher.

The bombers were relics from the First Great War - huge six-engined biplanes, almost as large as Dreadnought, with open cockpits and wooden wings held together by struts and wires. They were painted a solid dull grey, as if nobody could be bothered to give them more than a base coating and didn't even have roundels. The only defence they had was completely inadequate - two gunners, sitting back to back in the middle of the fuselage behind what looked like extremely small calibre guns that pointed out on opposite sides of the aircraft leaving very wide dead zones which neither of them could cover.

'Poor bastards.'

Mac expressed what they were all thinking; if the Prussians managed to get even a single fighter off the ground it would be a slaughter, especially if it were one of the larger MU10's.

There was worse news to come, though, when the Wolverines got close enough to get a good look at them. The bombers had so much trouble keeping their own weight in the air that they couldn't carry much in the way of a payload and there were only eight very small bombs, most likely two hundred and fifty pounders, hanging under each aircraft. They were totally inadequate for the job and would have to score a direct hit to do any lasting damage to an aircraft, something that was quite unlikely.

The aircraft were flying at their top speed, but that amounted to less than two hundred miles per hour and at that rate, the Prussians would have fifteen minutes warning from their troops along the border that a raid was on the way and would be able to scramble at least a few of their fighters again before the bombers got to them.

'Damn that general.' Abby's voice was low, but it came all too clearly over the squadron's private comm frequency and they knew exactly what was going through her mind - an already risky mission was going sour even before it had started and something had to be done before the whole outing failed dismally and lives were lost. 'Wolverine Leader to Nine, come in please.'

'Nine here, Leader.'

'What is the Prussian fighter squadron doing?'

'They are approximately ten miles from their base. I'm going to lose them in the ground clutter soon, but they should be on the deck in the next five minutes.'

'Thank you, Nine.' There was a click as Abby switched to the general frequency. 'Alright, Wolverine Squadron, listen up. This plan isn't going to work, so I'm changing it...'

'Is that wise, Leader? The plan has been discussed and approved by Imperial command...'

Abby cut Baryshnikov off as soon as she could. 'Thirteen, you know as well as I do that any plan of war need to be flexible. Don't worry, I'm not changing it too much, just enough to ensure that we have a chance of carrying it out and getting home alive.'

'Very well, Leader. Thirteen listening.'

'Thank you, Thirteen...'

Gwen grinned; she could almost hearing Abby's eyes rolling.

'As I was saying: change of plans. We'll be crossing the border in a few minutes, which means they'll be able to see us, even if they haven't got some other kind of early warning system set up. At the speed the bombers are going they'll have time to rewind at least a few fighters and get them back into the air, so Badger Squadron will go ahead and make sure they can't do that, while Wolfpack Squadron stays with Hammer Squadron, just in case there are any surprises. Got that Wolfpack Leader?'

'Got it. But I must say I would much rather be going on ahead and leaving you doing the babysitting.'

Abby laughed. 'I know you would, but the Harridans can handle these low speeds better than my B flight aircraft. Don't worry, there'll be plenty for you to do once you get to the target.'

'I certainly hope so, I would like some medals to send to my mother!'

There were a few chuckles at that, but silence quickly fell again; the pilots were nervous, knowing that they would be in danger soon.

'Right then, Badger Squadron on me, full climb to angels twenty, let's get above the cloud cover and try not to give the ack-ack any more warning we're coming than we have to. Badger Ten, follow as best you can.'

As Dragonfly surged ahead and tilted its nose up, Gwen pushed her throttle forwards and Wasp, who had definitely been sulking at being restricted to such low speed, came alive again under her touch.

'Nine, anything on your scopes?'

'Negative, Leader, the Prussian bombers are now home and there is no sign of any fighters being scrambled to meet you yet.'

'Roger, Nine. Let me know if that changes, please.'

'Roger, Leader.

The cloud cover was thick, hiding the Prussian fighter base, but every one of the Misfits knew how to navigate and weren't taken by surprise five minutes later when Abby broke the tense silence.

'Alright. Badger Five, you're going down first. Take B flight and buzz the airfield. Take a look at what's what, please. If you see a target of opportunity, take it, but don't waste ammo; we might need it. A flight, we're circling here until they report.'

'Roger, Leader. B flight, break into pairs and dive on my mark... Mark!' Derek's voice came over the radio just before the four aircraft of B flight peeled off neatly to either side of A flight and disappeared almost vertically down into the clouds. His orders were quickly followed by a howl as Mac did his own impression of the Wolfpack battle cry, but the Scotsman ruined the effect somewhat by breaking down into laughter half way through.

'Radio silence now, please, Seven,' snapped Derek, not amused.

'Sorry, boss.'

'Leader, this is Five. Twenty plus aircraft on the ground in the open, in a line next to the airfield. None of them are moving. Hang on, I see pilots running for machines. One moment, please, Leader. Six, the airscrew on that MU9 at the end is turning, let's try to change his mind about taking off.'

'Roger, Five.'

The sound of gunfire filled the airwaves momentarily before Derek's voice came back, emotionless and businesslike as always. 'Good shot, Six. Leader, this is Five. One enemy destroyed and at least one has a few more holes in it than is healthy. We're under heavy anti-aircraft fire, though, I count at least eight flak guns and they have another dozen or more heavy machine guns as well. Withdrawing.'

'Roger, Five, loiter out of range for now and well done.'

A new voice came over the radio now. 'Badger Leader, this is Wolfpack Leader. We are fifteen miles out. Taking heavy fire. Two bombers down. Request permission to engage ground forces.'

'Permission granted, Wolfpack. Happy hunting.'

'Thank you, Badger Leader.' Baryshnikov followed his words with something extremely excitable in Russian, then Gwen winced as an ear-piercing howl from the entirety of the Russian squadron, much louder than Mac's, made the small speakers in her helmet distort and squeal.

'I really wish they wouldn't do that...' Abby said, real annoyance in her voice. 'Right then, all Badgers listen up. We have to clear a path for those bombers. Badger Five, in two minutes start make full speed runs on the guns at the airfield, see if you can't take a few out, but keep an eye on the fighters and engage any that make a move. Ten, stay up here in the clouds for now, but when the bombers arrive feel free to go down and give the Prussians hell. A flight, we're going to fly the bombers' path and try to get the anti-aircraft gunners to keep their heads down until the bombers get past them... diving now.'

Gwen watched her wingman's yellow aircraft roll and dive, giving it a heartbeat to get ahead of her before following, not wanting to be too close when they went into the cloud.

CHAPTER 19

Gwen took a deep breath as she watched the altimeter plunging, but there was no time for anything else before Wasp burst out of the cloud and into the grey world beneath it.

It had been calm and peaceful in the sunshine above the clouds, but here the world was shadow and chaos.

Guns flashed from hundreds of positions on the ground, all pouring death up at the marauding aircraft.

Flak burst everywhere, innocuous-seeming puffs of grey that blossomed in the sky, sending shard of sharp metal pinging and whining off metal fuselages.

Tracer rounds reached up for grey aircraft, tearing large holes in them, ripping them apart one by one. Several columns of black smoke marked the path that the raid had taken from Muscovy, funeral pyres for the bombers which had already fallen.

Colourful Harridans screamed out of the sky, firing streams of metal at the ground targets.

A small ammunition stockpile next to a gun exploded, sending the twisted metal of the gun itself rolling along the ground, bowling over everything in its path - trees, vehicles, sandbags. Men.

There was a woman's screaming in Gwen's ears and she winced as she saw the wing come off a yellow and red striped Harridan. The voice cut off abruptly as the aircraft hit the ground and cartwheeled, flying apart, flinging debris every which way.

Gwen stared, her eyes wide and mouth dry, her gaze darting from one fresh horror to the next, unable to tear her eyes away, but at the same time wanting to block it all out. This was her first experience of a ground war, the other pilots, including Chastity, had fought in France, but she had only known the war over Britain, which had been solely an air war.

She froze.

It was only for a second or two, but that was enough for her to lose Abby.

Gwen searched and found her wingman almost half a mile away, already opening fire on one of the large flak guns. Small puffs of earth flew up into the air as Abby walked her machine gun rounds towards the gun, using them to sight, but then, when sparks began to fly from metal, she opened up with her cannon. The difference was immediate, as gaping holes appeared in the shielding around the gun and ripped apart everything around it.

The gruesome sight was almost immediately obscured by a mist that was earth brown tinged with red, but there had been more than enough time to see the result of large projectiles striking soft material and Gwen shuddered as the sight was burned into her mind for eternity. She swallowed bile and breathed deeply, trying to keep from vomiting as she banked Wasp hard and tucked in behind Dragonfly's wing.

'Welcome back, Two.'

'Sorry, Leader, lost you in the cloud.'

There was a brief silence that told Gwen that she hadn't quite been believed, but Abby didn't comment, she just got back to business. 'The bombers are nearly there, we have to draw some fire and make sure that as many of them get to the target as possible. Try to stay with me this time, please.'

'Roger, Leader.'

Abby took Gwen on a dipping and swooping ride, parallel to the path of the bombers. Dozens of guns that would have targeted the Muscovite bombers instead opened fire at them, but agile aircraft avoided it all with ease, confusing and confounding the gunners by darting this way and that, almost as if they were playing with the enemy.

Things became deadly serious over the airfield, though.

Derek hadn't been exaggerating when he'd said the aerodrome was heavily defended - there were a dozen or so guns in emplacements around the perimeter fence and at least twice as many in the nearby forest. Their combined had been far too much for B flight to handle on their own and had barely survived the couple of runs they'd made, but when the bombers came within sight of the airfield, most of them switched targets from the fighters to what they perceived as the true threat.

They were still several miles out, but their altitude made them easy targets. One by one the lumbering grey aircraft began to tumble from the sky and it was immediately apparent that, if the Misfits didn't do something about it, the mission would fail. Thankfully, though, with the majority of the guns now otherwise occupied, it wouldn't be so dangerous for the fighters to engage them.

'All Badgers, pick your targets and engage. Ten, we could really use you about now, please.'

Abby didn't wait for the acknowledgements to finish coming in before switching to the channel that just she and Gwen shared. 'Two, I've used too much ammo already. Take the lead and go for the big gun at one o'clock. You saw how I did it, now it's your turn.'

'Roger, Leader.'

Gwen dipped her right wing and banked towards the gun, lining up the shot whilst continuing to twitch and jerk Wasp about the sky with slight movements on her stick and rudder pedals.

She aimed slightly low, intending to walk the machine gun shots to the gun before opening up with the cannon just as Abby had and moved her thumb over the firing button.

Through her reflector sight she could see the men manning the gun frantically trying to swing it around towards her, their eyes wide in alarm, showing white, but they were too slow, they wouldn't be able to do it before she got to them.

She pursed her lips, judging the range and stopped her juking to fix the enemy in her sights. Her vision narrowed until it was just her, the men, the gun that was seeking to end her life and her thumb caressing the button on her stick.

'Pull up, Two! PULL UP!'

Abby's panicked shout broke Gwen out of her trance and she screamed as she saw the ground filling her vision. She yanked back on her stick, narrowly avoiding the gun she'd been aiming for, but it was too late; a tree loomed large, directly in front of her, its hooked and burnt branches reaching for her, seeking to drag her from the sky.

With a lurch, Wasp clipped the very topmost branches and faltered, her airscrew sending splinters flying in all directions. The aircraft was going fast enough to burst through, though, and was free again, but the tree had slowed her down and pulled her nose below the horizon. Wasp was close to stalling and only yards from cold earth.

Gwen swore and gritted her teeth, clenching anything and everything that could be clenched as she threw her throttle into emergency power and teased back the stick, simultaneously opening her flaps and lowering her undercarriage.

Wasp hit the ground and bounced, her wheels barely out in time, then fell and bounced once more, before finally responding to the power of her airscrew, shaking off a fine coating of sawdust as she levelled out and gained speed. The frozen earth raced by, only feet below and Gwen caught an impossible glimpse of a man's face, right in front of her, frozen like a deer in a hunting lamp as she bore down on him. She yelped as she jerked the stick back and the man disappeared, replaced by the solid grey of the clouds - in her panic she had pulled the nose of the aircraft into an almost vertical position. She pushed the stick forward and levelled off, just in time to prevent Wasp from stalling again, then withdrew her flaps and wheels and left the aircraft to fly herself, not giving a thought to her surroundings while she panted for breath and tried to clear her head.

'Gwen! Gwen!'

Gwen slowly became aware of the shouts in her ears and looked to her left to find Dragonfly on her wing. They were flying in a straight line and judging by the fact that there were no other aircraft around and no sign of the airfield, they had been for some time. Thankfully, though, as low to the ground as they were, they made very difficult targets for any isolated anti-aircraft guns they came across.

'I'm here. Sorry, Abby, I just... I don't know what happened.'

That was a lie, she knew *exactly* what had happened.

It was far too easy to think of the men she shot down as being just their machines, but what Abby's cannon had done to the men around that first gun... She didn't know if she could do that to anyone, not even the hated Prussians.

'Go back to base, Gwen, I can't have you here if you're just going to freeze, you'll just get yourself or someone else killed.'

Before Gwen could answer, Dragonfly pulled up and banked sharply, heading back towards the flashes and smoke that filled the mirror above Gwen's head.

It was Abby's disappointed tone more than anything else that brought Gwen back from the brink of disgrace and mostly likely grounding and expulsion from the Misfits.

A trickle of sweat ran down her cheek from under her helmet and she swiped the back of her glove across her face under her goggles then snarled at herself. 'Buck up, Stone, don't be a baby.'

She had no choice. She couldn't abandon her friends and her allies, she had to pull her weight and do what she could to ensure the survival of the remaining bombers.

She pulled the tightest turn she possibly could and headed back for the fight.

It had been no more than thirty seconds since her near brush with death, but in that time she had travelled more than two miles from the battle and she used the opportunity to take stock of what was happening.

A cold wave ran through her as she did a rough count of the number of large aircraft making their final approach to the airfield and came up well short. There were less than half of the thirty or so bombers that they had brought with them left to make their bombing runs, not nearly enough to carry out the objective and destroy all of the fighters.

A mile out, she took Wasp up to a hundred feet over the tops of the trees and picked her first target, but before she could even turn towards it a dark shadow rushed almost directly over the top of her. Gwen flinched and looked up as Wendy's whoop of joy filled her ears and her jaw dropped involuntarily at the sight of the enormous Dreadnought in a full power dive, swooping down like a gigantic bird of prey, going even faster than Wasp.

White hot fire lanced from Dreadnought's wings as the big aircraft reached the edge of the airfield. It impacted with something on the ground and a fireball, as big as the cathedral in St. Petersburg and shining just as brightly, sprang into being, rocking Wasp with the shockwave, even though she was still half a mile away.

Dreadnought pulled up from her dive, but couldn't avoid plunging into the roiling smoke and flames caused by the rockets and Gwen held her breath, unsure if even the big aircraft could survive such punishment. Not only did she survive, though, but she came out the other side with her guns firing, pouring an immense amount of metal down on the Prussians.

An explosion rocked Wasp again, a puff of grey smoke sending metal shards pinging off her left wing and she flipped the aircraft into an evasive barrel roll while she searched for the ack-ack gun that was targeting her. It fired again, betraying its position and she banked hard towards it and lined up her shot.

This time she didn't hesitate and Wasp juddered, slowing almost imperceptibly at the recoil from her cannon.

The gun disappeared below her and Gwen searched for her next target, not bothering to look at the result of her shots - she didn't need to; she knew she had hit it and hit it hard. The next gun was almost directly in front of her, one of the smaller machine guns, and it took only a couple of nudges on the rudder to bring it into her sights. She only had time to give it a two-second burst before it flashed past beneath her, but that was more than enough to put it out of commission.

'Welcome back, Two.'

Gwen glanced around and found the yellow Dragonfly on the other side of the airfield, climbing away from the smoking ruin of a large gun.

'Thank you, Leader. Forming up on you.'

'Negative, Two, do not cross the airfield at this time.'

Gwen opened her mouth to ask why, but immediately got her answer when the first of the Muscovite bombs finally detonated among the Prussian aircraft on the field. In the confusion and with the threat from the guns, she had almost forgotten that their actual target was the enemy aircraft and she took the brief respite provided by the bombers to check their status.

The wrecks of two MU9's lay abandoned at the end of the field, shot to pieces just before they took off, but the rest were still in the line that Derek had described. There was a gaping hole in what had been a neat and typically Prussian formation, though - a shallow crater, surrounded by twisted aircraft parts was all that was left of the six or seven fighters which had been obliterated by Wendy's rockets. Several of the machines nearest to the explosion had been tossed aside by the blast and were out of action for the near future, but around two dozen aircraft remained, completely undamaged, and as she watched, two MU10's detached from the surviving winding machines and leapt forward, accelerating almost before they had turned onto the airfield.

'Badger Three, there are two bandits taking off, heading in your direction. Intercept please, but be careful crossing the perimeter of the airfield; bombs are still falling.'

'Roger, Leader.'

In the end, there was no need for Bruce and Monty to intervene because by some stroke of luck a bomb struck the aircraft on the left, knocking out its right engine. Suddenly unbalanced, it skewed and veered directly into the path of its wingman, which could do nothing to avoid its fate and ploughed straight into it, finishing the job on both of them.

Direct hits destroyed two more fighters in the line and a couple of others were rocked by near misses, damaging them, but then the explosions stopped.

The guns had ceased firing while the bombs fell, their gunners blinded or taking cover, and an unnatural silence fell on the airfield as the loose earth, tossed skywards by the munitions, settled slowly to the ground.

'Is that it?'

There was a mixture of disappointment and anger in Wendy's voice that echoed what all of the Misfits were thinking, that the men and women in the bombers had made a huge sacrifice in an attempt to deprive their enemy of a precious resource, but their valiant effort had been in vain - they had done their part, but their leaders had given them inadequate tools for the job and more than half of the enemy fighters were untouched.

'Wolfpack Leader to Badger Leader, Hammer reports that they are out of bombs and turning for home.'

'Roger, Wolfpack Leader. Escort them, please.'

'Negative, we need to destroy the rest of those aircraft.'

'Badger Squadron can take care of them.'

Baryshnikov laughed. 'We're not letting you get all the glory! Wolfpack out.'

'Dammit, Wolfpack...' Abby growled. 'Alright, Badger Squadron, the sooner we take out the rest of the fighters the sooner we can get back to the bombers. Engage at will.'

Eight colourful aircraft immediately converged on the airfield from all directions, followed only seconds later by the large shape of Dreadnought, which rose above the trees to the north like the shadow of the Dark Scythesman himself.

The Prussian aircrew and fitters had finally realised that they had no hope of getting any of their aircraft off the ground and were streaming away from them, desperately searching for cover, when the first of the Misfits hit.

The Misfit fighters took it in turns to pepper the aircraft with machine gun and cannon fire, ripping holes in them, but it was Dreadnought which did the most damage once more. Wendy didn't have any rockets left, but her multiple gun turrets, each of which held at least two cannon, if not four, were just as effective against the soft targets and as she flew parallel to the line of aircraft they made good practice and literally tore them apart. She didn't escape unscathed, though, because the few remaining anti-aircraft guns opened up on that most tempting of targets, pinning her in a crossfire that tore holes in her tailplane and caused one of her engines to flame and die.

The enemy fire didn't last long, though, because the Misfit aircraft quickly targeted then silenced them.

Just in time for the Wolfpack to arrive.

The Russians were left with nothing to do, but it didn't stop them from wasting ammunition by liberally spraying everything in sight, including the hangars and barracks, but all they likely managed to do was ruin the Prussians' breakfast and shoot a few holes in their mattresses.

'That's it, good job, Badger Squadron, let's get to those bombers.' Abby deliberately said nothing to the Russians, showing her disapproval of their behaviour by ignoring them.

The Misfits broke off and headed east, searching for the Muscovite biplanes.

They found them only minutes later. There were three left.

'Damn you, Wolfpack...' Abby swore again, but this time under her breath and only on the Misfit channel, using a few of the colourful words that the squadron had been learning from Scarlet. 'Badger Squadron, let's clear a path. Engage any ground forces you see. Use all the rest of your ammunition if you have to.'

For the next half an hour, the Misfits raced ahead of the bombers, trying to draw the fire of any gun in their path and destroying them when they found them. They did the best they could, but ultimately they couldn't get all of them and the bombers were just too easy a target to miss. Two were destroyed by puffs of grey smoke that ripped apart machines and men in open cockpits alike and the last took a machine gun fire in one wing, putting two of its three engines on that side out of action. It struggled on valiantly, losing height all the while, but finally crashed into the ground only yards from the river marking the border, in plain sight of Murmansk.

Disheartened, the Misfits pushed their throttles to the stops and went home.

CHAPTER 20

Gwen and Abby were among the last to land and, by the time their aircraft had been pushed into place in their hangar, the Wolfpack pilots were already gathered in front of the mess. To the surprise and disgust of the British pilots, they immediately started celebrating, downing vodka as they sang and danced.

Abby, followed by every single one of her pilots, immediately descended on them.

'What the hell did you think you were doing up there? How *dare* you disobey my orders and leave the bombers to fend for themselves!'

A British officer who did something to cause a superior to say such words to them would at least stop what they were doing and, when invited to do so, explain themselves and try to justify whatever decision they had made.

Baryshnikov, however, only stopped laughing and joking long enough to shrug and give Abby a smile. 'The mission was successful wasn't it?'

He turned away from her and began to clap, shouting encouragement as a couple of his men started doing cartwheels around each other, but Abby grabbed him by the shoulder and spun him back around.

That got his full attention, but also that of his pilots and they stopped what they were doing to form a silent group behind their leader.

'On your toes, Misfits.'

Mac's muttered words were unnecessary, as every single one of the pilots was already moving to surround Abby. Most of them had never been in a brawl in their lives, but they were more than willing to jump in to support their friends if they had to.

The two groups glared at each other, waiting for their leaders to make the first move.

Abby looked at the Russian pilots, then at her own, before rolling her eyes. 'Oh for pity's sake. Come on.' She waved for Baryshnikov to go with her then stomped away out into the middle of the airfield without waiting to see if he would.

Baryshnikov said something in Russian to his pilots, dismissing them with a grin, then swaggered after Abby.

The Russians shot glares at the Misfits, but said nothing and just wandered away into the mess hall, where the sounds of laughter and singing soon rang out once more.

The British pilots turned to watch their leader, most of them wondering whether their circumstances were going to change in the next few hours.

'I'd give anything to be able to hear what they say.' Bruce whispered.

'Well, if you shut up, we might be able to make it out, yer big numpty!' Mac countered.

The Misfits did as he said and strained their ears, eavesdropping with all their might.

Abby watched the Russian stroll towards her, taking his time, an insolent grin on his face. He came to a halt in front of her and slouched, crossing his arms, waiting for her to make the first move.

Her anger had disappeared, but in its place was a white hot rage and if before she had wanted to punch that smarmy, smirking face, now she wanted to see it disappear in ignominy. She wanted to see the man standing before her reduced in ranks and forbidden the skies, although, she thought, it might be poetic to see him pilot one of the bombers he had so casually discarded. She wouldn't wish that fate on anyone, though; it was as good as a death sentence.

'How many pilots did you lose?' She spoke to him calmly, coldly, using a voice that her pilots knew only too well and feared hearing.

The man shrugged, oblivious to the thin ice he was treading. 'Only four.'

'*Only?*' Abby was horrified at his cavalier attitude to the loss of his pilots.

'That is a very small price to pay for such a great victory. *Our* victory, Group Captain.'

'And what of the bombers? More than thirty aircraft destroyed and a hundred men and women dead. An entire squadron, gone in a single morning.'

Baryshnikov gave her another of his grins. 'You don't think the plan was actually for them to destroy the enemy fighters, do you? Command knew they wouldn't be able to, they were only there to provide us with enough of a distraction to complete the mission and get out with minimal losses.'

'They were...' Abby swallowed, her mouth dry and her tongue a dead weight in her mouth. Her voice, when she found it again, was barely more than a croak. 'Did they know?'

'Of course they did! But they still went willingly.' He waved his hand dismissively. 'Put them out of your mind; they were inconsequential, barely trained and there are plenty more where they came from. Russia is a very large country and this has always been our way - sacrifices are made to ensure that the Empire survives.'

The fire which had died down at the thought of the poor men and women in the bombers knowingly going to their deaths, roared back into life and she took a quick step closer to Baryshnikov, putting her face only inches from his and, despite knowing it was beneath her, she couldn't help but feel gratified when he flinched. 'Whether those bombers were there just as a distraction or not is immaterial, but your insubordination is not. The Tsar put me in charge of the air defences in the north and if we're going to work together, then you're going to have to obey my orders, because they're as good as his.'

Baryshnikov gave her a small bow, smiling enigmatically. 'Very well, Group Captain. But we shall have to see if we work together again, won't we?'

'What do you mean?'

'No matter.'

He waved away her query, then reached out and took her upper arms in his hands. For a horrifying moment she thought he was going to kiss her, but instead he smiled at her and shook her once, as if he were speaking to a beloved comrade, not a superior. 'We shall have a party tonight and perhaps you will find a strong young Russian man or woman who takes your fancy and you will forget about all of this for a while, like we Russians do.'

He shook her once more and smiled broadly, then turned and walked away past the Misfits and into the mess where he was greeted with wolf howls by his squadron.

Abby waited until he had disappeared, then wandered back to her pilots. 'I suppose you heard all of that.'

She sighed at their nods. 'Much as we don't like what happened today, I'm just happy none of us got killed.'

'At least we destroyed their fighters.'

Abby glanced at Bruce. 'You and I both know that there are plenty more of them to come, but yes, we have to make sure we take full advantage of the brief window that the waste of so many lives has bought us. Let's go and see how our aircraft are, because at least a few of us have taken damage.' She looked pointedly at Gwen. 'Then I'm going to speak to command, see if I can find us a few targets; I *really* need to blow something up.'

'Gwen. A word please.'

Abby's cold voice stopped Gwen in her tracks and sent a chill running through her. She slowly turned to face her commander, the woman who had pulled her out of prison and given her a second chance. The last thing she wanted to do was disappoint her, but she had and it showed as she glared at her.

'Look, I'm sorry, I...'

Abby shook her head, cutting her off. 'All I want to know is - will it happen again?'

'No, it won't. Definitely not.'

'Good, because we can't afford that kind of thing; you almost got yourself killed this time, next time it might be me, or one of the others. Consider yourself warned - if it or anything like it happens again, then you are out on your ear. Understood?'

'Yes, ma'am.'

'Good.' Abby nodded, her scowl still in place. 'Well, now that my duty as your commanding officer is out of the way...' She sighed, her expression softening, and moved forward to envelope Gwen in her arms.

Gwen stood stiffly, for a couple of seconds, not quite sure what to do, but then returned the hug, squeezing Abby tightly.

Eventually, Abby pulled back. She smiled wryly, then jerked her head in the direction of the hangar. 'Come on, let's go have a look at what kind of mess you've made of squadron property.'

Every single one of Misfit Squadron's aircraft had sustained some damage or other. It was mostly just scratched paint, but there were a good few deeper scores and even a couple of holes which needed a bit more care than a polish and a coat of paint.

Wasp was one of the least damaged of the aircraft, her time away from the fight protecting her from much of the enemy fire, but her guns and airscrew would have to be dismantled to clean them of the wood shavings which had found their way into everywhere, a task that would require the rest of the day and much of the night to complete.

The only aircraft that would need grounding for any real length of time, though, was Dreadnought. Many of the brand new panels of her fuselage and wings would have to be replaced, along with the destroyed engine and most of her tailplane and rudder. Thankfully, though, none of her crew had been hurt, mostly because Wendy had installed more shielding around the guns after having lost several of them during the ill-fated attack on the French ports.

Wendy was looking very upset about being grounded yet again, but she soon bucked up when Abby spoke to her about fitting her rockets to other Misfit aircraft as soon as possible and Gwen was particularly happy when the big woman looked directly at Wasp, which was already being dismantled, and decided to start with her. The two engineers immediately started discussing plans, basing them on the ones that Wendy and Kitty had developed for Dreadnought, already debating how to install the necessary controls and wiring.

Abby watched the two women talking animatedly with a grin; as soon as she had given them something to engage their brains they no longer cared so much that their machines were out of action, but more importantly Gwen had forgotten her traumatic experience.

She made the rounds of the hangars, inspecting all the aircraft and making sure that repairs were under way, then went to the communications shed and requested a meeting with command in Murmansk.

With the Flea fighters out of the way there was a very small window during which the allies could act with relative impunity before more fighters could be shipped in. The obvious course of action was to attempt to destroy as much of the Prussian ground forces as possible, but in order to do that most effectively she would need the general to tell her what and where to strike.

She received an immediate reply saying that she was to report immediately and she commandeered a bike messenger to take her.

The first thing she did when she was shown into the same bunker as before was glance at the map and she smiled slightly when she saw that the figurine representing the fighter squadron had been removed. However, that smile faded when she saw that the yellow one representing the bomber squadron had gone as well.

'Group Captain.'

Abby looked up to see the general hobbling towards her.

She nodded respectfully. 'General.' She tilted her head in the direction of the map. 'You've heard then?'

'I heard that you lost my entire squadron of bombers, yes.'

Abby blinked at him in surprise. 'I assure you that I did my utmost to ensure their safety and bring them back. If anyone is to blame then it is Captain Baryshnikov.'

The general shook his head. '*No*, if anyone is to blame, Captain, then it is *you*; you were in overall command of the mission and it was you who changed the plan and abandoned the bombers to go racing ahead and get the glory for yourself.'

'Sir, that's not...'

He lifted his hand to stop her. 'I have spoken to Captain Baryshnikov, I have heard his side of the events and I have no need to hear yours to be able to read between the lines and see what he isn't telling me. I know you did what you could, I know your change of plans salvaged and made a success of a mission that was destined to failure from the start and I commend you for that. However, Baryshnikov has friends and his point of view, that it was your fault that the bombers were lost, will be heard in high places. Furthermore, he has asked to be taken from your command and given his independence and I have decided to grant him his request.'

Abby frowned and opened her mouth to protest, but closed it again immediately as her brain overtook her mouth. The general's solution to the problem was perfect - she would no longer have to deal with an insubordinate subordinate, the Misfits would no longer be in danger of being left in the lurch by unreliable allies, and they would be free to act in any way that they thought best, relying only on themselves. The only real downside was that the opinion of certain people would be poisoned against them, but that was of very little, if any, concern because, with any luck, the Misfits would be leaving before the month was up.

She smiled slowly and nodded. 'Thank you, sir.'

The general returned her smile, fully aware of everything that had gone through her mind and gave her a wink to show that it had gone through his as well.

'Now, on to the real reason you are here, Group Captain.'

Abby raised an eyebrow. 'And what is that, sir?'

The general laughed and waved a hand at the table. 'You want to know what you can attack next, isn't that so?'

Abby grinned. 'Yes, please, sir.'

CHAPTER 21

The general rightly pointed out that it would be almost pointless to attack the Prussian forces which were already in position at the front because they would be too well dug in and protected. Instead, he told her that it would be better to attack the columns that were still on the march and which would therefore be far more vulnerable.

He sent her away, promising that he would find a suitable column for them to attack and that very afternoon, Misfit Squadron took off to carry out their first raid on a mechanised column moving up through Finland towards the border with Muscovy.

The column was composed mostly of standard transport vehicles, but there were also a few mechanised cannon and tanks bringing up the rear. It was defended by a few antiaircraft guns mounted on wagons, but any return fire that came from them was ineffectual at best and the Misfits dealt with them harshly, destroying the only threat, before targeting the rest of the vehicles.

They left the convoy at a standstill, in complete disarray, with over half of the hundred or so vehicles disabled or destroyed and the road completely blocked by twisted metal, the morale of the survivors probably ruined just as effectively.

The Wolfpack were too busy celebrating the morning's victory to even think about flying another mission that day and by the time the Misfits got back the party Baryshnikov had mentioned was in full swing. The guards from the surrounding woods had been invited to join in and one of the bigger hangars had been appropriated to accommodate more than two hundred people, the Wolfpack Polikasparov fighters, which had previously been housed there, pushed out the back of the open structure to make room. Several large fires had been built to warm the space and the air under the half-cylinder of the simple building was smoky, fragrant and inviting.

None of the Misfits felt like they had much to celebrate, but Abby insisted that they at least make an appearance, in an attempt to keep up relations between the two squadrons.

The British immediately found out that there were absolutely no grudges being held by the Russians and they were wholeheartedly welcomed by one and all. Drinks were thrust into their hands and they were told to help themselves to the food that was roasting on the fires.

Gwen had been working on Wasp with Wendy while the squadron had been on the mission, but by the time the light faded they had finished the wiring and installation of the rocket mechanisms and were able to leave the fitters to complete the repairs while they went to the party. Neither of them really wanted to leave the aircraft unfinished, but Abby had as good as ordered them to at least spend a couple of hours socialising with the Muscovites, so they wandered over, wiping their hands on rags to get rid of the grease on them and putting their greatcoats over their work coveralls, but otherwise not bothering to make any effort to get dressed up.

Gwen had been too occupied with Wasp to have any time to dwell on the events of the mission, but now images came back to her, brought on by the sight of the fires and the meat roasting on them, so, while Wendy went over to Owen and gave him a big kiss which left a smeared of black oil on his cheek, she stumbled on shaking legs to where the vodka was being poured, suddenly finding she needed a stiff drink.

She downed the first one, to cheers from the soldiers manning the bottles, demanded a second and did the same, but saluted them in thanks with the third before wandering away to look for a relatively quiet place in the shadows where she could sit and nurse it while the trembling in her limbs subsided. She found a wooden crate to park herself on and leaned against the freezing metal wall of the hangar to watch the exuberant Muscovites celebrating.

'Penny for your thoughts?'

Gwen blinked and looked up to find Drake smiling down at her. 'I'm sorry?'

He tilted his head in the direction of the Wolfpack pilots. 'You were frowning in disapproval at our comrades over there.'

She looked over at the Muscovites and shook her head. 'I just don't understand how they can be so happy after losing so many people today and I'm not talking about the men and women on the bombers, although that's awful, I'm talking about the four of their *own* pilots they lost. *Four.* Out of only twelve in their squadron.'

Drake pulled another crate over, then settled next to her with a sigh.

'You've never really lost anyone in your squadron, have you? Misfit Squadron don't lose pilots, right?'

'No, nobody. But two pilots from my flight in my old squadron were killed my first time in combat.'

Drake nodded. 'Were you close to them?'

'Well...' Gwen grimaced and looked away from his intense blue eyes. 'Back then I wasn't letting anyone close to me. It was just after Richard had died...'

'So that's a no, then.'

'I suppose not.'

'Well, I have.' Drake said. 'Most of the men and women I was in the University Air Squadron with are dead, most of the men and women I went to France with are dead and most of the men and women I fought with over Britain are dead.'

Gwen blinked at him. She knew that casualties had been high in the RAC over the summer, that they had had to throw new pilots into the air with barely any training, just to try to hold back the Prussian tide, but she hadn't known that it had been as bad as that. It made it seem improbable, no, *impossible* that Misfit Squadron hadn't lost anyone except for Abby's sister.

'How did you cope?' Her voice was little more than a whisper, almost inaudible over the noise the Muscovites were making, but Drake heard her. Had been expecting her question.

'You remind yourself that your friends wouldn't want you to stop enjoying what little time you may have left and that they *definitely* wouldn't want us to give up and let their sacrifice be in vain. Then you go and have a few drinks, sing a few songs and put up a photo. And next day you go back to fighting the good fight and carry on living your life as best you can.'

Gwen considered his words then shook her head. 'You make it sound so easy.'

Drake just smiled, though. 'It's not, but I'm hoping you never have to go through something like that. However, I'm sure that if you ever do, you'll come out the other side looking to kick Prussian arses even more than you were before.'

Gwen laughed, then took a big swig of her drink. 'I'd like to think that, but my track record isn't so good.'

'Reacting badly to Richard dying isn't indicative of anything; he was your husband, a man you loved. Yes, people in your squadron are colleagues, friends... even lovers sometimes, but you go into your relationship with them knowing that one day they may die. You never thought that would happen with Richard, though, so you weren't prepared when it did.'

'I suppose not,' Gwen sighed and stared into her glass, 'but the Misfits have become like a family. I'm not sure I could handle...

A joyful shout brought her out of her brooding and she looked up to see Mac pelting across the hangar towards where two women were just arriving, one fair-haired and one dark. He grabbed the blonde and lifted her laughing into the air and swung her around before bringing her back down and kissing her extremely enthusiastically, to cheers from everybody in the hangar, all of whom had briefly stopped what they were doing to watch. The two were oblivious to their audience, though, and it didn't spoil their reunion one bit.

Drake chuckled. 'Now, *that* is a man who is trying to live his life to the fullest. Who's the blonde?'

Gwen frowned. 'I'm pretty sure that's Katerina, the girl he met in St. Petersburg, although I have no idea what she's doing here.'

Bruce had followed Mac across the room rather more slowly, but he greeted the second girl just as warmly before grabbing her hand and leading her across the room towards the drinks. Mac, though, was dragged in the opposite direction, out of the hangar and towards the barracks, drawing laughter from the Misfits, which he acknowledged with a wave and an embarrassed grin.

Drake laughed as well and glanced sideways at Gwen. 'That's what you need - a distraction to take your mind off things.'

'Hmmm, yes, I think you're right.'

Drake looked at her in surprise. 'I am? Really?'

Gwen nodded enthusiastically. 'Oh yes. Polikasparov has had his eye on me since the day we arrived. I think I saw him around here somewhere...'

'Why you...'

Gwen poked her tongue out at him and he punched her in the arm.

For a second, just a second, it was like they were children again, carefree and young, with nothing to complicate their lives, but then the moment was gone and Drake sighed. 'What are you going to do after all this?'

'I don't know. Maybe I'll go back to work for my parents, or start up my own company. What about you?'

'I'm going to retire and do something truly peaceful, like grow wheat or breed horses, and I'm going to live with my wife and never let her from my sight.'

He looked at her meaningfully and Gwen snorted. 'Is that some kind of proposal? Come off it, Digger, stop joking around! We haven't seen each other in more than a decade! You hardly know me!'

'I do! You're still the same tough, determined, intelligent...'

Gwen waved her free hand. 'Keep going; I quite like that.'

'...irritating, bloody-minded girl I grew so fond of.'

'I thought you were trying to butter me up?'

'I was.' Drake gave her one of his lop-sided grins. 'Was it working?'

She shook her head. 'Not really.'

He chuckled. 'Damn, I thought it was.'

She joined in with his laughter, but when he suddenly turned serious she realised he wasn't joking after all and it died on her lips.

'Look, Gwen, all I'm asking for is a chance to get to know you again when this is over and we have some time to ourselves. I'll take you to tea in Selfridges, or we can go to Hamleys like we used to.'

'Rudy, I don't...'

She knew she should tell him no, should tell him that she was falling in love with someone else, and she began to do so, but there was such hope in his eyes that she couldn't bring herself to do it. And anyway, all she was really doing was promising to have tea with him, something that they could and would do as friends without there having to be any complications.

'Alright,' she said reluctantly, 'I suppose we can do that at least.'

'Thank you.' He stood and offered her his hand, his crooked smile back in place. 'I don't suppose you'd care to dance?'

Gwen glanced past him towards where a few dozen Muscovites were standing in a wide circle, singing something very triumphant, accompanied by strange triangular stringed instruments, taking it in turns to enter the ring and perform extremely athletic moves that were probably quite dangerous as drunk as they were. 'Like that?' She looked Drake up and down. 'I'd quite like to see you try.'

His smile widened becoming his familiar cheeky grin. 'For you, anything, but maybe we could start with something a little less energetic, though?'

She shook her head. 'Sorry, I'm not staying; I just came to have a quick drink but now I have to get back to Wasp.'

Drake inclined his head, accepting her excuse, but his smile faded slightly. 'That's a shame, but who am I to stand between a woman and her aircraft? Perhaps next time.'

'Perhaps.'

He gave her a small bow. 'Goodnight, Goosy.'

'Goodnight, Digger.'

He backed away then turned and disappeared from sight into the crowd.

Gwen downed the rest of her drink, then climbed a little unsteadily to her feet and staggered towards the entrance of the hangar and out into the night, but, instead of heading to Wasp, she went round the side of the building and stood in the darkness, staring up at the stars, wondering what she'd just done.

She had no problem with being friends with Rudy; it wonderful to see him again after so long and remembering all the fun they'd had together, learning to fly, had been wonderful, but he'd never been more than a brother to her and she just couldn't see him as anything else. She should have told him that, shouldn't have given him false hope, but the thoughts he had already been having about settling down with her after the war were only going to grow and in the end her reluctance to hurt him would only hurt him more.

She cursed under her breath and kicked out at a nearby crate in frustration, but it wasn't empty like the one she'd sat on in the hangar and she hopped in place, clutching at her foot inside her work boot, hoping that the cracking noise had been one of the wooden slats breaking and not her toe. 'Oh, for crying out loud!'

'Gwen?'

'Hello, Kitty.' She put her foot down and hobbled around to face her friend, trying to put on a smile as she did.

'Are you OK?'

No, not even close. 'I'm fine, it's nothing. I just stubbed my toe.'

'Good.' The American smiled warmly. 'Did you see Mac and that girl?'

Gwen laughed, relieved that the conversation hadn't gone in the direction that she'd feared it would. 'Yes!'

'Apparently she asked for a transfer to be near him.'

'That's surprisingly romantic. I didn't thing Mac was the kind of person to inspire those kinds of feelings in anyone.'

Kitty laughed. 'I know! But they looked so happy, so much in love. The other girl who was in St. Petersburg, Natasha, came with her. She said something about regretting not having spent more time with Bruce or something. They've gone off as well - they had one drink, then she grabbed a couple of bottles and dragged him off, asking for a "tour of the base".'

Gwen smirked. 'That's the first time I've heard it called that!'

'Me too!' Kitty raised an eyebrow and gave her an inviting look. 'You know, I don't think *I've* had a proper look around this base either... Fancy going on a tour with me?'

'Kitty...'

'I know, I know - you need time. You can't blame a girl for trying, though, especially today, after seeing you almost...' Kitty sighed and looked away, staring into the darkness. 'I'm sorry, it's just that... Either of us could die at any time and I just want to be able to say that I actually had a chance to live first, that there was nothing I regretted not doing. Especially with you.'

She turned back to Gwen, her expression flat as she waited to be pushed away again.

Gwen met her friend's eyes and saw the longing, the desire and the sheer will to *live* evident in every fibre of her being. She suddenly realised that, while she had been hesitant and unclear about *how* to reject Drake's proposal, at the same time she'd had one thing very clear in her mind - that she *should* reject it because her heart belonged to someone else.

Hesitantly, not quite believing what she was doing, she held out her hand and smiled in invitation.

As Rudy had said - she should be living her life as best she could.

CHAPTER 22

Sergeant Jenkins and Wendy worked through the night and the next morning Wasp was back in one piece and had four thin silver tubes hanging underneath each wing, smaller versions of the rockets that were mounted on Dreadnought. Gwen rejoined the squadron and for the next three days the Misfits cut a swathe across Finland, terrifying the Prussians, who never knew when or where they would strike. They destroyed several more supply columns, but also a couple of mechanised ones, made up mostly of tanks. There were even a couple of heavily armoured Walkers in one of the columns - rare and incredibly expensive machines which were essentially boxes on legs, used primarily for carrying troops across rivers and minefields - and they made sure to obliterate them, knowing that they were almost irreplaceable.

Gwen soon found that the rockets were very inaccurate and that it was best to fire several of them in quick succession against grouped up targets. However, thanks to the explosive chemical formula that had been given to Wendy by a friend in the Chemists' Guild, a single hit was easily enough to destroy even the most heavily armoured of vehicles. Seeing her success, the other pilots clamoured for Wendy to install racks for the rockets on their machines, even volunteering to remain back from missions to give her time to do so, but Abby refused to allow it and so, for the time being, Gwen remained the only one with them.

Throughout it all, Gwen made sure not to think about the men she was killing. It was easier when she was attacking tanks because they were like the aircraft she shot down - she could convince herself she was just destroying the machines, but the times that they were sent against an infantry column she couldn't use that trick and she did her job, used her ammunition as best as she could, then emptied her guts as soon as she got back to base.

During this time, the Wolfpack was doing much the same as the Misfits, but seeing far less success and losing pilots as fast as the instructors could train them. The situation was so bad that the only surviving pilots from the ones who had greeted the Misfits when they had arrived in Muscovy were Baryshnikov and Polikasparov.

They were also running out of Harridans to put into the air, but when Abby commented on it in one of her daily calls to Dorothy Campbell, who was still stuck in St. Petersburg, she was told not to worry. Apparently, Whitehall had expected that to happen and were sending more fighters with convoys that were already scheduled for after winter.

On the fourth day everything changed.

First thing in the morning, the Misfits flew out to destroy a particularly large and tempting supply column, almost a hundred miles behind enemy lines.

The column was composed mostly of supply wagons, with no infantry or mechanised units, and was trying to rely on speed to reach defensible positions before they could be intercepted, but the attempt was in vain and the Misfits pounced on them like a cat on a ball of wool.

They played havoc with the Prussians, destroying numerous vehicles with every pass, but never once did they stop to think that it was too easy, that the convoy might have been bait in a trap.

Gruber grinned as he dived towards the childishly-coloured aircraft swarming around the tasty morsel he'd placed before them, like rats around poisoned fruit.

He was using their own tactics against them, the exact ones they had used against him in Northern England, and the fools had no idea of the red death descending upon them.

The sixteen red aircraft passed through five thousand feet, screaming down in a steep dive at much more than four hundred miles per hour. Hölle was actually outpacing the *Blutsaugers* of the rest of his squadron by some margin, moving through the air much more efficiently, but he didn't care one bit; it just meant that they wouldn't get in his way when he made his first kill.

And as to that kill...

His sharp eyes, aided by Swiss-made lenses had already picked out his two primary targets: the yellow *Dragonfly* of the leader of the Misfits, Abigail Lennox, without whom the Misfits would likely disintegrate, dissipating like so much smoke; and the absurd pink and black *Wasp* of Gwenevere Stone, the woman who'd had the temerity to defeat him then release him like a stream-caught fish, daughter of the designers of the Harridan that was causing his country so many problems.

Both would die under his guns, but the question was which to kill first.

He nudged his rudder, lining his sights up on first one, then the other, both blissfully unaware of him.

Which deserved to die in a heartbeat and which would he like to play with for a while?

'BREAK!'

Charles' shout gave them less than a second of warning, but it was just enough to save the Misfits from disaster.

Gwen kicked her rudder and threw her stick to the side instantly, but Wasp still lurched as her wing took a strike from something heavy.

'What the...?'

Her question was answered before she could fully express it when a blood-red machine flew past her, so close as to buffet her with its wake. She instantly slammed her stick in the other direction, reversing course and trying to get on its tail, but she had been going far too slowly, attacking ground targets and it was already gone. Two more red aircraft appeared in her vision, points of light winking from their wings and she threw Wasp into a twisting roll, substituting sky for ground for sky again in quick succession as she evaded their fire and they swept by, just as fast as their colleague and just as untouchable. Abby, however, had somehow managed to snap an impossible shot off and one of them went spiralling out of control, straight into one of the supply wagons below.

Gwen searched the air around her while she continued her manoeuvres, pinpointing the enemy fighters. There were more than a dozen of them, but they had all passed right through the Misfits and were climbing back up, a couple of miles away, regaining their height advantage. They weren't close enough to immediately affect her so she disregarded them for the moment and turned her eyes upwards, searching for anyone still lurking overhead. When she found nobody she stopped juking and took a deep breath, trying to calm her pounding heart.

'All Badgers, regroup on me.'

Even while she had been tossing Wasp about the sky, Gwen had never strayed far from her wingman and the rest of the Misfits joined them seconds later.

'Report.'

Gwen glanced out of her cockpit and winced at the gaping hole in her right wing - a cannon round had struck the red lion on her roundel dead centre, as if it had been an archery target, and there was nothing left of it. It wouldn't impair Wasp too much, though, so there was no need to report it as real damage and she kept the radio clear for the others.

'Badger Four. I have damage to my port-side aileron and controls are sluggish.'

'Badger Seven. Rudder's out.'

'Badger Six here, I've lost my starboard airscrew.'

Gwen immediately looked to Hawk, searching out Kitty, making sure that she was alright, but beyond her obvious frustration at her aircraft being damaged she seemed to be unharmed. The American met her eyes and smiled weakly, giving a thumbs up that Gwen returned, relieved.

'Badger Eight... I... I...'

Gwen's eyes lifted beyond Hawk and gasped when she saw Dove. Her cockpit was holed in several places and there was blood pouring down Chastity's face.

'Eight, what's wrong?'

'I...'

As Gwen watched, unbelievably, the young woman seemed to shake her shock away. She lifted a glove to her head, but dropped it immediately.

'Nothing, Leader. I... took some damage, but I'm fine. Badger Eight, Roger.'

There was a brief silence as Abby considered their options, but it lasted no more than five of Gwen's extremely rapid heartbeats. 'Right then, we need to get home as quickly as we can, but we're going to have to stay together and protect our injured. We'll stay as low as we can and make them come to us. If the Barons dive on us then turn to face, if not, continue course. A flight, form up on Four, B flight, form up on

Seven. We'll let them lead our turn as best they can, then we'll all form on Six. Ready? Execute.'

The two flights formed up on their two most damaged members and slowly turned towards home. Monty had the most problems changing course and he slewed around the sky like a drunkard as he tried to keep Raptor under control, but eventually they were all pointed east towards the border and then it was Kitty's turn to dictate their speed. She put her remaining airscrew to full emergency power, using her remaining spring tension at a prodigious rate, but even then she was barely able to make two hundred and fifty miles per hour.

Once they were settled, Bruce asked the question that was on all of their minds. 'Did anyone get a good look at Gruber's aircraft? I didn't see a triplane.'

'He was in the first aircraft down, the one with the black check pattern on its nose,' Abby said, 'and yes, I got a pretty good look while he was trying to kill Gwen. He's finally decided to catch up with the times, although he hasn't been very original while he's doing it.'

'What do you mean?'

'I mean that his new aircraft shares several design similarities with Wasp and Dragonfly. Gruber is trying to beat us by copying us.'

Gwen laughed.

There was a long silence before finally Abby came back over the radio. 'Two? Is there anything you'd like to share with the class?'

Gwen grinned and looked across at her wingman. 'Well, we've improved our machines since he last saw them and as soon as we get the chance we're going to improve them even more. His lovely new aircraft is already obsolete.'

Gwen laughed again and this time was joined by the rest of the Misfits, but Abby soon put paid to their good spirits and brought their minds back to the task ahead of them. 'Roger that, Two. But it won't matter very much if he kills us now, will it?'

'Leader, they're coming down.'

'Thank you, Five. Seven, Four, turn us around please.'

'Pull up and return to six thousand feet.'

Gruber gave the order to break off the run on the Misfit aircraft when he saw them turning. He really didn't want to go head to head with the British aircraft; he had read the reports and seen pictures of the damage their guns had been doing, ripping through even the thickest of tank armour. His aircraft would be blown from the sky with no guarantee that they would destroy any of the Misfits in reply.

A month ago he wouldn't have cared and would have sent his men anyway; the pilots had been new and unproven, but after two successful campaigns they had come together as a unit and with replacements so far away he didn't want to waste them unnecessarily.

He gazed down on the British Squadron, who were turning back towards the Muscovite border, still out of sight beyond the horizon, but only twenty minutes of flight time away and ground his teeth; unless he did something soon, they were going to slip away yet again.

Gwen squinted up into the clear sky. With the sun so low on the horizon the Prussians couldn't hide in it as they had over England, but the sky was still bright and relatively painful to look at and she had slotted tinted lenses into place to cut down the glare. 'They're still up there, Leader.'

'Roger, Two.'

'What are the bastards waiting for?' The strain was showing in Mac's voice as he fought against a machine that was more and more out of his control with every second; it seemed that it hadn't been just his rudder that had been hit, but some of his control wires as well and every so often they twitched in his hands as strands of the wires frayed and broke, making Jaguar act more like a skittish house cat than a predator.

'I don't know, Seven, but the longer they wait the better for us.'

The fifteen black dots high above swirled, moving in relation to each other and Gwen slotted more lenses in place, magnifying them. They were on the move. 'Leader, they're splitting up. They're coming down, but...'

'But what, Two?'

Gwen watched for a couple of seconds to make sure that the Barons were doing what she thought they were before replying. 'They're not diving straight at us, it looks like they want to get into a proper fight.'

'Dammit. I was afraid they'd finally work out what they had to do. Took Gruber long enough, though!'

The Misfits knew that they were in desperate straits, but even so most of them chuckled at the thought of the leader of the Barons and the reputation he had in the British press of being a good-looking but halfwitted figurehead for the Fleas. It was a reputation that was completely unfounded and not particularly credible, but the British propaganda machine insisted on spreading it to keep the spirits of the people up.

'Alright. We've got no choice. Mac, Kitty, Monty, hold this heading and make best speed for home. Everyone else, let's try to buy them time.'

Even though every single one of them knew that Abby might well be condemning the three wounded aircraft, there were no protests at her orders; there was nothing further they could do for their friends and the only chance they had was to make a run for it and hope that none of the Barons chased them down. Not that the remaining Misfits would have it easy, though; they were outnumbered three to one.

A glint of light, the sun reflecting off something up high in front of them, caught Gwen's attention and she looked up, dropping lenses over her eyes, seeking the source of the flash.

She smiled. 'I think I might have a better choice for you, Leader.'

'D flight, take the lame ducks, make sure they don't get away. Everyone else, on my mark, split into pairs and engage. Three. Two...'

'Sir!'

Gruber growled at his wingman's interruption. 'What is it? You have your orders, just carry them out!'

'Incoming enemy fighters, two o'clock high! I count at least ten, maybe more.'

'What? Of all the...' Gruber fumed and punched the instrument panel in front of him, his airspeed indicator shattering in a very satisfactory manner. There was nothing for it but to disengage; even though the Muscovite fighter squadron based nearby was reportedly nowhere near as good as the Misfits, their entry into the fight would tip the balance heavily in the favour of the British.

'Break off and head for base.'

Gruber slung Hölle onto its wing and jerked the control yoke into his lap, pulling the maximum G forces the aircraft would take, wanting the momentary taste of welcoming darkness it would give him.

'Badger Leader, this is Wolfpack Leader. We heard that you needed a bit of help.'

For once the Russian squadron was a very welcome sight. 'Yes, thank you, Wolfpack Leader. Can you escort us home, please?'

Baryshnikov laughed. 'Of course! It would be our pleasure. Coming down to you.'

'Negative, Wolfpack, stay up there, just in case the Barons come back.'

'Barons? Those aircraft belonged to the Crimson Barons?' Baryshnikov's voice had changed from jovial banter to something that was almost anger. 'Your man, Isaacs, didn't say that the Prussians attacking you were the Crimson Barons!' He swore in Russian, repeatedly and loudly. 'If I'd known...'

'What? What would you have done? Gone after them?'

'Of course!'

It was Abby's turn to swear, but she at least had the decency to turn her radio off first and she only came back on the air once she had calmed down. 'I'm sorry. Next time we'll let you know and we can handle them together.'

'Good. Do that.'

The Russian signed off and the two squadrons flew on in silence, broken only by fire from a single battery of anti-aircraft guns, which Abby and Gwen peeled off to deal with, and in less than fifteen minutes they crossed the border into safety.

Abby had called ahead and Medical staff were standing by when the Misfits landed, which was just as well, because Chastity made it only two steps from Dove before her legs gave way beneath her and she collapsed face-first to the floor, going into shock from blood loss. Not only did she have a shard of glass in her head, but the entire left side of her RAC flightsuit was peppered with small holes from where her cockpit had shattered and sprayed her. The suit had protected her somewhat, but the damage had added up and the blue fabric was soaked with red liquid. She hadn't said anything about being so badly hurt and Gwen wondered whether she'd actually been fully aware of her injuries with the shock and the blow to her head or if she just hadn't wanted to worry them.

While the medics took Chastity away on a stretcher, the pilots stood in a loose group, staring at the aircraft that were being wheeled into the hangars.

The three heavily damaged aircraft had gotten down safely, although there had been a terrifying moment when Monty had lost control and for a second it had looked like his left wing was going to hit the ground and send him into a cartwheel, but he had managed to recover just in time.

Only a couple of the other aircraft had escaped unscathed, but it would have been a lot worse if Charles hadn't warned them when he had. They were also fully aware that if the Wolfpack hadn't been in the air already and Charles hadn't been in communications range of them, then things would have turned out very differently.

'So...' said Mac. 'It looks like the Barons are here.'

Gwen frowned. 'I would have thought they'd be on one of the other fronts where the fighting was the heaviest.'

Bruce grinned. 'Maybe they heard we were here and thought they'd come and say g'day.'

Monty rolled his eyes at his wingman. 'Whatever their reason for turning up, they're here now and it complicates matters somewhat.'

'Why?' Abby looked around the group. 'Why does it make things more complicated? It's not as if we didn't know they would send more fighters. And who cares that it's the Barons? They're just another Prussian squadron, better than most, yes, but we've beaten them before and we'll do it again.'

She glared at them all, daring them to contradict her and when they didn't she nodded in satisfaction.

'Right then, buck the hell up, because we have work to do if we want to be back in the air in time to make a difference when the Barons, and whoever else they brought with them, start escorting the bombers over.'

One by one, Gruber removed the photos from the box and pinned them to the wall of his new office. As he did so, he took a few seconds to look at each of them, following the superb lines of the Misfit aircraft on them, lines that he knew by heart after staring at them for hours on end.

The photos were bad quality, dim and grainy, unfocused and poorly framed, taken from a camera concealed in a hat, but they were good enough to get a clear idea of the new machines. He still didn't know what the British had called them, but he could easily imagine how they handled - the smooth lines and sleek forms slipping through the air as he flew them in his imagination, in his dreams. They were remarkable machines, each showing Gwen Stone's unique touch, and copies of the photos were already being analysed by Herr Blume to see what could be learnt from them for the next generation of Blutsaugers.

He had been looking forward to burning at least a few of the photographs that day, anticipating being sent other trophies to go with the ones hanging in the mess in Bertha, but he'd been disappointed and instead he had to arrange for a box containing a red tailplane to be sent across the river.

He'd send it to Murmansk, though; it wouldn't do to let the other Misfits know he was aware of the location of their base until he turned up to raze it to the ground.

CHAPTER 23

True to Abby's prediction, the Prussians immediately sent a bombing raid up. They were accompanied by two squadrons of MU9's and another of HH190's.

The Misfits' aircraft were too beaten up to do anything about them, though, so, while the Wolfpack and a recently-reassigned squadron, an all-female squadron equipped with Polikasparovs called the "Night Witches", were sent out to intercept them, they spent their time patching holes, replacing Duralumin panels, Hawk's airscrew and the glass of Dove's canopy.

The afternoon brought with it surprise guests in the form of a fast scout aircraft carrying Dorothy Campbell, whose negotiations had finally concluded, as well as Freddy Featherstonehaugh and the photographer, Mr Jones.

While Mr Jones immediately began taking photographs and the sky commodore greeted the Misfits, the journalist barely stopped long enough to say hello before rushing to see Chastity, who was awake and recovering, but on bed rest for at least a couple of days.

Campbell shook her head as she watched him running at full speed around the corner of the mess hall, heading to the medical centre. 'He hasn't sat still the whole flight up. At one point I thought I was going to have to throw him out the door just to get him to stop asking me if the aircraft was going as fast as it could.'

Abby smiled. 'I knew those two had something going on, but I thought it was just a bit of a fling.'

'Oh, no. It's fairly serious. There's no ring involved or anything yet, but he did get her a pretty expensive gift in St. Petersburg.' Campbell grinned. 'Bet you can't guess what it was.'

'A Fabergé egg?'

'Not even close. He somehow got her measurements and persuaded Anton Petrov to make her a flightsuit.'

'Oh!' Abby's eyes widened.

Kitty nudged Gwen in the ribs to catch her attention. 'Who's Anton Petrov?'

'He's the man who made my flightsuit and Abby's. He makes arguably the best performance flightsuits in the world.'

Bruce overheard her and shook his head with a grin. 'Nah, that's Cobber Brown, down in Aussie - best Rooskin suits you've ever worn!'

Gwen chuckled. 'Well, if you don't fancy wearing a flightsuit made from Kangaroo leather or particularly feel like going all the way to Australia to get one, Petrov's suits are the next best thing. Mine is a bit of an antique - my parents got it for me for my sixteenth birthday, but Abby's is only a year or so old by the look of it, which is why she has controls for her lenses in her gloves and connectors for aircraft systems, which I don't.'

Kitty nodded slowly. 'OK... I'm guessing a flightsuit like that would be expensive then.'

Abby nodded. 'My flightsuit was a gift from the King - he gave it to me when he gave the Misfits permission to wear non-uniform flightsuits. I would never have been able to afford one otherwise and lord knows how Freddy did, but his timing is superlative; I'm fairly sure they had to cut Chastity's flightsuit off her.'

'I've always felt a bit bad seeing her in that bloody awful RAC monstrosity while we look so fabulous in our custom-made suits.' Scarlet said with a grin.

Abby gave her a scathing look. 'Quite apart from that, she'll be able to better use Dove's capabilities now, without the risk of blacking out.'

'That's what I meant.' Scarlet crossed her eyes at Abby and flounced away towards the mess, to the laughter of the rest of the Misfits.

Abby shook her head with a smile and turned back to Campbell. 'We were just about to take a break for dinner. Would you care to join us?'

'I'd love to, but please tell me there's a shortage of beetroot up here in the north.'

'No such luck I'm afraid.'

'Oh well, nevermind...' Campbell sighed then looked around and dropped her voice. 'Um. Do you think you can find us a table in a quiet corner so I can let you all know what's happening?'

'Wolfpack are still up, so it should be just us in there.'

'Good. Because the Tsar doesn't want the rank and file knowing how badly things are going.'

Gwen shared an alarmed look with Kitty, then together they joined the suddenly sombre procession into the mess hall.

Once they had gotten their food and were settled around a table in the corner of the mess hall near the fire, where the crackling and popping of the wood would cover their words a bit, the sky commodore began to fill them in on what was going on with the war on the Eastern Front.

They hadn't heard much of what was happening beyond their own theatre in the north, but what little had been filtering through had been generally optimistic. The reality, according to Campbell, was much different.

'The few successes you've been enjoying up here are the only one we've had. Greece, Yugoslavia, Bulgaria, Rumania, the Ukraine, the Baltic territories, they've all fallen and the Prussians have been pushing forwards along an eight hundred mile front. They've all but shot the Muscovite Air Service out of the sky and have been making deeper and deeper incursions for the last week or so.'

'Can the Muscovites hold them?' Abby leaned forward, propping herself up on her elbows and speaking barely above a whisper.

'The short answer is no. They have troops, millions of them, and they have the will, but they don't have the weapons. Only a few places are managing to hold out and most of those are the ones that have our tanks and guns, the rest are being overrun and the Prussians are driving towards St. Petersburg and Moscow.'

Campbell glanced around again to make absolutely sure that nobody was close enough to overhear her. 'The Tsar is making preparations to evacuate his family to the east.'

Mac growled. 'If he's buggering off, why the hell are we still here fighting for him?'

'Because the winter will stop the Prussian offensive further south, just like it will here. When that happens, the Muscovites will have at least a couple of months to build armaments and, combined with the supplies we bring in, that should be enough for them to mount a better resistance. But *only* if we keep these northern passages open to bring those supplies in. If the Prussians push us out of Murmansk there will be no way for us to help and Muscovy will most likely be lost.'

Abby nodded her understanding. 'So, what you're saying is that the Muscovites are throwing sticks and stones at the Prussians, trying to hold them back long enough so they don't conquer the whole damn country before winter comes and we need to hold on here so that we can bring in more weapons for the spring.'

'Essentially, yes. There is one good thing to report, though, and that is that the Ottomans have barricaded themselves in and insist on remaining neutral, which means that the route into Muscovy through Persia is closed for the Prussians, at least for now. We're looking at opening that up as a supply route as an alternative to the north, but we need to make headway in North Africa before we can do that and the Italians are making that bloody difficult at the moment. Plus, the Prussians are pushing hard towards Tsaritsyn and the Caspian Sea in the south to try to cut that route off before we can open it, so we may need the northern route for a bit longer than we thought.'

Campbell looked around the group before settling once more on Abby. 'And what about you? Are you going to be able to hold on here for a few more weeks?'

'If you'd asked me that question yesterday then I would have said yes. Definitely. Today, I'm not so sure.'

'Because of the Barons?'

'Yes. Their presence means we can't keep attacking the reinforcement columns like we need to. Any other squadron we'd be able to take care of and still do damage to the Prussian ground forces, but them...'

'Is it only the Barons you're worried about, though? There's nothing else?'

The sound of the Wolfpack returning from their patrol came from outside the hall and Campbell stared pointedly at Abby.

Abby's lips briefly twitched into a snarl. 'Things would probably be easier if we were working with a more disciplined squadron, but in the grand scheme of things I don't think it would make much difference.'

'Alright.' Campbell nodded and forked the last of her meal into her mouth, grimacing slightly as she chewed then swallowed, washing it down with a mouthful of kvass. 'Bleurgh, I can't wait to get home. I certainly hope the Arturo's got some proper British stores left for the trip back, even if it's just bully beef and spam.' She wiped her mouth with a napkin then sighed. 'Well, I've got to get moving; I need to get to Murmansk before it's dark. I'll be liaising with command there and hopefully we can work something out to delay the Prussians a bit.'

She stood up and gazed around the group, giving each of them a warm smile. 'Just keep doing what you're doing and I'm sure we'll come through this fine.'

The Misfits accompanied Campbell outside to see her off. Abby was mildly annoyed to see that an autocar had been provided for her, whereas she had had to make do with a bike messenger, but she said nothing, only put on a big smile and waved with the others.

Once the sky commodore's vehicle was out of sight, the pilots went back to their aircraft, joining the fitters who were just getting back from their own meal.

At the end of the day, the only aircraft that weren't yet airworthy were Raptor and Jaguar, which would require a long night of work by the fitters to finish. Supplies of paint had long since run out, though, (to the horror of the Wolfpack pilots) and most of the fighters had to be left with unpainted panels spoiling their colours. In fact, the only aircraft which was still completely as it had been when it arrived, apart from Hummingbird, Vulture and Bloodhound, which had seen no actual combat, was Dragonfly, a testament to her pilot's skill.

The Misfits woke the next day to a world which had turned completely white. Snow was falling in thick fluffy chunks and had settled, covering the airfield and buildings in a pristine blanket.

Gwen rubbed the sleeve of her dressing gown on the window to clear the condensation off and looked outside. 'It's beautiful.'

Kitty leaned over her shoulder, taking full advantage of the opportunity to put her arm around Gwen, who looked around to make sure that nobody was watching before snuggling against her. 'Yes. It is.' The tall American turned away from the view to gaze into Gwen's eyes. 'And so are you,' she whispered. 'Good morning.'

'Good morning.'

Gwen smiled up at her, but at a discrete, and at the same time knowing, cough from Scarlet, they separated and started getting dressed.

The night of the party they'd gone straight to the barracks, but unfortunately they'd only had a few minutes alone together before some of the other pilots arrived. However, Gwen found her pulse quickening when she recalled the feel of Kitty's hard body under her hands as they'd fumbled at each other's clothing, the feel of her silky skin and the way she'd gasped as Gwen had...

'You don't half look gormless with that big grin stuck on your face, Gwen.'

Scarlet's laugh snapped Gwen out of her daydreaming and she realised that she had been standing motionless with her shirt only half-buttoned, staring at Kitty. She gave the irrepressible Irishwoman a happy grin, but winced inwardly; slip-ups like that were fine around the Misfits, but if she did something similar in front of Drake he would know that she had as good as lied to him.

She resolved to speak to him as soon as she could, then hurriedly finished getting ready and followed the rest of the squadron outside, joining them in their delight in the novel circumstances.

Baryshnikov was with his squadron, preparing for takeoff. He had lost several pilots the day before, intercepting the bombing raid, and replacements had arrived just before midnight. The Wolfpack was going up with the three instructors on a training flight before breakfast to get the new pilots used to the Harridans so that they wouldn't be out of their depth when they went into combat, which meant it was just the Misfits on standby for any Prussian raids that came over that morning.

They wandered over to him and Abby asked him the question they were all thinking. 'Are you flying in this?'

He frowned as if he didn't quite understand the question. 'Of course! Why not?' He looked around them, at their fur coats hugged tightly around their bodies, silk scarves around their necks and uniform hats pulled low and laughed. 'Oh, my naive British friends, this is not winter! This is just, how do you say it? A bit of "brisk" weather! If we didn't fly in weather like this we would *never* fly. It would be like you British refusing to go up in the rain!'

He grinned at their doubtful expressions. 'Do not worry my friends, a bit of snow has never killed anyone. Except the Swedish. And the French.' He trailed off and walked away, laughing.

'Morning all.' Pemberton wandered over with Howard and Drake in tow, their aircraft prepped and ready.

Gwen nodded to Drake who gave her a dazzling smile in return.

'What do you think of flying in this weather?' Abby asked the squadron leader.

Pemberton grinned and dropped her voice so that the Wolfpack couldn't hear him. 'If the bloody Russkies can fly in it, so can we, what?'

The Misfits chuckled and Abby nodded. 'Indeed. I'm sure we'll be up soon enough as well, unless of course the Prussians decide that they want to stay at home and build snowmen. Have a good flight.'

'Thank you, ma'am.'

Pemberton nodded and went back to her machine, followed by Howard, but Gwen screwed up her courage and grabbed Drake to stop him leaving.

He looked at the hand on his arm and grinned. 'Did you change your mind about that dance, Goosy?'

Gwen smiled. 'Not exactly. I just need to speak to you about something.'

He laughed and gestured at the line of Harridans behind him. 'I don't know if you've noticed, but I'm supposed to be flying into a snow storm in a minute. Is it important or can we leave it for when I get back?' he frowned. 'Is something wrong?'

'No, no, nothing's wrong.' Gwen quickly waved away his question, not wanting him to be worried about her when he was in the air. 'It's not urgent, we'll talk when you get back.'

'Alright.' Drake nodded. 'Get the cooks to smoke me a kipper would you? I'll be back for breakfast. We can speak then.'

Gwen couldn't help but laugh; they'd had sleepovers a few times in each other's houses and he'd always insisted on kippers for breakfast, even though she hated them and couldn't stand the way they smell. She wouldn't be able to get near enough to speak to him properly if he was eating them, not to mention how bad his breath would be. She shook her head and punched him on the arm. 'Not on your life, Digger. See you soon.'

He winked, then turned and jogged off to his aircraft.

Gwen watched him go, dreading the conversation to come, then hurried into the warmth of the mess.

Freddy Featherstonehaugh was supporting Chastity as she hobbled in to join them at breakfast and saw her settled before he sat down himself. There was a thick bandage around her head and she was moving with exaggerated care, but she had a better colour to her skin and no longer looked like death warmed up. She wouldn't be fully recovered for a while but had been released from the medical bay after a good night's sleep during which Featherstonehaugh had refused to leave her side.

'Interesting coat, Mr Featherstonehaugh.' Abby pointed at the journalist's brown thigh-length jacket, which he had hung from a peg on the wall next to the long row of Misfit furs. It was of an unusual cut, with a particularly striking and complicated geometrical pattern of threads and beads decorating its front.

'Mr Jones and I were presented them by the Inuit during our mission for Imperial Geographic. They're caribou skin lined with wolverine fur.' He grinned. 'Which, I suppose, is a little bit of a coincidence, Wolverine Leader.'

'Let's call it a good omen, shall we?'

The journalist laughed. 'A good omen, I'll make a note of that.' He looked around the group. 'So, did I miss much?'

'Not half!' grinned Scarlet. 'Mac and Bruce have got girlfriends following them around the country.'

The journalist's eyebrows shot up at that. 'Really? That sounds absolutely terrifying.'

The Misfits laughed and Mac blushed in embarrassment, but Bruce just grinned proudly. 'We met a couple of lovely Sheilas in St. Petersburg and they've been posted to Murmansk.'

'They requested transfers here?'

'Nah! They were in St. Petersburg finishing their training as something called "morale officers" and when they graduated they asked to be assigned here.' The Australian shrugged. 'They got their choice no problem; it seems that nobody else wanted to be sent here. Don't know why, the weather's gorgeous!'

The pilots laughed again, all except Mac who was now scowling into his porridge.

'Remarkable! And you've been seeing these girls on a regular basis?'

Mac growled at Featherstonehaugh. 'Why the hell are you so interested in our love lives all of a sudden? Don't you know there's a war on?'

The journalist was taken slightly aback by the Scotsman's vehemence, but recovered quickly. 'I do apologise, Mr MacShane, but this is precisely the kind of thing I have been sent here to report on. The British people know about your successes in the air, they have heard of them over and over and never tire of them, but what they have never heard is *who* you are, what you are like as *people*. A story of this kind, a romance like this, a meeting of two cultures, so to speak, is something that will capture their attention and bring this war into their hearts, not just their homes.'

'Very well then, write your damn article,' Mac grumbled, not happy, but smart enough to see his point.

Featherstonehaugh gave him a bow. 'Thank you, sir.' He turned to Bruce, correctly assuming that he would get more out of him than Mac. 'Considering the sensibilities of the British people, is there anything that I might be able to report that isn't more suitable for the bordello?'

'Not much!' Bruce grinned happily, to further laughter from the pilots. 'Oh, there is one thing you might put in - the girls insisted on a tour of the base.'

Scarlet blinked at him in shock. 'We thought that was just a euphemism!'

Bruce grinned at her. 'Well, she didn't exactly call it a "tour", but there was this one thing that Natasha did with her tongue...'

'Back to the story, please, Bruce.' Abby interrupted hurriedly, not particularly wanting the Australian to go into lurid details while they were eating.

'Right oh, boss.' He grinned at her, before turning back to the journalist, who had paused in his scribbling to look up at him. Bruce gave him a wink. 'I'll tell you all about it later, eh? You can teach it to Chastity.'

'Bruce!'

Chastity looked horrified and had turned a bright red. Featherstonehaugh, though, was trying very hard not to laugh and waved for Bruce to go on.

'Anyway. The girls, both of them, mind you, insisted on a tour of the whole base. I think they're fans of the squadron - a bit like the civvies we met at the hospital, you know? Natasha says that Muscovite papers reported on how the war over England was going and they printed the stories that the British press reported on us. Apparently they made us out to be even bigger heroes than they did back home, held us up as examples to follow or some such.'

Abby rolled her eyes. 'I bet that impression didn't survive very long in your company...'

Bruce grinned at her. 'Actually, she was quite impressed with me later on when I...'

'Yes! Thank you!' Abby interrupted him again, putting her head in her hand and sighing. 'Honestly, I don't know what that poor girl sees in you.' Bruce grinned and opened his mouth to speak, but she quickly pointed a finger at him to forestall him. 'Do NOT answer that! Just get back to the story.'

Bruce shrugged. 'There's not much else to tell if you don't want to hear what happened in the barracks later. We just had a look around the base, admired the aircraft for a while, then found a nice quiet spot to... you know.'

Featherstonehaugh finished scribbling with a flourish. 'Excellent! The readers will love this, adds a wonderful human touch to what you're doing here.' He smiled. 'Is there anything else? Scarlet, I hear you're learning a fair amount about their culture, dancing and singing and whatnot. Is that right? How are you doing? Have you been learning the language as well?'

The Irishwoman grinned at him. 'I'm pretty fluent in swearing, would you like to hear some?'

The journalist returned her grin with delight. 'I would love to!'

Scarlet took a deep breath in preparation, but before she could begin to insult him, his lineage, his domestic animals and his dress sense, she was interrupted by a young soldier bringing two messages for Abby.

Silence fell as all eyes turned to the group captain.

Featherstonehaugh looked around. 'Is it the order to scramble?'

Mac huffed at him, still not quite having forgiven the intrusion into his private life. 'D'ya think we'd still be sitting here if it was?'

'No, I suppose not.'

'You'll know when it's time, lad; there'll be a bloody awful klaxon fillin' yer ears if they want us.'

Abby read the two messages, then looked up at them. 'This is a radio message from Owen. The Crimson Barons were spotted over the border five minutes ago, carrying out ground attacks on the troops stationed along the river. He had them on radar the whole time, but didn't know it was them until the Muscovites gave visual confirmation.'

Owen had been up in the air since well before dawn, watching for Prussian movements. With the snow coming down, the optical system in Charles' Vulture was almost useless, whereas Bloodhound's radar was unaffected.

'So, he knows where they are based.'

Abby nodded at Derek, who had seen the implications of the message before everyone else. 'He does. They've set up shop at the same airfield we attacked with the bombers.'

'So, why weren't we put into the air to stop them and when are we going to go and shoot the hell out of their aircraft?' Mac spoke through gritted teeth, his clenched fist banging the table to punctuate his words.

There was very vocal support of his suggestion from most of the pilots around the table, but Abby just shook her head.

'It wouldn't work; they have too many fighters now and they won't ever be all landing at the same time, low on tension. Also, I'm fairly sure they'd be ready for something like that. As for why we didn't intercept them, it's because they're not a priority target.'

'Of course they bloody are!' replied Mac. 'They shot down Penny, they...' He stopped, panting for breath, slowly bringing himself under control. 'I'm sorry, Abby. Why? Why aren't they a target for us?'

'Simply put, because the destruction of a single fighter squadron, even the Barons, will do nothing to save the Muscovites and we are better used against bombers and ground targets.' She waved the second piece of paper. 'So, at least for now, we're under strict orders to avoid any engagement with the Barons.' She looked around the group, making sure that everyone had understood, then glanced at the clock on the wall above the door. 'Come on, finish eating, then go get your flightsuits on; I doubt the Prussians are going to wait around much longer.'

The Misfits had just enough time to admire Chastity in her new Petrov flightsuit (it was white to match Dove and she looked absolutely stunning, especially with the Tsar's black fur over the top) before they were scrambled to intercept a Prussian bombing raid heading for Murmansk.

The snow-laden clouds were thick, but low, and above them was clear blue sky as far as the eye could see. They found the Polikasparovs of the Night Witches waiting for them at thirty thousand feet over the city and turned with them towards the approaching bombers.

There was something very familiar about the situation to Gwen and she smiled when she realised what it was - aside from the heavy clouds and the sun that was still low on the horizon, despite it being hours after dawn, the situation was very reminiscent of the interceptions they had flown over England; they were heavily outnumbered and being sent to attack bombers that were heading for a city.

She just hoped that the outcome would be the same as the majority of those interceptions.

'Wolverine Leader, this is Pinpoint, come in please.'

Gwen grinned at the callsign that Dorothy "Dot" Campbell had chosen for herself and there was laughter in Abby's voice when she responded. 'Pinpoint, this is Wolverine Leader, reading you loud and clear. I'm told you have some business for us.'

'Roger, Wolverine. One hundred plus aircraft, heading two eight zero. Fifty miles out at angels twenty-five.'

'Just like old times, Pinpoint.'

'Roger that, Wolverine. Prioritise bombers, please, repeat, prioritise bombers.'

'Roger, Pinpoint.'

'Thank you, Wolverine. Happy hunting.'

'Thank you, Pinpoint. Wolverine out.'

As soon as Campbell signed off Abby came over the squadron frequency. 'Right, you heard her, Wolverines, we're going for the bombers. Break straight through the fighter cover, only taking shots if they present themselves, then concentrate all fire on the bombers. When the fighters try to engage, do what you have to, but do not follow if they break off. Understood?'

Eight British and ten Muscovite pilots acknowledged her, but then they flew on in silence, heading almost due west towards the enemy formation, each of them preparing for battle in their own way.

The combined squadrons intercepted the bombers more than twenty miles before they reached the city and dived as a single unit, forming a solid wedge that they drove through the covering fighters, scattering them to the winds and destroying two, one by Abby and the other shared between Kitty and Derek, before cutting into the bomber formation. Several bombers went down to the concentrated fire of the Misfit pairs and the Muscovites accounted for two more, their four large calibre machine guns in each wing doing good work on the Prussian aircraft.

After having spent so much time attacking ground targets, which was very two dimensional work, the attack on the bombers was a welcome change for Gwen, a return to the freedom that was what she had loved so much about flying and that had made her want to dedicate her life to it as a child. She felt truly alive again for the first time since the raid on the fighter base as she followed Abby in and around the bombers, using the greater speed of their new springs to make longer runs than they had done previously and outrunning the fighters each time they tried to cut them off.

All too soon, the bomb bay doors of the bombers opened and they dropped their payloads. For several seconds, ironclad death fell screaming into the clouds far below, but then, as one, the Prussians turned and dived for home.

The Misfits pursued, the Polikasparov fighters with them, and they destroyed several more, but the bombers went into the clouds after only a couple of minutes and it became impossible to follow them, so they were forced to break off. They were more than happy with the morning's work, though, as more than a dozen enemy aircraft were littering the countryside for only a single Muscovite fighter downed in return.

The snow had worsened and visibility was very limited when the Misfits arrived back at Vaenga. The base was impossible to pick out from the surrounding countryside and if it hadn't been for a couple of flares, one placed at each end of the airfield, they might have missed it.

Landing was quite dicey; a foot or more of snow had accumulated on the ground and that provided a drag on the wheels that threatened to tear them off first, then, when that failed, tried to tip the aircraft nose first into the ground. The Misfits had been forewarned of the danger by Staff-Captain Polikasparov, Baryshnikov's second in command, before he took off, but they weren't quite ready for how bad it was and it was only by some judicious use of throttle and ailerons, that they were able to avoid disaster.

As soon as they had handed their aircraft over to the fitters for rewinding and refitting, they slogged through the snow to the mess hall, seeking to warm up over a cup of tea and a snack and found the four pilots of C flight inside.

'Owen? Shouldn't you still be up?'

The Welshman nodded at Abby's question. 'I did tell Campbell that I could stay up for longer, but she ordered me down, just in case the weather worsens more.'

'That's sensible, I suppose, but we won't have any warning if another raid come over.'

Owen shook his head. 'She told me to tell you that there wouldn't be any more interceptions.'

Abby blinked in surprise. 'Really? Why?'

'Apparently, very little damage was done to military installations this morning because the bombs mostly fell on civilian areas of the city. The generals are happy with that and feel that their resources are better spent against ground targets, which are a much greater threat.'

Abby stared at him coldly. 'And she agreed?'

'Yes...'

Owen was interrupted before he could say any more by swearing and disgusted comments from many of the pilots and he sat impassively, waiting for the chance to continue.

'Pipe down, everybody.' Abby's command was quiet and barely audible over the hubbub, but it was instantly obeyed nonetheless. 'Go on, Owen.'

'She said she agrees with their tactics *in principle* because the Prussians have to make a move soon and that will be with ground forces, so we have to weaken them while we have the chance.

However, she also said that she doesn't agree one bit with the callous way the Muscovites are treating their citizens.'

Abby stared into her tea for long seconds, deep in thought, but in the end, however much she hated it, she could only come to the same conclusion. 'They're right.'

Her words caused another uproar and she held her hand up for silence so that she could explain herself.

'We saw this in France and we saw this in Britain. Yes, air power can soften a target and destroy the ability to make war, but without troops and mechanised brigades on the ground you cannot hold or take a territory.' She looked around the group. 'Our job here is to prevent the Prussians from gaining and holding this territory, so, logically, our best chance is to weaken their ground troops as much as possible and if that means leaving the bombers alone, then so be it.'

She held her hand up again before her pilots could protest. 'The first time I met him, I told the Muscovite general what I thought about him putting civilians in danger and it didn't do a blind bit of difference, so nothing we say now is going to change anything. At the end of the day, though, if the Prussians cross the river into the city, the result will be a lot worse than the dozen or so bombing raids that we may or may not have been able to prevent. So yes, while I don't like it any more than any of you do, I agree with the necessity and in the long run it will probably save more lives.'

She took a deep drink of her tea, then met the eyes of her pilots one by one. 'Anybody got anything to say? Constructive, that is, and not just swearing.'

Before anyone could answer her, though, there were several almighty clangs from outside, like metal collapsing in on itself, that made everybody jump. There was a moment of silence and then mugs and chairs crashed to the floor as the pilots raced to the door.

At first they thought that the Harridan lying on its back only yards away had merely fallen victim to the snow and tipped over, but then they saw the holes in it and the blood dripping from the pilot as he hung limply from his straps, far too much of it to have just been from the impact.

CHAPTER 24

For one awful moment, Gwen thought that the man in the Harridan was Drake; his face and body were covered with blood, obscuring his identity, and, since they had run out of paint, the new recruits were flying unpainted Harridans, just like the instructors. However, a quick glance at the roundels told her that it was one of the Muscovite machines and she would have sighed in relief if it weren't for the fact that there was a man dying in front of her, full of bullet holes that shouldn't have been there if Wolfpack Squadron had stayed out of trouble like they'd supposed to.

More Harridans appeared as ghostly forms in the snowy sky and it became clear that the first wasn't the only one with damage. There was only one more mishap on landing, though, when the pilot of an aircraft with its undercarriage and almost half of its left wing missing tried to land on a single wheel instead of just pancaking. The stub of the wing inevitably dug into the ground and sent the aircraft into a spin that broke pieces off, but surprisingly didn't rip the sturdy Harridan apart. The pilot walked away from the experience bruised and dizzy, but in one piece.

Baryshnikov and Polikasparov landed easily, their experience with similar conditions telling, as did Pemberton and Howard. Another pilot got down safely after them, but had to be carried off to the medical centre with bullet or shrapnel wounds.

Of Drake and the final five Muscovite pilots there was no sign.

Pemberton leapt out of her Harridan as soon as it came to a halt and went storming through the snow towards Baryshnikov, tearing her gloves off as she went and Abby's eyes flew wide in alarm.

'Stop her, for pity's sake!'

Mac, Bruce, Monty and Wendy immediately sprinted as best as they can through the snow and grabbed the small woman only yards before she reached the Russian, and dragged her back to Abby.

'Let me go, damn you! Let me go right now! I'll have you bloody court-martialled with him if you don't BLOODY. LET. ME. GO!' Pemberton was only a couple of inches taller than Scarlet, but she was powerful and the four pilots were having trouble holding her back as she kicked and struck out at them, trying to get away.

'Squadron Leader!'

The pilots released Pemberton and Abby's commanding voice brought her up short before she could charge off again.

'Explain yourself, Squadron Leader. What the hell happened up there?'

The instructor stabbed her finger angrily at Baryshnikov, who was inspecting the damage to his aircraft with a fitter. Thankfully he hadn't noticed that anything was going on and was out of hearing. 'That bloody maniac led us straight into the Crimson Barons!'

Abby frowned. 'But the Wolfpack weren't supposed to have been anywhere near combat.'

'We weren't, we were well behind our lines, but then we got this call over the radio in Russian and we changed course. I didn't understand what had been said, so I thought it was just a routine call. I had no idea what he was doing until it was too late and we were too close to the Barons to break off. Then we just had to bloody get stuck into it with them. Drake was magnificent, he took down one of the blighters right away and drew away a couple who were on the new pilots, but then Gruber went after him...'

Gwen had only been half-listening to Pemberton's story as she searched the sky for Drake, expecting him to show up at any second, but at the mention of his name she turned to her. 'Where's Rudy?'

Her quiet voice stopped Pemberton dead and everybody looked at her.

'Where is he?'

Tears started to well up in her eyes, blurring her vision, but she brushed them away angrily and shouted at the woman, demanding an answer. 'Where is he!'

Pemberton shook her head. 'I'm sorry, I don't know; I lost track of him, but I'm pretty sure Gruber got him.'

Gwen hid her face in her hands and sobbed. She didn't feel it when first Kitty, then Scarlet wrapped their arms around her, everything was numb.

Some part of her was aware, though, when Baryshnikov strutted over to the Misfits.

The Russian was grinning. 'Did you hear?'

'Yes, we heard alright.' Abby was gritting her teeth, barely able to keep from shouting at the man.

Baryshnikov was oblivious, though, and he held up a couple of fingers. 'Two! We got two!' He gloated. 'Even you Misfits only got *one* the other day.'

'One.' Abby said coldly. '*You* only got one. *Aviator Lieutenant Drake* got the other.'

'Quite so, quite so, but he was under my command, so it counts for the Wolfpack. Where is he, by the way? I want to congratulate him.' Baryshnikov looked around and only then seemed to notice that fully half of his squadron and one of the instructors wasn't there. 'Ah, I see,' he nodded sagely, then shrugged. 'I am sorry, of course, but these things happen.'

Pemberton growled and the Misfits around her managed to grab her just in time before she could leap on the man.

Nobody had thought to restrain Gwen, though.

She closed the gap to the Russian in an instant and her fist shot out to hit him square on the nose, knocking him flat on his back, blood spraying onto the pristine white of the field.

The snow chose that exact moment to stop and the sun poked its way through the clouds, a beam of light illuminating the scene as if it were a work of art.

The silence went on for an almost unbearable length of time as Gwen stood over Baryshnikov's unconscious form, panting with fury, but at the same time aghast with what she had done, the intense feeling of satisfaction competing with the knowledge that she had done something forbidden and unforgivable.

She realised that she was still in a pugilist's stance like she'd been shown in basic training and forced herself to relax, taking a deep, shuddering breath as she dropped her fist to her sides and unclenched them. She winced at a pain in her right hand and flexed it experimentally, but it wasn't seriously damaged.

'Gwen, to quarters!'

Abby's sharp voice had her spinning in place to face the pilots. There was disbelief and shock on most of their faces, but pride and satisfaction on those of several. However, it was the anger, disappointment and dismay on Abby's face that made her stomach take a sickening tumble with the realisation that she was in a heck of a lot of trouble.

'Now!'

Without a word, Gwen started slowly towards the barracks building, unable to escape the feeling that she had been in the exact same position only months before and wondering if she would be able to escape her fate a second time.

Gwen paced up and down the long barracks room, tortured by thoughts of Rudy. She saw him torn to pieces by machine gun fire, blood everywhere, saw him going down in a stricken aircraft desperately trying to open his stuck canopy, had visions of him bailing out, his glidewings iced shut and not opening, his body tumbling over and over as it fell towards the ground so far below...

Every so often she would pause to look for him out of the windows. The clouds had broken up and the sun was shining weakly, the snow completely stopped. Conditions were perfect for flying, if a little cold, and if anyone had still been in the air they would have arrived long ago.

Nobody came, though.

'Gwen.'

She hadn't heard Abby come in and she whirled to face her. 'Is there any news?'

She thought that perhaps there had been a call over the radio to say that Rudy had put down in a field somewhere or bailed out, but any hopes that she'd had were dashed when Abby shook her head. 'No, nothing.'

'Oh.' Gwen sank down on the end of the nearest bed. She put her head into her hands and stared at the bare wooden floor, not really seeing it.

Footsteps approached and then Abby's boots entered her field of vision.

'The penalty for striking a senior officer in the Muscovite armed forces is death.'

It took a few seconds for the words to make their way through the haze of Gwen's grief, but when they did it was as if she'd been sprayed by one of the hoses on the Arturo and her eyes shot up to meet Abby's.

'But...'

Abby held her hand up, forestalling Gwen's protest. 'No need to start pleading for your life, though, you've been damn lucky; I've managed to strike a deal with Baryshnikov and he's not going to press charges.'

Gwen sagged in relief, her head returning to its cradle in her hands, but then she lifted it again and looked back at her commanding officer. 'A deal? What does that mean?' She swallowed. 'What do I have to do?'

'Don't worry, you don't have to do anything; I just told him he could keep the souvenir from the Baron I shot down - his ego was big enough for that to be adequate compensation for anything.' She grinned. 'In fact he probably would have let you slap him around a few more times if I'd insisted on it, he was so keen to get his dirty mitts on it.'

Gwen stared at her, astounded that she was going to get away with such a serious offence so easily.

Abby read her expression and smiled wryly. 'You're getting into a bit of a habit of breaking the rules - this is the second time you've done something that should have you thrown out of the RAC at best, at worst put in front of a firing squad - but it's not just you that's got a problem with military discipline, it's all of us: from Owen taking you up that night over London; to Mac and Bruce's drinking; to Wendy smuggling her weapons here; to Scarlet leaving Bagshot every night to meet Pewtall without permission - we're all guilty of something and me most of all for letting you all get away with it. Yes, we're Misfits and we aren't expected to obey all the rules, but there are limits even for us and we need to start getting a bit of, if not discipline, then some *common sense* into this squadron. We're going to be leaving here at some point and Cummerbund and his cronies are waiting for us back in London, or had you forgotten about them?'

Gwen nodded mutely and Abby chuckled. 'So had I, but I just had a nice long conversation with Dot and she let me know in no uncertain terms that our every move here is being scrutinised. She will try to make sure that no word of your little indiscretion makes its way into any of the official reports, but it is exactly the kind of thing that will give them an excuse to shut this squadron down, so we need to buck our ideas up.'

Gwen nodded. 'I'll try. And I'm sorry for hitting Baryshnikov.'

'Don't be; in the end you saved me from having to do it and that would have been a lot worse for us. Just apologise to him tonight and be on your best behaviour from now on, please.

'Roger, Leader.'

Abby held her hand out to her. 'Now come on, it's lunch time. We'll raise a drink to Drake with you later tonight, but we have a lot of work to do first.'

That afternoon the Misfits were sent to attack Prussian positions along the border.

Gwen used the white-hot anger she felt at Rudy Drake's death against them, showing no mercy, coldly and efficiently destroying all the tanks, guns and defensive positions she came across with guns and rockets, making sure to expend only enough ammunition to get the job done so that it would last longer and she could do more killing.

She felt no emotion, beyond that rage, felt no regret at the lives she took, but neither did she take any satisfaction in it.

The Fleas were taken completely by surprise by the change in tactics and scrambled fighters far too late to do anything to stop them, and the Misfits were already long gone by the time they arrived, leaving a swathe of destruction in their wake that extended almost two miles.

It was a drop in the ocean, though, compared to the immense force still arrayed along the front, ready to attack.

Gwen stood in front of the mirror in the barracks, tying the black silk cravat of her day uniform for the fifth time, trying to get it perfectly symmetrical through bleary eyes.

'Here let me.' Kitty appeared behind her and reached around to tie it with practised movements.

Gwen met her eyes in the reflection. 'I don't want to go; it feels too final, like he's really gone, like there isn't any hope.'

'I know.' The American woman put a hand on her shoulder. 'None of us do. But he *is* gone - we would have heard something if he was still alive; you know the Barons would let us know. So, we have to mourn him and move on.'

Gwen smiled sadly. 'He told me the same thing, the night of the party, he...'

She stopped, closing her eyes and taking a ragged breath, desperately fighting for control of herself. She didn't want puffy and bloodshot eyes making her look weak when she confronted Baryshnikov to apologise for knocking him out, something she wasn't at all sorry for and would do again in a heartbeat.

'There you go.'

Gwen opened her eyes and looked at her reflection. The cravat was better than it had ever been and the subtle makeup that Scarlet had helped her with was lovely, but her appearance really didn't matter; she wasn't dressing for Baryshnikov, she was dressing for Rudy, and Rudy wouldn't have cared how she looked for his wake, what would have mattered to him was that she was there tonight and that tomorrow she went on with her life.

When Gwen and Kitty walked into the mess hall it was quieter than it had ever been in the evenings. The Misfits had occupied a large table close to the door and the Muscovite officers had grouped at the far end of the room around the fire, letting the British have their private celebration, keeping their songs low and almost mournful, with no dancing going on and the conversations sombre, so as not to disturb them.

Gwen looked around the dimly lit space, trying to find Baryshnikov so that she could get the apology out of the way as soon as possible, but a nudge from Kitty called her attention to the wall next to the bar and all thoughts of the unpleasant man were pushed straight out of her mind as she walked over to it in a trance.

All the Russian trophies had been cleared from the middle of the wall and in their place had been plastered a dozen photographs. Taking pride of place in the middle of the wall was a large portrait of Drake in his dress uniform hat, looking more serious than he ever really was - one of the formal photographs that Mr Jones had insisted of taking of the entire party on the Arturo. The portrait was surrounded by more candid ones showing Drake in his day to day life. There was one from that very morning of him sitting in his Harridan, a dusting of snow on his aircraft and white clouds behind. Another showed him napping in front of the fire in the mess hall, his hat tipped over his eyes. Mr Jones hadn't been around the base long enough to take very many in Muscovy, though, and most of the photos were from the Arturo. There was even one of him and Gwen together in front of the dark shape of one of the Martinet fighters on the flight deck of the carrier. They were in profile, leaning in towards each other, deep in conversation, Gwen laughing at something he'd said.

It was one photograph in particular that caught and held Gwen's eye, though - it was of Drake on the deck of the Arturo, soaking wet, wearing white trousers and a white shirt, laughing merrily, his eyes sparkling and his head tilted back as he raked fingers through his hair to get it off his face. It was a remarkable picture, the photographer managing to capture his entire essence in one image, and Gwen reached out to touch it, a lump forming at the back of her throat.

'Officer Stone.'

The lightly-accented voice came from behind her and she turned to find Baryshnikov standing stiffly at attention. She was relieved to see that the only sign of her blow to his face was a slight bruising at the top of his nose and under his eyes; it would make her apology easier for him to accept if there was no lasting reminder of his humiliation.

He was wearing his light blue hussar's uniform, the gold buttons and braid shining brightly in the firelight, a red sash with a golden medallion draped over his shoulder and a long cavalry sabre at his waist. He seemed to be trying to make amends for his cavalier behaviour by sending Drake off with full honours and Gwen had to clench her fists to prevent herself from berating him and informing him that she would rather have her friend back than have his death honoured.

No matter what her opinion of the man, though, she had to do her duty and she drew herself up to attention and saluted him. 'Sir, I would like to apologise for my behaviour, it was...'

'Think no more of it, Officer Stone.'

He cut her off abruptly, rudely, but far from being offended, Gwen was relieved that she hadn't had to betray her principles.

The man gestured and Polikasparov stepped to his side. He was dressed in a similar uniform to his commander, but without the sash or quite so much gold braiding. He was carrying a long wooden box and he held it out to her.

She took it, puzzled and looked at Baryshnikov for an explanation.

'You were Lieutenant Drake's closest friend, were you not?'

'Yes, sir.' Gwen said slowly, not quite sure what was happening.

She glanced at the box. It was about a yard long and had a cross section of about six inches square. It was the right size for a sword or a gun, but was too light to contain either.

'I heard what he said about his ancestor losing his regiment's colours in the Crimean conflict.'

Gwen's eyes immediately shot upwards, to the place where the British banner usually hung, the one that Drake's eyes went to every time he came to eat. It was no longer hanging from the rafters; it was in the box in her hands.

'Would you see that this gets to his family, please, and tell them that it has long been one of our most prized trophies, not because of who we took it from, but because of how hard it was to do so. Tell them that we have honoured it for long enough and it is time that it makes its way home. That a Drake has finally brought it home to them.'

The man drew himself up and when he saluted, his eyes were on the images on the wall, not her. He held the pose for several heartbeats, then snapped his hand down and gave her a nod to her before going off to join the remnants of his squadron.

Polikasparov remained behind. He glanced around to check that his commander wasn't close, then leaned forwards to speak quietly to her. 'Wonderful punch.'

'Thank you.'

'And I thank you in the name of what little remains of the squadron; perhaps now he will be less of a Cossack in the air and more of a leader.'

'I didn't want to say anything, but you don't act or look like the rest of your squadron. I take it you're not a Cossack?'

'No, my father got me my place in this squadron. The rest of the pilots come from the Cossack regiments.'

'Why? Surely there were other squadrons better suited to you? More... I don't know... civilised?'

He laughed. 'There are plenty, but this is the best squadron in Muscovy and Baryshnikov is the best pilot. It was the ideal place to learn and get my own command as quickly as possible. But then the war...'

Gwen sighed. 'Yes. But then the war.'

'I am sorry about your friend. He was a great pilot and a very brave man.' There was no need to say anything more so Polikasparov just gave her a bow, glanced at the photos with a sad smile, then walked away.

Gwen turned and found that her friends were watching her, waiting for her. She took a deep breath then went over to them, putting the box with the banner carefully on the floor by the wall before taking the empty seat between Abby and Kitty.

A glass of vodka was on the table ready for her and looking around she saw that everybody had one, including Chastity, who didn't drink at all, even the weak kvass.

'We didn't know him as well as you did, so it's your lead, Gwen.' Abby said.

Gwen nodded and picked up the glass.

Without a word she lifted it, quickly followed by the others and, after a moment to remember her childhood friend, a moment in which she said goodbye to him and promised that she would carry on living as best she could, she drank it down.

CHAPTER 25

The Misfits had gotten to know Drake fairly well in the weeks they'd lived with him, but they hadn't known him long enough to have any stories to tell. Neither did the instructors, Howard and Pemberton, having met him only a few weeks before leaving England. It fell to Gwen, therefore, to say a few things about him.

She sorted her memories of him in her head, automatically discarding the ones that she knew would embarrass him, but then stopped when she realised that she no longer needed to worry about that and decided to just talk about him and see what came out.

'I owe my love of flying to Rudy. Before I met him, I fully intended to be *just* an engineer and definitely *not* an aeronautical engineer; that was going to be my little rebellion against my parents, but he persuaded me to go up in an aircraft and that was that - my life had changed. So you have him to blame for being stuck with me.'

Kitty frowned. 'Hang on, everyone says you built your first aircraft at seven, but now you're saying you didn't study aeronautical engineering before you met him. How is that possible?'

Gwen shrugged. 'I met him when I was six. I had a little bit of studying to do before I started Bumblebee, which is why she took me so long to build.'

The Misfits exchanged glances then broke out in laughter.

Mac leaned forwards. 'Gwen, dearest, please don't say things like that. I've spent half my life building aircraft on my own and between planning and construction each one has taken me at least ten months of working more than eight hours a day.'

Bruce grinned at him. 'I'm betting a six year old didn't spend most of her time drinking whisky, though.' He blinked and frowned at Gwen. 'You didn't, did you?'

An hour later, after a few more vodkas, Gwen stepped out into the night to take a breath of fresh air. She sat on a wooden bench under the overhang of the roof with her fur coat wrapped around her and her hands in its deep pockets, warm despite the freezing air, and leaned back to stare up at the stars. The clouds had drifted away and there was no trace of the storm left, but the snow was still thick on the ground and showing no sign of melting.

The door of the hall opened and a shaft of light pierced the frozen airfield. Gwen glanced to the side to see who it was, squinting against the sudden brilliance.

'Mind if I join you?'

'Please do.'

The dark shape that was Kitty settled on the bench next to Gwen with a sigh and leaned back to mirror her position, looking up at the heavens.

With no raucous party going on and the fitters having finished repairs for the night, the base was completely silent. There was not even any shelling from the front, usually audible as dull thuds even so many miles away. It was almost as if the world were back to how it had been only a few years ago.

Gwen searched out Kitty's hand in the dark and then shoved them both into her pocket.

'I wasn't sure if you would want company,' the American said, her melodic voice soft in Gwen's ear.

'I don't really, but that doesn't include you.'

Kitty's hand squeezed hers in the voluminous pocket and Gwen squeezed it back, grateful for the physical contact.

They sat like that for a while, watching their breath mist in the air above them and just enjoying the night and each other's company, but the silence couldn't last for long; there was too much to be said between them.

'I'm sorry. I know how much he meant to you.'

'Thank you.'

'I'm here for you, for anything. You know that. Is there anything you'd like to talk about? Anything you didn't want to say in front of everyone else, but want to get off your chest?'

Gwen began to say no, that she was fine, but stopped herself; that had been her response every time somebody asked how she was for so long, even though it wasn't true, that it had become automatic. She owed Kitty more honesty than that.

'I spoke to Rudy just before he took off and arranged to meet him when he got back. I was going to tell him that nothing was ever going to happen between him and me because, even though I loved him, I didn't love him the way I love you.' Gwen caressed Kitty's hand in her pocket. 'And I do love you.'

'I know.'

Gwen laughed and looked back up at the stars. 'In a way I'm glad I didn't tell him that this morning; I wouldn't have liked that to be the last conversation I ever had with him, but I hate that things were left unresolved between us.'

'Let me ask you something, did you ever lead him on? Did you ever make him believe that he had a chance with you?'

'I...' Gwen thought back to the night of the party when she had spoken to Drake. 'I didn't lead him on exactly, but I did say that I would have tea with him when we got back to London.'

Kitty gasped and stared at her in mock horror. 'Oh, dear! *Of course* he believed you were in love with him if you agreed to have *tea* with him!' She laughed gently, not unkindly. 'Come on, Gwen, you've got nothing to feel bad about.'

'But I...'

'But nothing! Stop torturing yourself, OK? He would want you to be happy, right? Even if it meant he couldn't be with you?'

'I suppose so.'

'Well then, stop being such a worrywart and bloody kiss me already!'

Gwen chuckled. 'Yes, ma'am!'

Gwen and Kitty stayed outside until their feet went numb. While their coats were warm and covered them to below their knees, their boots were RAC standard issue winter boots that were not even close to being adequate.

Gwen didn't want to go back in to the mess hall, though, so they hurried to the barracks where they knew the stove would be lit.

They sat next to each other on a bed in the middle of the room, their boots off and stockinged feet stretched out towards the old-fashioned iron stove, watching the flames consuming the wood from the forest through the grate in the side.

'Rudy asked me what I was going to do after the war and I told him I didn't really know, but that I would probably go back to being an engineer.' She looked at Kitty. 'What are you going to do?'

'I'm going to go home, back to Dayton, and see the family.'

'Oh.'

Kitty grinned at her. 'Don't look so downcast! I'm not going to stay there and you're welcome to come with me if you want. I just want to surround myself with familiar faces and kids for a while. Between my three brothers and all our cousins, there must have been about twenty kids been born in the last five years.' She sighed. 'I missed *them* most of all, when I left home to join the fight in Spain - their innocence, their laughter... There was none of that in Spain; the kids there were terrified, starving, with no strength to play, and France, what I saw of it at least, was much the same. I need to surround myself with some unconditional joy and love for a while to get over that.'

'Only for a while?'

'Yes. Only for a few weeks or so; children are great and all, but there's only so much shouting and screaming a girl can take before she wants to jump in an aircraft and just fly away.'

'And is that what you're going to do?'

'Yes. I want to see some of those places you've told me about, the ones your parents took you to.' Kitty chuckled. 'You know, before I shipped out to Spain, the furthest I'd ever been was New York. I'd never been out of the country, well, apart from one trip to the Canadian Dominion, but that barely counts. I want to see what this world has to offer.'

'Good for you!'

'Us. Good for us. That is, if you'd like to come along as my copilot.'

Gwen had been afraid that Kitty had plans for the future that didn't include her, that as soon as the war finished there would be no reason for the two of them to be together and she would just leave, but apparently not and, while Drake's plans for his future with her had been nice, Kitty's were perfect, what she would have dreamed about if she allowed herself to dream of a life after the war.

She smiled. 'Actually, I think *you* should be *my* copilot.'

Kitty laughed. 'Dream on! This is my damn trip, you're just tagging along. That makes me the captain and you the cabin boy!'

Gwen shrugged. 'Why don't we both just be pilots.'

Kitty frowned. 'You mean take two aircraft? That's a possibility, but I don't like the idea of going on long flights without being able to hold your hand or kiss you when I want to.'

'No, not two aircraft, just one, but a bigger one.'

Kitty grinned. 'Are you thinking of stealing Dreadnought, 'cos I think I could get behind a plan like that - the wife of one of my brothers has always hated me, I could land on her precious lawn and machine gun her roses...'

Gwen laughed at the image of the beautiful blonde woman behind one of Dreadnought's belly guns, laughing her head off as she poured hot metal into flowerbeds. She shook her head. 'Much as I would love to see that, I was thinking more along the lines of taking the Zeppelin I built when I was twelve. She might need a bit of work to get her airworthy, though. Her engines are still coal burning, so we'd need to convert them and we'd need to outfit her properly as well, but given a few weeks work, a month tops, she should be able to take us around the world in a bit of style and comfort. Do you think you could put off going home for that long after the war finishes?'

'There's nothing I would like more.' She leaned in and kissed Gwen. 'Thank you.'

The kiss deepened, but before they could lose themselves in each other the door opened and a blast of icy air washed over them. They hurriedly pulled back and made sure their clothing was in place; even though everybody knew they were together and weren't ashamed, Gwen still wasn't truly comfortable making public displays and Kitty respected her enough not to insist.

'Oi! Close the bloody door!'

Gwen looked at Kitty in shock; her accent had been almost perfectly cockney.

The American grinned at her. 'I like to collect accents. It's something I've done since I was a kid.' She looked up as the rest of the Misfits wandered over, shedding their coats before warming themselves at the stove. 'Don't I, cobber?' She said to Bruce in an Australian accent.

'Too right, mate!' Bruce replied with a grin.

'Gwen.' Abby approached them. There was a sheath of papers in her hands - the photographs from the mess hall. 'I'm going to send these to Drake's family, but I wanted to know if you wanted any of them first.'

She fanned them out but Gwen didn't have to look at them; she knew exactly which one she was going to take. 'I'd like this one, please.' She took the one of her and Rudy together on the flight deck of the Arturo, the first photograph that had been taken of the two of them together in more than a decade and the last.

Abby nodded. 'I'll have these and the flag taken to the Arturo as soon as I can, so that they can be stowed safely.'

'Thank you.'

Gwen stared at the photo and felt the tears welling up, unable to hold them back anymore.

'Mr Jones gave me one more photo tonight, but I didn't put it up on the wall because it's for you, although if you don't mind, I'd like to keep it for the squadron, to put up in the mess when we get home with the other trophies.'

Abby held out a photograph and Gwen lifted her swiftly blurring eyes to look at it.

After a couple of shocked seconds she began to laugh, but tears were streaming down her face as well, as all her pent up emotions escaped at once.

The image was framed absolutely perfectly, like a still from one of the old silent Hollywoodland funnies. The Misfits, as the supporting actors, their various expressions perfectly captured, were arranged around the two protagonists, who shared centre stage. The villain, Baryshnikov, had just got his comeuppance and his eyes were crossed, mouth open in an expression of dumb surprise, his arms thrown wide as he was knocked back by the force of the blow given him by the star of the movie, the hero, Gwen, the righteous rage on her face clear for all to see, her arm fully extended and her fist inches from the Russian's face.

The moment, when a measure of justice had been done, had been caught for all eternity.

CHAPTER 26

What the Muscovites considered to be winter was fast approaching, the weather worsening steadily and the port at Murmansk was beginning to ice over as the temperature dropped.

The Prussians were swiftly running out of time, but finally they were ready and launched their attack.

An artillery barrage, the likes of which hadn't been seen since the trenches of the Great War, was accompanied by a massed bomber strike, as the Prussians tried to weaken Muscovite defensive positions in preparation for a crossing of the all too narrow river that marked the border between Muscovy and Finland.

Despite knowing that the attack had to come soon, the Muscovites were taken completely by surprise by the ferocity of the assault. They had expected the attacks to be carried out at only a couple of strategic points along the line, but instead the Prussians came in devastating numbers along almost the entire length of the border, with far more troops and weapons than had been spotted moving up through the endless forests of Finland. At the same time, several divisions from the forces attacking St Petersburg broke off and began racing north, seeking to flank the Muscovite army.

It was a lighting quick assault, just as the Prussians had carried out so many times before, and the Muscovite fortifications were immediately overrun, the troops driven back in complete disarray. Even the Misfits and the Wolfpack, with the freshly repaired Dreadnought firing rockets and pouring metal down upon the enemy, could do nothing to prevent the rout as the Prussians swarmed across the border and raced into Muscovy.

However, where the Muscovites had failed to slow the Prussians, the weather succeeded.

While they had awaited the order to attack, the enemy troops had been comfortably billeted in warm barracks and they quickly became exhausted in conditions that they hadn't been prepared for. Likewise their equipment seized up - metal parts in weapons and vehicles alike stuck and refused to work, simply because their operators had no idea how to take care of them properly.

The Prussians' momentum was lost and the advance bogged down, then ground to a halt, the possibility of annihilating the Muscovite army in one fell swoop completely gone.

Over the next couple of days, the Muscovites mounted a resistance and took advantage of the let-up of pressure to dig in and fortify new positions from which they launched a few counterattacks, but were unable to force the Prussians back.

The two forces settled in and for a while it looked like a new front had been established some twenty miles inside the border, but the stalemate was broken when the flanking forces from the south arrived. They were comprised mostly of Finns, who were used to the conditions, and with their Prussian-supplied weapons they had no trouble brushing aside their badly armed opponents. Under threat of being surrounded, the Muscovites retreated and the Prussians resumed their advance, slower than before, but no less determinedly.

During this time it was almost as if there were a gentleman's agreement between the Fleas and the allied air forces. The Misfits and the Wolfpack were under strict orders to avoid engaging enemy fighters at all cost. They were told to concentrate solely on the ground forces to try to prevent their advance and, to Abby's satisfaction, Baryshnikov had been warned by Murmansk command of the dire consequences if he disobeyed.

The Wolfpack had taken a few more casualties, their machines shot down by anti-aircraft fire or damaged beyond repair and had finally run out of spare Harridans. There was no point in training new pilots to fly machines they didn't have, so Pemberton and Howard handed over their Harridans, before they and their fitters retreated to the safety of the Arturo. Vulture was packed up on a wagon and went with them; her optical instruments had been rendered almost useless by the almost constant cloud cover. To compensate, Abby ordered Charles to copilot

Bloodhound, giving Owen a rest and allowing the radar aircraft to be in the air almost constantly.

The Muscovites fought bravely, but they could do nothing to halt the Prussians. Thousands were killed and thousands more were cut off and forced to surrender.

The last day of the retreat was not much more than a rout, as the surviving men and women abandoned their weapons and equipment and ran through the snow, heading for the boats that were waiting to take them across the river to the city and the last line of defences.

The Prussians let them escape, knowing that their panic would be infectious and make the job of taking the city easier. They followed at a leisurely pace, conserving their strength, and set up along the river facing Murmansk.

Full winter was almost upon them, though, the ice spreading across the water, creaking and groaning as it expanded outwards from the banks, and the Prussians couldn't afford to wait too long before they tried to cross it.

When Abby walked in, the mood in the command bunker was more serious than she had ever seen it. The old general, Popov, and Dorothy Campbell, were discussing tactics, animatedly gesturing at the table, but the rest of the military leaders were just staring at the map, drinks in hand, not saying anything and the support staff manning the telephones were equally silent and morose.

'Abby!' Dot waved her over and she went around the table to join them. She didn't need to glance at the map to know what the situation was, but she did anyway and immediately wished she hadn't; there were fewer gold statuettes on the board than ever, not just in the north, but in the whole theatre, while the number of red ones seemed to have increased.

'Thank you for coming.' The sky commodore moved past Abby's extended hand to fold her into a hug, which surprised her, but only momentarily before she returned it.

They held it only briefly, though, before Campbell pulled back and her place was taken by Popov, who settled for a handshake, a smile and a respectful nod. 'Group Captain.' He nodded at Campbell. 'All yours, Commodore.'

'Thank you, General.'

They watched Popov wander away to join the rest of his command group, then Campbell turned to grin at her friend. 'Well, this is another fine mess Whitehall have gotten us into, isn't it?'

Abby nodded. 'Are we looking at another France, or is the situation salvageable?'

Dot waved at the map. 'The Muscovites are holding the centre and south, just. It's only really here that the situation is desperate, but as we've said before, if Murmansk falls, then the rest will follow and the Prussians know that. We have to hold the line.'

'And will we?'

'Maybe.'

Abby looked at the area around Murmansk sceptically, taking in the yellow markers that denoted the regiments which had retreated to the city and the ones that were thinly spread along the blue line of the river. There were already four or five times their number of red markers facing them and more than twice that amount on their way. 'How? I mean, all they really have to do is cross the river, the city itself has no real defences that I've seen.'

'You're right, it doesn't. However, the Muscovites knew this day was coming and have had a lot of time to make the river a deathtrap.'

Campbell led Abby over to the side of the room where there was a smaller scale map on the wall of just the city and the surrounding area, including the river. 'The Prussian commander is in a hurry; he's left his offensive too late and he only has days left before the weather completely closes in and has to find shelter in the city. He hasn't got time to try a crossing somewhere else and then besiege us, so he's going to have to come straight across, either directly into the city or very close by and we have some very nasty surprises in store for them.'

She ran a finger along the wide blue channel running past the city and Abby saw that it was marked with hundreds of red dots with only a thin passage between them. 'Mines in the water should deal with a good number of their heavier amphibious craft and Walkers, but they're really meant for ships, so anything with a shallow draught, like a troop carrier, will pass right over them. And that's where you come in - we're running low on ammunition so no more attacks on their dug-in troops, instead I need you to send as many of their boats and most especially those vulnerable troop carriers to the bottom as you can when they're out in the open.'

Campbell saw Abby's grimace. 'Yes, I know that neither you nor your pilots particularly like machine-gunning troops and you'd all much rather be duelling the Barons in the sky, but this is what we need you for right now.'

Abby nodded. 'Understood and we've come to terms with that. Don't worry, we'll do our jobs.'

'I know you will. I just don't know if it'll be enough, so make sure you're ready to evacuate at a moment's notice.' She tapped a point on the north coast, not far from where they had rendezvoused with the Muscovite aircraft the day they had arrived. 'Archangel has begun to ice up too and the Arturo has been forced to move out before she got trapped. She's here, at a place called Teriberka. There's a small airfield there and she will disembark fitters to dismantle Bloodhound and Dreadnought and pack them up for the voyage home.'

Campbell glanced around surreptitiously, making sure that nobody was nearby. 'Look, if the city does fall it's going to be every man and woman for themselves around here. The Muscovites aren't going to look after you, they're not going to fight to keep you safe, so don't wait around for orders, just go.'

'What about you?'

'There's no need to worry about me, I have my own evacuation plan. I'll meet you at Teriberka.'

Campbell grinned and Abby looked in her eyes, trying to work out whether she was lying or not. She chose to believe her and nodded. 'Alright. Just make sure that you do.'

CHAPTER 27

The Prussian assault began at dawn the very next day. This time it wasn't heralded by an artillery bombardment, because they hadn't yet been able to move any of their larger pieces up through the snow, but the bombers did their best to weaken the resolve of the defenders and pounded the city indiscriminately, not caring whether they struck military or civilian targets, their munitions raising dust and smoke, shrouding the city in a haze that the low-lying sun couldn't penetrate, plunging the Muscovites into near darkness. The explosions went on and on for long minutes as wave after wave of unmolested aircraft passed overhead, the sound of their engines drowned out by the continuous, deafening noise, but then suddenly it was over.

Into the expectant hush strode the first of the Prussian machines, the six immense heavily-armoured Walkers which had survived the allied aerial attacks to make it to the front. Their telescoping legs found solid purchase in the river bed as they stepped off the bank into it and their sharp prows easily broke through the as yet thin ice with ease.

The Muscovites opened fire, but their antiquated artillery, left over from the Great War, had no more effect on the heavily armoured machines than the bullets of the equally obsolete rifles of the common soldiers and they forged ahead, bringing their deadly cargo of men and tanks ever closer.

For a moment it seemed that the day would be lost as soon as it had begun, that the Prussians would be able to deliver their well-trained and well-armed troops directly into the centre of the city with their first assault, but then the first mine detonated.

The design of the Walkers was such that their bodies were held above the water and all that extended down were the legs. That meant that their profile in the water was far smaller than that of a normal amphibious tank or troop carrier and they were well into the minefield before the first of them was unfortunate enough to brush past one of the deadly cylinders.

The explosion ripped through the underbelly of the Walker as if it were paper, sending icy water rushing into it to consume its contents. Waves surged outwards, boiling and bubbling, rocking the other machines, which spread their legs to steady themselves without any problem and rode them out, but it wasn't only the water on the surface that had been disturbed and the shockwave that propagated through the depths set the mines swaying and bobbing on their chains.

A second mine pinged ever so gently against the leg of another Walker and instantly detonated, bursting it open, then a third and a fourth explosion threw plumes of white water up into the air, hiding the machines from view.

When the spray finally settled, only two Walkers remained.

The Muscovites soldiers along the river held their breath, waiting, hoping, praying for the roiling water to cause more destruction, but slowly the river calmed and resumed its tranquil appearance.

The machines remained motionless long after the last ripple had subsided and the defenders began to think that they might have been damaged, but the reason for their inactivity became all too clear when wave after wave of amphibious vehicles began to pour into the river along a wide front behind them. It seemed that the Prussian commander had enough sense to recognise that the troops contained in the surviving Walkers wouldn't last long on their own, that they would need reinforcements and had sent them.

The two Walkers lurched forwards again and almost immediately one of them ran into another mine, but its death was barely remarked upon because all eyes were on the hundreds of Prussian vehicles surging across the river, making light work of the freshly troubled water.

The grey machines, nicknamed "Toads" by the British, who had faced them in France, as much for how ugly they were as for their dual nature, were a cross between a tank and a boat. They were wide and squat and flanked by treads, which powered it forwards both on land and water - the steel slats which provided grip on land were wider than those on a normal tank and rotated through ninety degrees to form something like the paddles on a riverboat. It was heavily armed, with a large gun on the roof and several machine guns mounted on a rotating ring below it, but it had lighter armour than its more conventional cousins and they relied more on speed to protect the fifty men that they carried.

Mines detonated all along the line, destroying one, two or sometimes even three of the Toads at the time, but they barely made a dent in the numbers and the Prussians came on undaunted.

They were more than half-way across before the Muscovites unleashed their secret weapon.

There were rivers and lakes everywhere in North-Western Muscovy, from St. Petersburg to Murmansk, and much of life revolved around them. The adults and children alike used them for leisure, to bathe and fish, but also for other pastimes, the two favourite of which were skating, when they had frozen solid during the winter months, and sailing model ships.

Weeks back, when the possibility of a Prussian invasion had seemed inevitable, the local government had put out a call, asking for model ships. More than a thousand had been donated and with the water heated by the explosions and the ice melted, the way was clear for them to float from the sewage outlets of the city.

There was a bewildering variety, from a child's three foot toy steamer to an enthusiast's fifteen foot dreadnought. The military models were painted grey or dark blue, but most were decorated in traditional Russian fashion, with golden cogs, colourful hulls and burnished funnels. They were all of them hand crafted by artisans, who dedicate their lives to making them and no two was exactly alike, but they did share a single characteristic - they were all clockwork and not sail driven, so they weren't dependant on the wind. Strangely, though, they were also riding lower in the water than they should have been, and had grey floats, long thin tubes, bolted to their sides to compensate and hold them above the water.

Even with the ugly floats it was a lovely display, reminiscent of the mid-summer festivals that were held in most of the larger towns in the area, but it was one that disguised the deadly purpose behind it - the floats were magnetic and filled with flechettes, designed to pierce armour, and the boats themselves were so low in the water because they had been filled to the gunwales with high explosive.

Dozens of the beautiful boats sank, swamped by the wakes of the Toads, but many more attached themselves to the hulls of the machines and at least fifty of them bumped up against the last Walker.

Whistles blew in the city and the watching soldiers took cover wherever they could.

Seconds later, the models exploded, sending flechettes and shrapnel flying at high speed in all directions, pinging and whining off the stones of the buildings lining the waterfront, leaving deep gouges, some even thrown so far as to cut through the Prussian troops massed along the tree line. The damage it did to the vehicles on the river was far greater, though, and when the echoes of the immense blast faded, they were immediately replaced by a wave of noise as the Muscovite soldiers expressed their glee at the success of the absurd tactic.

Hundreds of Toads had been ripped apart and were sinking and hundreds more had come to a halt, immobilised, their treads torn off.

Of the last Walker, all that was left was a twisted lump of metal, swiftly sinking from sight.

At least fifty of the Toads had survived, though, and they were still powering towards the city, while behind them the next wave was advancing - hundreds of motorised boats packed with troops being driven carefully down into the river.

The Muscovites had inflicted heavy losses on the Prussians, but there were many *many* more soldiers to take their place and now they had no surprises left to throw at them.

CHAPTER 28

The Misfits, together with the six remaining Wolfpack Harridans and the eight surviving Polikasparovs of the Night Witches, circled a few miles east of Murmansk within striking distance of the river. They ducked in and out of the cloud cover, wondering if they would be needed and hoping that they wouldn't, that the Prussians would be beaten back by the Muscovite armies.

All too soon, though, almost before the smoke from the destruction of the Toads had cleared, the radio was crackling in their ears.

'Wolverine Leader, this is Pinprick, come in please.'

'Hello, Pinprick, this is Wolverine Leader. Congratulate Beetroot on the fireworks, please.'

'Will do, Wolverine. Guns free, repeat, guns free, but be advised we have incoming aircraft, fifty plus at five thousand feet, twenty miles out.'

'Roger that, Pinprick. Wolverine, attacking now.'

'Happy hunting, Wolverine. Pinprick out.'

'Wolverine Leader to all Wolverine aircraft, break into sections and engage at will.'

The section leaders acknowledged one by one, but Abby and Gwen were already diving.

'Independent fire, Two.'

'Roger, Leader.'

Gwen throttled back slightly to drop a couple of dozen metres behind Abby, still on her wing, still protecting her, but able to attack her own targets.

299

A quick assessment of Dragonfly's trajectory told Gwen which of the Toads Abby was going to attack and she nudged her rudder to line herself up others, grinning when she saw that the differing speeds of four of the amphibious vehicles were going to line them up perfectly for her. She dropped slightly lower, making her angle of attack slightly shallower, then opened fire.

From her perspective it was as if all four targets were stacked one on top of the other and all she needed to do to walk her fire from one to the other was to gently pull up on the stick.

Tracer rounds reached out, intersecting her targets and, as if by magic, wide black holes opened up in the machines one by one.

She poured a total of three seconds of fire into the four machines, less than a second for each of the targets, but a quick glance as she banked to follow Abby showed that all four of them were slewing off course or coming to a halt, fatally damaged.

'Good shooting, Two! Not that I'm counting, or anything, but that's four for you and only three for me. Coming around for another run.'

Gwen followed Abby as she banked hard, heading back to the river.

The other aircraft had made good practice among the Toads and there were now only a few dozen left. Gwen sighed when she saw the way they had clumped up in an attempt to avoid the wreckage of their friends, wishing that she had some of Wendy's rockets; one salvo would destroy most of them, but they had run out weeks ago when Wendy had no longer been able to find materials to make them with. She settled for lining up on three of them and repeated her tactics from before.

She settled back under Abby's wing and they banked around again, just in time to see her three targets going under the water, along with all of the other remaining Toads, destroyed in a single strafing run by the eight Night Witches.

'Not bad, Two, but you only got three that time.'

'*Only* three, Leader? I seem to remember you "only" getting three on your first run.'

'Ah, but that was just practice to get my eye in - I got five this time round.'

Gwen laughed. 'You did that on purpose! You knew there weren't going to be any left and lulled me into a false sense of security!'

'Maybe... But there's plenty of targets left - those troop carriers are looking very inviting.'

Gwen looked down. The boats carrying the Prussian troops were making their way across the river far slower than their armoured friends had and were indeed extremely inviting targets, sitting ducks in fact, and there were more than enough to go around.

She swallowed bile as she thought of the damage her guns would do among the men in the boats, remembered what they had done to hundreds before - no matter how many times she attacked troops on the ground, she never got used to it and she hoped that she never would. 'Roger, Leader.'

'Leader to all Wolverines, pull back and circle, we'll wait for the boats to get out into the middle of the river and then attack in sections. Use machine guns only, conserve cannon rounds in case there's more armour.'

She was about to say more, but she was cut off by Owen's frantic voice. 'Wolverine Leader, this is Nine. Those aircraft are two miles off bearing two seven zero and descending through angels four. It looks like they intend to intercept. Shall I call in Dreadnought?'

'Negative, Nine, the situation hasn't changed.' Abby hadn't wanted to put Dreadnought in the way of enemy fighters unless it looked like the Prussians were going to break through and make a landing in considerable force, but she was in the air over Vaenga, ready to come if needed. 'All Wolverines, change of plan. Break off and prepare to engage air targets.'

'I don't bloody see anyone, Leader.'

'Of course you don't; they're in the clouds, Seven! Just keep your damn eyes open! All Wolverines, rendezvous over the city and stay low!'

Gwen followed Abby as they raced back towards Murmansk. It was smart to use the city as cover; the varied colours, the uneven terrain and the smoke rising from the bombing raid wouldn't allow whoever was up there a clear run at them.

'They're right on top of you, Wolverine Leader.'

'Thank you, Nine. Does anyone see anything?'

Gwen followed Abby over the ruins of a church, its golden dome cracked and collapsed in on itself. They were weaving and banking, never once flying in a straight line, while never taking their eyes off the heavy cloud cover only two thousand feet above them.

A minute passed, then two.

The allied aircraft continued to weave around the city unpredictably, but the attack never came and in the meantime the Prussian forces were getting ever closer to the other side of the river.

Gwen caught glimpses of the fight every time they flew nearby and could see the Muscovite defenders taking potshots at the boats, but, as

Bruce put it, they were like "fleas biting a dog's arse," an analogy that Gwen found appropriate because in the end the Muscovites would be brushed away by a single swipe of the Prussians' mighty tail unless the Misfits did something quickly.

As if she'd read Gwen's mind, Abby's voice filled her ears. 'Nine, are you sure they're there?'

'Of course I am, Leader, they're just circling around you.'

Abby swore, forgetting to switch off her comms. 'All aircraft, form up and head back to the river, we have to hit those troops.'

The twenty-two aircraft formed up into one big wing and turned together towards the fighting, flying low over the roofs of the battered city.

'We'll attack by flights, not sections, first A, then B, then the Wolfpack, then the Night Witches. Stay together, stay low, stay fast and keep your eyes peeled until it's your turn. And whatever you do, don't fly in a straight line for long.'

They got to the river in seconds and Abby led A flight right in to engage the boats while the other aircraft circled, looking to cover them.

'Line abreast, A flight. Let's mow the lawn.'

Gwen moved up onto Abby's right wingtip, while Bruce and Monty did the same on the other side and together they dipped over the last of the buildings on the waterfront.

Suddenly the river was in front of them.

'Fire!'

The four machines opened up with their machine guns, literally mowing down the Prussian soldiers in a long line that stretched from one side of the river to the other, cutting a swathe through them fully thirty yards wide and almost a mile long.

The river so crowded with vehicles that it was impossible to miss and Gwen had to turn her head away from the carnage she was causing, so horrific was it.

Which was why she was the first to spot the dark shadow in the clouds above them.

'Bandits incoming! Four o'clock high!'

She barely got her warning out before the first of the aircraft broke into the clear, diving straight for her. It was instantly joined by almost a dozen more, but her eyes remained firmly fixed on the first, the one with the black chessboard patter on its nose - Gruber, the man who had killed Rudy Drake.

Abby looked up at the incoming aircraft and swore, then resolved not to do so again because her throat was getting sore from doing so.

She grinned when she counted only eleven red aircraft - it looked like the Barons hadn't had a chance to bring in new pilots and machines yet and for once the odds were going to be in the favour of Wolverine squadron.

The smile was wiped from her face immediately, though, when two more squadrons of fighters, MU9's, burst from the clouds and, despite her extremely recent resolution, she swore; she had forgotten that Owen had reported more than thirty fighters. She had to be tired to make such a stupid mistake.

A quick glance down told Abby that the situation was dire; even though A flight had destroyed dozens of boats in a single pass, the Prussians hadn't been deterred and they had to be dealt with straight away.

She came to a snap decision. 'All aircraft, turn into the enemy, but do not engage. I want one pass on the boats from everyone first.'

Everybody knew that making a ground attack while being chased by superior numbers of fighters was tantamount to suicide, but the pilots acknowledged determinedly; the outcome of the battle below, and perhaps the fate of Muscovy, rested on their shoulders. They had to turn back the Prussian assault, at all cost.

There was no more time for Abby to worry about her people, though, because the diving Barons had closed the gap to within firing range.

Gwen followed Abby as they stood on their right wings and pulled hard, trying to cut underneath the Barons. They were so low to the ground that her wingtip was only yards from the river surface, so close that she could see the men in the boats below ducking for fear of being clipped.

They hadn't completed even half of the turn when Gruber opened fire and she had to wrench her stick back to the left when something hit her right wing and rocked Wasp, threatening to pitch her into the water. It was only a single impact, though, and she smiled grimly, knowing from the angle of engagement that every round that missed her was going straight into the boats on the river. She wondered briefly if Gruber was aware of the damage he was doing to his own side. He must have been; he was too good a pilot not to, which begged the question, *did he care?*

Gruber answered her question effectively by continuing to fire, not letting up for even a split second as he shifted his aim to Bruce and Monty, who were following her and Abby round. She gasped as she saw Raptor struck twice, a large piece of orange metal flying away from her tailplane and spinning into one of the boats below, but then Gruber was past and they straightened out before tilting their noses up to point at the rest of the Barons.

As always, the impulsive man had raced ahead of his companions, seeking to win the glory for himself. Not only had that given the Misfits more time to react to the greater threat, but it meant that the rest of his squadron had to face the combined guns of the heavily armed aircraft of A flight.

Gwen found a Blutsauger in her sights and squeezed the trigger that fired her cannons. She saw pinpricks of light along the Prussian machine's wings flash into being at the same time, but, while her rounds impacted on the enemy aircraft, shattering the cockpit and ripping through the entire length of the machine, the return fire went just wide.

And then they were through the Barons, the enemy aircraft passing within yards of them on all sides, and into clear air.

There was no time for more than a quick breath before Abby took them back around, reversing their course with a snap roll and pulling hard to line up on the river again.

Gruber was coming around just as fast, followed closely by the rest of the Barons, now whittled down to seven by the superior marksmanship of the Misfits, but Gwen gritted her teeth and blocked them out of her mind as she followed Abby down towards the boats.

Faces were turned up towards them as they screamed out of the sky, expressions of sheer panic on most of the soldiers as they saw their death coming for them, but Gwen found herself staring at one man.

One man out of all of them was staring back at them, his face a mixture of defiance and resignation. He seemed to meet her eyes and she thought she saw him nod, but then he was gone, obliterated, along with hundreds of his fellow invaders as the four aircraft opened fire.

This time they went the length of the river and, if anything, the effect was even more pronounced. Boats broke apart under the weight of metal being thrown at them and men were tossed into the water, where they would almost certainly freeze to death, if their injuries didn't kill them first. Sparks flew and there were a couple of small explosions as some kind of ordnance was hit and ignited.

Gwen's machine guns clicked and fell silent, her ammunition expended, but it didn't really matter; the boats were past and the Misfits were climbing into the sky and banking to face the Barons.

Wasp lurched as something hit her and Gwen screamed as the instrument panel in front of her exploded, instinctively covering her face with her arms as glass rained upon her from the shattered canopy. She stared in shock at the enormous hole that was all that was left of the front of her cockpit, but came back to herself when Wasp jerked again.

She put her hands back on the stick and fought with it as more impacts struck her, automatically glancing up to look in her rear view mirror and find her attacker, but the mirror wasn't there; it had been vaporised by the cannon round that had first struck her.

Wasp lurched one more time, but this time it was different from the others; it wasn't an impact, it was something else, something worse and the aircraft fell completely silent as the spring beneath Gwen's seat stopped supplying power to the aircrew - the cannon round that had passed through the instrument panel, that had almost killed her, had killed Wasp. It had severed the drive shaft that connected the spring to the airscrew.

She could glide and try to put her aircraft down, but with nowhere close enough and enemies in the sky with her that was impossible and there was only one alternative.

'This is Two. I'm bailing out.'

Gwen swallowed the lump in her throat and fumbled with the quick release mechanism that held her in her seat, then stood up, the radio wires and heater tubes pulling out with sharp pops, cutting her connection with her aircraft for the very last time.

'Thank you, Wasp,' she whispered, giving the stick a last push to point her nose at the boats below, then dived out.

'This is Two. I'm bailing out.' Abby heard the words, but didn't quite register their meaning until she saw Wasp stop manoeuvring and start slowing, falling back behind her as the aircraft lost power.

'Gwen...'

There was nothing she could do for her wingman so she put her out of her mind and searched the sky for the man who had shot her down.

Gruber had overshot Wasp as the Misfit aircraft had slowed unexpectedly and was banking around to come back.

'Three, take Four and engage the rest of the Barons. I've got Gruber.'

'Roger, Leader.'

Some part of her felt Bruce and Monty leave their positions off her left wing, but she didn't see them go; her whole focus was on Gruber.

Gwen missed the trailing edge of Wasp's wing by inches as she tumbled head over heels towards the ground, less than a thousand feet below and approaching rapidly. A pull on the lever at her side had the first panels springing out from her glidewings, slowing her dizzying spin and she deployed the other three in quick succession to bring herself fully under control and begin her guide.

She looked back just in time to see Wasp nose into the river a mile or so away. She broke up on impact, cartwheeling over and over and took four boats with her to the bottom of the river, refusing to go quietly.

She watched until the last pink panel had disappeared below the waves, then looked around to get her bearings. The city was a few miles away to the north so she turned east, away from the river and picked out a clearing among the trees, within easy gliding distance, to set down in.

With a safe landing ground chosen, she had some time to assess how the fight was going.

B flight and the Russians were over the city, too far away to see clearly without using lenses, which she couldn't slot in place and keep control of her glidewings at the same time, but the rest of A flight were still quite close and she watched Bruce and Monty coordinating perfectly as they engaged the Barons, wheeling around each other and creating confusion among their enemies with each twist and turn. However, for some reason Abby hadn't joined them, but was coming back around, heading towards her.

Some instinct prompted her to look over her shoulder and she gasped in shock at the sight of Gruber's aircraft, only a few hundred yards away and aiming directly at her.

Abby had expected Gruber to look to engage her after he'd shot down Wasp. He didn't, though, and instead performed a neat Split S that took him towards the elegant black and silver shape that was Gwen under her glidewings.

'No...'

She couldn't believe that Gruber would actually open fire on a pilot who had bailed out. Technically there was nothing in any rule book that stated that you couldn't do it, but every pilot just *knew* that it wasn't done. That it was wrong.

And yet...

Gwen yanked on the lever to close her wings and tucked herself into a ball just as Gruber opened fire. She dropped from the sky, once again tumbling uncontrollably, but her desperate action had gotten her out of his sights and the deadly stream of metal passed over her head, the noise deafening, so much louder outside the protection of a cockpit. During the brief times when she was the right way up, she saw Gruber pushing his nose down further and further, trying to adjust his aim, but he couldn't compensate enough for her acceleration and just flew past harmlessly.

Gwen's relief was extremely short-lived, though, because her manoeuvre, while it had been the only one available to get her out of trouble, had taken her straight from the frying pan and into the fire because she was now far too low and travelling far too fast.

She opened a single panel of her glidewings, but didn't have the time to allow the resistance they provided to completely stop her spinning, so instead she tried to judge when she would be more or less parallel to the ground and yanked the lever, spreading the wings wide.

She screamed as the straps wrenched her back and nearly passed out from the pain as one of her shoulders gave way with a pop that she felt throughout her entire body. She knew that giving in to the welcoming blackness would mean a sure visit from the Dark Scythesman, though, so she kept screaming, forcing blood to her head and using the tactics that pilots used in the air to claw on to consciousness, all the while fighting for control.

She managed to slow her descent a fair amount, but she was still going far too fast when she hit the top branches of the trees.

Abby watched, aghast, as streams of incandescence, bright in the dimness of the northern morning, reached out from the red aircraft towards the angelic form of her wingman.

She blinked, thinking that her eyes were playing tricks on her, when the silvery shape seemed to wink out of existence, but her pilot's eyes soon picked out the black ball which had replaced it and she laughed in joy when Gruber overshot his target. She tried to follow Gwen down

with her eyes, wanting to see her safe, but all too soon she lost sight of
her against the backdrop of the trees and the snow.

Her eyes snapped back to Gruber.

He had to die for all he'd done.

Gwen opened her eyes and found herself looking up at the sky
through the branches of a tree as they waved sedately back and forth
in the breeze. A small bird landed above her and looked at her, tilting
its head to one side, assessing then discarding her as a threat, before
opening its mouth to trill a call.

Gwen smiled at it and yawned, idly wondering what she was doing
lying there, why she was being so lazy; she was fairly sure that there
was something she was supposed to be doing.

She became aware of faint popping noises coming from somewhere
in the distance. They seemed vaguely familiar and she frowned as she
tried to recall something, anything, to explain her situation. The trees
gave her no clue, though, so she went to roll onto her side to better
look around, but gasped as pain flared from her left shoulder. The
sudden agony brought her memories back in a rush and she groaned
as she saw again her beautiful aircraft disintegrating, then growled
when she remembered what Gruber had done.

That anger spurred her into action and she reached across herself
with her right hand, fumbling for the glidewing release mechanism on
her left side. She found it, but it was slick with liquid and when she
pressed down on the mechanism a pain in her side made her gasp. She
persevered, gritting her teeth and the straps finally fell away, but then,
when she ran her hand over her side searching for the injury, she came
across something sharp poking out of her.

Alarmed, she lifted her head and looked down at it.

There was a branch, about an inch thick, embedded in her side.
Liquid was spurting from the hole it had torn in her flight suit and she
clutched her hand to it in panic; the piece of wood must have nicked
an artery or something and, if she didn't stop the bleeding soon, she
would fall unconscious and die.

She scrabbled at it briefly, sobbing, but stopped when she realised
that, even if she did pull the piece of wood out, she wasn't going to be
able to do anything about the bleeding; she had no medical equipment,
the city was miles away and everybody was far too busy with the
Prussians to come and look for her. She was going to die where she
was and, if she was lucky she'd be found when the thaw came in spring,

but if she wasn't... Well, the wolves in the forest would be a bit less hungry that winter.

She lay back down in the snow and closed her eyes, resigning herself to her fate.

Only slowly did it enter her awareness that she wasn't actually losing consciousness, that, if anything, her head was clearing with each passing moment and that there was almost no pain in her side, aside from a dull ache, which was probably nothing worse than a bruise.

She opened her eyes again and struggled to sit up, then took a closer look at the wound. She pulled off her glove and touched the liquid that was now only slowly seeping through the hole in the leather and laughed in relief when her fingers came away clear, not red; it was just water from the pockets of her G suit. She grabbed the branch with her bare hand, getting a better grip on it, and pulled it out, hissing as it scraped her ribs, but welcoming the pain as proof that she was still alive.

Holding her arm to her, she rolled awkwardly over onto her knees, then struggled to her feet. She swayed slightly, suddenly feeling quite faint, but a few deep breaths cleared her head enough for her to take in her surroundings. The trees seemed thinner to one side of her and she thought that she could hear the sound of running water from that direction so she bent to close her glidewings, surprised to find them completely intact, a testament to their marvellous design, then slung them over her shoulder and started walking, thinking that the best way to not get lost in the forest was to find and follow the river.

After less than a hundred yards the trees opened up and she found herself on the wide banks of the Tuloma, the river that ran past Murmansk.

The city was only two or three miles away and she had a clear view all the way to where the troop boats were now beating a hasty retreat, under fire from the defenders. More importantly, though, without the canopy of the trees above her, she could see the aircraft in the sky.

She crunched across the stones of the bank towards a large rock, then sat down and pulled lenses, which had proved far tougher than her, into place over her goggles.

She could worry about getting to the city later, after the show was over and she'd seen her friends safely home.

Gruber had been so hell-bent on murdering Gwen that he hadn't noticed Abby until she was right on top of him, her guns blazing. He immediately flung his aircraft on its side and spiralled out of the way, but he was just a millisecond too late and a series of small holes appeared in his left wing.

Abby swore; in her fear for Gwen's life she had forgotten to switch back to her cannons after the run on the boats and if she hadn't made such a blatant blunder, he would most likely have been dead already. She remedied her mistake, flicking the selector so that all her guns would fire, and tried to bring Gruber back under her sights, but he was a slippery character and every time she managed to get a bead on him and fired he jerked away. She got one solid hit, though, and watched happily as a piece of his left flap went spinning away into the forest below, but she wasn't satisfied; she wouldn't be that until the man was falling from the sky in the wreckage of his shiny new aircraft.

Bullets flashed past her own aircraft, but they didn't come close to worry her. She had been perfectly aware that two of Gruber's Barons were on their way to help him, but she also knew that, with the way she was moving around the sky following their leader, they would find it impossible to hit her.

She smiled grimly as she remained stuck behind Gruber's aircraft; he might have tried to copy Wasp and Dragonfly, might have tried to make a hybrid between them of the best they had to offer, but he just didn't have the knowhow that Gwen Stone had. He wasn't nearly the genius that she was.

And he wasn't half the pilot that Abigail Lennox was.

A short burst ripped another chunk from the red aircraft and it faltered. Caught mid-manoeuvre, unexpectedly, Gruber hesitated, and the red aircraft swam into Abby's sights.

She depressed the trigger.

Two shots came from her cannons, blowing holes in the enemy aircraft's wing, but that was all before silence fell.

'No, no, no, no, no, NO, NO!!!' She screamed her rage, pumping the button on her stick and switching back and forth between machine guns and cannon, but it was no use, she didn't have anything left.

Tracer rounds flashed past her cockpit and Abby realised that she had flown straight and level for too long. She pushed the stick forwards away from the bullets, the red of her rage replaced by blood rushing to her head as she dove away, heading back towards the city and the safety of the rest of her squadron.

Gwen hadn't been able to remain sitting for long and she whooped and jumped up and down as Kitty shot down another MU9, her four that she had been able to see. Her celebrations were tinged with sadness, though, because she had also been forced to watch as, one by one, the Wolfpack and Night Witches had been shot from the sky, until only Baryshnikov and Polikasparov were left. She was too far away to tell whether any of the pilots had managed to bail out, but she certainly hoped they had, although many of them had been over Prussian lines when they had been destroyed and would likely be in captivity. They did take a creditable amount of MU9's with them, though, whittling them down to about half the original force.

The fight that truly interested her wasn't the one over the city, though, it was the one taking place almost directly over her head.

Abby and Gruber had been circling the area where Gwen had been shot down, ducking in and out of sight behind the trees and each time she saw them the story was the same - the yellow aircraft stuck to the tail of the red one, snapping at its heels, but unable to finish the job.

However, when next they reappeared it looked like the dogfight was nearing the end and Gruber's aircraft lurched from a hit and flew straight for a long second.

'Go on! Shoot him! Shoot the blighter!'

Gwen went up on her toes in excitement, knowing that Abby wouldn't let such a golden opportunity escape, expecting the red machine to be ripped apart at any moment, but the shots never came and she was forced to watch in shock as Abby dove away from the fight and flew at maximum power along the river, back towards the city, pursued by the two Barons that had been attempting to get her off of Gruber's back.

She turned her gaze back to Gruber's aircraft, hoping that Abby had only backed off because it had already sustained fatal damage, hoping that it would crash in short order, but it didn't, it just flew across the river, back towards the Prussian lines. Gwen stuck two fingers up at him as he disappeared behind the trees and wished him landing trouble, then turned her attention back to the fight over the city, but there was nothing to see there either as both sides disengaged, backing off to lick their wounds.

She sighed and picked up her glidewings, grunting in pain as she looped the strap over her good shoulder and the weight pulled on the scrape over her ribs then began trudging towards Murmansk; hopefully someone there would give her a lift back to Vaenga and wouldn't think she was a Prussian and shoot her.

She had gotten less than a hundred yards when something whistled over her head, almost low enough to touch and she ducked, wincing as her shoulder complained, but then smiled when she saw what it was.

'Fancy a lift?'

Scarlet grinned at her from the cockpit of Hummingbird. She had the canopy open and was leaning on the lip of it as if it were one of Lord Bagshot's racing machines and she was picking up a good-looking man from the side of the road, all while effortlessly holding the machine stationary just inches off the ground.

Gwen laughed and handed Scarlet her glidewings to stow before hopping onto one of the stretchers the Irishwoman had had bolted to the side of the machine so that she could pick up casualties.

'So, where would you like to go?'

Gwen grinned. 'Second star to the right and straight on till morning?'

'Sounds good to me! Hold on to your hat!'

Scarlet laughed as Hummingbird leapt into the sky and banked towards home.

CHAPTER 29

Hummingbird was the slowest of the Misfit aircraft, so the rest of the squadron had landed by the time they got to Vaenga and the pilots rushed over to meet them.

'Oh, Gwen, I'm so sorry.' Kitty was one of the first to arrive and she put her arms around Gwen as she sat up on the stretcher, shivering, fumbling with the catch of the safety belt with frozen fingers.

The American quickly pulled back, though, at her stifled scream. 'What? What is it?'

'My shoulder.' She could barely squeeze the words out between clenched teeth as she clutched at her arm, fighting to hold onto consciousness.

Kitty's skin took on a greenish tinge at the sight of the dislocated limb and Gwen looked at it and forced a smile through her own queasiness. 'Will you still love me if I'm a hunchback?'

Kitty couldn't help but laugh and reached out to take her hand, but was pushed out of the way when medical personnel arrived and began lifting Gwen onto a proper stretcher.

The jostling set off explosions of black behind Gwen's eyes and the world faded away again, but a sudden thought brought her back from the brink and she recovered just enough to clutch at Kitty's arm. 'Come with me, please. Don't let them cut my flightsuit off.'

'Of course, darling.' Kitty nodded, biting her lip with worry and strode beside her as the orderlies carried Gwen away.

Abby watched her wingman being carried away, barely conscious, then stared down at the frozen ground, kicking at it angrily with the toe of her boot. Despite the fact that it had been the right decision and the *only* decision under the circumstances, it had been her order to make another run on the boats that had gotten Gwen hurt and Wasp destroyed and she couldn't help but feel responsible.

She looked up, startled, when Scarlet planted herself in front of her and poked her in the chest.

'I saw what Gruber did, the question is, what are we going to do about it?'

Bruce frowned. 'What is she talking about, Abby? *What* did Gruber do? I saw him shoot Wasp down, but that's just the fortunes of war.'

Abby turned to him and saw that the rest of the Misfits were also waiting for her answer. Apparently, they had been too busy with their own fights to see what the Prussian had tried to do, all except Scarlet. 'Gruber made a run at Gwen after she bailed out. He would have killed her if she hadn't closed her glidewings in time and gone into free fall. She was only a few hundred feet up, though, and couldn't get herself back under control in time, which is why she's hurt - she had a bit of a rough landing.'

'What? I didn't see that!' Bruce was furious. 'I wish you hadn't told me and Monty to back off... Wait until I get my hands on him! Next time I see him in the sky I don't care, I'm going to get the dirty bastard!'

'You'll do nothing of the sort, Bruce. None of you will.' Abby stared at him coldly, before looking around at the rest of the pilots, making sure that they got the same message. 'Our priority remains the ground troops. Once the Prussians give up on trying to cross the river we can do something about Gruber, but I do not want people seeking him out in the air until then; killing one man and destroying a single fighter isn't going to do *anything* to stop the Prussians. It might have done over Britain, but not here.'

'But...'

'But *nothing*, Bruce. Those are my orders and you will obey them. There is more at stake here than just our personal grudge with Gruber and we can't let it distract us from our job, because that way he wins just as surely as if he'd shot us all down.'

The pilots grumbled, but all saw the logic behind Abby's command.

All except Scarlet. 'That's not good enough.' She shook her head and stomped away, heading towards the medical centre.

Abby watched her go, then looked around at everyone else. 'I swear, we *will* make Gruber pay at some point, but unfortunately that might not be for a while.' She took a look at her chronograph. 'Ten minutes for a bathroom break and a cup of tea, then be ready for takeoff. I expect the Prussians will be trying again soon.'

When the doctor put Gwen's shoulder back in its place she had passed out from the pain, but when she regained consciousness she felt much better. Her body ached all over and her shoulder throbbed, but she was warm and she no longer had to fight to form a coherent thought.

'You're awake.'

Gwen turned her head, groaning as her neck muscles protested and found Kitty and Scarlet sitting by the side of her bed. She frowned at them. 'Shouldn't you be up in the air?'

Kitty shook her head with a smile and reached out to take Gwen's hand. 'It's after sunset. We've already flown two more sorties.'

'What? How long have I been out?'

'About six hours; the doctor gave you something to make you sleep. Apparently you have a concussion along with the dislocated shoulder and you lost a fair amount of blood from a pretty deep gash on the back of your head.'

Gwen reached up and found a thick bandage wrapped around her head. She hadn't even noticed she'd taken a knock there; she'd been too concerned about her arm and side, although it certainly explained how fuzzy she'd been.

'You'll be fine, the doctor said you mustn't use the arm and should stay off your feet as much as possible for a few days. Oh, and he's also grounded you for a couple of weeks.'

Gwen blinked at Scarlet, who was trying hard to keep a serious expression but failing dismally.

The Irishwoman broke first and then they were all laughing, but after a few seconds Gwen suddenly found herself crying instead.

Kitty slid onto the bed and put her arms around Gwen with exaggerated care, holding her and rocking her gently as she sobbed.

When she finally managed to stop she pulled back slightly and grimaced at the mess she'd made of the lapel of the American's uniform shirt - it was soaked through with tears and slimy with a judicious amount of snot. 'Sorry about your shirt.'

The American shrugged. 'It's alright, I'll just use one of yours until you can wash it.'

Gwen smiled weakly. 'You can have as many of my shirts as you like, but I don't love you enough to do your laundry, sorry.'

Kitty chuckled and leaned forwards to brush Gwen's lips with hers, but pulled back with a start when Scarlet cleared her throat; they'd forgotten that there was someone else in the room with them.

The Irishwoman grinned at them. 'I hate to interrupt you lovebirds, but I've got a few things to do.' She stood and leaned over Kitty to give Gwen a peck on the cheek. 'I'm glad to see you looking better and I'm sorry about Wasp.'

'Thank you.'

With a last nod, Scarlet grabbed her fur coat, then went out into the night.

'Does she have a date or something?'

Kitty shrugged. 'No idea. Probably, knowing her. You hungry?'

'Starving.' Gwen gave her a cheeky grin. 'Are you going to bring me dinner in bed?'

'Hopefully one day soon we'll be able to stay at a hotel and have room service in bed together, but tonight you can damn well walk to the mess hall! There's nothing wrong with your legs, lazy!'

Gwen moued in mock disappointment, but allowed Kitty to help her up and get her dressed.

When she was ready she waited while the American changed her shirt, smiling as she did indeed put one of hers on; it looked much better on Kitty than it ever had on her, especially the way it stretched tightly across her chest.

Kitty saw the direction of Gwen's gaze and smiled, toying with the top button of the shirt. 'Are you sure you're hungry? Because we could just stay here; everyone's at dinner, they won't be back for a while...'

'I...' Gwen began to answer, but was cut off when her stomach growled angrily.

Kitty laughed. 'Sounds like you've got an angry mountain lion in there! We need to feed it before it dies of starvation.' She grabbed Gwen's coat and wrapped it carefully around her shoulders before giving her a kiss.

She sighed and leaned her forehead against Gwen's. 'I can't wait for this to be all over so I can have you all to myself.'

'Me neither.' Gwen stood on tiptoes to give her another, deeper kiss, then clung onto her for the short walk to the mess.

Scarlet didn't turn up for dinner that night and she wasn't in the barracks when the squadron woke up before dawn the next morning. In fact it wasn't until they were finishing their breakfast, nursing cups of tea while they waited for the call to scramble that she finally turned up, exhausted and covered with dirt, but looking very pleased with herself. She put a canvas bag on the floor by her usual chair then went and stood at attention next to Abby.

Abby barely looked up at her from her tea. 'I was just about to put you on a charge for dereliction of duty; it was your turn to make the tea this morning.' She glanced up and frowned when she belatedly noticed the state of Scarlet's flight suit. 'What the hell have you been doing?'

Scarlet grinned and placed a small metal canister on the table. 'Present for you.'

Abby picked up the cylinder then raised an eyebrow at the Irishwoman. 'Photographs?'

Scarlet nodded.

'Of what?'

'It's a surprise.'

Abby looked across the table at the photographer. 'Mr Jones, when you've finished your breakfast, would you mind?'

Jones downed the rest of his tea quickly and grinned. 'Looks like I'm finished.' He stood, grabbed the canister and rushed out.

All eyes went to Scarlet, but she just ignored them. 'Any food left? I'm starving.'

She wandered away to the buffet table, strutting even more than usual, fully aware that her fellow pilots were watching her and started filling a plate from the leftovers, studiously keeping her eyes on the food. When her plate was piled high she wandered back, took her seat and began to eat.

'Scarlet. Darling.' Abby said sweetly.

Scarlet made a show of finishing her mouthful and swallowed before replying. 'Yes, Abby?'

'Will you be alright to fly when we're called?'

Scarlet nodded. 'Of course, but it might not be necessary; I think the Prussians might be a bit more hesitant to attack this morning. They've got a bit of bad news to assimilate beforehand.'

'Really? And what would that be?'

The Irishwoman refused to say anymore, though, and just smiled as she went back to her food.

Dawn came and went and still there was no call from Murmansk for the squadron to take to the air.

Scarlet finished eating and leaned back in her chair, sighing in satisfaction and patting her belly.

Abby gave her a dirty look, then stood up. 'I'm going to go call Dot and see what's going on.'

She started to walk away, but Scarlet called out, making her stop. 'Tell her that the devices the Muscovites put together for me worked a charm, please.'

Abby stared at her, but the Irishwoman just smiled innocently, meeting and holding her gaze without flinching and in the end the group captain just stuck her tongue out at her then left.

Abby didn't even get half way to the radio shed, though, before a soldier came running from it with a message for her and the klaxon sounded for the squadron to scramble.

She grabbed the piece of paper from the man and read it as the rest of the pilots came streaming out of the mess hall behind her.

While most made a beeline straight for their aircraft, Wendy ran up to Abby, an expectant look on her face.

Abby smiled at her. 'Owen reports no enemy in the skies.'

'Yes!' Wendy pumped her fist in glee, then turned and sprinted for the waiting Dreadnought, calling for her gunners to get on board.

Abby laughed at her enthusiasm, then shoved the paper back at the soldier before running for her own aircraft.

Completely forgotten, Gwen watched them take off from the steps of the mess hall. 'Happy hunting, Misfits.'

The previous day, Dreadnought had joined the Misfits in repelling the second assault, taking advantage of the fact that the Prussian air bases were much farther away than Vaenga and that they needed more than twice as long as the allies to rewind and rearm and be back over the battleground.

The Misfits carried out a wholesale slaughter, turning the incoming assault back before it had even gotten half way across the river, and when the Barons and their fellow Fleas finally did arrive, the British were long gone and they found nobody to fight.

The Prussians had coordinated their third and last assault of the day a bit better, though, and Dreadnought had had to stay at home.

If the Misfits had been outnumbered the day before, this time they were doubly so, as not only did they have less allies than the day before, but the Fleas had been reinforced with another squadron of MU9's. The Misfits ran amok among the enemy fighters, halving the number of MU9's and even shooting down a few Barons with only minor damage in return, but there were too many of them and they were unable to get anywhere near the river to support the Muscovites.

Without any harassment from the air, the Prussian transports made it all the way to the far bank. The Muscovites had few nasty surprises set up on the river banks, just as they'd had for the boats, but they were insufficient to turn back such a large force and they had to commit their few reserves, even bringing up civilian volunteers, like Abby had feared, but, instead of mothballs and handbags, they were equipped with hunting rifles, bows and rocks and acquitted themselves passably well.

It had been a very close-run thing, but after several hours of bloody fighting the Prussians were repelled. However, the Muscovite defenders had taken extremely heavy casualties and it was unlikely that they would be able to withstand another such assault.

Inexplicably, though, despite it being clearly demonstrated that they had to have air cover if they were to have any hope of their attack succeeding, that morning the Prussians threw everything they had into the river without any.

The attack came on three fronts. Their main assault came straight across the river, just as it had the previous day, but they also launched two simultaneous assaults further upriver one of which was composed mostly by a few dozen Toads which had arrived during the night with other reinforcements.

While A flight and the two remaining Wolfpack aircraft took care of the main assault and B flight the secondary one, Abby sent Dreadnought to handle the amphibious vehicles; her heavy guns would make short work of the armour. However, Wendy found not only the Toads there, but also several batteries of anti-aircraft guns that had been moved into position during the night and she was forced to move off to a safe distance after sustaining minor damage. It was only a minor setback, though, and the problem was solved by simply swapping Dreadnought and B flight - the faster aircraft were much harder targets for the Prussians to hit and their cannons were just as effective as the ones on Dreadnought against the armoured Toads.

Once more the Prussians suffered heavy losses, but they refused to give up and stuck with the assault well beyond the point where they should have given up, as if expecting some miracle. It never came, though, and in the end what little was left of the enemy forces limped back to the Prussian lines and the Misfits were released back to Vaenga.

Mr Jones was waiting for them in the mess hall with the explanation for why they had been alone in the sky that morning.

There were eight images in total, an entire roll of the special low-light film that Scarlet used on her scouting missions, and they clearly showed her activities of the night before.

At the Irishwoman's prompting, Mr Jones began to lay the photographs on the table one by one, giving the pilots time to take in each one before moving on to the next.

The first showed a row of buildings, barracks and hangars, flanking an airbase that was very familiar to them.

'Scarlet, please tell me you didn't...' Abby shook her head in disbelief.

'Just wait.' The Irishwoman grinned. 'It gets better.'

The second photograph showed the interior of one of the hangars, filled with about a dozen aircraft, instantly recognisable as *Blutsaugers*, except for the one at the front which had a check pattern on its nose.

The Misfits couldn't help but laugh at the third. Scarlet's camera had a timer on it and she had used it to good effect - the image was of Scarlet standing under the cockpit of Gruber's machine, giving the V for victory sign that the King had made so popular during the bombing raids on London. A large canvas bag was over her shoulder and she held a metal sphere, slightly larger than a tennis ball, in her other hand. Over her shoulder could be read Gruber's name and the name of the aircraft - *Hölle*.

Derek chuckled. 'Hell? That's a cheery name for an aircraft.'

The fourth image showed the side of the aircraft again, but this time the ball was stuck to it, at the wing root.

The fifth image showed the side of a different aircraft, an MU9 this time. It too had a ball on it.

Abby frowned. 'There weren't any MU9's in that hangar.'

'Nope.' Scarlet shook her head. 'They were in the other hangars.'

'*Hangars? Plural?* How many did you go into?'

The Irishwoman shrugged. 'All of them.'

'Weren't there any guards?'

'A few, but they weren't expecting to be paid a visit by the Pitiless Pixie now, were they?'

'The what?'

Scarlet grinned. 'That was the nickname they gave me at the Infiltration and Sabotage school you sent me to before France. Y'know, because I'm small, Irish, and show no mercy to my enemies.'

There was more laughter at that, but it was short-lived because the Misfits were impatient to see the rest of the images and Abby motioned for Mr Jones to turn over the next image.

The sixth brought more laughs. Scarlet had taken a can of paint and a brush with her and had scrawled "The Misfits were here" on the wall of one of the other buildings on the base, the mess hall by the looks.

The seventh photograph was from inside Hummingbird's cockpit and showed Scarlet's hand holding some kind of radio device. The background through the window was blurry, but they could just make out the shape of the hangars, a hundred yards or so below.

The eighth and final image was taken from a greater distance, but the image was still perfectly clear.

Every single one of the hangars was a wreck, but one of them had been split open like a melon hit by a cricket bat and there was a fire raging in the debris.

When Abby looked a question at her, Scarlet shrugged. 'I had no idea what kind of bang those explosives were going to make, so I put a couple on some hydrogen I found at the back of one of the MU9 hangars. I don't think I really needed to.'

Mac laughed. 'I'd say not!'

Abby surveyed the photographs and nodded in appreciation. 'While I was rather annoyed by your behaviour this morning, I have to say that you've probably done more in one night to change the course of this war than the entire Muscovite army. Bloody well done, Scarlet.' She picked up the photograph showing Scarlet in front of Gruber's aircraft. 'This is *definitely* going up on the wall and I'm quite tempted to send Gruber a copy.'

The Misfits laughed started up a debate as to how they would get the photo safely to the Crimson Barons, but fell silent and looked up when a Muscovite soldier burst in, grinning and waving a message slip. He handed it to Abby, then shouted something in Russian to the rest of the room, making every single officer, including the two surviving Wolfpack pilots, cheer and jump out of their seats to start dancing.

Abby raised her eyebrow at them, then read the slip of paper. 'I don't know what the fuss is about; all this says is that the Prussians are in full retreat back into Finland and there's a cold front on its way from the Arctic that will be here the day after tomorrow.' She looked up from the message to smile at them. 'Misfits, we're going home.'

Gruber surveyed the wreckage of the hangars through the window of the transport aircraft as it took off, on its way south to rendezvous with Bertha in Italy. With the loss of the fighters, his time on the god-forsaken northern front was finally, thankfully, over.

It hadn't been a very auspicious end to the campaign, but it wasn't as if it had been his fault; he had carried out his orders as best he could and been successful in driving the Muscovites back to Murmansk. No, the fault with the defeat ultimately lay elsewhere and the men responsible for it would be punished accordingly, just as he had punished the men responsible for the fiasco of the night before.

He craned his neck to peer back and found that he could just make out the bodies of the officer and three men who had been on guard duty, swinging in the wind down below in front of the mess hall. They had insisted that they had been patrolling, as assigned, but they were obviously lying - no doubt they had been in a warm corner of the mess hall with a bottle of schnapps.

He found that he wasn't angry, though, on the contrary, he was almost amused with how things had gone and a little grateful for the Misfits for giving him the perfect excuse to leave. He hadn't done what he'd wanted, he hadn't killed any of them, but he would have the last laugh - he had sent a coded message only half an hour before, setting plans in motion. Desperate plans that he had hoped he wouldn't need, but had put in place for just such an eventuality as this one.

He settled back in the deeply padded seat as the airfield dropped away and smiled contentedly; he wasn't leaving the north empty-handed by any means and, if everything went well that night, he would have another prize to add to the one that was bound and drugged in the seat opposite him.

He was looking forward to making his guest feel welcome aboard Bertha, where they would have some nice long conversations about Misfit Squadron and about Aerial Officer Gwen Stone in particular.

<h1 style="text-align:center">CHAPTER 30</h1>

Arrangements were made for the Misfits to rendezvous with the Arturo the morning of the day after and all that remained to do was to pack up and say goodbye to their hosts.

Baryshnikov arranged another party, like the first one, in one of the hangars, and again he invited the soldiers from the surrounding woods. More than half of them had been reassigned to defend the city, but they had been given permission to come back for the night, although sadly there were a lot less of them and not all of those that came were in one piece. Their injuries and losses did very little to put a damper on their mood, though, and they celebrations were just as raucous as ever.

Dorothy Campbell would be travelling in Dreadnought with Wendy and Gwen and she arrived soon after dark bringing with her General Popov and a few of the general staff with her. Instead of making things awkward, like high-ranked officers were wont to do every time they turned up to such celebrations, the generals were made very welcome, especially because they brought with them fresh supplies of food and alcohol that had arrived that afternoon on a train from St. Petersburg.

When everybody who was coming was there, Polikasparov called for silence and gathered the Misfits together in the middle of the hangar where they could be seen by everyone. Baryshnikov then stood on a crate to address everyone, speaking in Russian while Polikasparov translated for the British.

'Tomorrow, our allies, our *friends*, leave us. Perhaps we will never see them again, although I hope that they might have enjoyed themselves so much that they decide to come back in the spring.' The

Russian grinned at the Misfits, knowing full well that they had no intention of doing any such thing. 'Just in case they don't, though, we have a gift for them. This gift is not just from the Wolfpack or the soldiers of this base, though, but from *all* the people of Murmansk and Russia, every single one of whom have been following our fight here in the newspapers and on the radio.'

Abby caught Dot's attention subtly and raised an eyebrow, wondering if what the man was saying was true, whether the Tsar had been using the Misfits as a means to raise the morale of his people just like the King was in Britain.

Campbell nodded and shrugged as if to say *are you surprised?*

Abby chuckled silently and shook her head before looking back at Baryshnikov, who had been handed a small black box by Polikasparov. He held it above his head and turned in place so that everyone could see it.

The box was about two feet wide, six inches tall and maybe a foot deep, lacquered black like Gwen's Japanese chest, and decorated with blooming flowers and red berries which shone warmly in the light of the fires. It was a simple, yet elegant expression of tradition Russian art and craftwork, but the true value of the gift was hidden within and, when everybody had had a chance to see it, Baryshnikov faced the Misfits once more, then carefully opened it.

Music from a Tchaikovsky ballet filled the hangar as a four-inch tall ballerina, unfolded herself from under the lid.

Normal music boxes had a static figure that turned slowly about itself, the illusion of actual movement given only by mirrors in the lid, this one, however, was a clockwork wonder; the dancer was similar in construction and articulation to the automatons they had seen in the ballet, just on a much smaller scale.

She was dressed in a simple white, form-fitting dress, that went from her neck to her calves, but curling out from between her shoulder blades were a pair of breathtaking and fully articulate wings, like those of a swan or an angel, and as she raised her arms above her head and began to move in time to the rhythm of the music, those wings moved too, in perfect harmony with her.

Involuntarily, entranced by the figure, the Misfits moved forward to get a better look.

Baryshnikov smiled at the wonder on their faces, then, holding the lid open so that it didn't snap closed, he slowly tipped the box towards them.

The pilots gasped and Gwen had to fight the impulse to leap forward and catch the figure before it fell, but incredibly it didn't, it just kept dancing, parallel to the ground, seemingly completely unperturbed.

'How does it do that?' asked Scarlet.

'It's got to be magnetic. Right?'

Gwen looked at Baryshnikov for confirmation of her theory and received a nod in reply. 'Very good, Miss Stone. Its feet contain powerful magnets.'

He winked at her, then brought the box back to the horizontal before slowly starting to close the lid.

As the music came to a natural end, the automaton somehow detected that the dance was finished and it performed a deep reverence, before sitting, folding itself over and draping its arms over an extended leg, a pose that Gwen recognised from a piece called the "Dying Swan" which had moved her almost to tears when she had first seen it at eight, seeing in it the death of a creature of the air, much like she herself was.

The lid closed, hiding the dancer from sight and everybody in the hangar took a breath, as if a spell had been broken.

Baryshnikov spoke into the silence, displaying the box to the pilots once more. 'Gold from Siberia, Alexandrite from the Urals, wood from our very own trees and the finest clockwork automatons from the master craftsmen of St. Petersburg. You each have one of these to take home, so that a piece of Russia will always be with you.' He handed the box to Polikasparov, who gave it in turn to a soldier, who took it away. 'They are on your beds waiting for you. Please try not to forget they are there when you are drunk and knock them onto the floor!'

While the Misfits laughed, the Wolfpack leader said something to the soldiers surrounding them, then grinned at the British pilots.

'Hip hip!'

The hurrah from the soldiers was deafening, continuing on and on and in the end Baryshnikov just laughed and shrugged - it seemed that his comrades hadn't quite got the message that it was supposed to be three cheers and not just one long one. He stepped down from the crate and hugged each of them in turn, crushing them in a traditional Russian bear hug, although he took care with Gwen and received as good as he gave from Bruce and Mac.

When he was done he shouted something else in Russian and was received by another cheer, just as loud as the one they had given the Misfits.

'What did you say to them?' Gwen asked him as the soldiers went back to their celebrations.

He grinned. 'I said what every true Russian *loves* to hear, I said "let's drink."'

Natasha and Katerina were among the soldiers at the party and, as soon as the music boxes had been presented and the party got back under way, they latched on to Bruce and Mac as if there were no tomorrow, which, in a way, there wasn't.

Natasha had been one of the soldiers who had been sent to the front and she had been injured by a splinter of shrapnel from an explosion. It wasn't too serious, but she was in some pain and walking with a limp. She also had a sad look in her eye, as if she were haunted by what she had seen. None of that stopped her from grabbing Bruce and dragging him off into the darkness after only a couple of drinks for a "proper goodbye" as she put it, though.

Katerina had remained in the woods around the airfield and had visited Mac a few times when she'd been off duty, but they hadn't had much time together, so they took full advantage, dancing and drinking in the hangar before slipping away quietly after an hour or so.

The rest of the Misfits broke up into groups and sought out those Muscovites who were engaged in activities that they enjoyed: Scarlet automatically went for those who were singing and dancing; Derek, Chastity, Charles and Monty looked for those engaged in more intellectual pursuits; Dot and Abby found a quiet corner to speak; and Wendy and Owen danced together with those engaged in more romantic activities. Gwen's head wasn't up to dancing or drinking much, though, so she just sat in a corner with Kitty, sipping kvass and watching the fun.

The party started to wind down around midnight, but many of the soldiers kept drinking and the last of them didn't wander away to their barracks, carrying unconscious companions and the remaining alcohol with them, until well after one in the morning, letting the fires burn down and leaving the debris where it was to be dealt with in the morning.

Finally, the base was completely silent and dark and appeared deserted except for the two figures slowly walking around the perimeter fence.

During Katerina's first visits to Mac it had been hard for the lovers to find somewhere private to be; military installations don't typically have many places where two people can be alone. She had had a brilliant idea, though, and the third time they met she had told him to wrap up warm and taken him into the woods. There, she had set up a small bivouac, no more than a few old canvas sheets draped between some trees, but it was enough to shelter them from the elements and they could even build a small fire underneath it to warm the air slightly. That, combined with their fur coats, made their time together not only comfortable and peaceful, but also quite magical.

They had spent their time that evening making love, but also talking a great deal. Mac had told her all about his life in Scotland, the beauty and solitude of the highlands, and the work he did with his aircraft. He had even told her about the local whisky that he loved, which put vodka to shame. She had laughed at his claim, saying that nothing was better than vodka, then told him about her childhood, growing up in a small village in Siberia called Liniovsk, which was more or less the same size as his own, before going to the school in the nearest town.

Neither of them had mentioned the fact that Mac was leaving in a few short hours until they were walking back to the base.

'Come with me. I can talk to Dot Campbell; I'm sure one more person on the ship won't make any difference.'

Katerina sighed and shook her head. 'I can't, William.' She refused to call him Mac and had almost hit Bruce when he'd referred to him as "Mad Mac" one night. 'I have to stay; my country needs all the soldiers it can get.'

'But one soldier isnae gonna make a difference!' Mac always made an effort to enunciate properly when he was with her, because of her difficulty with English, but in his consternation he slipped back into a more familiar way of speaking.

She stopped, pulling him around to face her and stared into his eyes. 'How can you say that? You are a *Misfit* - you *know* what one person can do.'

'Yes, but I'm a pilot, I have an aircraft.'

'And I have just a gun, is that what you're saying?'

Mac took a deep breath and shook his head, knowing that he was getting into an argument that there was no way of winning. 'No, of course not. You are much more than the gun that you carry.'

She nodded curtly. 'Too right, mate.'

Mac winced, chuckling as she tried to imitate his accent and failed dismally, ending up sounding more like Bruce, which wasn't particularly flattering. She'd known it would make him laugh, though, and had done it to try to lighten the mood. It had worked and he put his arm back around her as they started along the path again.

'We will write to each other and then, when the war is over, maybe you can come in your aircraft and carry me away to Scotland.'

Mac smiled. 'I would love that, Kat. No matter how long it takes, I promise - I'll come and get you and then we'll make a home together.'

'And I will teach you to make vodka.'

He laughed. 'Yes. I'll make vodka with you. I'll probably be chucked out of the clan, but I'll make vodka with you.'

'Good, because we will need it to wean the babies.'

Mac stumbled to a halt as what she'd said caught up with him, but then grinned widely. 'Aye, lass, we'll need it for the bairns.' He grabbed her and pulled her into his arms and locked his lips to hers.

She pulled back fairly quickly, though and slapped his roving hands away. 'Stop that, William! You know I can't arrive back to barracks after curfew, not even for you. Not even on our last day together.'

'I know, lass, I know. Sorry.'

They began walking again, slightly faster than before, but still arm in arm, heading towards the buildings and the main gate.

Light flared twenty yards in front of them as someone came out of the communications shed and they both shielded their eyes and squinted, trying to see who it was.

'Tasha?' Katerina called something out in Russian and the shadow, clearly female, despite wearing one of the shapeless but incredibly warm grey parkas that the Muscovites had all been issued with, turned towards them.

There was a faint whir and Katerina sagged back against Mac with a sigh. He caught her, staggering slightly as he took her full weight, but then there was a hammer blow to his head and all he knew was darkness.

CHAPTER 31

Mac opened his eyes and groaned. His head hurt like he'd emptied an entire barrel of whisky and washed it down with a bottle of vodka.

Vodka...

'Kat!' He rolled over, fighting against a wave of dizziness and found her lying beside him. 'Kat! Kat, darlin'!'

He pulled her to him and went to pat her cheek, but stopped. Her eyes were sightless, the light of the full moon making them glow with a life that they would never have again.

'Oh, Kat, my sweet darling...' Mac groaned as he softly rocked her back and forth, clutching her to him tightly as if he could squeeze life back into her. 'My bonnie wee lassie...'

He wanted nothing more than to stay there with her, to hold her to him and weep, but there would be plenty of time for that later.

After he got revenge for her.

He kissed her, then laid her gently back down, pulling her hood forwards over her face, before pushing himself up and staggering towards the communications shed to raise the alarm, taking great gulps of air as his head spun.

Two men were stationed in the communications shed at all times, even with the party going on, but they were both dead, shot, and Mac spared them only a quick glance before lunging for the button which activated the klaxon that sent the squadrons into the air.

Nothing happened.

He thumped it with his palm several times, swearing when it refused to work, but then saw that the wires leading to it had been cut, as had the ones connected to the radio.

No help was going to be forthcoming from the shed so he would have to find it elsewhere.

He stumbled to the door and back out into the night, already breaking into a shambling run towards the guard post at the gate beyond the hangars, more than half a mile away, praying that the men there were still alive and had some means of summoning help.

What was Natasha doing, though? Why kill everyone who saw her? She had a legitimate reason for being on the base, she didn't need to sneak around.

Unless...

Unless she was getting rid of anyone who wasn't deep in sleep or too drunk to stop her before carrying out some plan.

Which implied that it could be stopped.

Mac growled; his head hurt too much and his thoughts were just spinning round in circles, not making much sense. He just needed to put one foot in front of the other and find someone who would know what to do. Then he could get back to Katerina.

The mess halls were silent, no lights on in either the eating areas or the kitchens, neither were there any mechanics or fitters working late in the machines shops. However, a faint light was shining through a crack in the blackout curtains of the hangar where the Misfit fighters were kept and Mac veered in that direction, hoping that perhaps one of the squadron's fitters had snuck back to do some late night adjustments, something that they often did.

He pushed his way through the curtain and looked around, squinting in an effort to see in light that was only just brighter than that provided by the moon outside.

Movement to his side made his pilot's eyes flash in that direction and he caught sight of a shadow moving among B flight's aircraft. He opened his mouth to call out, but immediately stopped when he realised that whoever it was, they weren't acting like a pilot or a fitter, they were being altogether too stealthy.

The figure disappeared momentarily from his view as it went under Hawk, but then, when it came back out the other side and moved to Jaguar, he got a better look and he snarled when he saw that the figure was blonde and wearing a Muscovite parka - it looked like he'd found Natasha.

She had no idea he was there - he could sneak up on her and stop her himself.

He padded as quietly as he could across the hangar, pausing only to grab a spanner from a workbench and snuck up behind the person as they bent to go under Dove.

When she straightened up again, he was ready for her and he hefted the tool. 'Natasha.'

She whirled around and Mac swung the spanner.

Almost too late he realised that it wasn't Natasha, it was Polikasparov.

He pulled the blow, only just managing to stop the heavy metal before it impacted with the man's head.

'Sorry, I thought you were, you were...' Mac stuttered and came to a halt when he noticed the metal ball in the man's hand and registered the one hanging from the wing of Dove - the balls were identical to the ones that Scarlet had used to destroy the Prussian aircraft.

Polikasparov saw the direction of Mac gaze and knew that the game was up. He dropped the explosive and shoved his hand into his coat pocket.

Before he could bring out his gun, the spanner struck him on the temple and he fell to the ground bonelessly, like a sack of spuds.

'What the *hell* is going on?' Mac muttered to himself, frowning down at the Russian pilot.

A sound from outside, a high pitched whine followed by a chuff, answered his question. It was the unmistakable sound of an aeronautical steam engine starting up.

Mac bent down and grabbed the man's gun from the ground and, as an afterthought, searched him for the small radio that sent the signal for the balls to explode; hopefully without that Polikasparov wouldn't be able to destroy the aircraft if he somehow managed to regain consciousness before he could be secured.

Mac staggered back outside and started running towards the next hangar in line. 'I'm too old for this...' He paused at the corner of the hangar, panting for breath, tired beyond all measure, and threw the detonator into the bushes between the buildings; he didn't want to risk it falling back into the hands of the saboteurs and just had to hope that they didn't have another. He gulped down deep breaths of the cold air, blinking to clear the sparks from his vision, then willed himself to stumble on.

The next hangar in the line was where C flight's machines were kept. It was dark, but the doors were wide open and the blackout curtains pulled back, as if an aircraft were about to take off.

The engine noise increased suddenly, changing in pitch and, to Mac's horror, Owen's radar aircraft, Bloodhound, began to nose its way out.

Mac reached deep inside, summoning what little energy he had left for one last sprint.

He ran for the back door of Bloodhound, reaching it just as the aircraft started to turn onto the taxiway and began accelerating towards the end of the airfield. He fumbled with the latch, but lost his grip when the aircraft bumped over the uneven surface. He gritted his teeth, knowing that he wouldn't be able to keep up with the machine for very long and lunged for it again. This time the door swung open, almost sending him flying, but he recovered quickly and he dived inside, falling full length inside the compartment that held the radar apparatus.

He lay there panting, fighting to get his breath back, being rocked back and forth as Bloodhound raced down the taxiway far too quickly - whoever was in the pilot's seat was playing with fire, risking everything to get the aircraft off the ground before someone could stop them.

With no time to lose, Mac forced himself to get up and staggered down the gangway towards the cockpit, breaking into a half-run, going as quickly as he could among machinery which jutted out unevenly on all sides, all the while swearing at how absurdly long the aircraft was.

He was almost at the cockpit when Bloodhound decelerated, braking hard at the end of the taxiway with a loud squeal, and he stumbled, taken by surprise, and clutched at a bank of monitors to regain his balance, but was thrown sideways into one the bulkhead and tumbled to the floor as the aircraft veered sideways, swerving onto the runway.

He gasped as something snapped in his chest, but adrenaline surged and he pushed himself back to his feet, clinging onto one of the engineer's seats as the machine came to a halt and the airscrews on the steam engines started cycling up to full power for takeoff.

He was out of time.

He took the last few paces to the cockpit at a sprint.

'Stop! Shut down the engines!'

He stood in the doorway of the cockpit, hanging onto the frame, fighting for breath through the pain in his side, but holding the pistol steady, pointing it at the woman sitting in the pilot's seat.

Natasha slowly turned to look at him.

She took in the gun, then met his eyes coldly. 'You will not shoot me.'

'I bloody well will if you don't shut down the damn engines.'

Her eyes narrowed as if she were assessing the truth of his words. Finally she nodded. 'Very well.'

She turned back towards the instrument panel, but then suddenly spun back towards him. There was a whirring noise and Mac flinched as something whined off the bulkhead next to him.

Out of reflex, he fired.

Natasha's eyes went wide and her hand spasmed, the gun dropping from it to hit the floor with a clang. She frowned at him, seemingly puzzled, then slumped and rolled slowly out of the seat.

Mac hurried forwards and started the engine shutdown process. He only just managed to complete it before darkness finally claimed him.

Mac regained consciousness up when the medical staff tried to put him on a stretcher to carry him out of Bloodhound. He waved their hands away irritably and struggled to his feet, then moved to the door that was just behind the pilot's compartment and looked out.

He snorted in amusement; it was just as well the Prussians had stopped sending bombers over at night because every single one of the base's lights was on and the airfield was lit up as bright as day. Brighter, in fact, considering the weakness of the sun in winter at such high latitudes.

The entire base had been roused by the sound of the engines, everyone not unconscious from drink anyway, and there were soldiers rushing around everywhere.

'Mac!'

Mac looked to his right to see Owen coming around the nose of the aircraft.

'I'm surprised to see you on your feet, when I looked in on you, you were out cold and snoring to wake the dead...' Owen went white as he realised what he had said. 'Oh, I'm so sorry, Mac, really. I wasn't thinking...'

Mac shook his head. 'Dinna fash yerself, man. Kat was a soldier and we both knew that either one of us could die soon enough. I just didn't expect...' Mac broke off as a lump rose in his throat and he brushed away a tear angrily; he hadn't cried for more than twenty years, he wasn't going to start now. 'Polikasparov!' He said, suddenly remembering the saboteur. 'He was putting explosives...'

Owen held up his hands to forestall him. 'He's in custody and Scarlet is disarming the bombs as we speak, although things are still a bit hairy; apparently the detonator is missing. Neither Polikasparov nor Natasha had it, so people are worried that there's some other bastard running around who might set the bombs off at any moment.'

Mac shook his head, wincing at the pain the movement provoked. 'I took it off Polikasparov and chucked it into the woods so he couldn't use it if he came round too quickly. I suppose I'd better go tell that to Abby. Sorry about the mess I made in your cockpit by the way.'

Mac gave Owen a weak smile, then stepped down from the doorway, but stumbled, gasping at the pain in his ribs. 'Dagnabbit....'

The medical staff, who had been loitering, watching him warily, immediately leapt to grab him and he had to slap them away again. 'Gerrof! Go bother someone who's actually hurt!'

Even though they didn't understand his words, they understood his tone perfectly and backed off as Mac stomped away towards the base buildings a few hundred yards away. They followed him at a safe distance, though, keeping an eye on him and Mac didn't say anything; he was feeling increasingly light headed and short of breath and had no idea if he was going to be able to make it all the way.

Thankfully, the rest of the Misfits saw him coming and rushed over to meet him.

'Mac! You look bloody awful! Rough night?'

Mac snarled at Bruce in reply, but saw the pain in the man's eyes and realised that the humour was just his way of trying to cope with the crushing blow that he had also received, his feelings manipulated and his trust betrayed.

Mac reined himself in, his expression softening slightly and he nodded sympathetically at his friend, then looked at Abby. 'The detonator's between hangars one and two. I chucked it into the woods. You can tell Scarlet she doesn't need to brick it; she's safe.'

Abby nodded. 'That's good to hear. Well done, smart thinking.' She glanced at Chastity. 'Run along and let her know, please.'

'Yes, ma'am.' Chastity nodded and sprinted off towards the hangar.

Abby frowned as she watched Chastity go. 'I wasn't *actually* telling her to run...' She shook her head with a sigh. 'That girl...'

She grimaced then turned back to Mac. 'The Muscovites wanted to take Katerina away to put her with the rest of the dead before they send her home for burial, but I wouldn't let them until you'd woken up and had a chance to see her. She's in the medical shed.'

Mac nodded gratefully. 'Thank you.'

'And while you're there, get yourself patched up for pity's sake.'

Mac grumbled, but didn't argue, instead he asked the question that had been on his mind since the moment the woman who had come to mean so much to him had died. 'Why? Why did they do this?'

Abby shrugged. 'It's too early to know. Polikasparov is already on his way to St. Petersburg for interrogation at General Popov's orders, so we have no idea of his motives yet, but we found a camera disguised as a button and a small shortwave transceiver of Prussian design in Natasha's kitbag on Bloodhound, so it looks like she's been working for the Prussians for a while.'

The words registered with Mac, but the more he tried to grasp their meaning, the more it slipped away and he swayed, blinking rapidly in an attempt to remain focussed on the group captain even as his eyes kept wanting to slide off to one side.

Abby saw and stopped speaking, shaking her head. 'Stubborn man.' She waved to the medical staff, who were still hovering and they immediately came forward. 'Go to the med centre and get your wounds seen to.'

He automatically began to brush the men off, but Abby stopped him with a growl. 'That's an order, Mac.'

'Yes, ma'am.' Mac sighed and, with a great show of reluctance, let them lie him down on their stretcher. 'But only because you insist; I don't really need the help.'

Abby smiled at him fondly. 'Of course you don't, Mac.'

It was only weeks later, after Polikasparov had been thoroughly questioned, that he revealed why he had betrayed his country.

When Polikasparov was growing up, his father had travelled the world, working in various aviation companies. One of those companies had been based in Bavaria and Polikasparov had gone to school there for a year. He had befriended another boy and, even after Polikasparov had left, the two had continued to correspond as they grew into men, sharing ideas as well as ideals.

That boy had been Hans Gruber and he persuaded Polikasparov that the only way for the Russian Empire to survive intact was for them to surrender to the Prussians before the country was completely destroyed.

A few words in the right ears had been sufficient to get Wolfpack squadron assigned to the new Harridan fighters, putting Polikasparov in the right place both to spy on the Misfits and to whisper in

Baryshnikov's ear and get him to make overly aggressive decisions that put the British in danger.

When all else had failed, he had been contacted by Gruber and ordered to help Natasha carry out the plan to salvage at least something from the defeat.

Polikasparov was executed in the New Year, but insisted to the last that he had only been acting in the best interests of his country.

EPILOGUE

'It was bitterly cold the next morning when the Misfits left Vaenga for the rendezvous with Arturo on the north coast of Muscovy, the promised front already making its presence known with temperatures that were well below zero Fahrenheit.

They were glad to put the place behind them for good - they had felt welcome there, certainly, but it had never been a home for them like Badger Base, or even Bagshot Hall had been, not because of the lack of comforts and luxuries, but because the people that usually surrounded and supported them, the people that had become their family, hadn't been there.

Mac's heroics of the night before had left him barely conscious and in no fit state to fly - the projectile from Natasha's clockwork gun had left a deep crease in his head that left him with a severe concussion and he had two broken ribs from falling sideways in Bloodhound. Dorothy Campbell had offered to take his place, but she hadn't received the training in carrier landings that the Misfits had, so Gwen, despite her injuries and the objections of the Muscovite doctor, was assigned to fly Jaguar, with Chastity on her wing, while Mac rode in Dreadnought.

The eleven Misfit aircraft formed up over Vaenga, waiting for the transport aircraft carrying Freddy Featherstonehaugh, Mr Jones, and the skeleton crew of fitters, who hadn't been sent ahead overland the day before, to join them, then headed directly for the rendezvous, just over forty miles away.

The pilots relaxed and joked over the radios, already looking forward to a good rest, but they had one last, extremely unpleasant surprise left for them in Muscovy.

'Smoke! There's smoke!'

They were ten minutes into the flight when Charles' call had them frantically searching the sky for enemies.

'Where?'

'Behind us.'

'Misfits, coming about.'

Abby led them in a wide turn to face the smoke rising in the distance, leaving the transport to continue on without them.

Gwen pulled down lenses to try to make out the source of the dense black cloud rising into the sky. It was miles away, coming from somewhere near the city. She gasped. 'Oh, my lord, the civilians...'

The smoke wasn't coming from *near* the city, it was coming *from* the city - Murmansk was aflame from one end to the other and above, through the smoke, could be seen mass ranks of Prussian bombers going home, their craven deed done.

'Why?' Scarlet said, her voice thick with emotion.

'They're denying it to the Muscovites.' Derek said, his tactical mind instantly recognising the ramifications. 'The Prussians were going to use the city as their base here in the north and now that they can't, they're taking it away from their enemy.'

'They're also being complete bastards,' Bruce added.

'That too,' agreed Derek.

Abby sighed. 'Well, there's nothing we can do for the poor buggers, now and we have a ship to catch.'

The Misfits reversed their course again and accelerated to catch up with the transport, all their joy at going home gone, along with the city they had invested so much into defending.

They had done their duty, succeeding where everyone had expected them to fail, but they couldn't help feeling that, at the very last moment, they had let down the brave men and women they'd been sent to help and hadn't been there for them at the most crucial moment.

'Tinman to Badger Leader, come in please.'

'Badger Leader here, go ahead Tinman.'

'We have you in sight, Badger, welcome back.'

'Thank you, Tinman.'

'We have a message for you from London. Message reads - congratulations Misfit Squadron, mission accomplished. The kettle is on, come home safely. George R.'

Gwen's heart swelled with pride at the demonstration of the high regard that the King held them in and she smiled as she glanced across to Hawk, on the other side of Swift in the B flight formation.

Kitty was already looking at her and Gwen laughed, Murmansk momentarily forgotten, when the American blew her a kiss; home beckoned, along with a very appealing future.

ABOUT THE AUTHOR

Simon Brading's interest in aviation began when he was very young and at thirteen he joined the RAF section of the Combined Cadet Forces of Dulwich College with the aim of becoming a pilot. However, when he was 18, had reached the rank of Flight Sergeant in the CCF and was trying to get into a University Air Squadron, he was told that his eyesight wasn't good enough to be a pilot, so he had to move onto plan B... something else.

He tried his hand at many things before it occurred to him that he might have a few stories to tell. He never lost his interest in flight, though, and hopes to add a PPL to his very basic and probably extremely expired glider license.

www.simonbrading.co.uk

For news of special offers, upcoming releases, exclusive content, competitions and events, please follow me on social media.

Instagram - @sibrading
Facebook - Simon Brading Author
Tiktok - @SimonBradingAuthor

In addition, souvenirs and merchandise, including T-shirts, badges, stickers and more, are available from the Misfit Squadron store on REDBUBBLE at -
https://www.redbubble.com/people/misfitsquadron/shop

ALSO BY SIMON BRADING

The "Displacers" series - a young adult time travel adventure series for all ages.
The Pirate's Heir
The Secret of the Ancients
The Whitechapel Plot
The Price of Greed
The Time for Vengeance

The "Misfit Squadron" Series - a Steampunk series set in an alternate World War 2.
The Battle Over Britain
The Russian Resistance
A Misfit Midwinter
The Lion and the Baron
The Maltese Defence
Tales From the Second Great War
The Siege of Gibraltar
The King's Mission
The Home Front

The Dismal Futures books - stand-alone science fiction tales suitable for adults.
Empath
The Lifeboat at the End of the Universe

The "Twin Ambitions" series - ballet books for children ages 7 and up.
Fight to Dance
Back to Basics

The "Ni Hon - The Two Books" Series - a young adult series set in a dystopian future Japan.
The Black Book

Others
Public Enemy